D1086022

FLAMENCO IN THE TIME

OF

MOONSHINE AND MOBSTERS

David C. Edmonds

This is a work of fiction. Names, characters, businesses, places, events, locales, and incidents are either the products of the author's imagination or used in a fictitious manner. Any resemblance to actual persons, living or dead, or actual events is purely coincidental.

Published by St. Petersburg Press
St. Petersburg, FL
www.stpetersburgpress.com

Copyright ©2019

All rights reserved. No part of this publication may be reproduced, distributed, or transmitted in any form or by any means, including photocopying, recording or other electronic or mechanical methods, without the prior written permission of the publisher, except in the case of brief quotations embodied in critical reviews and certain other noncommercial uses permitted by copyright law. For permission requests contact St. Petersburg Press at www.stpetersburgpress.com.

Design and composition by St. Petersburg Press
Cover design by St. Petersburg Press and Pablo Guidi

Paperback ISBN: 978-1-940300-10-8
eBook ISBN: 978-1-940300-09-2

First Edition

For all my children—Chris, Julie, Alex, and Davy

Other Titles by David C. Edmonds

"Toto, I have a feeling we're not in Kansas anymore."
Dorothy—*The Wizard of Oz*

CHAPTER 1

Brooker Creek Nature Preserve
Tarpon Springs, Florida
Halloween, 2019

I wish someone could explain what happened to me that night. Was it the location? The date? The weather? Nothing about it was logical. Even if it had been daylight, which it wasn't, it's never a good idea for a woman, by herself, to drive down a secluded road that's bordered by swamp on one side and forest on the other.

And especially not in a low-slung Toyota Prius.

The road—if you could dignify it with that word—was single lane and one-way, and I was driving in darkness. Not just the darkness of night, but the darkness of storm clouds and overhanging limbs. No road markers either, and the only light other than my headlamps was an occasional flash of lightning. But I didn't care. It was Ramón's birthday. He was exhibiting his paintings at a Halloween art show, and I was going to surprise him with a flamenco performance.

The thought gave me a tingle. Oh, those dark Gypsy eyes and the way he spoke Spanish with an Andalusian accent. The way we melded on the floor as if we'd been dancing together all our lives. And the things we did afterward, at his place or mine.

My cell dinged with a text from Selena, my other dance partner.
Where R U, Amy? We may have trouble!!!!

I tapped the phone display on the steering wheel.

"What's wrong?" I asked.

"It's Ramón!" she said in a shrill voice. "There's this woman with him, been clinging to him like a nagging wife. They're arguing in that Gypsy language."

She told me this in Spanish, in the flat intonation typical of second and third-generation Spaniards who'd grown up in Tampa speaking English. "Who's the woman?" I asked.

"*Quien sabe?* I don't have a clue … and I'm not getting near her."

"What does she look like?"

"Like an escapee from a caravan."

"Oh, God, she could ruin this. Is everything else ready?"

"Ready. Director's right here with the lighting technician. We've also got five or six extras from the Tarpon Springs Performing Arts Center, all dressed as Gypsies."

"Hispanics?"

"Greek, but the audience won't know the difference." She chuckled. "And, oh, we also have this Greek guy, Nick something-or-other. He'll do the blanket scene."

"What blanket scene?"

"The cape throw-down."

I rolled my eyes. "For God's sake, Selena, you can't keep adding stuff."

"Oh, stop worrying. It'll work out. Only thing that concerns me is the time. It's not even seven, but it's already dark. This is the west side of the bay. Old folks. Retirees."

"Does Ramón know what we're planning?"

"He's too busy selling his paintings. And get this: you know that semi-nude he did of you?"

"Which one?"

"Gypsy at Midnight, where you're propped up in his bed like a little—"

"What about it?"

"Sold for five-hundred dollars, boobs and all. Imagine that. You'll be hanging in the study of some old geezer with white hair."

She burst into laughter. I didn't feel like laughing, not after what she'd told me about the Gypsy. Ramón had assured me there was no one else, but I knew women, and I had enough Gypsy blood to know she wasn't haggling with him over the price of a painting.

"Amy, are you still there?"

"Still here. This trail's a nightmare. There's water running over the road."

I slowed for a speed bump. A deer sprinted out of the foliage. Then I came to an unmarked fork. Right or left? I dialed down the volume on my radio and strained my eyes for a sign.

Nothing but the sounds of crickets, frogs, and other night creatures that probably wanted to eat me. Worse, a misty fog was rising from the swamp, catching the beams of my lights and filling the car with damp, swampy smells.

Was I even on the right road? This was the kind of place to film a horror movie.

I pushed the thought from my mind and took the fork to the right, hoping to see a marker or building; anything other than swamp and cypress trees. Instead, I came to a barricade of orange construction barrels, all with reflectors and a large sign.

DANGER. SINKHOLE. DO NOT ENTER!

A sinkhole? Here? I shouldn't have been surprised. This was Florida, where entire houses and even people disappeared into sinkholes. I remembered seeing it on TV—the biggest sinkhole ever. It had swallowed the road, the surrounding swamp, an abandoned tractor, and three or four acres of cypress trees.

I slammed the gear into reverse and was backing up when an image appeared in the rear-view monitor. Another deer? I stopped. A woman in white appeared next to my window.

Even scarier, she had a faint glow about her, as if she'd sprayed herself with a luminescent liquid. She placed a hand on the window and sauntered by without a word, disappearing into the fog like a character in an old Dracula movie.

How I turned around without going into the marsh, I don't know, but I was soon back on the road, my heart in my throat, trying to stay focused.

The fog thickened. Who was she and what was she doing in this wilderness? I half expected her to appear on the road in front. Or in the seat beside me. A chill came over me, and I was about to call Selena just to hear a voice when I rounded a curve and there it was: Brooker Creek Environmental Education Center, three large buildings looming out of the fog like a fairy wonderland, all lit up for their Halloween art exhibit.

Never again, I told myself. No more trips down lonely back roads.

The parking lot was full, mainly SUVs and family vans, glistening with dampness in the beam of my lights. I parked where they'd told me, in a space marked Staff Parking—right next to Ramón's new BMW. Just the sight of it caused my heart to jump.

I called Selena again. "Outside," I said. "Is everything ready?"

"Thank goodness," she shot back. "We were getting worried. Meet you at the door."

"Is that woman still with Ramón?"

"Still there. Ramón looks like he wants to kill her."

The jitters I usually get before doing a new number at an unfamiliar place came on stronger than usual. I did a quick check of my makeup and hair in the visor mirror and stepped outside to smooth the wrinkles out of my flamenco dress.

Would Ramón like it? Would the audience? *Oh, God, please let this go well.*

Something shrieked. Loud. I swirled, expecting to see that woman of the swamp, but there were only the cars, the damp smells, and the croaks and chirrs of nightlife. This was a new one for me. The best venue for flamenco is a smoke-filled, wood-floor dive that smells of sweat and wine, or the backroom of a bodega amid casks of aging wine.

But flamenco in a swamp. How weird was that?

I drew in a breath of damp night air and followed the Jack-o'-lanterns up a meandering boardwalk to the building.

CHAPTER 2

Selena was waiting on the veranda, dressed in a traditional flamenco dress with ruffles and lace. She was about a decade older, and thicker in the hips, but she had the natural looks of a dancer with her olive complexion and raven hair pulled back in a bun.

"Do you need the bathroom?" she asked.

"What I need is a stiff drink. How's my lipstick and eye shadow?"

She pulled me into the light. "Perfect. They'll think you're Salma Hayek."

"Is that woman going to be a problem?"

"Oh, stop worrying. We're doing Bizet's *Carmen*. She'll make a nice prop with her fiery looks. Isn't that what flamenco is about—passion and conflict?"

That wasn't the conflict I wanted, not when my stomach was already doing somersaults, but I dropped my protests and followed her inside.

The place was so large and crowded that hardly anyone noticed us in our flamenco outfits. Patrons mingled on the floor, some dressed in Halloween attire. The artists stood or sat along the walls with their paintings and crafts, and a percussive flamenco played over the sound system.

The Greek dancers hurried over as soon as they saw me, looking like fortune tellers in their shawls and swirling skirts. Selena gave them instructions and spoke with the lady in charge. Then our guitarist, Javier, dressed as always in a puffy-sleeved white shirt with black pants and a red scarf around his skinny waist, came over and gave me a big hug.

"Does Ramón know what we're planning?" I asked him.

"I haven't told him. It should be a surprise."

I wanted to ask about the woman, but by then the director was on the floor with her microphone. "Ladies and gentlemen, your attention, please."

The room quieted. Assistants ran brooms over the place; others set up temporary rope barriers. I tried to calm myself with the thought the people here were art lovers, not flamenco aficionados. They wouldn't know if I missed a step or not.

You can do it, I told myself. Breathe deeply. Make Ramón proud.

The lights went from bright to dim. Javier's guitar strummed—fast strokes that signaled something big was afoot. The Greek cast of faux Gypsies moved into position, a dazzling display of red scarves, fluttering fans, lace and ruffles. A second guitar kicked in. Ramón? I couldn't see him, but I imagined him glancing around, looking for me.

Selena stepped from the shadows and into the light, stamping her feet and clapping her hands the way she did so well. She belted out her opening line in Gypsy Romani, as cracked as if she were singing in a thieves' den in Seville.

Love, love, love is a rebellious bird,
that nobody can tame.

Bizet's *Carmen* came to life in rousing strums and rhythmic claps. This was my cue, my moment, my night to impress my lover. I clasped the castanets in my hands, pulled in a deep breath, and danced into the light.

Selena and I did a little fandango around each other, our hands in the air, stamping our feet in a rhythmic dance with the guitars. The audience clapped with us, their faces aglow behind the ropes. Ramón, looking like a torero in his embroidered vest and black pants, his hair pulled back in a ponytail, moved his chair onto the floor.

But something wasn't right. Where were the smiles of joy? Why was he avoiding my eyes?

It had to be that woman.

I stole a glimpse of her next to his exhibits. She was glaring at me, hands-on-hips and fire in her eyes, all gypsied up in bracelets, large hoop earrings, and long skirt and bandana.

Ignore her, I told myself. Concentrate on the performance.

I struck a castanet against my knee and played a down-stroke. This brought out the male actor from Tarpon Springs, looking like Zorro in his cape and black Spanish hat. He handed me a rose, swept off his cape in dramatic fashion, and twirled it in tune with my castanet rolls. I almost laughed at his blinking eyes and a false mustache. But when he spread his cape on the floor as if to invite me to lie with him, I danced to him in teasing fashion, clicking the castanets and glancing from him to the cape.

Suspense was in the air. The guitars strummed, high and then low.

In a single motion, I kicked away the cape and gave him a dismissive sniff. The guitars hit it as perfectly as gunfire in a firing squad. My would-be lover picked up his cape and retreated, looking downtrodden. Selena punctuated it with yet another scorched line.

The bird you thought you'd caught,
flapped its wings and flew away.

I twirled around with my castanets and focused on Ramón, sitting there with his guitar. Would he fall under my charm, or would he walk away like the soldier in his first encounter with Carmen? I didn't know, but for me at that insecure moment my dance was more than a performance. It was a love dance, a song, a poem, a cry for him to prove his loyalty. In other words, it was real flamenco, where love is at stake and hearts are broken.

He put away his guitar, but Javier kept up the beat. Selena clapped and stomped. I danced over to Ramón, closer and closer, and did a roll of castanets in his face.

He glanced up and then down at his guitar.

Please, Ramón, please. This isn't a game.

I did another castanet roll, and right on cue, the faux gypsies dashed out and began their pretend protest, all talking together.

"He's mine, I saw him first."

"No, he's mine. Go away, woman."

I dismissed them with a scoff and a beat from Javier's guitar. The women backed away like angry vixens, fanning themselves and flashing thigh flesh. I leaned over Ramón again, this time with the rose, close enough to smell his cologne. Close enough to feel his body heat. I waved the rose under his nose as if it contained a romantic potion … and dropped it at his feet.

He leaned down and picked up the rose.

Javier slapped his guitar at the same moment.

Please, Ramón. Stand up. Dance with me.

He looked up as if he could read my thoughts. Great drama was in the air. Selena clapped. Javier's guitar strummed, high and low. Ramón stood, lifted his arms and brought his hands together in rhythmic claps. Yes, he was going to do it. The world was right.

His hands traveled from my legs to my waist and on up my arms—hybrid flamenco with a touch of tango, which my great-grandmother Carmen had choreographed back in the early '30s. He pulled me into his arms. Our bodies melded. I could feel the heat, the love, the passion. I wanted to kiss him. I wanted that other woman to know we were lovers.

And I was staring into his eyes when she stepped onto the floor.

"*Puta* flamenco!" she shrieked and flung a painting at us.

Javier's guitar fell silent. The dancing and clapping stopped. She flung another painting, a semi-nude of me. Then she knocked over his display and charged onto the floor.

"*Cuidado!*" Selena cried. "She's got a knife!"

CHAPTER 3

Peple dove to the floor as if she had an assault rifle. Women and little kids dressed like goblins ran for the exits. Ramón just stood there like a petrified tree.

I also froze in horror and might have ended up with a knife in my heart if not for the Tarpon Springs' actor. He flung his cape over her head and grabbed her from behind. The knife clattered to the floor. Still, she kicked and ranted and called me every dirty word I'd ever heard in Gypsy talk and some I hadn't.

A burly man in uniform hurried into the fray. The main lights came on, bathing the room in a harsh glare. The director and a few spectators gathered around, some of them filming the fuss on their cells. This made the Gypsy even more furious. "*Puta!*" she screamed, spitting out the words. "I will kill you! Kill Ramón too! Kill his children!"

I looked at Ramón. "Children?"

"Three!" she cried. "Didn't he tell you?"

Ramón turned away as if he couldn't bear to face me. The woman kept ranting.

Pregnant with his fourth child.

Abandoned us like dogs.

Wanted in Spain for armed robbery and murder.

She pointed a finger as if to summon all the demons of hell. "You will pay for this. I will put a curse on you. You will regret the day you stole my husband."

Behind me, someone was translating her words into English.

The pain of betrayal spread over me like cancer, and when the tears came, I pushed through the crowd for the exit. I had to get away. To escape. Drown myself in the swamp. How could this happen? Why hadn't I checked his background? Why had I believed his every word?

People stood aside as if I were contagious. A woman touched my arm. "I'm so sorry. Happens to lots of women. Been there, done that."

I mumbled a thank-you and hurried outside, into the freshness of the damp night air. People were there too, staring as if they could see right through my flamenco dress to my crying soul. I broke into a trot—only to slip on the wet boardwalk and go sprawling.

I cried in pain. I pounded my hands on the boardwalk, right there on my knees in the fog beneath a string of overhead lights. In front of a mob of spectators who looked like bereaved relatives at a Halloween funeral. A woman helped me to my feet. Others gathered around, asking if I was okay. Then Selena appeared at my side.

"Oh, my God, oh, my God. Are you hurt?"

"I'm okay."

"No, you're not. You're bleeding. Look at you."

She yelled for a doctor and tried to pull me inside. I yanked away and hurried along the boardwalk. A woman scooped up her child as I passed, and by the time I reached my Prius and started the engine, I could barely see through the tears and blood.

I backed up so fast that I scraped the side of Ramón's BMW. "Bastard!" I shrieked, and I angled into the driver's side again, knocking off the side mirror. Too bad I didn't have a container of gasoline. Or a pistol to shoot it full of holes. Shoot myself too.

People came running. I ignored them and took off in a fury, spinning the wheels.

The fog had grown thicker, but I didn't care. Didn't care either that I was driving too fast, blowing past an oncoming car. My life was over. My love gone. I would forever be known as the humiliated flamenco dancer. A stupid woman who'd fallen for a married Gypsy.

My cell rang. Selena's name appeared on the dashboard display. I punched the button.

"Are you okay?" she asked in a shrill voice.

"I'm fine."

"No, you're not. You need to turn around. You're driving the wrong way on a one-way road. You also damaged a car."

"So what? It was Ramón's car."

"No, Amy, you hit the director's car. She's on the phone now, calling the cops."

She was still talking, saying something about leaving the scene of an accident, when that damn mystery woman appeared in the glare of my headlights.

In the middle of the trail.

I've heard of drivers who in a moment of panic hit the accelerator when they thought they were hitting the brakes. That may have happened to me. Or it might have been a demonic force. All I know is that my car sped up, taking me straight into the barricade barrels. They flew this way and that. The darkness of the biggest sinkhole in Florida loomed into my vision, and then I was plunging into the abyss.

CHAPTER 4

Rays of sunlight filtered through an overhead canopy of foliage and Spanish moss. An owl hooted. I heard mysterious birds singing around me, birds I did not know and whose plumage I could only imagine, and they were speaking to me in Spanish.

"Stupid woman. Stupid woman."

I sat up, and it all came back. The jolt of the airbag. Water filling the car. Water up to my chest. Water filling my lungs.

"Stupid woman. Stupid woman."

Yes, I was stupid. Stupid to fall for Ramón and stupid for caring. Yet I was alive. Or maybe I was in purgatory. But did purgatory have trees and singing birds and sunlight when the last thing I remembered was gloomy darkness?

I stood, using a low-hanging limb to pull myself up … but quickly sank back down. Trees and forest swirled around me. My vision blurred. I had a momentary urge to vomit.

In time, the forest stopped moving. The birds started their infernal racket again, and when my stomach settled, I realized that a low mist hung over the forest, making my surroundings even spookier. I checked myself for injury. Hands scratched and bleeding. Fingernails broken. My expensive dancing shoes gone. My beautiful flamenco dress was also covered with muck and vegetable debris, and the knot on my head was oozing blood. No wonder I was nauseous. I should be in the hospital, not lying in the wilderness by myself.

But where were the ambulances and medics?

Where was Selena?

And what about that woman who'd stepped in front of me?

The woman. Did I hit her? Dear God, no!

Those last sickening moments came into my head—swerving to miss her, the car fishtailing and straightening out. The impact of the barrels. But there'd been no impact from the woman. No jolt. Surely I missed her. Surely she'd have flagged someone down.

But why had no one come?

Again I pulled myself up with the help of a limb and tried to get my bearings. This wasn't where I'd gone into a sinkhole. No barrels or barricades. No road either. Nothing but swamp to my back, a dark lagoon to my front, thick forest all around, and a little footpath.

The only thing that made sense was that I'd crawled out of the water in a daze, meandered around the forest, and passed out under a tree. Yes, that had to be it. The preserve had lots of walking trails. A miracle I hadn't been attacked by alligators.

The thought chilled me. Images of bears and panthers filled my head. And pythons so huge they could squeeze the life out of an alligator. I needed a weapon—a club, a spear—and was hobbling around, looking, when an object where I'd been sitting caught my eye.

My Apple iPhone, still in its leather holster.

I scooped it up, opened the holster, and pressed the power button. *Please, dear God. Let it work.* The Apple icon appeared. Yes. I waited for it to power on. Then I punched in my four-digit password. Yes, there it was, all the icons, notification of 94 percent battery power, and two text messages—both from Selena.

Call me, please. I'm worried.

Where R U? Did you get my message?

I touched her number and waited, but there was no ring. Nothing. Not even that annoying little twirling circle. Shit! Why didn't things work when you needed them? I glanced into the overhead, up where birds sang and things moved in the foliage. Maybe that was it. The signal couldn't penetrate. I looked down the trail both ways. Nothing but soupy forest. What I needed was an ambulance. Not a trek through this jungle.

Alone.

Had Ramón tried to call? I looked at my messages and voice mail again. Nothing. Bastard! Probably in bed at this moment, humping his little Gypsy wife, begging her forgiveness. The thought hit me like a kick in the stomach. Why should I care?

I drew in a sharp breath and set off down the trail, barefoot.

CHAPTER 5

Frogs croaked. Butterflies floated around me like tiny angels, and giant trees loomed up on both sides. No wonder they had turned this place into a state park. Any other time I'd have appreciated its wildness, the creepers and bright red trumpet flowers, the bromeliads and orchids that seemed to festoon every tree, the vines that trailed into the water.

But not while I was lost and hurting and my heart broken from betrayal.

At last, I came to a small opening, a boggy place covered with palmettos and reeds. Buzzards circled above me as if waiting for me to die.

Please, dear God, let my phone work.

It didn't. 9-1-1 didn't work either. Maybe I could send a text. I opened Selena's message and keyed in *Help!!! Am injured on Brooker Creek trail near sinkhole.*

The text went out with an electronic swish that some genius had created. The word Sending showed on the display. Then came a short reply.

Message not delivered.

What was wrong with this stupid phone?

Siri, what about Siri?

"Hello, Siri, I need help. Siri, are you there? Siri."

No reply. Nothing, and for a fleeting moment I wanted to fling Siri and that useless phone into the water. This was ridiculous. I cupped a hand to my ear and listened for the sounds of traffic or music, anything at all to guide me. But there was only the chirp of crickets, the hoot of a distant owl, the smell of swamp, and those annoying, chattering birds.

"Stupid woman. Stupid woman."

"Just shut up!" I yelled, and flung a pine cone as if that would quiet them, but all it did was intensify the pain in my head. God, did it hurt! It was also bleeding, running down my face and dripping onto my dress. I needed to ice it. Needed to bandage it. Needed to rest.

I trudged over to the swamp. What I imagined would be dark and murky and stinky was as clear as a glass of tap water. Here and there it bubbled up like a spring. It was also shallow and filled with minnows and schools of fish and green turtles, some tiny, some as large as my hand. Just the sight of water made me realize how thirsty I was, my mouth dry and cottony.

A snowy egret alighted on a downed tree trunk and looked around. I watched, expecting an alligator to spring out of the water and devour it. Nothing happened. No alligators. No snakes either. Unless they were hiding amid the cypress knees and roots that bordered the water, or lurking beneath the floating lily pads. Waiting.

I picked up a stick and threw it into a little reed island.

Birds fluttered up, shrieking their protests. The egret glided away in silence. I flung a few more sticks to be certain, and finally hiked up my dress and put a foot in the water.

It was marvelously cold. I bent down to drink, but bending was painful, so I waded into deeper water, still glancing around for hidden dangers.

Fish scurried away. The egret returned. Other birds strode along the water's edge, pecking and chirping as if they had no concerns. I took another step, turning this way and that for danger. An owl hooted as if to say it was okay, and I thought how hauntingly beautiful it sounded—a love song in the morning, a call for companionship.

Damn that Ramón.

I sank into the coolness and scooped up water in my hands, cool, refreshing water with a mild earthy taste, better than the tap water of Ybor City. I drank. I splashed water onto my face. I rolled onto my stomach and dunked my head, trying to get sand and blood out of my hair, and I was wringing out the wetness when there came a shriek so piercing the birds fell silent.

There she stood, this apparition from hell who'd caused me to wreck. This woman who'd scared me out of my wits. Her appearance was so startling I scarcely noticed she was about my age, skinny and pale with scraggly black hair and a shapeless nightgown that reached her ankles. She even looked like me. She said nothing. Didn't have to. The look on her face said it all, and she was pointing at something behind me.

I turned to look. The egrets and the other birds were gone, and in their place, creating a V-shaped disturbance in the water, came an alligator as large as a log.

CHAPTER 6

With a yelp, without thinking, I bounded out and dashed down the trail, screaming, holding my wet dress up to my hips, uncertain how far or fast an alligator could run.

At last, exhausted and out of breath, I stopped and glanced back, gasping for breath. No alligator. No girl either. Only the trees and swamp and mist and the birds that were laughing at me. "Stupid woman! Stupid woman!"

Damn this place! Damn the people who ran it. And damn Florida. No warning signs. No barriers. That monster could have swallowed me and no one would have known.

"Hello!" I called out to the girl. "Are you there? Hello!"

Her silence was as maddening as my useless phone. I traced my footsteps back, but every tree with its gnarled roots became a place for alligators to hide. So did every bush, every shadowy depression and every outcrop of reeds and elephant ears. I yelled into patches of palmettos. I hollered up and down the trail. I even looked into the dangling Spanish moss and vines. But there was no trace of her, nothing, nada, not even footprints. How could that be?

I wrung water out my dress, retrieved my cell, and was wondering what to do next when I heard the drone of an engine, low pitched, almost like a vibration.

A rescue helicopter? Were they looking for me?

The sound grew louder. I hobbled back toward the opening. The noise became a roar. The foliage vibrated. Butterflies scattered. I lifted my arms. Surely they'd see me, standing there in my wet dress and scraggly hair, waving my arms like a refugee from a shipwreck.

A dark shadow appeared through the treetops. Then it was directly overhead, not a helicopter, but a low-flying biplane, one of those double-wing things like the crop-duster that tried to kill Cary Grant in *North by Northwest*.

"Hello! Here I am! Hello!"

A blast of wind shook the trees … then it was gone.

What was wrong with them? No dipping of wings to signal they'd seen me. No circling about. Just gone—like that crazy girl of the swamp. The only sign it had even been there was the lingering smell of exhaust fumes.

I tried my cell again. Still nothing. Now what? Best to strike off in the airplane's direction. There must be a nearby airfield. Otherwise, why would it be flying at treetop level?

I found a broken tree limb for walking and trudged off toward the morning sun, passing in and out of shadows so deep that the air temperature dropped.

At first, it seemed promising. No uneven ground or ravines. I even caught a whiff of wood smoke, sweet and pungent, and for a moment I remembered a camp-out with friends—girls sitting around a blazing fire, telling scary stories, their faces aglow in the illumination.

And now I was living one of those scary tales.

Foliage coiled around me. The trunks of fallen trees took on the form of alligators, and every overhanging vine was a snake waiting to drop on my head. Worse, it grew darker, as if the forest had swallowed the light. The hideous hoots, shrieks and croaks grew louder. I came to a swollen stream that was bridged by a fern-covered log. And just when I thought it couldn't get worse, rain began to fall, with thunder and flashes of lighting.

Dear God, why couldn't this be easy? Where were the hikers? Where were all those beautiful nature trails described on the Brooker Creek website?

This was the kind of place that only Tarzan would love.

Something growled. A twig snapped. I hurried to the log, bounded across, and tumbled to the opposite side, ready to do battle with whatever was stalking me.

A squirrel scurried across the log and climbed a tree. But no forest beast. Only the trees with their dangling foliage, the falling rain, and the rush of water.

Damn this jungle and damn Ramón and damn that girl who'd caused the wreck! If I got out of here alive, I would sue her. Sue Brooker Creek too.

The rain stopped, but the headache and nausea came back. I trudged on, growing weaker with each step, not daring to rest, not in this tangled forest with its croaks and shrieks.

My head pounded. My breath was coming in labored spurts, and blood was running down my cheek. I stumbled and fell against a spreading oak that was covered with little crimson and blue flowers. Probably poisonous, but who cared? Just another hazard of this cursed place.

I sank onto its roots and looked at the ruffled hem on my dress. Maybe I could rip it off to staunch the bleeding. Hadn't Scarlett done that for wounded soldiers in *Gone with the Wind*? I pulled at it. I jerked. But it didn't give. Damn it, what kind of material was this? I even tried to tear it with my teeth, but it was as hopeless as the likelihood I'd get out of this jungle alive. I could almost sense the angel of death, hovering back in the cool shadows, waiting to take my soul away, leaving my corpse for the animals.

Would Ramón miss me? Would he care? Would anyone? Not my mother. She'd gone to Spain "to find herself" at age fifty-something and was dancing flamenco in one of those little tourist dives in Granada. My dad had died of cancer when I was a child. My ex had moved to Miami with his gay partner after the divorce. The only person who might miss me was my old abuelita, but she was suffering from dementia and rarely recognized me.

And that was when reality struck, sitting on the ground with my back against a tree, bleeding out and too weak to even tear a flamenco dress for a bandage. Everyone I'd ever loved had left me. I had no one. And now I was going to die all alone, right here amid the crimson and blue flowers, with the sweetness of honeysuckle in the air.

I closed my eyes and surrendered.

CHAPTER 7

An owl hooted. Another one answered in the distance. The trees rustled. Peace came over me. I heard singing, the same beautiful hymn I'd last heard at a funeral.

Amazing grace, how sweet the sound,
that saved a wretch like me…

All in my head, I told myself, nature's way of preparing me for the final journey.

"Amy?"

I looked up, and there she stood again, almost luminous against the darkness of the forest, staring down at me. "Come with me," she said in Andalusian Spanish.

"Where?"

"Through the forest, to the river, beneath the trees."

"Are you real?"

She did not answer. Instead, she leaned down and laid a hand on my head. A shock ran through me, as if she'd touched me with a low voltage electric wire. "Your time has not yet come," she whispered, and pulled me to my feet.

Amazing how much stronger I felt, how my injuries had stopped hurting, how I could even see and hear better.

I once was lost, but now am found,
T'was blind but now I see…

A herd of deer sauntered by. They didn't scatter the way deer normally do. I turned to ask the girl again if she was real, but where she had stood before, there was only the forest with its giant trees and tangled vines.

"Hallelujah! Praise the Lord!"

I opened my eyes and found myself still on the ground, leaning against the tree. The singing had stopped, but there were other sounds, like someone preaching.

"Amen, brother!"

"Praise Jesus!"

How I managed to struggle up and stumble ahead, I have no idea. The preaching continued but gave way to singing and more hallelujahs. The sounds grew louder and more animated. Through the foliage, I saw movement and swatches of white.

My spirits soared. Around a bend and there they were, a congregation of black worshipers dressed in white robes near a creek bank. Some stood in waist-deep water, getting baptized. Men in straw hats stood on the bank with guns, and behind them, which didn't seem strange at the moment, were horses, mules and wagons.

Thank you, dear God.

The pastor, if that's what he was, dunked another saved soul. Again there were shouts of "Hallelujah!" Again the chorus sang "Amazing Grace," loud and clear, in voices that had never sounded so divine. I staggered down toward them, not thinking how I must look in my drenched clothing and disheveled hair with blood running down my face.

The singing stopped. The pastor looked up. There were gasps. They splashed out of the water, stumbling and tripping as if running from alligators, the strong helping the weak, and the entire bunch retreated toward the mules and wagons.

"Wait!" I cried in a voice so weak I could scarcely hear myself. "Help me. Please."

A guard pointed his rifle. "Get thee behind me, demon!"

I stumbled closer. "I'm Amy. I was—"

A gun fired. A bullet kicked up dirt near my bare feet.

I turned to run. And there stood that damn girl again, looking as if she'd just climbed out of a grave. My legs gave way, and the ground came up to meet me.

CHAPTER 8

Anyone who has ever had the flu knows that miserable feeling of hurting all over and seeing or hearing things that may or may not exist. That's what it was like for me, trying to get comfortable in a bed that smelled of cigarettes while people came and went like ghosts in a haze. First, it was a man, a doctor, I thought, until I saw his full beard, battered hat, and old-fashioned overalls that gave him the look of a character out of *Grapes of Wrath*.

"She ain't no ghost," he said, leaning over me with his lantern.

"That don't make a lick a sense," said a woman. "She's alive."

The man leaned so close I smelled his foul breath. "You sure she's alive?"

"Sure looks alive to me. Been talking in her sleep."

"Sweet Jesus," the man said. "Clarence is gonna have a hissy."

He stalked out. A door slammed. The woman yelled after him, "Wait a minute, Virgil, we need to talk!" Virgil didn't answer. The woman touched my arm. "You git some rest now, honey. Clarence ain't gonna touch you again. Sal neither."

Who the hell were Clarence and Sal? And why were these people speaking in country hick English? Something filmy closed around me. I listened for voices again, but the only sounds came from crickets and a whippoorwill outside the window, in the ghostly moonlight where alligators ruled the swamps. In my feverish dreams, I heard the strum of Ramón's guitar. I smelled cigarettes, coffee, and a wood fire.

Then, a rooster crowed outside the window.

I sat up, thinking I was back in Ybor City where chickens roamed the streets. But as the dream faded, I realized I was on a lumpy cot enclosed in mosquito netting, and someone had bandaged my head and dressed me in a gauzy white nightgown.

Where was this place? I swept back the mosquito net and tried to make sense of my surroundings. It had an earthen floor, exposed studs on the walls, a musty smell and a rusted tin roof supported by saplings, everything rough with nails sticking out.

And somewhere a woman was singing about her love for Jesus.

Jesus loves me, yes I know,
For the Bible tells me so…

A rooster crowed again, loud and abrasive. The singing stopped. There was a clattering sound, like banging on a pot. "If you don't pipe down," yelled a woman, "I'm gonna wring your scrawny neck!"

I crawled out of the cot, tested my balance, and crept to a screened window. Oh, God, I was still in that scary swamp with its trees and early morning haze. Chickens clucked and scratched the way they did in Ybor City. A heavyset black woman, red headscarf and all, stood over a steaming mix of clothes in a pot, stirring it with a stick. Her clothesline stretched from a small tree to a post, and on it was pinned an assortment of bib overalls, flannel shirts, sheets, socks … and my flamenco dress. Surely she hadn't boiled my dress in that pot.

"Hey, Pearl."

A bearded white man in overalls lumbered past the window. Was that Virgil, the man I'd thought was a doctor? He spoke to the washwoman and pointed to her bare feet. She jumped and did a little dance, and they both laughed. Then Virgil followed a footpath back toward the trees where another fire was burning, this one beneath a large copper boiler.

Five or six black men worked around it, stacking wooden kegs, chopping wood or pumping water from a long-handled water pump. A coiled tube ran from the boiler to a smaller copper pot. Was that a whiskey still? The only thing that made sense was that it was a replica for tourists.

Either that or I'd stumbled upon something I wasn't supposed to see.

The door opened. I flinched, but it was only a skinny white woman. She was younger than me, late teens, and might have been pretty except for her stringy blonde hair and a swollen black eye. Her fingernails were broken and dirty, and she was dressed in a shapeless nightgown.

"Lordy mercy," she said. "Just look at you, all up and around. Are you okay?"

"Bathroom," I mumbled.

She directed me through a crude door into a room that was little more than an attached shed with a wood plank over a smelly hole in the ground. Good Lord, how could people live like this? No running water or tissue either, but there was a bucket of Spanish moss, a washbasin of clean water, a sliver of broken mirror, and a comb and shaving gear on a shelf. The room was too dark and the mirror too small to see how wretched I must look, so I put myself together as best I could and went out to find the girl waiting with a cup of coffee.

"I fixed breakfast," she said, "scrambled eggs, bacon, grits, and black coffee. Ain't got no cream though. You must be starving, hiding in them woods all this time. Here, drink this coffee."

I took the coffee and gulped it down. "Who are you?"

"Donnie Sue, the girl that saved you from them maniacs. They thought you was Carmen's ghost. Jesus musta been looking after you."

"Where is this place?"

"You don't know?"

"All I remember is driving through Brooker Creek Park."

"Ain't no park here. All we got is swamp and trees."

"This isn't Brooker Creek?"

"The coloreds call it Bogger Creek."

"Bogger?"

"Like the bogger man. It's because of the ghost sightings. This swamp is scary."

"Is the center nearby?"

She gave me a blank stare. "Ain't never heard of no center."

"Do you have a cell I can use?"

"A what?"

"A telephone."

"Ha! You think this place has a horn?" She burst into laughter. "Look around you, girl. Only thing we got is a old icebox. Closest horn is Tarpon Springs, but that's five miles."

I glanced around for my iPhone. Before I could ask, she took it out of her pocket, looked at it a second, and thrust it into my hand. "Here's your cigarettes."

Cigarettes? Did she think my cell was a cigarette case? I opened my mouth to explain, but just as quickly closed it. She stepped closer and put a palm against my cheek. "Fever's gone. Are you one of them Catholic girls?"

"Is that a problem?"

"Ain't no problem long as you accept Jesus as your Lord and savior. You able to walk?"

"I think so."

"Good. Let's eat in the kitchen. But we gotta hurry. You don't want Clarence to find you."

"Who's Clarence?"

"You saying you don't know Clarence?"

"Never heard of him."

"You don't remember what he done to you?"

"Clarence didn't do anything to me. I was in a car wreck. Drove into the water."

"Your name's Carmen, ain't it?"

"My name is Amy. Who is Carmen?"

"You telling me you ain't Carmen?"

"No, I ain't Carmen. I'm Amy."

"Well, whoever you are, they thought the gators ate you and turned you into a ghost. Now come on to the kitchen. You need to git food in you and git outa here."

CHAPTER 9

The kitchen was as crude as the rest of the cabin. A wood-burning stove radiated heat. Black pots and skillets hung from nails on the walls, and on a rough wooden shelf sat dishes, fruit jar preserves, and cooking utensils. The only thing on the table, other than buzzing flies and a spoon for eating, was a bucket of water, a Bible, and a plate of food covered with a dishcloth. Donnie Sue motioned me into a cowhide-covered chair. I shooed away the flies.

"How long have I been here?" I asked.

"Since yesterday. I worried you wouldn't wake up in time to git away from Clarence."

"When does Clarence get here?"

She glanced at an old alarm clock. "Forty minutes. We got time to bless the food." She put one hand on the Bible and another on mine. "Lord God, thank you for this food we are about to eat. Thank you for saving this girl from Clarence and the beasts of the woods. And please keep me and her safe. I ask these blessings in the name of our Lord, Jesus Christ. Amen."

I said, "Amen," wiped the spoon on my gown, and tore into the eggs and grits. I had a hundred questions for her, like who was Clarence, who was Carmen, and who was the girl in the swamp, but time was short and I hadn't eaten for a day and a half. Donnie Sue refilled my cup from an antique-looking coffee pot and stepped to the screen door.

"Pearl," she called out.

"Yes, ma'am."

"Fold her things and put'em in that cotton sack."

"Yes, ma'am."

"Something for her to wear too."

"Yes, ma'am."

"And don't you breathe a word to Clarence."

"Ain't telling nobody, Miss Donnie. Don't see nothing. Don't hear nothing."

What on earth was this place? A washwoman who could double as Mammy in *Gone with the Wind* and a scrawny white teenager who looked like she'd been battered by her boyfriend. I raised my cell and took a photo of her standing in the door.

"Tell me about Clarence," I said.

Donnie Sue slammed the screen door and turned back. "You honestly don't remember?"

"I told you I have no idea who Clarence is."

She sat down and glared into my eyes. "Look, Amy, if that's your real name. That lump musta knocked the senses out of you. So you listen, and you listen good. Clarence works for Sal. When Sal's got a problem with one of his gals, he sends'em to Clarence. That's what he done with Carmen. Dumped her in the gator hole."

"Gator hole?"

"That's what the coloreds call it. They say you can see lights at night … hear them girls screaming. Sometimes a tree just falls in and disappears. They say it ain't got no bottom."

I didn't like the way this conversation was going, and I liked it even less when she told me the girl he tried to kill—Carmen—looked a lot like me.

"Spanish looks and all. Just like them other girls. Some couldn't even speak the King's English. Every single one of them gals wore fancy clothes and lacy underwear. Like you. All that Spanish stuff they wear at Rosa's."

The screen door opened with a screech. I jumped, thinking Clarence. But it was Pearl with a bundle of clothes.

"You choose," she said and dumped them on the table.

They were stiff from being on a clothesline and had a soapy smell.

Donnie Sue picked out a plain blue dress with puffed sleeves that looked like it had come from an old Sears catalog. "Ain't no time to iron it," she said and handed it to me along with a pair of bloomers that must have been designed by nuns in a convent. "Hurry up, now. Virgil's loading the wagon. You can ride with him to the airstrip, then hike to Keystone. From there you—"

An airplane buzzed overhead, throwing a quick shadow over the screen. Donnie Sue ran to the door and turned back, her eyes wide.

"Shit. You gotta git out of here. Now."

It usually takes an hour to pull myself together in the morning. Take a shower. Blow-dry my hair, put on makeup. Choose what to wear. But not today, not with a killer named Clarence at the airstrip a half-mile away, coming to finish the job. So off came the nightgown and on went the grannie clothing.

Donnie Sue wrapped a scarf around my head and tied an old pair of stub-nosed shoes on my feet, yapping away in fast-fire country Southern.

Pray to Jesus.

Get past the airstrip and keep going to Keystone.

Hitch a ride to Tampa with the Rolling Store.

She opened a Hav-a-Havana cigar box and took out two five-dollar bills. "Clarence's," she said, "but he ain't gonna miss it. It's small payment for what he done to you. Now go. Virgil's waiting. But don't let him play no snake tricks on you. He ain't right in the head."

"What will you tell Clarence?"

"Tell him you stole food from the smokehouse and ran back to the swamp. Jesus'll forgive me for lying. Now come on."

I followed her into the misty outdoors, past Pearl at the clothesline, past a smokehouse with its pungent smells, around clouds of floating butterflies and along a path beneath the trees. She pointed to a stack of oak saplings that had been cut into sharpened stakes.

"Tomato stakes," she said. "Take one. You can use it to kill vipers."

I grabbed the heaviest one I could find and looked up to see Virgil in his bib overalls and hat, pulling up in a mule-drawn wagon. On it were five or six wooden kegs from the whiskey still. He pointed to my feet. "Look out for that snake."

I froze. Virgil burst into laughter. Donnie Sue said, "You stop it, Virgil. That ain't funny. Now git this girl outa here. And don't let Clarence git her or I'll skin your hide."

"Yes, ma'am."

Donnie Sue handed me a small paper package. "Your dancing frock," she said and threw her arms around me. "Worse come to worse, you ask Frenchie for help."

"Who is Frenchie?"

"Lafitte. The pilot. Only decent man we got around here. Now go."

I climbed aboard with my package and tomato stake and sat on the floor behind the kegs. The wagon had a strong smell of whiskey and manure. Donnie Sue waved and said, "Pray, girl. Pray to Jesus. You hear?"

"I hear."

"He'll protect you." She waved again and said, "Abyssinia."

"What's Abyssinia?"

"It means I be seein' ya. Now git. Hurry."

Virgil popped the reins and away we went, following a rutted trail beneath moss-laden trees. Donnie Sue followed a short distance behind in her bare feet, swatting at deer flies.

"When you git to Rosa's, ask if they got a job for me. You hear?"

"I hear."

"Abyssinia," she said again. "And don't forget to pray to Jesus."

I nodded and waved goodbye, confused as ever. Who were these people? The day before, I'd been concerned about being eaten by alligators. Now, every shadow took on the shape of a man named Clarence. As if to magnify the danger, the mule cut loose with a loud blast of gas that wafted over us like an evil omen. Virgil bellowed with laughter. I held my nose until it passed.

"How far to the airstrip?" I asked him.

"It ain't far."

"Can you see it from this trail?"

"We ain't there yet, so you can't see it."

I shook my head in frustration. "Is the airstrip next to the road?"

"It's close."

"Listen, Virgil, here's what I want you to do. I want you to let me out just before we reach the airstrip. Forget you ever saw me. Okay?"

"Yes, ma'am. We ain't there yet, but I see Clarence."

CHAPTER 10

My heart almost stopped. I lifted my head and there he came, a man in white shirt, suspenders, and fedora hat, dodging around the ruts. His flared pants and boots and the pistol around his waist gave him the look of a Nazi in a war movie.

"I'm jumping out now," I said to Virgil. "Get as close to the bushes as you can."

"Which side?"

"That way." I gestured to the right.

Virgil yelled "Gee!" and pulled to the right.

I hopped out the back and stooped behind the wagon, waiting to get closer to the bushes, keeping as low as possible, hoping Clarence wouldn't see me.

"Whoa!" Virgil yelled and stopped the wagon.

"No, don't stop," I said. "Keep moving."

"Watch out for that snake."

"Damn it, Virgil, go!" I slapped the side of the wagon and dashed through a patch of saw palmettos, and would have kept going except for the swamp. Mist hung over the water like a curtain of doom. Giant cypress trees loomed up around me, bell-bottomed and covered with creepers. I crouched behind the nearest one, in ankle-deep water, and realized too late that the creepers were poison ivy.

Worse, Virgil and that damn moonshine wagon hadn't moved.

I crouched lower. A snake slithered across the water. Then it was

Clarence, yelling at Virgil. "Damn it to hell, you stupid moron. How come wadn't you at the strip on time?"

"Miss Donnie Sue, she was—"

"I don't give a goddamn about Donnie Sue. Is that swamp girl at the shack?"

"I ain't seen no girl."

"Don't you lie to me, Virgil. They called from Tarpon. Said they found her—alive."

Virgil sputtered words I couldn't make out. Clarence said, "Virgil, you are one stupid son of a bitch. That girl was big stuff in Ybor City. She gits away and talks to the sheriff, we'll all go to the chair. Understand? It'll be worse if Sal finds out. He'll fry your ass in oil."

There was silence. Clarence lit into him again, demanding to know if he'd seen me. Virgil let out a little whimper that sounded like a sad dog. Then Clarence said, "You git this wagon to the strip. Move it. I'll take care of the girl."

The wagon rolled on. I waited, wishing I had a shotgun instead of a tomato stake, not daring to breathe. Had Virgil pointed me out? Mosquitos and no-see-ums buzzed around me, biting my face and arms. I caught a whiff of cigarette smoke. The crunch of feet came closer, and still closer. My heart pushed against my ribs.

I pressed myself into the poison ivy. *Please, God, please.*

"Come on out, little girl. I know you back there."

A roar filled my head. The world seemed to go black. Then, as if the gateway to hell had opened, there he stood, this man who wanted to kill me for reasons I didn't understand.

"Well, well," he said, "and they thought you was a ghost."

I backed into the water, balancing myself with the stake.

He stepped closer. "Go ahead and run into the swamp. Them gators'll save me the trouble."

"I'm not who you think I am."

"Well, listen to you, speaking English. How'd that happen?" He came right up to the water's edge and pointed to the package that contained my flamenco dress. "What's that?"

"It's from Sal. He said to give it to you."

"He what?"

I clutched the stake in my right hand and tossed the package with my left. He caught it with both hands, and that was when I struck with the tomato stake—on the left side of his head.

His hat fell off. He staggered back, crying in pain, cursing, fumbling for his pistol.

I whacked him again and again. Hard. Blows to the head. Blows to his arms and hands. He went down, his cries growing louder, but I was in such a fury, ready to kill, to exact revenge for all the injustices inflicted on me by Ramón and this damn wilderness, that I might have driven the stake into his heart except for the girl of the swamp.

Her appearance was so sudden and unexpected, coming from behind a cypress tree in her white nightgown, and her face so pale and ghost-like, that I almost bolted.

She said nothing, nada, but the way she shook her head and finger was unmistakable.

Before I could speak, she turned and melded into the foliage in her bare feet, leaving Clarence on the ground in a fetal position, and me standing over him with my stake at his throat.

I pressed the stake a little harder.

"Why were you trying to kill me?" I asked.

His hair was down in his eyes. There was blood on his face. He mumbled something I didn't understand. I asked again. He groaned louder.

"Did Sal put you up to it?"

He broke into sobs and whines, which angered me even more. "Damn you, Clarence. I asked you a question. If you don't answer, I swear to God I'll kill you. Understand?"

"Yes, ma'am."

His answer didn't sound like the "Yes, ma'am" of respect. More like the "Yes, ma'am" of contempt, so I delivered a vicious blow to his hand. He groaned and cursed some more, and I had my stick in his throat when he said, "It was Sal. I had no choice."

"Why did Sal want to kill me?"

"He don't tell me nothing. Maybe you was cheatin' on him. Maybe you stole his money."

I kept probing but got nowhere, and I was about to start running again until a naughty thought came into my head. "Listen, Clarence, you know what Sal says about you? Says you're an ignorant white trash piece of shit. Says he's going to send his boys to take over your operation. They'll dump you and Virgil in the gator hole. Understand?"

"Sal said that?"

"All the time. Just wait until he hears I bested you and got away."

He went silent. It was time to go, but I wasn't about to leave him with the pistol. "Listen, Clarence, I want you to take out your pistol, slow, and put it on the ground."

"Can't. You done went and broke my hand."

The holster flap was open. I used the stake to fish it out and push it away, threatening to stab him in the throat if he moved. Then I scooped up the pistol and stepped away. It was heavier than I imagined and had an oily smell. I didn't have the foggiest idea how to use it, but just to have it in my hand gave me a feeling of power.

I poked him again. "I'm leaving, Clarence, but I'm telling you this. You ever come near me again, I'm going to put a stake through your heart. Understand?"

"Yes, ma'am."

"And one more thing. Watch your back with Sal. I'd get him before he gets you."

CHAPTER 11

I stumbled along the rutted trail, passing in and out of patches of fog, glancing behind to be sure he wasn't following. Pine limbs and trumpet vines hung so low I had to keep pushing them back. Deer flies swarmed. The "Habanera" from Bizet's *Carmen* came into my head again, and every few heartbeats a snake or some other creature slithered into the brush.

A clearing appeared in front, all sunlight and brightness, with crows circling in the overhead. I crept closer, my senses on full alert. Yes, there it was, a narrow runway that cut across the trail at an angle. A windsock hung limply from a pole. The yellow biplane was there too. The mule and wagon stood next to it, with Virgil and another man transferring kegs to the plane.

Now what? They'd see me if I tried to cross the runway, but I couldn't wait. What if Clarence was already on his way with a posse of moonshiners?

I tried to skirt the field to the left. The crows spotted me and put up such a fuss that I dashed into the foliage. Once they settled I tried again, only to find myself in an impenetrable swamp. Damn it. Now what? The only other possibility was going around the field to the right, but it would set off the crows again and take me too close to Virgil's wagon.

Fatigue came over me. My head ached. I hurt all over. Maybe I should rest a few minutes.

I glanced down the trail, didn't see Clarence, and sank against a large oak tree. Crows still circled and cawed in the overhead. Mosquitos and deer flies swarmed. I brushed them away and was pulling the scarf over my face when something moved in the brush.

Clarence?

No, I would have seen him. Someone or something was coming. I struggled to my feet. The brush parted in front, and out stepped a man in a leather jacket and boots.

"Who are you?" he asked.

He stepped closer. I backed away and aimed Clarence's pistol at him. He raised both hands. "Hey, put that thing down. I not going to hurt you."

He said this in an accent that sounded French. "Are you Lafitte?" I asked.

"*C'est moi.* Are you that … how you say, girl of the swamp?"

"What if I am?"

"Because Clarence after you."

"Is Keystone that way?"

He shook his head. "Best you not go to Keystone."

"Why not?"

"Clarence's friends."

The crows above us seemed to multiply. I glanced around like a cornered animal. Couldn't go to Keystone, couldn't go back, couldn't wait here, and wasn't about to splash into the swamp.

"If you going to shoot me," Lafitte said, "you better click off safety."

I glanced at the pistol, and in that moment of doubt Lafitte yanked it from my hand. He popped out the magazine and ejected a cartridge. "This is Clarence's. No?"

"What if it is?"

"How you get it?"

I explained or tried to. Lafitte's eyes grew wide. "You kill him?"

"I only broke his hand."

He tromped over to the trail, took a long look, swatted at insects, and came back. His jerky motions and the way he kept glancing around told me he was as unnerved as I was. "How much you weigh?" he asked.

"What does weight have to do with it?"

"The airplane. Is important. How much?"

"A hundred twenty-five."

He grimaced as if to say I needed to lose weight, then stepped closer and laid his hand against my cheek. "Are you hurt?"

"I'm okay."

"You not look okay. You need doctor."

He led me along the edge of the runway, keeping to the bushes until we came out behind a dilapidated shed that reeked of motor oil. A buzzard was perched on the rusted tin roof, and through an open back window I saw barrels, boxes, and tools as well as the airplane and Virgil's wagon. "You wait here," Lafitte said.

"What if Clarence comes?"

He handed me the pistol. "You know how a Luger to use?"

"What's a Luger?"

He rolled his eyes. "The pistol. I show you later. Wait here. Don't let Virgil see you."

He stepped around the shed and hurried over to the airplane. I sank to my knees with the pistol and tried to stay alert, but I was so weak I wanted to crawl into the bushes and sleep. Damn that Ramón. This whole thing was his fault. If he hadn't lied to me, I wouldn't have driven into a sinkhole. Wouldn't be in this stupid jungle either. Or stuck with a bunch of crazy moonshiners from the southern wild.

I took out my cell, snapped a couple of pictures, and tried to listen to their conversation. Virgil wanted to watch the take-off. Lafitte said no, that Clarence and Donnie Sue needed the supplies he'd brought from Tampa. The three of them loaded Virgil's wagon with bags and boxes, then Virgil rolled away. Lafitte spoke to the other man and motioned me over.

At first, I thought the other man was black, but as I approached him and saw the headband and muscles, the dangling earrings and the Bowie knife he carried in a red waistband, he took on the appearance of a scary Indian warrior.

"This is Popsicle," Lafitte said. "My mechanic. He not speak English."

I looked into Popsicle's acne-scarred face and said, "Nice to meet you."

He nodded and spoke to Lafitte in French. They glanced at me as if trying to decide what to do. Lafitte said, "*Bon,*" and held up a single finger. Then Popsicle stepped to the airplane and wrestled out a single cask.

"For the weight," Lafitte said. "Now we have only five barrels."

"How much do those barrels weigh?"

"Same as you … fifteen gallons a barrel. Now come on. *Allons.* We have to go."

I didn't protest about being reduced to gallons and let him help me into the plane, seating me on a cushion with my back to the pilot's seat, in a tiny space with evidence of Clarence's recent presence. He'd left cigarette butts, Baby Ruth candy wrappers, and a newspaper. The oak casks had the distinctive smell of moonshine and left barely enough room for my legs.

Lafitte handed me a green blanket. "You fly before?"

"Not in one of these. What is it?"

"A De Havilland. Gipsy Moth Two. A hundred twenty horses."

I had no idea what that meant and didn't care so long as it would fly. Didn't care about the cramped space and smells either. All I wanted was to get away from this cursed place. Through the open door, I saw Popsicle putting the keg in the shed and covering it with a tarp.

"Attákapas," Lafitte said.

"A what?"

"Attákapas Indian. From Louisiana. Place called Grand Coteau. We were in school together." He looked at his watch and pulled on a leather helmet with ear flaps.

"*Allons!*" he yelled to Popsicle and motioned with his arm.

I had a hundred questions for him, but by then Lafitte had climbed into his seat and Popsicle was trotting to the front of the plane. Lafitte clicked things I couldn't see. He mumbled to himself. I heard the word "Magneto," which meant nothing to me.

"Contact!" he hollered through the open door.

"Contact!" answered Popsicle.

The plane shook, but nothing happened. Good lord, was this one of those antique planes that could be started only by hand-swinging the prop?

"Contact!"

"Contact!"

Still nothing. What if the plane wouldn't start? What if Clarence showed up? This exchange of shouts and shakes went on two or three more heart-stopping times before the engine sputtered to life. A cloud of smelly white exhaust blew over us. Lafitte buckled in and closed the door. Popsicle gave a thumbs-up, and a few seconds later we were bumping and rolling down the runway, passing the moss-covered trees of Brooker Creek on each side.

Yes, thank goodness.

We made a U-turn at the end of the runway and sat there a moment, presumably for the engine to warm and Lafitte to check the instruments. The plane vibrated and shook. Exhaust fumes burned my eyes. *Come on, come on*, I wanted to say. *Get this thing in the air.*

"Is everything okay?" I asked.

"*C'est bon.*"

Bon? How could things be bon when people wanted to kill me and I had a splitting headache and was sitting in the back of a smelly airplane that was loaded with moonshine and might blow up any second? I picked up the newspaper on the floor. The *Tampa Tribune*.

What was this? The *Tribune* was defunct. Even weirder was the headline—WHO MURDERED THE LINDBERGH BABY?

"*Merde!*" said Lafitte.

I twisted around. "What?"

"Clarence. In the wagon with Virgil."

CHAPTER 12

Lafitte gunned the engine. I sank lower, my feet against the kegs. We bounced along the runway, the barrels rattling and shaking. Lafitte mumbled *"Allons"* again and again, each *allons* more desperate than the last, and I was certain we were going to marry the cypress trees at the end of the runway when at last we lifted into the air, banked, and flew away.

It took a long time for me to settle down. We were still over land, but a large body of water was off to the right. The gulf? No, we were heading east, into the sun. I twisted around and tapped Lafitte on the shoulder. The roar of the engine and whistle of wind was too loud for conversation, so I had to shout.

"IS THAT TAMPA BAY?"

"NORTH SHORE. THAT'S TAMPA OVER THERE."

He pointed to a small country-looking town set amid trees and water. How could that be Tampa? Tampa had skyscrapers and six-lane highways.

I picked up the newspaper. It was dated Monday, May 16, 1932, and had a photo of President Herbert Hoover and a story about Amelia Earhart's planned flight to Paris. Until that moment, I'd tried to rationalize all the bizarre happenings—the whiskey still and Donnie Sue, the way people dressed and talked, the disappearance of Brooker Creek Center, the girl of the swamp, and now this. I twisted around to Lafitte.

"WHAT IS THE DATE?"

"MONDAY THE SIXTEENTH."

"SIXTEENTH OF WHAT?"

"MAY."

May? It was October when I'd gone into that hole.

"WHAT YEAR?"

"YOU NOT KNOW YEAR?"

"I WAS IN AN ACCIDENT. BUMPED MY HEAD. CAN'T REMEMBER THE YEAR."

"IS 1932. NOW HOLD ON. ABOUT TO LAND."

We dropped lower and still lower, banking left and right, passing over rooftops that looked like cigar factories in Ybor City. People looked up and pointed. Wind and air pockets knocked us this way and that. My stomach churned. I held a hand over my mouth, willing myself to not throw up all over Lafitte's plane.

We buzzed a pasture at the edge of a housing area, scattering cows, chickens, and even a horse, almost clipping the tops of trees. Then we did a long banking turn and touched down in the pasture. A dog chased us, animals stared. We did a U-turn at a fence line, the engine roaring and kicking up dust, and finally came to a stop.

Lafitte pulled off his flap cap and turned to face me. "You okay?"

I tumbled out the door and threw up Donnie Sue's breakfast.

When I recovered, I found myself amid a dozen or more kids, most of them dirty-faced and dressed in rags. An older man yelled at them in Spanish to stay back. A truck appeared, and three or four rough-looking men began wrestling out the whiskey kegs and loading them onto the truck. "Only five?" one of them asked Lafitte.

"Sorry," Lafitte answered. "I'll get it later."

Within a minute they were gone, leaving behind a dust trail and more unanswered questions. Lafitte handed me a smelly towel to wipe my face.

"Where are we?" I asked.

"Ybor City. You not live here?"

I broke down in tears. "I don't know where I live. I can't remember."

"Poor baby," he said and put his arms around me. "Not to worry. I take care of you."

He helped me through a barbed-wire fence. A crowd had gathered on the other side, staring and pointing, speaking Spanish. Dogs barked. The sun beat down on my head. The world seemed to be swirling. I stumbled and would have fallen except for Lafitte.

"Almost at doctor's house," he said. "They take care of you."

"You're leaving me? What about Clarence?"

"Clarence know nothing about this place. Not to worry. Abyssinia later."

"What?"

"I said I be seeing you later."

We came to a large house with a porch, shutters and wrought-iron fence. A man came out and spoke to Lafitte in French. And then I was lying in a plush bed in a wall-papered room where a young woman in a lab coat gave me a spoonful of something with a vile, bitter taste.

"It'll help you relax," she said in Spanish.

Instead, it sent me back into that hellish jungle of trees and swamp and alligators and snakes, and Clarence and Virgil in a wagon that was stacked full of corpses of young women.

The girl of the swamp was there too, holding up a sign that read WELCOME TO 1932.

CHAPTER 13

Someone shook me awake. It was daylight. The crow of roosters told me it was morning, and it all came back when I sat up and stared into the face of the same young woman who'd helped me to bed. Not until then did I notice her dark complexion and how pretty she was.

"Feel better?" she asked in Spanish.

I wiped the sleep out of my eyes. My arms itched. The injury to my head hurt. So did my heart. "Where am I?" I asked.

"Doctor Antonio's home. You've been sleeping for"—she looked at her watch—"twenty hours. Did you know you talk in your sleep?"

"What did I say?"

"Sinkholes, alligators, somebody named Clarence." She handed me a glass of water. "I need to ask you some questions."

"Not until I go to the bathroom."

She helped me across the wooden floor and into a bathroom. The evidence of 1932 was all around—in the claw-foot bathtub with ivory faucets. In the overhead pull chain for flushing. And in the screened window for ventilation and a freestanding vanity. There was also a new toothbrush, Pepsodent toothpaste, and a bar of medicated soap that smelled like something my grandmother would make.

I stepped to the tiny mirror over the vanity and stared in horror at the wretch I'd become. Only days ago, Ramón had told me I was the most beautiful girl in the world, always talking about my smooth olive complexion, my long dark hair, and even the dimple. Now he would hardly recognize me with my scraggly hair and swollen face that was covered with insect bites and poison ivy rash. There was also a blood-stained bandage around my head and dark shadows beneath my eyes.

What I needed was a week or two at a spa, except I had no money. How could I pay the doctor? Where was I going to live? How was I going to survive in this new world?

I opened drawers and found an unopened box of Kotex pads, a bottle of Carter's Little Liver Pills, castor oil, Phillips' Milk of Magnesia, and Lydia Pinkham's menstrual medicine. Good God, how could people live like this? My bathroom at home was filled with everything a woman needed—makeup kit, shampoos and conditioners, hair blower, perfumes, lotions, eye rinse, fingernail clippers, scissors, and tissues.

"Señorita," came the nurse's voice through the door. "Do you need help?"

"I'm fine. Just give me a few minutes."

Breakfast was waiting on a tray when I came out—boiled eggs and toast, beans and rice, black coffee and chunks of apple with rusty nails sticking out like toothpicks.

"What is that?" I asked, pointing to the nails.

"Dr. Antonio says it's the quickest way to get iron into your body. It also represents the sin of Eve. Just don't swallow the nails."

I sank onto the side of the bed. Did they also put rusty nails in coffee? I stirred in cream, watched it blend with the coffee, and took a sip. Pure heaven. The nurse, whose name was Soledad, picked up her clipboard. "Is your name Carmen?"

"My name is Luz Amelia, but you can call me Amy."

She jotted it on her clipboard. "Amy what?"

I shrugged.

"You know your first name but don't know your last?"

Again I shrugged, thinking it best to say as little as possible.

"Tell me about your accident."

"Can I finish my breakfast?"

She left the room. I ate and glanced around at crucifixes on the walls, prints of Jesus, a small table on which rested a grotesque carving surrounded by candles and flowers. Weird, I thought. Probably a Cuban deity, but no more weird than finding myself back in 1932.

The door opened. Soledad came back with more coffee. "Tell me what happened," she said, pulling up a chair next to the bed. "You must have been reliving it in your dreams."

"All I remember is I woke up in the woods. Wandered around until I found these people. Then Lafitte helped me."

"Who?"

"The airplane pilot, Lafitte."

"Oh, him." She broke into a grin. "His real name isn't Lafitte."

"What's his real name?"

"Who knows? All I can say is he's Cajun French." She gushed over him a while, talked about how cute he was, and added that he and the doctor had been friends since the war.

"What war?"

"The Great War. How old are you, Amy?"

"I don't know."

"You look about twenty-five, so that's what I'll put. Birthdate …1907."

I didn't object to her taking six years off my age, but the image I'd seen in the mirror told me she was being kind. The questions went on. Where are you from? What is your profession? Do you have any best friends? I answered that I didn't know on the theory they'd put me in a straitjacket if I told the truth.

"What about relatives?" she said. "Surely you must remember something about them."

I closed my eyes and let my mind wander back to my dad, who'd come to Florida from the Maya Riviera, and how he loved the US and even served in the Marines in Vietnam, and how proud he was of his Mexican heritage and the beauty of palm trees that married the sea, and how he sometimes complained about the injustice of being treated like a second class citizen. And I thought of my mom, Florentina, whose life was filled with music and flamenco and who wore provocative dresses decorated with bright colors and who danced barefoot in moonlight, but who was now dancing flamenco in Spain. And I thought of the light of my life, my old abuelita Sonja, who also danced flamenco in her youth, and who must be wondering what happened to me.

"Well?" said Soledad. "Do you remember anything?"

I shook my head. After a while, she said, "Let's try some name associations. I'll name a comic strip character and you respond with the first thing that comes to mind."

I braced myself, thinking I'd better not play this game.

"Popeye," she said.

The taste of spinach came to mind, but I held my tongue.

"Superman."

"Someone strong."

"Good, Amy, how about Tarzan?"

"No."

"Dick Tracy?"

I shook my head.

"Little Orphan Annie?"

"Sorry."

She made a notation on her chart. "Okay, let's try memory retention. Can you recite the names I just gave you?"

"Sure. It's Popeye, Superman, Tarzan, Dick Tracy, and Little Orphan Annie."

"Good. None of those names are familiar to you?"

"No, but now I'm interested in reading the comic strips."

She laughed, took my blood pressure, said it was slightly elevated and was writing in her chart when the door opened and in walked Dr. Antonio with his stethoscope and white smock.

"*Muy buenos días*," he said in an accent that sounded like he was from Spain. After the pleasantries, he listened to my heartbeat and conferred quietly with Soledad. He also looked at what she'd written, and finally he sat in the chair beside me. He had a pleasant face, but there was no smile beneath his bushy mustache or in his dark eyes.

"It's too early to be certain," he said in his Castilian Spanish, "but from what you've told Nurse Soledad you could have either retrograde amnesia or dissociative amnesia." He explained that one is caused by serious head trauma and the other by a deeply disturbing event. "It's possible you have both. And there are rumors about—"

"About what?"

He exchanged glances with Nurse Soledad. "Rumors we'll save for later."

"I'd like to hear them now. Someone was trying to kill me."

"Who was trying to kill you, Amy?"

"Some redneck named Clarence. They also talked about Sal, said I was his girl."

"Are you his girl?"

"I don't even know who Sal is."

He laid a hand on my arm. "Listen, Amy. Is it okay if I call you Amy?"

"Of course."

"Good. So listen to me, Amy. Do you know who runs this town? People like Sal. He and Charlie Wall and Santo Trafficante. Also a long list of other gangsters. They control the clubs. They run bolita. They bring rum from Cuba. They bring moonshine from the swamp, and Lord knows what else they bring."

"But … but, how do they get away with it?"

"Amy, Amy, *por favor*, where have you been?"

He was still lecturing, talking about payoffs and corruption, bolita war, shotgun slayings and mayhem, when his speech was interrupted by a loud knocking from somewhere out the door. I sat straight up. Sal? Clarence? The doctor and the nurse exchanged puzzled looks. I glanced around for an exit. A window. A door. Where was the pistol when I needed it?

"I'll check," said Soledad, and went into the hallway.

There were muffled voices—a man demanding something I couldn't make out and a woman who sounded frantic, and then Soledad was back.

She closed the door and glanced at me as if to say the end was near.

"Well?" said the doctor.

"They want to see Amy."

"Who?" I asked, trying to remain calm.

"The woman says she's your sister."

"That's crazy. I don't have a sister. Don't let them in. They could be—"

The door swung open and in they marched.

CHAPTER 14

I jumped up so fast the tray clattered to the floor. Dr. Antonio also stood. "What's the meaning of this?" he asked. "You have no business—"

"Just calm yourself," said the man. "All we want is to see her." He pushed around the doctor and looked into my face, bringing with him the smell of cigars. I backed against the wall. He was shorter than me, but his double-breasted suit gave him the looks of a mafia don. So did his fedora and big rings on his fingers.

"What the hell happened to your face?" he asked in Italian-accented Spanish.

"Spanish flu," said the doctor. "It's contagious."

The man backed away and yanked a handkerchief from his breast pocket. The woman also kept her distance. She was about my age, and her hoop earrings and dark Mediterranean skin gave her a distinctive Gypsy look. She also bore a striking resemblance to my Tía Rosario, right down to her raven-colored hair and dark eyes.

"Who are you?" I asked.

"I'm Natalia, for heaven's sake, your big sister."

Her Spanish had an Andalusian accent, nothing like the Spanish of Ybor. She'd know the minute I started talking I wasn't her sister.

"I'm not sure if I know you or not," I said, trying to feign her accent.

"How can you not know me? We grew up together."

"She had a bad accident," said the doctor. "A head injury. Amnesia."

"Amnesia? Is that like … don't remember?"

The doctor shrugged. Natalia said, "Sal did this to her, Sal and those damn moonshiners." She stepped closer to me, her heels clicking on the wooden floor, her eyes wide with concern. "You poor child. Do you even know your name?"

Everyone in the room stared. Outside the house, a dog barked. Children laughed and played. A man was hawking fresh chicken, and I wondered if my life would ever be normal again.

"Your name is Carmen," Natalia said. "Carmen Amaya. Don't you remember?"

"Are you saying I'm a flamenco dancer?"

"Of course you are. Everyone knows you."

I sat down. Carmen Amaya was my great-grandmother, a well-known flamenco dancer who disappeared in 1932. Was she the girl of the swamp? Was she the reason for me being here now, because I'd been obsessing about her in 2019?

"Natalia asked you a question," Vito said. "We need to establish your bona fides. Are you or are you not Carmen Amaya?"

"Leave her alone," said Natalia. "Can't you see she's injured?"

"She can still answer questions."

"That's enough," said the doctor. "She needs rest, not an interrogation." He motioned toward the door with his thumb. "Give her a few days … come back later?"

"She's in grave danger," said Natalia. "Just give me a few minutes … in private. Please. There's something I need to show her."

The doctor turned to me.

"It's okay," I said.

He quit the room, but not before glaring at Vito as if he'd brought leprosy into his house.

Nurse Soledad, who had remained silent, picked up the contents of the spilled tray. "We'll be outside with a gun," she whispered. "Scream if you need help."

At the door, she paused and turned to Natalia. "I'm giving you five minutes."

Natalia waited for the door to close and turned back to me, and when she spoke, her words were in Caló, the Gypsy language of Andalusia. "They're gone, Carmen. It's okay."

I'd learned Caló from my abuelita and sometimes spoke it with Ramón, but I wasn't fluent, so I answered in Spanish. "I'm not pretending. I honestly don't know if I'm Carmen or not."

"But you understand Romani?"

I nodded.

"And you dance flamenco?"

"I think so."

"So you're one of us, *verdad*?"

I wasn't exactly Gypsy, but I had the blood, so again I nodded.

Natalia stepped closer. "That rash … is it Spanish flu?"

"Poison ivy. Who told you I was here?"

"Lafitte told me."

"The pilot?"

"Isn't he nice?" She talked about him in the same glowing terms as Soledad—tall and handsome and daring, sexy French accent, and how she'd love to go up in an airplane with him—and I was wondering what was so awesome about him when Vito flung out his arms.

"Would you stop it? He's nothing but a coon-ass hick who flies an airplane."

"Not a hick," Natalia shot back. "He's a war hero. You should see his medals."

"When did you see his medals?"

Natalia stepped over to him and brushed dandruff off his shoulders, and that was when I noticed his Italian looking shoes. They were bright and shiny and had the kind of soles to give him extra height. "Oh, Vito, Vito. That was long ago. You're the only man in my life."

I rolled my eyes. "Listen, didn't you say you wanted to show me something?"

She gave Vito a peck on the cheek and began digging in a side pocket of her handbag. "Here it is," she said and handed me a photo of great-grandmother Carmen. The same photo hung over the fireplace in my grandmother's home in 2019 Ybor—Carmen all done up in a sexy Flamenco dress that I'd copied for my performance with Ramón. The same dress Donnie Sue had cleaned and bagged for me. We looked so much alike that I could be the one in the picture.

Natalia plopped down on the bed beside me. "It's you, Carmen, and I'm going to prove it." She fumbled at the upper button of her blouse and fished out a medallion she wore around her neck, a spoked wagon wheel. "Do you know what this is?"

"A Gypsy medallion?"

"Precisely. We sometimes tattoo it on our bodies." She lifted her skirt and there it was, an identical image on her right inside thigh, red spokes and green wheel, next to the garter belt that held up her stockings. She touched my leg. "You have one just like it."

My hand went defensively to my thigh. The music from Bizet's *Carmen* began drumming in my head. I didn't have a tattoo anywhere on my body, at least not before. I hadn't seen myself nude since waking up in this scary new world. Was it possible that through some weird time warp I'd morphed into Great-grandma Carmen?

With a tattoo.

Natalia pulled her skirt back into place and smoothed out the wrinkles. "Don't you remember how you showed it when you were dancing? How the men at Rosa's loved it? 'Show us the tattoo!' they'd yell. 'Tattoo, Tattoo, Tattoo.' Remember?"

By then Vito had taken an interest. "Well, come on, girl. Pull it up and show us."

"Back off," Natalia said. "This is just for us girls."

Vito took a cigar out of his pocket, bit off the end, spit it out, and lit up with a gold-plated lighter. Smoke rose around him, filling the room with cancerous odors. I wanted to protest but didn't have to because the door opened and in marched Nurse Soledad.

She glared at Vito like a traffic cop. "You can't smoke in here."

"Says who, little girl?" He took another puff and defiantly blew a smoke circle.

Soledad yanked the cigar out of his hand, took it to the bathroom, and flushed it, leaving Vito with a stunned look on his face. When she came back, she spoke to me. "Five minutes are up. Are you finished with them or do you need more time?"

"Give me a couple more minutes."

She shot another glare at Vito and backed out the door.

"Well, come on," Natalia said. "Let's see the tattoo."

The music in my head picked up again, the guitars, the castanets, the handclapping and foot-stomping. Was I Carmen, arisen from the dead? Or was I Amy? I glanced over at Vito to be sure his back was turned, took a deep breath, and lifted my gown.

CHAPTER 15

Natalia stood for a better look. I didn't dare look. Suppose I had "died" in that 2019 sinkhole and been brought back as Carmen? Was that what happened when people died?

"Oh, my God, oh, my God," Natalia said and burst into sobs.

Vito came tromping over. "Is she or isn't she?"

Natalia yanked down my gown like a protective mother. "I'll tell you later. Why don't you wait outside? Give us some privacy."

Vito flung out his arms again. "What the hell is it with bossy women?"

"Just go. Get out. I need to talk with Carmen … alone."

Carmen? She'd called me Carmen. The castanets and hand-clapping grew louder. Vito sauntered to the door like a defeated dog. I waited for the door to close and pulled up my gown again. No tattoo. Only a smooth white thigh that was untouched by poison ivy. Relief flooded over me. "I'm not Carmen," I said. "Why did you let on to Vito?"

She pulled up a chair where the doctor had sat. "Because I wanted you to be Carmen. I prayed you were Carmen. I heard about the sightings … the girl of the swamp. I thought it was Carmen. It gave me hope. But now … now—"

Her voice broke. She covered her face and cried so hard it almost brought me to tears. I rubbed her back and was wondering if I should tell her I wasn't the girl of the swamp either when she stopped crying and pulled herself together. "Listen, Amy."

"Who told you my name is Amy?"

"The pilot … Lafitte. He told me. But I'd like to hear it from you. What happened to you back in that swamp? Do you remember anything?"

I told her the same thing I'd told Soledad, but she kept firing questions like an interrogator, asking about things I wouldn't know, like my work at Rosa's. Finally, I held up a hand to stop her. "Listen, I'm tired. My brain's not functioning. Can't we talk about this later?"

"Don't you get it, Amy? There may not be a later. Sal murdered Carmen. He tried to murder you. He knows you got away. He'll come after you. He's afraid you'll go to the G-men."

"The what?"

"Government men. Bureau of Investigation. Untouchables. You've got to get out of Ybor. I figure you've got three days before Sal kicks in the front door. The only question is who finds you first, the mob or J. Edgar Hoover. They all want you."

In spite of my weakness, I paced around the room. Somewhere a dog barked. A truck rumbled by, and in my tortured mind I pictured Vito dragging me out by the hair and taking me back to the swamp. I stopped in front of Natalia. "Wouldn't it be best if I explained to the G-men?"

"Are you crazy? You'd just end up in jail yourself."

"Why would I go to jail? Did Carmen do something illegal?"

She looked at me as if I were hopeless. "You don't remember, do you? Half of Ybor is on the wrong side of the law, just trying to survive in this stupid Hoover depression. As I see it, you've got two choices. One"—she held up a finger—"hop on the next Greyhound out of town."

"Is that what you'd do?"

"Hell, no. This is my home. Sal's not going to scare me away."

"So what would you do?"

She hitched up her handbag. "What I'd do is kill the sonofabitch, make him pay for what he did to you and Carmen … and those other girls. It's the only way you'll be safe again."

She said, "Abyssinia," gave me a big hug, and headed for the door.

"Wait," I said.

She stopped and turned around. "Yes, Carmen."

"I'm not Carmen."

"Let me ask you something, Amy, or whatever your name is. Do you want Sal and Clarence to pay for their crimes?"

"Of course, but—"

She waved her hand in front of my face. "No buts. They'll come after you anyway. Makes no difference whether you're Amy or Carmen. But if you're Carmen, or if they think you're Carmen, they'll come sooner and make more stupid mistakes."

"Why is that?"

"Because Sal was in love with her."

"He murdered Carmen because he was in love with her?"

"No, Amy, he murdered Carmen in a jealous rage." She dabbed at her eyes "Here's what happened. Carmen was terrified. She wanted to escape, so she cooperated with an agent … good looking guy named Aloysius Pruitt. I'm not sure what their relationship was, but Sal thought she was fucking him. Now Pruitt's dead. Shotgun blast to the head. Right in front of Carmen. Everybody knows Sal did it, but they can't prove it, not without Carmen."

The image of a bloodied corpse popped into my head.

"Something else you should know, Amy."

"What?"

"The G-men. They think Carmen was in on Pruitt's murder … think she set him up. It's okay to kill another mobster, people like Sal. It's good for the community. You can get away with it. But you don't kill a G-man. They'll come after you with their Chicago typewriters."

"Their what?"

"Tommy guns, machine guns."

In case I missed the point, she pretended she was aiming a machine gun at me and shot me full of holes. "Pow-pow-pow! Dead. They want to make an example of Pruitt's killer."

By then, my head was pounding and my stress level was in the danger zone. It was bad enough to be stuck in 1932 with no resources, no money, and no contacts. Bad enough to be injured and hurting, and to have a murderer named Sal after me. Now I had to worry about Elliott Ness and his Untouchables. And J. Edgar frigging Hoover.

Natalia put her hands on my shoulders. Her dark eyes were glossy. "You should rest, Amy. You look like you're about to drop." She hugged me, said, "Abyssinia," and stepped out the door.

CHAPTER 16

No sooner had the door closed than I regretted not asking when she was coming back, where she lived, and a hundred other things about the scary world of mobsters, molls, bootleggers, and G-men. But I needed rest and was trudging toward the bed when Soledad pushed into the room with her clipboard and a pitcher of lemonade.

She settled me against a pillow and picked up the photo of Carmen. "Nice picture."

"That's not me."

"How can it not be you? You're wearing your flamenco dress."

In the fog of all that had happened, I'd forgotten about my flamenco dress. "Where is it?"

"In there," she said, pointing to a large armoire. "All pressed and prettied up. We put away your cigarette case too. We don't want you smoking in your condition."

"Cigarette case?"

"Blue one. It was in your pocket."

It took me a moment to realize she was talking about my iPhone in its leather case. The same iPhone on which I'd downloaded 1932 newspapers in my research on Carmen.

"Where did you put it?"

"In a safe place."

"What about the pistol?"

"We don't allow patients to bring guns."

"But is it here?"

"You can have it back in a few days." She poured me a glass of lemonade and sat in the chair next to my bed. "I hope to God you're not Carmen."

"Why?"

"Isn't it obvious? Carmen attracted attention. She had a reputation. If it gets out you're Carmen, we'll have every newspaper reporter in Ybor knocking on our door."

"Did you know her?"

"Only by reputation. People say she was the most famous exotic dancer since Mata Hari."

"What's wrong with that?"

"Because she hung out with a bad crowd, people like Sal and Charlie Wall. They even say she was romantically involved with that big writer … Heming something or other."

"Hemingway?"

"That's it. The doctor has his books."

"Wait. Are you saying Carmen and Hemingway were like, you know … *amantes*?"

"You know how people talk."

I was glad I was already lying down or I'd have fainted. My great-grandmother sleeping with Hemingway—and also with Sal and a G-man. What a slut.

"Something else you should know," Soledad said.

"What?"

"That man who came with your sister, Vito. Do you know him?"

"That woman is not my sister. As for the man, no, I don't know him."

She took a deep breath. "Well, word around Ybor is … he works for Sal. That's why Dr. Antonio didn't want him in here."

By then I felt like running out of the place screaming. Was there anywhere in Ybor that was safe? Was this God's punishment for falling in love with a lying, cheating Gypsy?

"Are you okay?" Soledad asked.

"No, I'm not okay. What if Vito comes back?"

"He won't." She took my hand and looked at me with those big dark eyes. "From now on, we'll keep the doors locked. Also keep you out of sight."

"But I can't stay here forever, hiding."

"You don't have to. Lafitte should come tonight. We'll work out a plan."

"Tell me about Lafitte. You said he and the doctor were in the war together?"

"In France for two years. Dr. Antonio was the squadron doctor. Lafitte was a pilot. They say he shot down seven German planes. You should see his medals."

CHAPTER 17

Lafitte didn't come that night or the next. Natalia and Vito didn't return either, but I paid a heavy price for their earlier visit. It rained almost every night, with thunder and lightning. Things shook and rattled. I heard footfalls and voices and saw movement in the shadows. In my tortured mind I was certain Clarence or Sal would crawl through the window. Or Vito. Or the G-men would kick in the door. Ramón's Gypsy wife also visited me in my dreams, sometimes materializing at my bedside as a witch or a putrid corpse, laughing, calling me Carmen.

"I'm not Carmen," I protested.

"Of course you're Carmen. The stain is on your soul."

She said this so many times that I began to wonder if I was Carmen, even without the tattoo. Everything else had been stripped away: my bank account and possessions, my job and friends, my home, even my identity. So maybe it wouldn't be so bad to think of myself as Carmen. Carmen had a job, an identity, a history.

Amy had nothing.

Even when it didn't rain, I paid a price. I wanted to get out and jog like I did at home, wanted to go to the gym for a strenuous workout, wanted to rehearse my dance routine, but the only exercise I got was from puttering around in the doctor's backyard vegetable garden like an old woman, straw hat and all. I was also tortured by the sounds that came through my window at night, in the ghostly moonlight beyond the drapes—the beeping horns and traffic, the jingle of the night watchman's bells as he made his rounds, and the beautiful strains of *La Vereda Tropical* that spilled over the walls of some distant club.

What was it like out there? I imagined lovers hand in hand, and rowdy crowds going in and out of speakeasies, and torrid affairs like characters in a Somerset Maugham novel. But I knew nothing other than what Soledad told me.

I asked her if I could use the doctor's portable Remington typewriter. She said of course and gave me typing paper and showed me how to change a ribbon, correct mistakes, and pull the return for new lines. So I typed away, beginning with the spooky road that night in Brooker Creek and all that followed—everything from my disastrous performance to my meeting with Natalia and Vito. I even wrote about my loneliness, and I borrowed a line from Hemingway that had always stuck in my mind: *Night is not the same as the day ... all things are different ... and the night can be a dreadful time for lonely people...*

No one would ever see it, but at least it gave me something to do other than a backyard garden or reading newspaper stories about soup lines and poverty and Herbert Hoover's declining popularity and how Al Capone had been diagnosed with syphilitic dementia. Carmen's disappearance still made the papers, but the more sensational news was about Babe Ruth, Amelia Earhart, the Lindbergh baby, and Jack Benny's new radio show.

Not that I could listen to Jack Benny. The doctor had a beautiful Marconi, a floor model as large as a washing machine. I tried it while he was tending patients, dialing across the spectrum for news or music, but there were only static and garbled sounds.

Soledad said it was because God intended people to work during daylight.

And maybe she was right, because as soon as darkness settled over the city, and the doctor was in his slippers and I was back in my room, it worked beautifully.

Sometimes I cried myself to sleep, absurdly thinking about Ramón. Were all guys like him, cheating and lying their way into women's hearts? Why couldn't men be like Dr. Antonio, who'd saved Soledad from a dismal life in the cigar factory when she was sixteen? Now she was more than a nurse to him, which was obvious from the sounds I heard from their bedroom next door—the creak of a bed, the moans of pleasure—while I lay in misery in my bed.

Alone.

CHAPTER 18

fter about two weeks, or maybe three, I found myself alone in the house for the first time. And for the first time snooped like a thief, looking for my iPhone, starting in Dr. Antonio's bedroom. I looked in the closet, in an armoire, and every drawer, but I found only condoms, clothes, shoes, a Bible, prints of Jesus on the walls, and another pagan altar that Soledad had fashioned with flowers, seashells, candles, a rag doll and figurines of Caribbean gods.

Did she still worship those old gods?

Dr. Antonio's office was more interesting. It was all wood paneling with shelves and medical books, and war medals and certificates on the walls, and photos of airplanes, and the doctor in uniform with his wartime buddies. Lafitte was in the photo too, in his pilot's uniform.

Lafitte, the man who saved me from Clarence. Why hadn't he come to visit?

There were also books in French and Spanish by authors I loved—Victor Hugo, Alexandre Dumas, Gustave Flaubert, Leo Tolstoy and Hemingway's *A Farewell to Arms*.

Hemingway. Had he and my great-grandmother been lovers? I opened the book and thumbed through it until I reached the page where Frederic is reunited with Catherine at a hospital in Milan: *When I saw her I was in love with her. Everything turned over inside me. She looked toward the door, saw there was no one, then sat on the side of the bed and kissed me...*

I closed my eyes and imagined Lafitte sitting on the bed beside me, kissing me, telling me in his funny accent how he would fly me away.

A car drove past. I rushed to the window. Not them. I put away the book, opened the top desk drawer and there it was: my iPhone inside a Hav-a Havana cigar box. Clarence's ugly pistol was in the box too, smelling of gun oil and metal, but at least the doctor had placed a soft cloth between the pistol and my cell.

Had he examined the leather case and seen things that would create more problems? Or had he assumed it was just another cigarette case? It was the same size and shape. Better yet, the leather holder concealed the glossy black screen and buttons.

I opened the case and pressed the little power button on the side.

"Please," I said aloud. "Please have power."

The Apple symbol appeared. Yes. I plopped into the doctor's chair and entered my 4-digit passcode. The icons appeared, and notification of 67 percent battery power.

Yes. I clicked on the icon for the *Tampa Tribune*, a paper I'd downloaded in my other life in my search for news about Carmen. Would it open?

Yes.

Skip the front pages. Hurry. Skip to the back.

Yes, there they were, winning bolita numbers.

This was better than insider trading information. This was a sure thing. Maybe I wouldn't have to make a living as Carmen after all. Maybe I could make it as a fortune teller.

If I dared.

I shoved away a copy of *Grey's Anatomy*, grabbed the doctor's ink pen and pad, and jotted down winning numbers from the most lavish establishments in Ybor—El Dorado, Serafina, and the Lincoln Club— places that generated millions for the mob.

Hurry, I told myself. Get the information before Soledad and the doctor returned. I used only the first initial for each club, and I did it for today, Friday and Saturday, and was working on Monday when a slamming car door caused me to jump.

I put away the phone and scooted back to my room in time to hear the opening front door. Soledad bounced into my room with a package wrapped in brown paper, all smiles until she saw me. "Are you all right? You look like you've seen a ghost."

"I'm fine. What's in the package?"

She stepped closer and looked into my face. "Good, no more swelling. You're beginning to look normal. Even getting some sunlight." She handed me the package.

"What's this?"

"Open it."

I tore it open and found a black skirt and white blouse with ruffles, colors that blended with my hair and complexion. But the cut and style were 1930s awful. Padded shoulders. A blouse front that lapped over the buttons in double-breasted fashion. Sleeves that terminated in an open flare. And a tubular skirt that was almost ankle length, as depressing as the depression.

"Well," said Soledad. "What do you think?"

"*Perfecto.* It's me." I managed a smile. "When can I wear it?"

"Tonight. Lafitte is stopping by for a drink."

My stomach did a little flip. "Tonight?"

"He's been calling every day asking about you. He wanted to come before, but the doctor wouldn't let him, not until you…"

"Until I what?"

"Recovered. Looked better."

I sank onto the side of the bed. Lafitte wanting to see me? I'd only seen him once, and had been so weak and scared and on the run that all I remembered were his boots, leather jacket, airplane, and Cajun accent. Still, I'd fantasized about him and even dreamed about him. I'd also heard Soledad and Natalia gushing over him like he was Valentino, talking about his war exploits and medals. But there was also that little thing that he bootlegged for Sal and Clarence.

"Is this going to be like a date?" I asked Soledad.

She sat down beside me. "Don't you want to see him?"

"Well, yes, I want to thank him for rescuing me. But look at me. I'm a wreck."

"Oh, stop worrying. You look fine."

"Doesn't it trouble you he works for Clarence and Sal?"

"Everybody in this city works for crooks, Amy. People have to make a living."

"I don't have shoes."

"I have shoes. If they don't fit, I'll get you a pair. Get you a hat and purse too."

"Tell me what you know about Lafitte."

"Ask him yourself. He'll be here at eight. Now try on your clothes."

CHAPTER 19

As eight approached, Soledad brought me stockings along with an ornate bottle of perfume and another package that contained a medieval-looking corset. She had changed into a long, tube-shaped burgundy skirt and matching blouse as if she was the one going on a date, her dark hair pulled tight and tied in the back like a flamenco dancer.

I looked at the corset with its hooks and dangling straps. "Is that necessary?"

"It is if you wear stockings."

"What if I don't wear stockings?"

"You don't want him thinking you're a *puta*, do you?" She handed me the corset. "Better hurry. He'll be here in a few minutes."

My only experience with vintage underwear was with Victoria's Secret that I'd worn for lying, cheating Ramón. Back then, 87 years in the future, it had been lacy panties and a miniature garter to hold up fishnet stockings. Now it was granny white underwear from waist to thigh, a corset that smelled like rubber, and hosiery that only Sister Agnes would love.

I sucked in my stomach and strapped the corset around my waist.

Good God, what was wrong with women? They should have burned this stuff centuries ago.

A few minutes later, feeling like I was wearing a chastity belt, I clipped on Soledad's hoop earrings, put on makeup, dabbed on lilac-smelling perfume, put on white shoes, and inspected myself in the mirror. The shoulder pads didn't help. Neither did the wide lapel. Or the dark hem. I preferred the short skirts and feathers of the Twenties fashion. Jazz and Charleston, wild women and speakeasies, but I was stuck in the depressing Thirties.

"You look lovely," Soledad said. "How do you communicate with him?"

"English."

"You speak English?"

I wasn't ready to admit my native language was English, which would require an explanation, so I said, "Just enough to communicate."

The doorbell rang while we were sitting in the living room around a coffee table with cheese, flickering candles, and a bottle of illegal red wine, listening to ragtime from Radio Tampa on the Marconi that was nothing but static during the day.

Soledad dialed down the volume. I jumped up like a child. Dr. Antonio, smoking his pipe with the aromatic tobacco and dressed in the dark suit he usually wore during the day, headed to the door. I heard laughter and conversation in French.

Footfalls came closer … and there he stood, the pilot who'd saved me from the swamp, now dressed in a suit with a ridiculously short tie, his hair slicked down, his face deeply tanned.

He studied me for the longest time with those dark French eyes as if trying to decide if I was the waif he'd found in the swamp. "Amy," he finally said. "Is you?"

I nodded, speechless, unable to take my eyes off him, or even notice the roses he carried. He was taller than I remembered, with erect posture and chiseled features, looking like he'd stepped out of a romance novel. No wonder Soledad swooned over him.

Get a grip, I reminded myself. He's a bootlegger working for thugs and murderers.

Soledad, grinning like she'd won the Florida lottery, took his flowers and accepted his kisses on both cheeks. She spoke to him in Spanish. All I heard was my name. They chatted a moment, and then Lafitte turned to me, took my hand, and said, "Good to see you again."

He had a nice soapy smell, and even that sent a jolt of electricity through me. I couldn't ever remember being so jittery around a man and almost lost my voice saying it was good to see him too. He seemed to be struggling to find words as well, and I think we were both grateful when the doctor motioned us into chairs and poured wine.

We raised our glasses in a toast. Dr. Antonio spoke in French and Spanish, giving thanks for the pleasure of being together again with an old friend from the Great War and a new friend from the prohibition wars. "*Santé*," he said, and we all clinked our glasses together.

At first, we tried a four-way conversation, but since we weren't comfortable in a common language, it went nowhere. The doctor and Lafitte chatted a few minutes in French. Soledad and I chatted in Spanish. After a while, Lafitte stood and put on his fedora as if to say it was time to go. "Ever been to El Dorado?" he asked in passable Spanish.

"Isn't that a bordello?"

There were uncomfortable looks all around. Dr. Antonio said, "It's one of those all-purpose places, gambling, dining, and other things … upstairs. The dining part is respectable."

"Is it safe?"

He waved his hand back and forth. "No more dangerous than anywhere else in Ybor."

"I hope that's not where Sal hangs out."

"It's run by a different set of crooks. G-men don't go there either. Too Spanish for them."

I hurried to my room and checked El Dorado's winning bolita number for the day—51. Should I place a bet? Was it right when I knew the winning number in advance? *Do it*, said the greedy little devil in my head. *It's compensation for the agony you've had to endure.*

"Right," I said and grabbed a shawl. On the way out, I took a final look in the mirror. Earlier, I'd been horrified by the hat Soledad had pinned to my hair in rakish fashion, like a beret worn sideways. Now I thought it gave me the looks of a French artist. Yep, not so bad. Maybe Lafitte would knock it off in a passionate kiss.

Soledad appeared in the doorway, one hand on her hip and a teasing smile on her face. She waved the front door key at me. "Well," she said, "what do you think?"

I shrugged. "He's okay."

"More than okay. I saw how you almost fainted."

She handed me the key. "We won't wait up for you."

CHAPTER 20

Lafitte guided me down the front steps to a car beneath an oak tree, all aglitter in the porch lights. The sparkles of fireflies and familiar chirrs of crickets should have comforted me, but this was the first time I'd been outside the house at night, and I glanced into the darkness as if Clarence was lurking behind a tree with a tomato stake.

"What kind of car?" I asked Lafitte.

"Ford's latest model, a '32 sedan."

Knowing how men are about their toys, I walked around it, taking in the spare tire on the rear, a hood that looked a mile long, prominent fenders, and a boxy shape that gave it a gangster look. Lafitte opened the door and helped me into the passenger seat. It smelled new, but there were no interior lights, and the front seat was barely wide enough for two.

"Flathead V-8," he said.

"What's a flathead V-8?"

"Powerful enough to outrun coppers, bootleggers, G-men."

He climbed into the driver's seat and shifted the floor stick into neutral. "Much easier to start than old Model-A. Watch what I do." He explained each step as he opened the fuel line, turned the key in the ignition, pulled and pushed the choke, then pressed the floor starter. It whined and whirred. There was a smell of gas. The engine came to life with a ragged idle. It smoothed after a few adjustments and settled into a throaty pulse.

"Ready?" Lafitte asked. He revved the engine into a masculine vroooom-vroooom.

"Rock and roll."

He shook his head as if to say how strange I was and shifted the stick into gear. There was an awful grinding and crunching of gears, and we lurched into the night.

"Where's the seat belt?" I asked.

"Seat belts only for airplanes."

"What about a radio?"

"Ha, you are funny girl. One day, maybe they make with gramophones and telephones. Radios too. Maybe put wings so will fly."

"How about air conditioning?"

"On a car?"

"Why not? You can close the windows and ride in comfort. No outside noise or wind messing your hair. They'll also have navigation. Put it on the dashboard right there—a small electronic screen like they have in the movies. With a map showing where you are. It'll move with the car. Speak to you, tell you where to turn."

"Ha, you read Buck Rogers comic strips?"

"No."

"Where you come up with this?"

"If I told you, it would be so shocking you'd run off the road and get us both killed."

He roared with laughter. I laughed too and thought how nice it was to be able to laugh again, to dress up and get out of the house, to speak English, to be with good company. Lafitte patted the seat space beside him with his right hand. "More comfortable if you move over."

"Why?"

"Softer. Try it and see."

I slid over, even though there were only a few inches between us.

"Better," he said. "Now we not so loud talk."

He took my hand in his and on we drove, beneath the stars of a moonless sky. There were no street lights and precious few signs. Hardly any cars or people either, or brightly lit homes. Only an occasional pedestrian with an oil lamp or a dim glow in a window. The people we saw, and there were only a few, wore bandanas over their mouths and noses like bandits in an old western.

"Why are they wearing bandanas?" I asked.

"Evil gases of the swamp. The cholera it brings, and lung diseases. Carried by witches. Only way to protect is with bandana or scarf."

"Why aren't you wearing a bandana?"

"Ha, if Kaiser Wilhelm and the flying baron not kill me with their guns and airplanes and exploding shells, then vapors of the night I am not afraid."

I almost laughed at his garbled syntax, but mine would be worse if I attempted to speak French. "Tell me about the Dorado," I said. "What's so special about it?"

"Is like New Orleans, outside and in. People from all over, even rich Americans from Tampa, drive fancy cars. Come for gambling and Spanish girls."

"Don't they have girls in Tampa?"

"Not like here."

Things changed as we approached 7th Avenue. Storefronts were lit, but only dimly. No noisy pedestrians as in 2019, and the few I saw were leaning against buildings, sitting on blankets, or as slump-shouldered as relatives at a wake. There were also dogs and mule-drawn wagons, and people pushing wheelbarrows or pulling carts, or riding bicycles, and masked men on horseback, looking like they were getting ready to rob a bank.

"Horrible depression," said Lafitte. He shifted down for a traffic light. "Back in Twenties was almost like Bourbon Street, happy people. Now look how sad."

"Do you think Ybor looks like New Orleans?"

"Ybor has taste of New Orleans but not *joie de vivre*. Not imagination either. Just look at street names. All numbers. Boring. Where they come up with 7th Avenue? Should have exciting names like in New Orleans— Royale, Dauphine, Toulouse, Burgundy."

"It's called *Septima* in Spanish or sometimes *La Setima*, and it's too historic to change."

"Fine, keep it, but rename the others."

The light changed, but we stopped again for a streetcar with sparking cables and flashing red and green lights. Lafitte rattled on—"Rampart, Basin, Canal, Esplanade. But look where we are, corner of 7th Avenue and 15th Street. Blah!"

"What would you name this street?"

"A Spanish name, or Cuban or Italian, like the people here."

A car behind us beeped its oou-gah sound, and three or four horses galloped by, leaving traces of horse sweat and leather in the air. We sped on, Lafitte still rattling off New Orleans street names—"Chartres, Poydras, Loyola, St. Charles." Here and there I caught whiffs of Cuban coffee and cigar smoke, but the overwhelming essence as we rumbled along the brick streets of Ybor was exhaust fumes and horse manure.

"Carondelet, Toulouse, Conti, Gravier."

"Would you stop it? You made your point."

We turned right, drove a block to 8th Avenue, paused for a skinny dog, and stopped in front of El Dorado, a building of wrought iron balconies, ornate posts, and party lanterns, all lit up in red, yellow and green. "See," said Lafitte, "Looks like the quarter. They should name this street—"

"Shut up, please."

Uniformed attendants helped us out and took the keys for valet parking. A couple of beefy men in double-breasted suits and fedoras stood outside, looking into faces of arriving patrons. They patted Lafitte for weapons, looked into the handbag Soledad had provided for me, and held open the door.

I took Lafitte's arm, and we stepped into a world I knew only from books and movies.

CHAPTER 21

There was music, laughter, and singing, just like modern Ybor except for the smoke-filled air and the formality of dress, the men in suits and vests and fedoras, and the women in hats and tubular outfits with feathers and dangling necklaces. All the tables were full, and they were handing cups over a crowd jammed up at the bar. Some stood around with cups in their hands, others at dice tables or a roulette wheel, or seated at tables where clients played cards like in a saloon of an old Western.

"Why is everyone drinking coffee?" I yelled into Lafitte's ear.

Again he looked at me like I'd flown in from Mars. "Not coffee, Amy. Liquor, wine, beer, rum. They serve in cups in case of raid."

"We could be raided?"

"Maybe, but not to worry. We escape by tunnel."

"This place has a tunnel?"

"Amy, poor Amy. You not remember? Every place in Ybor has back door for quick escape. They warn if police come. See up there ... on balcony."

I followed his gaze up to a railing that ran along the interior from side to side. On it stood three Tommy gun-toting guards, looking down on the crowd.

"Is okay," Lafitte said. "We safe here."

I wasn't so sure about that and hugged his arm a little tighter. Several people looked up from their tables as if they knew me, or knew Lafitte, and again I felt a stir of uneasiness. Suppose Sal had spies in the place? Or suppose there was a shootout?

A slender man in a tuxedo led us through the melee to a plush dining area in the rear. It was also crowded but not as noisy as the front. He held the chair and said, "Señorita," the way they did in classy restaurants in Spain. He also placed a cloth napkin in both our laps and lit the candles with all the dignity of a funeral director.

Lafitte removed his fedora like a gentleman. A server named Aurelio took our order for cabernet sauvignon, and almost immediately a sommelier in a red vest appeared to uncork the wine. He poured each of us a cup and left with the bottle. We ordered the special of the night, sautéed grouper, and after we settled in with our wine, and with the pianist playing "How Deep is the Ocean," I said to Lafitte, "I don't get it. This is the Thirties, deep depression, people sleeping in the streets, and yet in here it's all party."

"Is Ybor," he said. "Gambling, vice, girls, employment in cigar factories." He leaned closer. "Listen, Amy, you are mystery woman, like dropped from sky."

"Is that a question?"

"Logical, not you think? A jungle. A running girl like Jane of the jungle. Who she is?"

"Didn't Clarence tell you?"

"Why Clarence tell me?"

"You work for him, don't you?"

His smile vanished. "I work for *moi*, for myself, Lafitte. Not Clarence. Only transport his whiskey. Is what I do is for living. Pay for airplane. Everyone in Ybor is prostitute for crooks. People have to survive."

"But you talk to Clarence, don't you?"

He took a swallow of wine. Fire was in his eyes, and I felt the heat rising to my face as well. "Look," I said. "Sal and Clarence tried to kill me. They probably killed Carmen … and other girls. So all I'm asking is—"

"Cigarettes, señorita? Señor?"

A skinny cigarette girl who couldn't have been older than fifteen stood at the table with her tray of Camels and Lucky Strikes, held by a strap around her neck. Lafitte asked if I smoked. I said no. He said he didn't either and waved her away. I watched her saunter across the floor where a young couple was dancing, holding each other as if they were deeply in love, the way Ramón and I used to dance.

Lafitte waved a hand in front of my eyes. "What were you saying?"

"Nothing. Let it go."

"No, I not let go. I may in the war kill. May God's commandments break too, but I not conspire with murderers like Sal and Clarence."

His expression was like a little boy wrongly accused, so I reached over and put my hand over his. "Listen, I know you're not a bad person. A bad person wouldn't have saved me from Clarence. If it wasn't for you, I'd still be hiding in the swamp." I touched my cup to his. "Thank you. Merci a thousand times."

He did not answer, but I saw the softening in his face, so we sipped our wine and listened to the pianist, and just when I thought the cloud had passed, he said, "You not to answer my question."

"What question?"

"Girl in swamp. Snakes and bootleggers."

"Didn't Dr. Antonio tell you about my amnesia?"

He sighed. "*Bon.* You not want to talk, I answer for you. *D'accord?*"

"You're going to tell me how I ended up in the swamp?"

"*Mais,* why not? Pretend my name Amy. Someone ask me question. Okay?"

I sat back with my cup of wine. This could be good. "Go ahead. I'm listening."

He grinned, which lessened the tension, and began speaking in a mock-female voice. "*Je ne sais quoi* I was in that swamp. No idea. Was like … how you say … poof! Opened eyes and there I be, trees, serpents and people who want to kill me."

"Don't forget alligators."

"Ah, yes, *cocodrillos.* But wait, I not finished. Here is second answer. I know exactly why I in swamp. I know who I am. I know where I from. But am I gonna tell Lafitte? *Non.*"

"Are you saying I'm hiding something?"

There was a smattering of applause for the pianist who finished his number and lit a cigarette. The young couple on the dance floor headed to their table, holding hands as if all was well in the world, but at our table, we sat looking at each other with suspicion. Lafitte finally said, "We all have secrets, Amy. We save discussion for later. *D'accord?*"

Maybe it was the sincerity in his voice or the mangled syntax. Or maybe it was that indefinable little glow I'd felt for him since he'd flown me out of the swamp. Whatever the case, I said, "Okay," as if it were an "I do" at a wedding. He smiled. I smiled back, and just when I was beginning to relax, Natalia came sashaying into the room on the arm of Vito.

They waved and settled at a nearby table, Vito in a double-breasted suit with a black tie, and Natalia in a glittery red outfit that would stop a fire truck.

"Why they here?" Lafitte asked. "*Pourquoi?*"

"Maybe a coincidence."

"I not in coincidence believe."

I didn't either and glanced at them again. The server was at their table, but Natalia was still looking in our direction as if she'd rather be with us. Or with Lafitte.

As if that wasn't uncomfortable enough, the lights dimmed and went out.

CHAPTER 22

The music stopped. Groans filled the air. Someone said "Ybor" as if it were an explanation. There was laughter, but for me, it was a moment of terror. Was this a deliberate act to darken the place long enough for Vito to put a knife in my back?

I scooted around the table to Lafitte's side. He wrapped an arm around me, his hand warm on my back, pressing my skin through the thin fabric of my blouse. I leaned into him.

"Is okay," he whispered. "Happen all the time."

Matches and cigarette lighters flared. Yellow pools of light blossomed around us. Servants hurried around with scented lamps and candles. Conversation picked up, and by the time our salad came to the table, my heartbeat was back to normal.

"Do you know that man with Natalia?" I asked Lafitte.

"He scare you?"

"I hear he works for Sal."

"Not anymore. Now he work for Trafficante. They try to … how you say—muscle in on Sal's operations. Is way things are in Ybor. One gang fight another."

Even in the fog of my confusion, it struck me that maybe that was why Natalia wanted to get rid of Sal, not for vengeance, but to remove an obstacle to Vito's ambition.

"Not to worry," Lafitte said. "Is okay."

The room grew stuffy and smoky without the ceiling fans. Couples came and left. Tuxedoed servers made their rounds. Cigarette girls sauntered from table to table in high heels and fishnet stockings, but over at Natalia's table there was turmoil. She jabbed a fork in our direction, hostility in her eyes. "I don't take orders from you," she said loud enough to turn heads.

"What's going on with them?" I asked.

"Natalia create dust storm everywhere."

"Maybe she'd rather be with us."

"Ha, ruin my dinner."

The main dish arrived. We ate, and Lafitte was telling me about black coffee, crawfish, and accordions in Cajun Louisiana when Natalia and Vito got into it again. She was on her feet. "DON'T TELL ME TO CALM DOWN!"

"Big mistake," I said. "It's never a good idea to tell an angry woman to calm down."

Natalia snatched up her purse and marched to our table. "We need to talk," she said to Lafitte and stormed away.

A stab of jealousy shot through me. "Are you and Natalia like…"

"Months ago."

Right, I thought. Gypsy women like Natalia—and Ramón's wife—didn't create that kind of stir unless something was going on. "Why did you break up with her?" I asked.

He reached over and took my hand. "Hey, Amy, I with you tonight, not Natalia. So let's—"

"Señorita."

It was the cigarette girl again. "That gentleman over there," she said, pointing in the direction where Natalia and Vito had been sitting. "He asked me to say hello."

I squinted my eyes. All I could make out in the dim light and smoky haze was a man with dark hair and mustache and a woman puffing on a cigarette through one of those long holders.

"Who is he?" I asked.

"He didn't say."

"Carmen admirer," Lafitte said. "Look, they waving."

I waved back and returned to my food, and by the time tiramisu arrived, we were chatting like a first-date couple. He asked about me, and I wanted to tell him how I'd grown up in a family of dancers in Ybor and how my old abuelita spoke to me in Caló and how I'd majored in creative arts at the University of Tampa and was working on my masters, and how I'd survived a bad marriage and gotten myself involved with a lying cheat like Ramón. But I couldn't, so I told him I had flashes of memory as a flamenco dancer. And he resumed his story about growing up in Louisiana, telling me his widowed mom had fallen in love with the village priest, a Jesuit from Holland, and the priest was his father, which accounted for his height.

"Did they marry?"

"*Mais, non, cher*, he was priest."

He seemed uncomfortable talking about it, so I asked how he became a flyer.

"Me? I only eighteen. America not yet in war, but French recruiters, they come to Louisiana, looking for men to fight for France, so I—" He stopped in mid-sentence and gestured toward the couple that waved. "Look, now they leave."

The man waved at us again, but instead of leaving, he and the woman came straight toward us. "Oh, my God," Lafitte said. "You know who that man?"

"Who?"

"Hemingway."

CHAPTER 23

I t happened so fast that all I could do was absorb his name before they stood before us, Hemingway tall and broad and dressed in a dark suit with blue tie, vest, and fedora, looking down at me with uncertainty in his eyes. The woman with him, nursing her cigarette in a long holder, didn't seem to care one way or the other.

"Carmen?" Hemingway said. "*Eres tú?*" Is it you?

I stood, not sure how to answer. He threw his big arms around me, gave me a crushing hug, kissed me on both cheeks, and introduced the woman with him as a playwright, Dorothy something-or-other, and then introduced himself to Lafitte as Ernesto.

They shook hands. Lafitte, who was also standing, spoke to him in French. All I understood was the word *guerre*. Hemingway removed his hat, plopped down at our table without being invited, and motioned for the server.

"A Spanish Rioja," he said in a commanding voice.

The server shuffled a bit. "I'm sorry, *caballero*, but the depression makes it—"

"No problem," Hemingway said. "Bring us the best you've got. *Tinto, por favor.*"

"*A sus órdenes, caballero.*"

The woman asked Lafitte where he was from. He said the Cajun country of Louisiana, and they began speaking in French. Hemingway moved his chair next to mine. "What in God's name happened to you,

Carmen? Rosa said you'd fallen off the face of the earth."

I wasn't comfortable lying and was on the verge of saying I wasn't Carmen until Lafitte jumped into the conversation in his broken Spanish.

"Is okay, Carmen. Tell Ernesto about your car wreck."

"You were in a car wreck?" Hemingway asked.

"*Sí, Ernesto. Un accidente muy grave.*"

I told him the same thing I'd told the doctor and said it affected my memory and apologized for not being able to recall any previous meetings with him, and I explained this in short, halting sentences, trying to emulate Natalia's Andalusian accent.

Lafitte seemed to be enjoying my discomfort, smiling now and then, even encouraging the charade by asking, "Would you like more dessert, *Carmen?*"

I kicked him under the table.

Hemingway loved to talk, and as I listened I tried to resolve conflicting reports about his Spanish. Some claimed he spoke it poorly; others that he had a native facility. I rated him in between, but with the flavor of northern Spain. He was also loud, getting attention from tables around us, and before long he was telling me about his accidents and injuries, and his new life in Key West, and how much he missed bullfights and flamenco and the foods of Spain, and how he hoped to go back and write another book about the turmoil.

"Spain is going to hell," he said, waving his arms like an Italian. "It's those damn fascists. They're getting encouragement from Mussolini. The Pope's no better. What was he thinking by banning tango? The only man in Spain with any sense is Unamuno."

He touched my arm as he spoke and even placed a hand on my thigh. I pushed it away. "I have an idea for your next book," I said.

"Tell me, woman. Let's hear it."

"Okay, suppose there's a war in Spain, the republic against the fascists. Don't you suppose foreigners will join both sides, like your hero joined the Italian army in *Farewell to Arms?*"

"It always happens."

"So let's suppose an American goes to Spain and joins the fight."

"On which side?"

"Oh, come on, Ernesto, your hero wouldn't fight for the fascists, would he?"

"Hell, no."

"Well, the hero would be like you, an adventurer. The plot should be … oh, let's see. He's a demolition expert. His job is to blow up a bridge before the fascists cross it."

"You should be the writer," Hemingway said. He took a cigarette out of a little silver case and offered me one. "Gitanes. Isn't that your brand?"

"No, thanks, I'm cutting down."

He shrugged, lit up, and leaned forward again. "Okay, you were telling me your plot."

"Well, it wouldn't be a Hemingway without a love angle, would it?"

"Love and war go together. What kind of wine is this?"

"I don't know. You ordered it. You like wine, don't you?"

"No, Carmen, I just like to swirl it around in a coffee cup." He drained the cup in one long gulp, winked, and waved over the server for another round.

I shook my head. Was this real, sitting here next to the great Hemingway, his face illuminated in candlelight? Too bad I didn't have my cell.

He leaned into me again. "What were you saying about love and war?"

"I said I'd put in a beautiful señorita. But someone has to die."

"Kill the woman?"

"No, Ernesto. You did that in *Farewell to Arms* … and every woman in the world hates you for it. This time you should kill the man, but after he does something heroic, you know, like sacrifice his life for the cause. Let the bell toll for him, not her."

"Say that again."

"I said you should kill your hero."

"No, not that. What did you say about the bell?"

I leaned closer and said, "Bong, bong. Let the bell toll for him, not the woman."

"She's right," said Dorothy, who'd been listening. "Kill the man. You can't trust them anyway." She shot Hemingway a why-are-you-ignoring-me look.

Lafitte, who had contributed nothing to the conversation, spoke up in his limited Spanish. "You know what I liked about *Farewell to Arms*?"

"The war scene," Dorothy answered. "It's what all you men want. Bang, bang, explosions. Dead soldiers. Didn't you get enough of that in the war?"

Lafitte glared at her. "That's not what I was going to say."

"What then?"

"Loyalty. Frederic is loyal to the woman he loves. It made me want to … cry."

From the way it grew silent—everyone at the table staring—you'd think he violated some sacred tenet of manhood. The expression on Dorothy's face morphed from hostile to friendly, and I knew at that moment that here was a man I could love, a man who would stand by his woman to the end. "Here's to loyalty," I said and raised my mug.

"Loyalty," they all said, and we clinked our mugs together.

The talk about war and writing went on, Hemingway dominating the conversation, sometimes mock shooting the enemy with his arms, and what was worse, his interest seemed to be in me, which didn't sit well with Lafitte, who was beginning to look miserable.

Dorothy also looked miserable, sitting there in her brimmed hat, adding to the room's toxic air with puffs from her cigarette in its long holder.

"Enough about war," I said, and pushed my chair closer to Lafitte. "I'm ready to play bolita."

"Me too," said Hemingway. He put on his hat. "Let's get a table closer to the action."

That wasn't the answer I wanted. I'd hoped Hemingway would take the hint and leave. Lafitte gave me a resigned look and called for the check.

"No, no," Hemingway said. "It's already on my tab."

Lafitte didn't look pleased with that either but thanked him anyway, and we all headed to another section to place our bets. Dorothy hung onto

Hemingway's arm like a drunk sailor, stumbling in her heels, and my head was also spinning from the wine.

"I'm sorry about this," I said in Lafitte's ear, holding his arm to keep my balance.

"Is Friday night, Amy. We not control who shows up. Natalia come, I not stop her. Your boyfriend come. We not stop him either."

"Damn it, Lafitte, he's not my boyfriend. He thinks I'm Carmen."

"Are you?"

"No, hell no, and I'm tired of pretending. I'm going to tell him the truth right now."

"No, Amy. Not to ruin his evening. Is only another hour."

He took my arm, and we were standing there, drawing unwanted stares, when a balding little man with a potbelly, thick mustache and heavy jowls came over and threw his arms around me.

"*Por Diós*, is that you, Carmen? Rosa said you've been out of town."

CHAPTER 24

Introductions followed. I didn't catch his name, only that he and the workers were excited about my upcoming visit to his cigar factory.

"Next Saturday," he said. "Bring your friend."

"But I'm not Carmen. I'm—"

He cuffed a hand over his ear. "Say that again. Can't hear with all this racket."

Lafitte stepped forward. "CARMEN SAY NEXT SATURDAY SHE SEE YOU."

"Saturday," the man said. Then he and his wife melded into the crowd.

I turned to Lafitte. "What is wrong with you? I'm in enough trouble already."

"You flamenco dancer, no?"

"What if I am?"

"Then you not disappoint the workers. Is at Hav-a-Havana. Don Ignacio is owner."

"Don Ignacio?"

"Big man in Ybor. Friend with gangsters. Also in love with Carmen."

I rolled my eyes, and a short while later we were seated with Hemingway in a noisy room with at least a hundred other laughing, smoking, chatting, drinking-from-a-cup, half-inebriated patrons, near a spinning roulette wheel.

"How do we play bolita?" I yelled into Lafitte's ear.

"You choose a number between one and one hundred." He waved over a tuxedoed server and asked for forms and pencils. I heard talk of lucky numbers, and a woman saying her dead husband had told her the winning number in a dream. Hemingway bet a dollar on 98, the last two digits of his birth year. Dorothy placed a dollar on 29, her age, and Lafitte chose 32, saying it was his lucky year because he'd met me in 1932.

"How about you?" Lafitte asked me. "What's your lucky number?"

Maybe it was my imagination, but it seemed as if the noise level went down and every eye in the place was on me, which made me even more self-conscious. It didn't help that someone said "Gypsy," either as a slur or a misguided notion that Gypsies have intuitive powers.

Lafitte made it worse by plunking another dollar on the table.

"Whatever Carmen chooses, I'm adding a dollar."

"Me too," said Hemingway.

The server who'd passed around the forms stood off the side, waiting for us to decide. As if that wasn't stressful enough, Natalia materialized from the crowd again, trailed by her pock-faced, cigar-smoking, dandruff-on-his-shoulders, height-challenged, mafia boyfriend. Damn her, was she trying to ruin my relationship with Lafitte?

She pushed around the table in dramatic fashion, all jangling jewelry and flowing scarves, until she stood behind me. She placed both hands on my shoulders and leaned down next to my face, bringing with her the smell of jasmine and cigarettes.

"Well, well," she said. "Look who we have here, a famous writer, a famous playwright, a famous war hero, and my famous Gypsy sister, the one and only Carmen, the Mata Hari of Ybor City. You should all stand and take a bow."

I twisted around to face her. Vito looked as embarrassed as the rest of us and tried to lead her away, but she jerked free.

"PUTA BASTARD. If I want to talk to my sister, I'LL FUCKING TALK WITH MY SISTER. If you don't like it, leave." She waved her hand. "Go! *Vete!*"

A thick-necked server who probably doubled as a bouncer came over to reason with her. She cursed him in Spanish and Romani, *puta* this and *joda* that, which brought over more bouncers.

"*No hay derecho!*" she screamed at them. "You have no right," which in Spanish is about the strongest protest you can make. Then Vito got into a scuffle with the bouncers, cursing and shouting, losing his hat in the process, and it didn't end until both he and Natalia were more or less dragged out of the place, Vito yelling he'd have the place shut down.

This set off a flurry of mumbles around us, with words like lowlife Gypsies, thugs and whores.

By then, I was ready to crawl under the table. It wasn't supposed to be like this. Back at the doctor's house, I had imagined a romantic dinner with just the two of us—candlelight, wine, conversation and a cool night breeze off the bay. But now ... now I was also the Gypsy sister of the crazy one, sitting at a table with a man who thought he'd slept with me and another who probably wished he'd abandoned me in the swamp.

"Well, that was interesting," said Hemingway. "She should have been in the war."

Lafitte placed a hand over mine. "Next time I take you to a quiet place. Okay?"

"You promise?"

"Promise."

The blast of a horn interrupted us. It grew so quiet I heard the clatter of dishes in the kitchen. Then a man in black tie and tails ascended a stage and rang a bell. Beside it rested a glass jar filled with ivory balls numbered from one to a hundred, all white and shining.

"Fifteen minutes to midnight," he said in Spanish and English, speaking through a megaphone. "Fifteen minutes for your final bets. This could be your lucky night."

Lafitte and Hemingway waved their dollars at me again. Dorothy took out a dollar. "Ernesto says you read palms. Can you predict the winning number?"

"Maybe."

"Then let's hear it."

"Look, here's the thing. All of you know I was in an accident. A head injury. Memory almost gone. But every day I get flashes of things. Future things. Like this morning at breakfast."

"What happened at breakfast?"

"Well, there was this big crystal bowl on the table—"

Dorothy said, "You have a crystal ball on the breakfast table?"

"Bowl, not ball. It seemed to be swirling. I saw things in it."

"Saw what?" Hemingway asked.

"A number, Ernesto."

His eyes bored into mine. "What number?"

"Well, I wasn't thinking bolita but maybe if I had another bowl."

Lafitte waved over the server. "Bring us an empty bowl."

"Crystal," I said, "and two candles."

CHAPTER 25

By the time the bowl came to the table, we were down to ten minutes. I turned it upside down. Lafitte and Hemingway lit the candles with cigarette lighters. I wrapped the shawl around my head like a fortuneteller and placed a candle on each side of the bowl. It glittered in the flickering light. Then, with a silent prayer to get it right, and with the three of them looking on, I leaned forward, clasped the bowl in both hands, and glared at it as if I were a fortune-teller, mumbling the first thing that came into my head—in English.

Speak, bowl, full of light. Let me hear your song.
Secret numbers, souls that wonder … if this could be the night.

People at other tables stared, and when someone said, "Gypsy," my inner street performer came out. No longer was I acting for Hemingway, Dorothy, and Lafitte; I was performing for the entire caravan. I swayed my upper body back and forth. I moved the bowl around, and I chanted like a spiritualist at a séance.

Speak, bowl, full of light. Let me hear your song…

People gathered around—cigarette girls, servers, guests, even the bouncers—as if they expected the table to levitate. I muttered words in Gypsy Romani, like a chant, and in one final act of the absurd, I said, "Yes, yes, yes!" like I was having an orgasm, and came halfway out of my chair before sinking back down as if drained of energy.

"Are you okay?" Lafitte asked, touching my arm.

"I will be. Just give me a second." I shoved away the bowl and blew out the candles, then I took off my shawl, leaned back, and waited for the surrounding people to drift away.

Dorothy pushed closer. "Did you see the winning number?"

"I don't know if it was the winning number or not."

"We're running out of time," she said. "What number?"

"Fifty-one."

The bell rang again. "*Cinco minutos*," said the announcer. "Five minutes."

Lafitte pulled another dollar from his pocket and handed it to me. "A dollar for you and another for my bet." Hemingway and Dorothy also shoved a dollar at me, saying my performance was worth it even if the number was wrong. Then, with just a couple of minutes left, and with their three dollars added to the five Donnie Sue had given me, we placed our bets—eight dollars for me on 51 and a dollar each for them.

The seconds passed. The room settled in anticipation. My mind buzzed. At odds of a hundred to one, I could win eight hundred dollars. But what if the number was wrong?

The man in black tie and tails bounded onto the stage again. "*Damas y caballeros*," he said, speaking through a megaphone. "Ladies and gentlemen. *Cubanos, Españoles, Italianos y Americanos*. Are we readyyyy? *Estamos listos*?"

This continued in English and Spanish until the entire place was shaking with affirmations. The man began picking up the numbered balls and dropping them into a velvet bag, mixing them with his hand as the bag filled. When the last ball was inside, he tied the bag with a drawstring, stepped off the stage, and handed it to a young woman at a table.

"Shake it," he said. "Mix them up."

The woman shook the bag and passed it to another table, and on it went, each person shaking and turning it this way and that, some kissing it or making the sign of the cross.

This went on for at least ten minutes, but at last the bag was back in the hands of the man in tails and tie, and even he gave it a final shake. "Now," he said, "which one of you beautiful señoritas wants to pick the winning ball?"

A young woman in a red dress lifted her arm. The man handed her the bag and told her to select a single ball by feeling through the fabric of the bag.

"Just the outside," he said. "Don't open it."

The woman crossed herself like a good Catholic and made a big show of feeling through the bag. "This one," she said in a girlish voice.

The man tied a red ribbon around the bulge she'd chosen, and took the bag back to the stage. He picked up a large pair of bright red scissors and waved the scissors around, snipping the air. "Ladies and gentlemen. Are you readdddy?"

"*Coño*," Hemingway mumbled. "It looks like a bull castration."

Lafitte put an arm around me. "If you win, keep quiet. No celebration."

"Why?"

"Because is dark outside. Maybe thieves waiting to rob the winner."

There was momentary foot-stomping and applause. Then it grew so quiet I heard a passing car. Lafitte squeezed my shoulder. Hemingway cocked a bushy eyebrow. With great flourish, the man in tails snipped the bag just above the bulge.

He untied the ribbon that secured the bulge and took out the ball.

There was a drumroll from the musicians.

The man held the ball aloft. "The winning number is … FIFTY-ONE!"

I almost collapsed in relief. There were cheers from another table, a woman waving her arms, saying she'd just won ten dollars. Hemingway, Dorothy and Lafitte, who'd won a hundred each, sat there in open-mouthed disbelief, and I could hardly believe it myself. Eight hundred dollars was a huge amount, considering the average pay in Ybor was less than twenty dollars a week. A few more nights of this and I could afford one of those nice houses on Bayshore Boulevard. A Packard in the garage. A housecleaner, a new wardrobe.

Maybe my plunge into 1932 wasn't so bad after all.

We clinked our cups together and took a sip. The band struck up "I Don't Know Why." Couples headed to the dance floor; others gathered up their things to leave. The outside doors opened, and the surrounding air grew cooler and more refreshing. Lafitte pulled me onto the floor, and I came into his arms as if we were lovers.

I don't know why I love you like I do.

I don't know why, I just do….

Our faces touched. His breath was warm on my cheek. "This is crazy," Lafitte said, caressing my back. "Woman of mystery. Girl of the swamp. Reader of crystal bowl."

"Is that a question?"

"I meet you one time, in swamp, and now … now I want every night be with you."

He probably used that same line on Natalia and his other conquests, but I liked it anyway and I liked him, so I cocked my head toward Hemingway. "Why don't we collect our winnings and tell them goodnight?"

"Bon idea," he said and led me to the payment window.

A little man with thick eyeglasses, visor, and elastic armbands on his shirt sleeves tended the window. Two thick-necked men stood on either side. A sign said we had ten days to collect. A half dozen other winners stood in line, including Dorothy and Hemingway, swaying to the music. Hemingway, never shy about anything, sang along with the vocalist.

You never seem to want my romancing.

The only time you hold me is when we're dancing.

They collected their money. We moved to the window. And that was when a loud pop sounded outside the building, like the blast of a firecracker.

There were other pops, and then the rat-a-tat of automatic fire.

Doors slammed shut. The music stopped. The payment window shut. The men guarding it took off at a run. Lafitte said "*Merde!*" and grabbed my arm. "*Allons!* Out of here."

"Is it a raid?"

"Not a raid. Police not come in shooting."

Glass shattered. An explosion shook the building. There were shouts and screams and someone yelling, "Douse the lamps!" and within moments, the entire place plunged into darkness.

CHAPTER 26

Panic turned to stampede. Bodies shoved past other bodies. Someone collided with us in the darkness. Not one person but many, sweeping us along in a flowing, screaming, crushing mass of humanity, like a raging river of debris from a flash flood.

I screamed for Lafitte, who was probably shouting for me. But there was no communication in that madness, only an ungodly collision of trampling feet, smoke, acrid smells, shrieks, and flashes of gunfire through the open windows.

Stay on your feet, I told myself. To fall would be certain death, and for a crazy moment I thought of Hemingway running with the bulls in Pamplona.

The flow took me against a table, pinning me against it. The pressure grew. It hurt. I couldn't move, couldn't do anything except cry and scream, and I was leaning over the table, trying to pull free, when a luminescent glow appeared to my front.

There she stood in her tattered clothing, the girl of the swamp, amid the crowd that was flowing around her, the same girl who'd saved me from the alligators. She motioned with her hand as to say, "Come this way."

What happened next may have been divine intervention, like Jesus raising Lazarus from the dead, or it may have been the force of pushing bodies. The table slid forward, relieving the pressure on my thighs. I climbed atop the table, scooted to the other side, and crawled beneath it. The girl vanished, but the table kept sliding.

I clung to the legs and slid with it, praying to God, Jesus, and the Virgin that it wouldn't overturn and crush me, and that the building wouldn't catch fire, and that whoever was shooting wouldn't come inside and kill everyone, and that Lafitte, Hemingway, and Dorothy were safe.

At last, the table came to rest against a wall. The flow of people and shouts and screams diminished. So did the gunfire, leaving only the acrid smells. Lamps and lanterns were lit, and when I heard voices near me, I crawled out and struggled to my feet.

"Señorita," said a tuxedoed worker holding a lantern, "are you okay?"

I wasn't. My beret was gone, my shoes missing, my thighs felt as if a truck had run over me, and I couldn't stop shaking, and I was desperate to find Lafitte.

"You need to go that way," said the man, pointing into the darkness.

"Where?"

"This way." He lifted his lantern, and I followed him around a mess of overturned tables, chairs, and other litter, past injured people that sat against a wall or lay on the floor, tended by workers. I looked into their faces as I passed, praying one of them wasn't Lafitte—and almost stumbled on a body that lay face down in a puddle of blood.

I bent over him.

"No, no, no, señorita. Someone shot him. Get out. The police are—"

The front door burst open and in they came, a steady flow of uniformed policemen and men in suits and fedoras, all with pistols or shotguns, shouting orders.

"Hurry," the man said. "They'll arrest you." He hustled me into the shadows, around more litter and toward the stairway, telling me to watch out for broken crockery.

"What was the shooting about?" I asked.

"We may never learn the truth."

He led me to the back of the stairway, grumbling about the stupidity of it all, and opened a door marked *Emergency Exit*. "Down there," he said. "It's the escape tunnel. Just follow it." He handed me his lantern. "Good luck, señorita, I'm so sorry this happened."

He shut the door behind me, leaving me alone in the dim glow of lantern light.

Good Lord. Only a short while ago I'd been fantasizing about a mansion on Bayshore Boulevard, with a Packard and servants. Now I was a refugee in the escape tunnel. Were rats down here—like in the sewers of Paris? Would I have to slosh through human waste?

Down I went in my stockinged feet, into the shadowy darkness and earthy smells of a world I didn't know. Al Capone's world. Now my world.

There were candles along the walls, dimly illuminating a narrow passage that seemed to go on forever. Water dripped and ran down the wall in little rivulets and through a small channel on the side. My lantern cast spooky shadows. I half expected to see skulls and bones and long rotted corpses. Instead, I saw the evidence of panic, scattered on the floor in shawls and high heels—a man's jacket, cigarette cases, handkerchiefs, hats, even a tote bag.

I found sandals that fit. They didn't match, weren't the same color either, but I didn't care. I needed something to cover my feet.

A door slammed. The candles flickered. I stopped and listened, and breathed the smells of mildew and mold.

What if there was no exit? What if that harmless-looking man had locked me in this hole for his own evil purposes? I heard squeaks, like an army of invading rats, and I think if the girl of the swamp had appeared I'd have died of a heart attack.

I ran. I stumbled and almost fell, and kept running until the tunnel ended in another stairway. Someone had even painted an exit sign and up-arrow on the wall.

Up I went, holding the rail for support, and came to a door marked SALIDA. I pushed it open and found myself in fresh air that had never smelled so good, in a dimly lit room with other people, all looking like survivors from the *Titanic*.

Lafitte wasn't there. Neither was Hemingway or Dorothy.

"Are you the last?" asked a sad-eyed young woman sitting on the floor, her arms cradled around her knees. I set the lantern on a table and told her the shooting had stopped, the police had arrived, and, yes, I'd seen injured people.

She burst into tears. Others tried to console her. I also felt like crying.

I stepped out the door, into the cool night air with its tobacco smells and buzz of crickets. Lanterns hung from trees—yellow glows amid swarming insects—and below them, in little pools of light, stood a cluster of people, almost everyone with a kerchief over their mouths.

"Lafitte!" I yelled. "Ernesto? Dorothy? Are you out here?"

CHAPTER 27

Out from the shadows came Lafitte, his hat gone, his hair a tangled mess, jacket rumpled and stained like Cary Grant after that airplane incident in *North by Northwest*. Dorothy was there too, holding a shawl over her mouth, and Hemingway with his necktie pulled to one side.

I rushed into their arms, but we were so caught up in emotion that it took a long time before any of us spoke. In time I learned the tunnel terminated in the back room of a small grocery store called the Blue Ribbon, a half block from El Dorado. No one knew who was behind the shooting, but there was speculation and animated debate, and grumbles about bolita wars, crime syndicates, crooked police, and union thugs, and how the country was going to hell, and good citizens like us were caught in the middle.

"Who gives a damn?" said Hemingway, slurring his speech. "Important thing is we're safe." He said there was an all-night clandestine bar at the hotel where they were staying, and that it was within walking distance, and they had piano music and wild patrons, and we could party in his room. "Let's go," he said in Spanish. "Drink and celebrate our survival."

"Not me," I said. "I've had enough partying."

"Oh, come on, Carmen. Where's my party girl?"

"She needs rest," Lafitte said. "Is her injury."

Hemingway complained a bit more, saying it wasn't even two yet. Dorothy straightened his tie and tugged on his arm. "Come on, Ernesto. It's late. I'm tired too."

"*Diablo*," he said and gave me another crushing hug. Dorothy said, "Abyssinia," whatever that meant. Then they struck off into the darkness, holding hands, Hemingway belting out an old song like a drunk sailor.

Lady of Spain I adore you,
Right from the night I first saw you…

Lafitte put his arm around me, and we stood there in the glow of lanterns, listening to Hemingway until his singing faded into the night. Hemingway in 1932. Mobsters and moonshine. A bolita shootout. A scary tunnel. Was this real? A part of me wanted to wake up in my old bed in Ybor and learn it was only a dream. Another part liked my new life with this handsome war hero who seemed genuinely interested in me.

In me, Amy Romano, just a little girl in a woman's body, a girl lost in time.

And that's when it struck me, another of those universal truths. It wasn't love only that drove women to men. It wasn't just physical attraction or the need for sperm to create a child. The real reason was a woman's underlying need for security, for safety, for protection from the monsters under the bed. At least that's how I felt, standing under that oak tree in the darkness with Lafitte's Arm around me, his face illuminated by hanging lanterns.

"*Allons*," he said and pulled me into the darkness. "Now we find car."

The power was still out, and there were no ambient lights, not in houses and not even the heavens, thanks to the limbs of overhanging trees.

"What does Abyssinia mean?" I asked.

"Ha, now I know you from Mars."

"Well?"

"Is slang, Amy, from Mussolini. He always talk about invading Abyssinia. Is in Ethiopia, so now people joke and say Abyssinia. Say it slow and sound like … I be seeing you."

"Like the song?"

"What song?"

"Billie Holiday." I sang a couple of lines:

I'll be seeing you
In all the old familiar places…

"Beautiful," Lafitte said. "Who is Billie Holliday?"

How we stumbled down the street in that gloomy blackness without colliding with a tree or pedestrian or stepping in horse manure, or getting mugged or stabbed to death by derelicts, I do not know. People passed us in the dark, people we could not see but only hear. Were they going home? Had they been at El Dorado?

Or were they lovers, taking advantage of the darkness?

Lafitte must have read my thoughts because he pulled me to him and our lips met in a wonderful moist fusion of passion, right there on a no-name street in darkness lit only with fireflies, somewhere in Ybor in 1932. Our bodies pressed against each other. I felt his hardness. I heard his whispers, and I don't know how long we would have carried on if it hadn't been for the clop of hooves and the sound of wagon wheels.

We stepped aside. The wagon rolled past with a whiff of air, leaving behind the familiar smells of horse and sweat and the bad memory of Virgil and Clarence in the swamp.

"Idiot!" someone yelled from the darkness. "Put a bell on that damn mule."

The sounds faded. Lafitte pulled me to him again, but the magic was gone, so we resumed our journey, rounded a corner, and there it was, in the glow of red, yellow and green party lanterns, and a snarl of police cars, men, and ambulances.

"Dorado," Lafitte said as if he'd just discovered buried treasure.

I thought he'd ask for the valet, but he said he had an extra key and wasn't about to risk an encounter with police. I couldn't see a thing other than an occasional glow in a window or the flash of fireflies, but Lafitte must have had the vision of a night owl, because we found the car in a nearby parking lot that was lit by lanterns and were about to climb in when a church bell began its toll for two in the morning.

"Uh oh," I said. "Witches are loose." I twirled around.

"Why you do that?"

"The gypsies say bells at night bring *brujas* out of their caves—witches. Only way to protect yourself is by twirling." I twirled again. He made the Sign of the Cross. Then we climbed into the luxury of leather and new smells, and he soon had his flathead V-8 fired up and running.

He shifted into gear. "Now I take you home on one condition."

"What condition?"

He leaned over and kissed me. "You promise tomorrow night we together again."

"It's already tomorrow."

"You know what I mean."

"I know what you mean, but I have a condition too."

"What condition?"

"That you don't take me to another shooting."

"Ha, tomorrow night we to a quiet, romantic place go. Candlelight and good food. No guns, no Hemingway. Just Amy and Lafitte."

"Amy and Lafitte," I answered and slid next to him. He put an arm around me, and we drove into the darkness of a moonless night, the headlights illuminating unpaved streets: no signs, no street lights, no other cars, no pedestrians, and no lights at houses either. Only the fireflies, thousands of them, maybe millions, blending with the stars and flickering on and off like little semaphores, something I'd never seen in my other life.

"Do you believe in guardian angels?" I asked.

"You have guardian angel?"

"The girl of the swamp. She stopped me from killing Clarence."

I told him how she'd appeared just as I was about to lay more blows on Clarence's head, and how she saved me from an alligator, and how she appeared again during the panic at El Dorado. He listened, then squeezed me tighter and slowed down, and by the time we reached the doctor's house and parked in front, I was almost ready to confess the whole story.

"My mother is guardian angel," he said. "Spanish flu take her, but I always feel her presence. She read to me poetry when I was little."

"Do you have a favorite poet?"

"Christopher Marlowe. His 'Shepherd Song'" He whispered a few lines:

Come live with me and be my love,

and we will all the pleasures prove…

I knew the works of Christopher Marlowe, but didn't tell Lafitte. "More," I said.

"Is all I remember, but the poem, it make me think of you. Make me want to put you in airplane and fly you to Louisiana. Take you away from bad men. Make you my love."

"You're crazy."

"Ha, I only fly airplanes, but you, Cher Amy, you see ghosts. You twirl to scare witches. You read the tomorrow in crystal balls."

"Bowls."

He pulled me to him, and again we kissed like teenagers, right there in the narrow front seat of his flathead V-8. In front of the doctor's house beneath the stars, amid the fireflies.

"Love," he said, using the Spanish word, *amor*. "I believe is emotion most important in the world. Love makes earth turn. Makes birds sing and flowers to bloom."

Maybe it was because he spoke those words in tortured Spanish—*Creo que la emoción más importante en el mundo es el amor.* Or maybe it was the fuzziness in my head or the resentment at Ramón. Or maybe it was just him, his attempt at poetry, his talk of loyalty, of *amor*. Whatever the case, a fire ignited inside me, and I didn't stop him from kissing me on the neck, beneath my chin, and down to my breasts. Our hands were all over each other, in places I'd never tell, and I'm not sure I'd have refused if he'd suggested we get into the back seat.

"Amy?" he whispered.

"What?"

"Come home with me. Tonight. Be my love. Stay with me."

"No, Lafitte, this is going too fast."

He sighed and straightened up, and we sat there a while longer, cooling our passions in the night air, watching the fireflies and listening to the crickets, not one of us moving. What were women like in 1932? Did they sleep with men on the first date? The third? Or not until they had a ring on their finger?

"I come for you tomorrow," he said, "same time. *Non?*"

"Abyssinia tomorrow," I whispered and let him walk me to the door.

CHAPTER 28

I drifted in and out of sleep. One minute I'd be running through that tunnel with no end, crying for help. The next I'd be awake, the wind rattling the windows. I smelled orange blossoms. I heard the rumble of thunder and the clock strike three, and from the next room came the sounds of the doctor and Soledad, turning in their beds.

Were they doing it? At three in the morning? While I was in bed alone.

Alone.

The next time darkness closed around me, I found myself in an airplane with Lafitte, heading to New Orleans. Not as Amy the flamenco dancer, but as Carmen with a tattoo. The Gulf of Mexico stretching to the horizon. Starry sky above us. Lafitte with his hand on my thigh.

"Why to wait until tomorrow?" he whispered.

He put the controls on automatic pilot, flattened the seats into a bed, and pulled a blanket over us. The tiny cabin that before had been cramped was now a spacious bedroom.

The engine droned. We flew on. Billie Holiday sang "I'll be Seeing You," and despite the absurdity of the dream, I felt those wonderful, moist kisses again. I felt his lips on my breasts, on my stomach, on my thighs. Down there. *El amor.*

It was his body I embraced around the pillow, his body I lay beneath.

He whispered poetry to me in French, in words I didn't understand but that made perfect sense. We were one, Amy and Lafitte, bodies and souls joined in a love dance, a mile-high over the Gulf of Mexico. The airplane undulated, up and down. It swayed. My head spun. I cried out in pleasure, and just when I thought my heart would burst with love, there was a knock at the airplane door.

"Amy, wake up. Are you all right?"

I sat up, alarmed, my heart about to beat out of my chest. The room was spinning. My stomach felt as if I'd eaten a can of dog food. The pillow that had been Lafitte was now a crumpled mass. And Soledad stood next to the bed in her nightgown, holding a mug of coffee.

"That must have been some dream," she said. "You need to get up. Hurry."

"What's wrong?"

"We heard about last night. It's on the news. Are you okay?"

"I'm okay. Just need sleep."

"No, get up and get dressed. Hurry. We'll be in the dining room."

She handed me the coffee and left without another word. The bedside clock told me it was only a few minutes after eight.

I hurried into the bathroom. A glance in the mirror. A wrinkle here, a dimple there, darkness under the eyes. Splash water on my face. Brush my teeth. Pull a hairbrush through my hair. Why in God's name did Soledad wake me so early? Did it have anything to do with Lafitte?

Oh, those marvelous kisses.

I pulled on a robe and stuffed my sore feet into slippers. Then, I gulped my coffee and stumbled out of the room and down the hall, my heart still beating against my ribs.

As I came closer, I smelled the aromatic smoke from Dr. Antonio's pipe and heard static from the radio. They were in the dining room, Soledad standing near the Marconi with a look of despair and the doctor sitting at the table with his newspaper and coffee. His vest was unbuttoned and he had on his reading glasses that were always slipping down his nose.

"What's going on?" I asked.

Soledad switched off the radio. Doctor Antonio motioned me into a chair and looked at me over the top of his spectacles. "Are you okay? That business about last night is on the radio."

"What are they saying?"

"Another bolita shootout. Three dead, maybe more. But that's not the issue."

"What's the issue?"

He pushed back his spectacles and pointed to the window. "See for yourself."

The old dread swept over me again. I arose with as much dignity as I could summon and traipsed to the window like the accused entering a courtroom.

Down the street, only a few houses away, stood two men in dark sunglasses, both dressed in suits and black fedoras, leaning against a black automobile. They were too far away to make out their faces, but in my tortured mind they were Sal and Clarence.

"G-men," said the doctor. "I think they're waiting for back-up."

"Back-up for what?"

"To raid the house."

I didn't know whether to flee out the back door or feel relieved. Sal and Clarence wanted to finish the job; the G-men would want to question me before they beat me to death.

"How do they know I'm here?"

"Because it's their job. They investigate. Someone must have recognized you last night."

No sooner had he said it than there came a sharp rap at the door.

Soledad, her face drained of color, smoothed back her dark hair with both hands and headed to the door, her ponytail with the red ribbon swaying. The doctor whipped off his glasses and re-lit his pipe with a shaking hand.

I stood there, too paralyzed to move, waiting for the G-men and their handcuffs.

"Why can't I sneak out the back?" I asked the doctor, my voice weak.

"They're trigger happy. They might shoot if you run."

The door opened and closed. I expected to hear gruff voices. Or the rat-a-tat of machine gun fire. Instead, it was a familiar woman's voice. There were footfalls. Then crazy Natalia swept into the dining room in her feathered hat and heels, looking as beaten and bleary-eyed as I felt. She shot me a glance and turned her gaze on the doctor. "Why isn't she ready?"

"We didn't expect the G-men. This complicates everything."

"Complicates what?" I asked. "What's going on?"

"You'll see," Soledad answered. "Come on."

CHAPTER 29

She guided me into the bedroom she shared with the doctor and, there, on the brass bed beneath a turning ceiling fan, lay one of her nurse's white outfits.

"Put it on," she said. "You will be me."

"You?"

"Me, Amy. It's the only way. Then you're going to walk out the front door with Natalia."

"To where?"

"Out of here, that's where. Now hurry. *Darte prisa.*"

My headache grew worse. This was the second time I had to change in a hurry, and I wasn't sure the plan would work. Soledad's skin was darker than mine. So was her raven-colored hair. We didn't look that much alike either. She had a waist like a wasp and a rounded butt that would stop construction work. Not to mention those beautiful Cuban features that came from a rich mixture of Caribbean native, African and Spanish blood, whereas my Gypsy-Moorish-Spanish ancestry gave me more of a Mediterranean look.

I was also a few inches taller. But it wasn't like I had a choice.

Again, I sucked in my stomach and strapped the corset around my waist. Then I pulled on the dress and was buttoning up when Natalia took a toothpaste-looking tube from her makeup kit.

"Chocolate and cinnamon," she said. "It'll give you a nice Soledad tone."

"Wait, you're going to do a black-face on me?"

"Brown-face. Now shut up and hold still."

Next came a wig the same color as Soledad's hair. It even had a ponytail and red ribbon. There were more touches and adjustments, more preening and fussing, and when we finished and I went out, smelling like chocolate and cinnamon, Dr. Antonio looked me up and down. "Perfect," he said. "Let's do the test."

"What test?"

"Newspaper test. Soledad already went out for the *Tribune*. Now it's your turn."

"But you already got the paper."

"Only the *Tribune*. They just delivered *La Gaceta*. Go get it."

"Are you serious? What if they try to talk to me?"

"*Por Dios*," said Natalia. "Show some backbone. They're two houses away."

Soledad walked me to the door, opened it a crack, and put her hands on both my shoulders. "You can do it," she said. "Paper's on the curb. Walk slowly, the way I do. Put some sway into your hips. When you pick up the paper, stand there a second or two and scan the front cover."

She pushed open the door. "*Anda.*"

I set off, my heart in my throat, one foot in front of the other, trying to walk like Soledad, wishing I'd gone home with Lafitte, thinking how ridiculous I'd been to refuse him like a nice girl who didn't sleep with guys on a first date. The stupid girl. The girl about to get gunned down on the street.

The morning was warm and humid. The G-men's gaze seemed to burn right through my nurse's outfit to my deceitful heart. A dog barked. The makeup on my face felt as artificial as a mask. I heard traffic and beeping horns, and chirring crickets, and the clang of streetcar bells.

Then I was at the curb, looking down at *La Gaceta*.

I scooped it up and scanned the front page, expecting to see photos of bodies and a headline about the shooting. But the shooting had been too late to make the morning papers, and there was only a black and white picture of the bonus marchers in Washington, DC.

A truck rumbled by. It smelled of tobacco and exhaust. The men in the truck waved and whistled. I waved back, thinking that's what Soledad would do. The truck stopped. The men stuck out their heads. Were they coming back? Did they think I wanted a ride? I made my way back to the house, hoping I wouldn't faint or have a heart attack and die on the front lawn.

Soledad met me at the door. "Good," she said. "Perfect."

"Did the G-men notice?"

"Stared like you were Harlow. You should be in the movies."

"Harlow is blonde."

"Aha, you're getting your memory back. That's good, Amy." She glanced at the clock. "Twelve more minutes, then you go."

"Why wait? Why not now?"

"Because I always leave at nine sharp. They know that."

"But why would they wait for you to leave before raiding the house?"

Soledad shrugged and looked at Natalia for help. Natalia said, "Don't you get it? The G-men aren't all bad. They don't want Soledad to get hurt."

"How do you know that?"

"Because I know. Because I have friends. Now shut up and eat your breakfast."

"I'm not hungry."

"Eat," said the doctor. "You don't want to go out there on an empty stomach."

The way he said it sounded like a combat mission over Germany, so I drank another cup of coffee and picked at my eggs. Meanwhile, Natalia gave me instructions. "We go out the door together. You turn one way, I go the other. Then we link up at Lola Milagros."

"What is Lola Milagros?"

"*Por Dios*, Amy, you know who Harlow is but don't remember Lola?"

I shrugged. "So how do I get there?"

She looked at me like I was helpless and gave me instructions. Soledad said, "We'll send your things over later, once you get settled in."

"Settled in where?"

"You'll see."

The minutes ticked by. Natalia sat down, stood up, and walked around mumbling to herself. The thought of going anywhere with her made me wonder if it wouldn't be better to just surrender. Everyone else kept glancing at the clock or gazing out the window.

At five minutes before nine, I picked up the note pad on which I'd jotted down winning bolita numbers—numbers I'd planned to place myself. But what if I didn't make it past the G-men? What if they arrested me? I called Soledad into the bedroom. "Listen, last night some winning bolita numbers came to me in a dream."

"You see numbers in your dreams?"

"It's happened before. Can you place a bet for me … at Serafina's?"

"Of course, Amy. No problem."

I wrote the number on a pad and gave her the other five dollars Donnie Sue had given me.

"That's a lot of money for a bet," she said.

"It's a certain thing. If I were you I'd also place a few dollars on that number."

She promised to do it for me, and we stepped out to find Natalia waiting at the front door, looking like she'd rather be anywhere but here.

"Time," she said. "Let's go."

The doctor handed me a tote bag and a small wallet.

"What's this for?"

"Change of clothing in the bag. The wallet's for coffee money."

"But … but—"

He hugged me, wished me good luck, and opened the door.

CHAPTER 30

I followed Natalia back into the humid morning air with its chirring crickets and fresh morning smells. My headache was better, but my feet were still sore and my legs were aching.

A glance told me the G-men were still on the street, staring.

"You better not faint on me," Natalia hissed.

"Why would I faint?"

"Because you're jittery, that's why. Because you've got a hangover."

"You don't look so calm yourself."

"That's because I'm the one taking the risk, not you. I've got to walk right past them, whereas you, dear Amy, you go in the other direction."

"Maybe they'll come after me anyway."

"No, Amy, you're sweet little Soledad. They don't give a damn about her."

Another black Ford drove up and stopped behind the G-men. Out of it stepped two more agents in sunglasses and hats. "Don't panic," Natalia said. "This is exactly what we expected—a nine o'clock raid."

"How do you know that?"

"Didn't I tell you I have friends?" She gestured down the street, away from the G-men. "When you get to that corner, at the trees, you turn left. Then you get your little behind to the Columbia … change out of that nurse's outfit. It's like a red flag. Understand what I'm saying?"

"I'm not deaf. Why don't I go straight to Lola's?"

"Because you don't have time. That's why. And stop asking questions.

Soon as they learn they've been suckered, they'll be swarming all over Ybor, looking for a nurse. Now get going, and don't be like Saul's wife and look back."

"Who is Saul?"

"For God's sake, Amy. Don't you remember the Bible guy whose wife turned to salt?"

"That was Lot, not Saul."

"Lot, Saul. Whatever." She gave me a dismissive wave and struck off toward the G-men.

The corner she'd pointed out with its trees and fence was only about a half-block away, but it seemed like a mile. It also looked like the fence line I'd crossed with Lafitte after he'd landed his airplane. Lafitte. Would we still be able to get together tonight? Oh, those kisses.

Stop it, I told myself. Right now there were more important matters.

At the corner, I hazarded a glance back. All four agents were still there, talking with Natalia. Maybe this would work. Maybe. I hastened my step despite my aching thighs, praying I'd be able to get to the Columbia before they came after me.

It was cooler beneath the trees. Wilderness to my right. Clapboard houses to the left, all shaded with live oaks and dressed up with flowering crepe myrtles and oleanders—a rainbow of pinks, reds, and lavenders—and as I walked, I caught whiffs of baking bread and Cuban coffee, and the sweetness of honeysuckle and freshly cut grass.

The sound of an approaching car set my heart into panic mode. Was it *them*? It sputtered past like the Joad jalopy, kids waving from the rumble seat. A barking dog chased them. I breathed again, and even laughed at a sign on a tree—*Get her a Hoover for Mothers' Day*, illustrated with a smiling woman pushing a vacuum cleaner.

There was more traffic on 22nd Street, which I knew well, and even in my rush to get away I remembered Lafitte's complaints about Ybor's numerical street names. Things got noisier as I approached downtown Ybor—kiosks selling magazines and newspapers, shoeshine boys in knickers and caps, a man holding up a JESUS LOVES YOU placard.

Beggars were also on the street, and men, women, and children in tattered clothing who looked like refugees from the dust bowl, all crusty-haired with dirt tattoos on their faces, some of the women wearing bonnets as if they'd escaped from *The Handmaid's Tale*.

And finally, the place where I performed as a flamenco dancer in 2019, the world-famous Columbia Restaurant, corner of 22nd Street and 7th Avenue. It looked the same. But was it? Were they suffering like everyone else? Did they have those wonderful dishes like *Caldo Gallego* and *Paella Valenciana* on their 1932 menu?

I stepped to the door and reached for the handle.

Locked. The damn place was locked! A sign read, *Open at Ten*.

Good Lord. What was Natalia thinking? Already people were staring. It had taken at least fifteen minutes to get here, maybe twenty. By now the G-men would be at the doctor's house. They'd know we had conned them and would be looking for a nurse.

I glanced around. Where to go? Surely something was open. Maybe that building on the other side of 7th Avenue. I hurried across, almost tripping on the trolley tracks. The building had a big sign over the door—*PACO'S TATTOO PARLOR*.

A couple of rough looking sailors stood in front, leaning against the building.

"Ain't open yet," said one of them in English. "You a nurse?"

The other one reached for my arm. "Hey, sweetie. I'm injured. Can you heal me?"

I jerked free and hurried on, scattering a group of clucking chickens. Back in my other life, I knew every little shop, bar, and bistro on 7th Avenue. Knew the buildings too. Some looked the same, but the names were different. Here was a coffee house called El Buen Gusto. Closed until ten. A five and dime. Closed. A butcher shop called Jorge's Carnicería with pork sausage for 10 cents a pound. Closed.

For God's sake, it was Saturday morning. Why wasn't anything open? No phone booths either. Superman would have a tough time finding a place to change. Yet for all that, there were cars and trucks and horse-drawn wagons on the street—Fords and Chevrolets and Cadillacs, and brands like Packard and Hudson that I knew only from old movies.

Newspaper boys in knickers hawked their papers, yelling about bonus marchers in Washington DC and the suicide of the Lindbergh babysitter. Hands of beggars reached out to me—women sitting on blankets. A blind man rattling his cup. Skinny little kids with cardboard placards on which they'd scrawled MUST WE STARVE?

There were also Indians on the street—bronzed Seminoles in their native dress, dangling ornaments, and distinctive hairstyles, some of the women with babes strapped in blankets—strolling around as if wondering how their world had been taken over, bricked over, and rearranged by these impoverished rag-tags.

A skinny woman grabbed my arm. "*Señorita, por favor.* My baby is sick."

Her face was so piteous that I gave her a quarter from the wallet the doctor had given me. Her eyes opened wide as if surprised at such a large amount. "God will bless you," she said. But all it did was attract four or five ragged little boys with sad faces and outstretched hands.

Another block and I came to a gathering of young boys and girls at the Rivoli Theatre and Cine, waiting in line to see a double feature, *Tarzan the Ape Man* starring Johnny Weissmuller, and a cowboy movie called *The Montana Kid.*

Was the ticket window open?

Yes, and people were entering.

CHAPTER 31

I stood in line, drawing stares in my nurse's dress, wishing I could make myself invisible. Across the street, a group of noisy protesters was marching in a circle, waving red banners and holding up placards that read HUELGA, the Spanish word for strike. A group of counter-protesters was there too, dressed in Spanish berets, chanting, "*Que viva España!*"

I'd always heard of the animosity between Cubans and Spaniards, and there it was, light-skinned Spaniards on one side, darker complexioned Cubans on the other, trying to outshout each other. The language around me was also Spanish—Castilian Spanish—with now and then a smattering of musical Italian or lyrical Cuban.

At last, I paid a nickel for entry, followed the crowd into a lobby that smelled of popcorn and cigar smoke and looked for the ladies room. A sign on the stairway directed people of color to the balcony. The ladies room also had a "Whites Only" sign. No one challenged me, so I marched in with my bag and found myself face to face with a woman in the uniform of an usher, holding a bundle of towels in her arm.

Was I white enough?

She studied me with her eyes as if trying to decide but said nothing. The charge was two cents. I gave her a nickel, then wet the towel and stepped into a stall.

How long it took to change out of my wig and clothing and scrub off the coloring, I don't know. The problem was the hat Soledad had stuffed into the bag. It had all the charm of a Nazi war helmet and looked like a green volleyball she'd cut in half and decorated with a ribbon, a faux flower arrangement, a fishnet, and a feather.

"Señorita, are you all right?"

"I'm fine." I pulled the flush cord and put on the hat. The good news was that it covered my ears and forehead, but when I exited the stall as a different person, whiter than when I went in, the towel lady gawked in disbelief.

A desperate fugitive would have shot her. All I did was put a finger to my lips.

People were still coming into the theatre, mainly kids. I crossed the lobby with my bag, breathing easier in my hat and green dress, and was almost at the door when I saw him: a G-man leaning against the ticket window, unmistakable in his black suit and fedora hat.

He looked up from his newspaper. Would he notice my white stockings? Did I still have chocolate on my face? Worse, the towel lady was peering out the ladies room.

Out the door I went, back onto 7th Avenue with its noise and protesters, trying to walk naturally. Another G-man stood in front, next to his black Ford. There were no shouts. I didn't drop dead from fright, but I felt his cold blue eyes on me.

Damn that Natalia! Why had she sent me to the busiest part of Ybor?

With every step, I fought back an intense desire to break into a panicked sprint. Or dash across the street and seek refuge with the protesters.

A yellow trolley rumbled by and stopped in front of the Red Lion Saloon at the intersection with 20th Street, its cables sparking in the overhead. Should I?

Yes.

I climbed aboard without looking back.

The driver took my fare, smiled, and said, "*Gracias, señorita.*"

I grabbed the overhead swing straps for support and made my way down the wood-planked floor to a vacant seat in front of the colored section. Yet even there, on a hard wood seat, it seemed as if every man, woman and child in the trolley were staring.

Did they know? Could they see the fear in my eyes?

More passengers boarded. Men dressed in knickers and golf caps; women with ribbons and bows, curls and ringlets, bonnets, and those ugly, tubular-shaped outfits. Others looked like factory workers in straw hats and vests, and still others with red kerchiefs around their necks.

And still we sat there, the doors open, everything and everyone reeking of tobacco and body odor, the newspaper boys selling papers through the open windows, the protesters holding up placards and slapping their hands on the side of the trolley.

"Come on, come on," I mumbled under my breath. "Let's move."

A young woman with a child sat down beside me. She smiled like she knew me, the way defenseless moms sometimes do. Her teeth were stained and crooked, in need of cleaning and braces. I returned the smile, and was wondering if people went to a dentist in 1932 when a man who looked like a Russian revolutionary in a Lenin cap, red armband, and rumpled dark jacket came aboard and began handing out pamphlets.

"It's so wrong," said the woman beside me.

"What's wrong?"

"The way they treat workers. They fired me because I was pregnant."

"That's not right," said a man in the aisle. "What this country needs is revolution."

"Amen," said another voice. "Line them up and shoot them."

This set off complaints all around, passengers mumbling their grievances, getting louder, and before long even the air seemed to take on the taste of injustice.

Shoot the blood-sucking factory owners.

Herbert Hoover too.

And Lindbergh. Shoot him too.

The man in the Lenin cap, holding the overhead swing strap for support, looked down at me. "What about you, señorita? Do you support our cause?"

It grew quiet, everyone staring like I was a dangerous counter-revolutionary.

I raised a fist and shouted, "*Huelga!*"

The woman beside me also shouted, "*Huelga!*" Others chimed in. Then everyone except the blacks were pumping fists in the air and calling on the workers to strike.

The streetcar shook. The baby started crying, and while this was going on, I looked out the open window. The G-man was still there in his black suit and fedora, leaning against his black Ford and talking to a policeman, probably about the veterans' march on Washington, DC.

At least they weren't turned in my direction. Maybe I was safe. Maybe I'd get away.

Or so I was thinking until that damn towel lady came rushing out of the theatre with the other G-man, pointing toward the streetcar.

CHAPTER 32

A few weeks before my world collapsed, I'd read a story about a woman in Ybor who hijacked a streetcar because of its delays at stops. If I'd had Clarence's gun, I'd have taken over as well. But I didn't have a gun. I was trapped.

I closed my eyes and waited. But then, as if by the magic of a *deus ex machina* in a Greek play, the conductor closed the door, flipped the switch, and away we went, rumbling on the rails, the bell clanging, horn blowing, leaving the towel lady and the G-men behind.

Thank you, deus ex machina. Thank you.

The elegant Club Asturiano flew by the open window. So did the Ybor City square, and Rosa's, and a palm tree island in the middle of 7th Avenue. I kept glancing out the back window for G-men in hot pursuit. They had to be back there, closing the distance in their black Ford. Best to get off at the next stop. Otherwise, they'd get ahead of us and climb aboard.

I pushed around the standing passengers and was already at the exit when the car stopped in front of Las Novedades, a restaurant that had suffered the indignity of a detachment of Teddy Roosevelt's cavalry riding their horses into the dining room.

Noisy protesters were there too, waving red banners. A separate crowd was demonstrating against prohibition, with placards like REPEAL THE 18th AMENDMENT. And there were counter protesters shouting, "*Que viva España!*"

Good Lord, what would Teddy's cavalrymen do—join the protesters or trample them into the dirt? Most of the exiting passengers scattered. I pushed through the Cuban protesters as if I were one of them, chanting "*Huelga! Huelga!*" like a tobacco worker, and dashed down 15th Street.

The streetcar rumbled away, bell clanging, horn blowing. The protesters stopped their chants. I scooted over to a moss-draped oak and hadn't been there more than a few seconds when the black Ford showed up at the corner.

It slowed and there they were, Dick Tracy clones in their dark suits and fedoras, looking out the open windows. This brought the protesters back to life. I flattened myself against the tree and prayed they hadn't seen me. At least there were no alligators. Or poison ivy. Or Clarence.

The protesters quieted. I stuck out my head.

The Ford was gone.

It took a while for my heart to stop racing and to realize 15th Street was where Natalia had told me to meet her, near the streetcar stop. Again I went rambling, my tote bag and elbows brushing palmettos that grew wild beneath the trees, until I came to an old woman with one of those god-awful white bonnets on her head, sitting in a rocker on a porch.

She spat a stream of snuff juice into the palmettos. "What you looking for, *mija?*"

"Lola Milagros."

"Other side of Setima. That way. Watch out for the traffic. People don't care anymore."

I thanked her and hurried back through the protesters, across the trolley tracks, and down the side street, hastening my step and glancing over my shoulder for a black Ford sedan.

Another half block, and there it was: LOLA MILAGROS SALÓN DE BELLEZA.

A beauty parlor? What was so secretive about that? Why couldn't Natalia have just told me?

A sign in the window advertised their services—massage, pedicure, manicure, hair styling and coloring, dandruff treatment, body hair removal, and facials. A separate sign welcomed patrons in Spanish, English, and

Italian. And another read: *We also speak Cuban.*

I glanced around to be sure no one was following and shoved through the door.

CHAPTER 33

The eye-burning clouds of cigarette smoke didn't help my mood. Neither did the sharp smell of ammonia. Aside from that and the ceiling fans, and a Victrola that was playing "All of Me," the place didn't look that different from a 2019 beauty salon—mirrors and beauty products on one side and a long row of women, young and old, in padded chairs on the other. The attendants in their blue smocks didn't look that different either, except they were Latina instead of Asian.

An attractive older lady at the counter glanced up and smiled.

"Oh, my God. Is that you, Carmen?"

She planted kisses on my cheeks and spoke to me in Castilian Spanish. "Thank goodness, you're back. We heard the most awful things. Are you well?"

There was no escaping it. I was Carmen, so I mumbled something to the effect that I was okay and happy to be back, and then Natalia was at my side.

"*Por Dios*, Carmen, what took so long?"

"They almost got me," I said and explained what happened.

She glanced at the door. "You didn't bring them here, did you?"

"I'm not stupid. Why didn't you tell me the Columbia doesn't open until ten?"

"How would I know? I don't go there for breakfast."

By then, everyone was staring as if I were the girl of the swamp, which in a way I was. The woman who kissed me, who I guessed was Lola, barked at them to get back to work. She led me to the back, sat me a padded chair, and examined my frazzled hair and broken nails.

"You poor thing," she said. "What you need is the full Lola miracle treatment.

"Exactly," said Natalia, who had followed us to the back. "She's had a rough time. Please ask your girls to not question her."

"I already told them."

Lola took the bag that contained the nurse's outfit and left to deal with other customers. As soon as she was out of earshot, I asked Natalia who would pay.

"It's on Lola. Carmen brings in business."

"But I'm not Carmen."

"Yes, you are. Nobody will ask you to prove your bona fides."

Before I could protest, an attendant placed a tub of warm water at my feet and asked me to take off my shoes and stockings.

"Give us a minute," Natalia snapped. "We're talking."

Natalia waited for her to leave and leaned closer. "Couple of things you need to know. First, I instructed them to not give you the *pan* shave. Definitely not. *De acuerdo?*"

Pan is the Spanish word for bread. "What's a *pan* shave?"

"For God's sake, girl, don't you understand Cuban talk? *Pan* is that sweet thing that men want between your legs. Carmen always got hers shaved. They know about the tattoo. You don't have a tattoo. And one more thing. Don't talk to the girls."

"Why not?"

"Your accent, for God's sake. It's not Andalusian. Why do I have to explain everything? You don't sound like Carmen. Not at all."

"Maybe it's because I'm not Carmen."

"Look, Amy, or whatever your name is. It's not like you have a choice. Sal is going to come after you no matter what. So are the G-men. You're a marked woman, but I can help you."

"What's in it for you if I pretend to be Carmen?"

"Does it matter?"

"Murder always matters."

"It's not murder, Amy. It's self-defense."

I wasn't into cold-blooded murder, but this wasn't the time or place to argue. Besides, the attendant was already back with an armload of towels.

"Ready?" asked the girl.

"Everything except the *pan*," Natalia said.

Natalia went off to another chair. The girl looked down at me. "Where's your cigarette case?"

"I kicked the habit."

"Really? That's amazing. I wish I could stop."

Despite being told not to talk to me, she began massaging my feet and lower legs and yammering in a lilting Cuban accent about the latest hairstyles, saying no one wanted the Clara Bow nowadays but they were getting lots of requests for the Jungle Jane image. "Maureen O'Sullivan," she said. "She's Jane in that Tarzan movie. Have you seen it?"

"Not yet."

"Oh, my God. You've got to see it. Tarzan without a shirt—nipples and everything." She fanned her face. "Can you imagine? It's illegal to go shirtless in Florida, even at the beach, but you can see a movie with a half-naked man. And what a man."

I made a mental note to see the movie and fell into a heavenly sleep. Someone else trimmed and darkened my hair and did my nails and massaged my face and shoulders. Now and then I heard chatter about the bolita shootout, and there was talk about the "blood-sucking" owners of the cigar factories. Or a president who didn't give a damn about Spanish-speaking immigrants or the starving veterans of the Great War. Lindbergh also came in for a bashing, but there were also moments of silence, and in those moments it seemed as if everyone was turned in my direction, conversing in hushed tones.

"That's Carmen over there," I imagined they were whispering. "The slut who sleeps with Hemingway and the mafia. The girl who killed a G-man."

The thought chilled me. Suppose there was a reward for Carmen?

Suppose this whole thing was a set-up? Suppose the feds would burst into the place at any moment?

Patrons came and left. The Victrola played scratchy tunes by Louis Armstrong, Billie Holiday, and even a Carlos Gardel tango. Almost every woman had a cigarette case on her armrest. And I was trying to stay awake when Natalia shook my arm.

"Finished," she said. "You look terrific."

I stood and examined myself in the mirror. What a difference from a few days ago. Would Lafitte like it? Would I still be able to see him tonight?

"Stop admiring yourself. We've got to go."

"Where are we going?"

"My place. Trolley passes in a few minutes."

"Why can't we go to the doctor's?"

"For God's sake, Carmen. They just raided his house. They'll be watching."

"But what about Vito? Won't he be at your place?"

"It's not like you have a choice."

"I could always walk out the door."

"Try it. I figure you'll last about ten minutes."

An attendant helped with my stockings and shoes. I put on my ugly hat with its bird-nest looks. Then Lola and the other girls gathered around as if I were a celebrity. They hugged me and wished me well. Lola squeezed my arm. "If you ever need an alibi for murder," she said, "or a shovel to bury Sal, we'll be happy to help."

Everyone laughed and nodded. I thanked them and followed Natalia out the door, into the tobacco-scented air of 15th Street that Lafitte wanted to rename and along a shell sidewalk beneath the oaks. "You see," Natalia said. "Everybody knows what Sal did to you. No one would blame you for killing him."

"I don't think the G-men would see it that way."

"The G-men would give you a medal. It's Sal they want, not Carmen."

I stopped and faced her. "Listen, Natalia. Get this through your skull.

If Sal crawls through my window and I shoot the bastard in self-defense, that's one thing. But I will not conspire with you or anyone else to kill him in cold blood. *Entendido?*"

"Fine, whatever you say. Only problem with that scenario is you'll never see him coming."

In case I didn't get the message, she curled her fingers into a pistol and fired two rounds into my chest. "Boom, boom. Dead."

CHAPTER 34

Back in my other life, I'd always left beauty parlors feeling like a new person. Hair nice and shiny, nails trimmed and polished, a bounce to my walk. Now I glanced into the shrubbery and parked cars as if death lurked in every shadow, thinking this was no way to live. Every car could shield a gunman. Every pedestrian was an assassin. Natalia seemed equally spooked, and we were both looking over our shoulders when we came to the trolley stop.

Protesters stood around with their placards and literature. Some were unshaven and rumpled as if they'd been sleeping in the park. Others looked angry and hostile. All wore red kerchiefs, and their placards could have been written by Marx himself.

STRUGGLE OF THE MASSES!

THROW OFF YOUR CHAINS!

A small knot of Seminoles stood there too, watching the protesters in stony Indian dignity. "What are they protesting?" I asked Natalia.

"Everything—wages, working conditions, the weight rules."

"What's a weight rule?"

"Christ, Amy, don't you remember anything? Management wants a uniform cigar, same weight, same length, same everything. Makes sense. Right? But the workers want it the way they roll it—fat cigar, skinny cigar, short cigar. To hell with quality. They won that battle. Now they're up in arms because owners are firing lectors and replacing them with radios."

"Why are they firing lectors?"

"Didn't I just tell you? Radio, R-A-D-I-O."

"I know how to spell radio. But I asked about lectors."

"Do you even know what a lector is?"

"It's someone who reads to the workers. Right?"

"Right. They're supposed to be reading informational stuff … like what's playing at the theatres. Or entertaining works by famous authors—Tolstoy, Fitzgerald, Victor Hugo. Right? It allows them to dream, to imagine great things. But do the lectors do that? Hell, no. Now they're reading Marxist trash by that radical professor at Salamanca."

"Unamuno?"

"That's it, one-world egalitarianism. Wants to take away the gains from all our hard work and share with the lazy *culos* of the world. What a bunch of *puta* garbage."

A battered truck roared by, its muffler busted. In the open back stood ragged men, women, and children with farm tools, looking more defeated than angry. A large sign on its side read:

IN HOOVER WE TRUSTED

NOW WE'RE BUSTED

The driver honked his horn and waved. The protesters waved back with their flags and placards. "Damn Cubans," Natalia mumbled as if they were a scourge. "Just look at them. Can't even spell their names. And that's not the worst part."

"What's the worst part?"

"Resistance groups, debate clubs. The hot topic now is thesis, antithesis, and synthesis. More Marxist crap. Also dialectical materialism, whatever that is. Can you imagine? Do you know the meaning of any of that *mierda*? Does anyone?"

She got so worked up, ranting in her Castilian Spanish, that some of the protesters took notice. I wasn't about to provoke her further by saying I'd always had a favorable view of lectors, or that maybe the workers had legitimate grievances, or that maybe she should shut up.

A clang of bells alerted us to the approaching trolley, its lines sparking in the overhead.

It glided to a stop in front of us, a bright yellow boxcar with a cigarette advertisement on its side: *More Doctors Smoke Camels than any other Cigarettes.* The protesters chanted, *"Huelga! Huelga! Huelga!"* Counter protesters chanted, *"Que viva España!"* Passengers got off the car and scattered in every direction.

We climbed aboard, paid our fare, and took a seat behind the conductor.

Again, the doors remained open, just like earlier that day, and we sat there while the chants grew louder and protesters banged their hands on the side.

"Puta Cubanos," Natalia mumbled. "Don't they understand half the country is out of work? They should be grateful for the jobs they have."

The conductor, a dark-skinned man with kinky black hair and a thin mustache, swiveled around and glared as if to tell her to shut her Spanish mouth.

"What's your problem?" she snapped at him.

"Look, lady, you need to watch your tongue."

"Oh really? This is a free country. I'll say what I damn well please."

He pointed to the door. "Either you calm down or get out."

Natalia sat forward and shook her finger in his face. "Who's going to throw me off? You or your trouble-making strikers on the street?"

He didn't answer. Instead, his dark gaze fell on me. A flash of recognition showed in his face. Was he the same conductor who'd picked me up in front of the theatre? Had the agents told him to be on the lookout for a woman in a green dress and white stockings?

Please, dear God, no.

Without a word, he flipped a red switch at the controls, picked up his coin-box, and stepped outside, leaving the doors open. "What's he doing?" Natalia said.

"I think he recognized me."

Natalia scooted over to look out the window. *"Mierda!"*

"What?"

"Black Ford behind us. He's motioning to them."

CHAPTER 35

Without thinking, I jumped into the driver's seat and slammed the door. The conductor raced over and pounded on the glass. "Open this damn door!"

I looked at the controls on the dashboard—BRAKES, MAGNETO, THROTTLE—all in red block lettering. I released the brake lever.

The car inched forward.

"What are you doing?" yelled a passenger. "Let the driver in."

I flipped the magneto switch. Nothing happened. The conductor was now kicking the door, cursing and shouting. In the mirror I saw the G-men, trotting along the side with drawn pistols.

I pushed the throttle and rang the bell. The motor whined and away we went, rumbling east on 7th Avenue, picking up speed.

"ABYSSINIA!" I shouted like a madwoman.

"ARE YOU FUCKING CRAZY?" Natalia screamed in my ear.

In the side mirror I glimpsed the conductor and the G-men running after us. I pushed the throttle all the way forward and held down the horn button.

"Hold on!" I yelled back. "We'll stop in a minute."

We barreled past 16th Street, horn blaring, bell clanging, scattering protesters with their signs. A horse-drawn wagon crossed in front of us on 17th Street, the driver snapping the reins in wide-eyed terror. Buildings and side streets went by in a blur. Trucks, autos, and wagons pulled to the side. Women grabbed their children. Even dogs ran for safety.

By the time we reached the intersection with Angel Oliva Senior Street, passengers were bunched up at the doors, ready to jump. Others were yanking on the "Stop" cord, creating an endless ding, ding, ding, while still others yelled at me to stop.

Easy for them. They weren't wanted by the feds. They weren't in jeopardy of going to Old Sparky for a murder they didn't commit.

Natalia put her hand on my shoulder. "Please, Amy. Stop this damn thing and let's get off."

"We'll stop on Twenty-second. Get ready to jump."

Somewhere a siren sounded, or it may have been the wail of passengers.

Streets and stops flew by—19th Street, 20th Street, a blur of placards and staring pedestrians. The passengers at the doors were getting angrier.

"You'll get us killed."

"You passed my stop."

"*Puta loca.*"

A flock of chickens scattered, but not fast enough. Feathers flew past the windows and stuck to the windshield. Off to my right, a black Ford was racing beside us.

"Shit!" I mumbled and ran the traffic light at 21st Street.

By then passengers were hovering over me, yelling and cursing.

A man reached around me for the controls.

I bit his hand. He yelped. Someone else tried to wrestle me out of the seat.

I struggled with him, I cursed, and that was when we slammed into the rear fender of a tobacco truck on 22nd Street. The truck spun toward the tattoo parlor and flipped on its side.

The trolley jumped the tracks.

Passengers screamed. Or maybe it was the screech of iron wheels on brick. The power tongue that attached us to the cables broke loose and flapped side to side like the sword of a Viking warrior. Down came wires and cables, popping and sparking like a fireworks display.

We skidded to a stop near the front door of the Columbia but not before leveling a light post, destroying a kiosk, and scattering newspapers, magazines and chickens.

Acrid smoke rose around me. Passengers pushed out the doors. Words like "Crazy bitch" came at me from all directions. Natalia stumbled out the door with other passengers, and the next thing I knew, the feds were standing over me with drawn pistols, looking like the Men in Black in their dark suits and sunglasses.

The conductor was there too, his company hat pushed back on his head, his face contorted by rage. "Communist *puta*!" he shouted and lunged at me. The agents grabbed him and dragged him off, and I imagine if they hadn't done so, he'd have pummeled me with his fists.

It was over. This time there'd be no cavalry to the rescue. No knight in shining armor.

No deus ex machina.

CHAPTER 36

They cuffed my hands in front, then frisked me for weapons and helped me down to the sidewalk in front of the Columbia next to the Spanish tiles where I'd stood earlier that morning dressed like a nurse. What was I thinking? What was wrong with me?

The only positive was that I'd lost that ugly hat.

I glanced around, half expecting to see broken bodies and blood, but there were only the outraged passengers, the tangled cables and wires, and the overturned truck that was now on fire.

"Look," said one of the agents in English. "Bastards were hauling shine."

"Why do you say that?" asked the agent holding my arm.

"Blue flame. Only thing burns like that is shine."

He dashed over to the truck and came back grinning. "Yep, just like I thought. Broken hooch bottles everywhere … in a tobacco truck. Looks like it was the good stuff."

"Anybody inside?"

"Nope, no blood either."

"Whose truck is it?"

"Sal's. He's the only one bold enough to haul shine in broad daylight."

Great, I thought, now Sal had another reason to kill me.

By then, onlookers were peering out windows of nearby buildings, and coming from all directions, and cars stopping, and protesters with their placards and red flags. Cops were there too, yelling to get back, saying the truck could explode any second.

And sure enough, it went up in a muffled fireball of heat and debris, showering the area with broken glass and tobacco leaves.

"Holy Christ!" said an agent. "Let's get out of here."

They brushed tobacco leaves off themselves and out of my hair, and then half dragged, half shoved me through the crowd, stopping here and there for a newspaperman to snap our picture. The agents posed and prepped like male models, hats at jaunty angles, cigarettes in mouth, all puffed up like they'd busted Al Capone.

"Smile for the camera," said the fed on my right. "You're going to be famous."

I covered my face with my cuffed hands, and when we resumed our walk, I saw Natalia, crazy Natalia who got me into this mess.

She lifted a finger to her lips as if to say, "Don't tell them anything."

Damn her. None of this would have happened if she'd kept her mouth shut. She must have wanted me to get caught. Either that or she was naïve about clandestine matters, which seemed unlikely for anyone with Gypsy blood.

The black Ford I hated was waiting on the street like a funeral hearse. Four or five cops stood around it in boots, hats, and flared riding britches. "We'll take her," said a wiry little man with sergeant's stripes, speaking in Cuban Spanish. He rattled off a litany of my crimes—hijacking a streetcar, destruction of city property, endangerment of citizens.

The feds didn't understand a word and indicated as much by shrugging and looking at each other as if English was the language of the gods. I didn't offer to translate and neither did bystanders. Curses in Spanish and English flew around like brickbats. Tempers flared, and it didn't end until one of the agents growled, "Murder, goddammit, she's wanted for murdering one of our boys!" and shoved me into the back seat of the Ford.

He slid in after me, bringing with him the smell of a man who didn't use deodorant. Other agents jumped into the front and slammed the doors.

The little local cop yelled in the window, "*No hay derecho!*"

They ignored him, and away we went, siren blaring, the local cops following in their cars.

The driver, the oldest looking of the three agents, said, "What a crazy bitch."

"Must be on the rag," said the other man in front. "Women get like that."

"My wife's like that if she don't get her Lydia Pinkham."

"I don't smell nothing," said the man beside me. "Maybe I oughta check."

"You keep your hands off her. She's Gypsy."

"I thought she was a spic."

"Gypsy spic."

"How you know she's Gypsy?"

"Because she's Carmen, asshole. Everybody knows Carmen is Gypsy."

"I thought Gypsies look like A-rabs."

"It's Arabs, asshole, not A-rabs."

The agent beside me took out a pack of Lucky Strike, lit up, and shook another out of the pack for me. "Wanna smoke?"

I shook my head.

"You speak English?"

Again I shook my head, thinking it best not to confess to anything.

"Damn Gypsies," he said. "They should learn the language if they live in America."

The man in the front seat twisted around and stared into my face. "She don't look Gypsy."

"That's because of how she's dressed," said the driver. "Normally she'd be all gypsied up in scarves and hoop earrings, offering to read your palms, maybe offering other things too."

"What other things?"

"The hell you think? What kind of podunk hole you grow up in?"

"If she don't speak American, how'd Pruitt communicate with her?"

"Bedroom talk. Miracle his cock didn't rot off."

"You think Gypsies have hex power?"

"How else you explain Pruitt? He wasn't no dummy."

At first, I'd been terrified of these men in their black suits and fedoras.

Now, listening to their ignorance, I almost laughed. If my abuelita could hear them, she'd repeat her mantra—*Curses work only if you believe in them.* Which raised the question of how could three waspish looking guys who worked for the federal government believe such superstitious *tonterías*?

Or maybe it wasn't nonsense. Hadn't Ramón's Gypsy wife put a curse on me?

They went on, relating stories about sorcery and witchcraft as if I'd escaped from the Bible. The man beside me quoted a verse from the Book of Deuteronomy, "Let no one be found among you who practices divination or sorcery, or who casts spells."

"Exactly," said the driver and threw in a verse from Micah. "And I will cut off sorceries from your hand, and ye shall have no more tellers of fortunes."

The biblical quotes about sorcery and witchcraft went on for so long that I began to wonder if G-men were recruited in Baptist seminaries, and by the time we drove into a parking lot, they were warning one another to not look into my eyes.

"Don't even tell her your name," said the driver. "She could hex your whole family."

The men in the front seat stepped out. I thought they'd open the back door for me, but before that happened, the agent beside me frisked me a second time. He felt my breasts, then ran a hand up my dress, beneath my panties, and tried to insert his fingers. As if that wasn't disgusting enough, he tried to kiss me.

"No!" I cried, "*No hay derecho*," and wiggled free.

"Fucking witch."

The door opened and they pulled me out. By then, the local cops had also arrived. They trotted over in their boots and were making their case about jurisdiction. In Spanish. I interrupted to complain about the agent, but before I could finish, two of the G-men hustled me along a shell walkway to an unimposing one-story building over which fluttered the Stars and Stripes.

A sign near the doorway read US POST OFFICE, YBOR CITY, FLORIDA.

CHAPTER 37

We entered a door marked *Employees Only* and followed a narrow corridor to the offices of the US Bureau of Investigation, which I'd since learned was the daddy of the FBI. A bouquet of tobacco smells enveloped me. There were wanted posters on the walls in black and white, and faces and names I knew only from history books—Dillinger, Baby Face Nelson, Ma Barker, and Bonnie and Clyde—and newspaper clippings of agents in suits and fedoras handcuffing bootleggers and pouring moonshine into ditches.

The clatter of typewriters stopped. So did the scratch of pens on paper. Workers looked up from their desks or mimeograph machines and put down their cigarettes. People came out of side offices, and it seemed as if even the wanted posters were staring.

An older man with thinning hair and thick glasses asked me if I spoke English. "No espeak *Inglés*," I mumbled, shaking my head. Which was kind of funny since English was my native language and the reason I knew Spanish was that I'd grown up in a bilingual community.

"Where's Cheena?" he asked.

A well-dressed Asian woman about my age stepped out of a side room, smoothing down her jacket. She had big brown eyes and straight black hair and couldn't have been more than five feet tall. The older man pulled her to the side for a hushed conference. The agents who'd arrested me joined the conversation. They glanced at me. I couldn't hear every word but caught Pruitt's name, along with bits of talk about Gypsies and witchcraft.

Hijacked a streetcar.

Seduced Pruitt with a hex.

Don't make eye contact.

The woman marched over and looked straight into my face. "*Hola*, Carmen."

"I'm not Carmen," I said in Spanish. "They arrested the wrong person."

"Are you saying you don't know me?" She said this in an accent I didn't recognize.

"I heard them calling you Cheena. Is that your name?"

"No, it's Luzviminda. It's a Philippine name, but everyone calls me Cheena, meaning Chinese, because of my looks. I'm going to walk you through the process."

"What process?"

"Same as before. Mug shot, fingerprints, interrogation."

"What do you mean same as before? I've never been here."

"Oh, please señorita. I'll also be the translator."

I was still seething at the G-men for their lewd remarks and wanted to do something about the creep who'd felt me up. By then, they'd removed their jackets and hats and were holding court with other agents in their white shirts and shoulder holsters, bragging how they'd arrested me. One of them must have said something funny because they burst into laughter.

I pointed at them with my cuffed hands. "They're the ones who should be arrested."

"For what, señorita?" She reached over and took a shard of glass from my hair.

"Molestation. Insulting a prisoner."

In case they didn't hear me, I said it again, louder.

They turned to face me. The agent who'd run his hand beneath my panties caught my eyes and sniffed his fingers like a pervert.

"*Sucio asqueroso!*" I yelled at him. Dirty creep.

Cheena tugged at my arm. "Stop it. You'll just antagonize them."

"Oh, really? What are they going to do, arrest me?" I nodded toward them again. "The lanky one. Blond hair. What's his name?"

"That's Gerhardt. Why are you asking?"

Gerhardt noticed the attention he was getting and started toward us, grinning.

"Gypsy giving you trouble?"

"It's all right," Cheena said. "No trouble."

That seemed to satisfy him, but I wasn't about to let him off. I turned to Cheena. "You know what this *huevón* did? Ran his hand up my dress, inside my underwear."

"What's she saying?" he asked.

I pointed my cuffed hands at him and narrowed my eyes in what I hoped was a sinister look. Then I cocked my arms upward and snapped them straight as if hurling a lightning bolt. "*Puta pendejo*," I said. "I just laid a Gypsy curse on you."

The lights dimmed, went out a few seconds, and came back on.

Gerhardt backed away, his eyes wide. Cheena also stepped back. If she was anything like Soledad, she'd grown up in a culture of dark magic and believed in curses.

"What are you doing?" she said. "Are you crazy?"

"Yes, I'm crazy. I'm also a Gypsy *bruja*. Tell him what I said. Those exact words. Also tell him I just laid a curse on him, a Level One."

"What's a Level One curse?"

"Just tell him, for God's sake. Do your job."

She translated, glancing at me as she spoke. Gerhardt swallowed hard but avoided my eyes.

"What's a Level One?" he asked, his voice shaky.

"Tell him he'll know by tomorrow, but I'd advise him to scrub his hands and keep his windows locked. Doors too. It could get ugly."

Cheena translated. Gerhardt swallowed again and hurried back toward his friends, leaving me alone with Cheena. She also looked troubled, and for the first time since going into that sinkhole, I didn't feel helpless. I had power.

Gypsy power.

Curses work only if you believe in them.

144

Cheena seemed to read my thoughts and gave me a pleading look. "Listen, señorita, I'm not your enemy. All I'm trying to do is get us both through this. *Estamos de acuerdo?*"

"*De acuerdo.* I know it's not your fault."

"How did you make the lights go out?"

A coincidence, I assumed, but thought I could use it to my advantage. "Telekinesis," I said.

"Teleki what?"

"The power to move things with my mind. I can do worse. Much, much worse if that bastard touches me again."

CHAPTER 38

Cheena took a deep breath, then led me to her desk and motioned me into a chair. I found it odd they hadn't posted gun-toting deputies to keep me company. I couldn't imagine them leaving Bonnie and Clyde alone with a little woman like Cheena. Hadn't I supposedly killed one of their agents? Maybe I should kick something over to get attention.

"We'll do the same thing as before," Cheena said and picked up a box on the floor. She took out the wallet Dr. Antonio had given me. "This yours?"

"It looks like mine."

"I'm going to open it for our inventory. *De acuerdo*?"

"Why do you need my permission?"

"Because that's the way we operate." She unsnapped the wallet, pulled out my money and began counting. "Twenty-five dollars and fifty-five cents. Is that right?"

I nodded.

She jotted the amount in a ledger and reached back into the box. Out of it came that god-awful green hat that I thought I'd lost in the streetcar crash. "Fashionable," she said and examined it as if being careful to not offend me. "Yours?"

"It was a gift. Not exactly my style. Do you want it?"

"We don't accept gifts."

She made another notation and handed me a possession form to sign.

While I was signing, she took forms out of her desk, inserted carbon paper between them, stuck them in an Underwood typewriter, adjusted the forms, and began typing.

"Your full name is Carmen Amaya-Perez. Right?"

"No, Cheena. My name is Amelia Romano, but you can call me Amy."

She stopped typing and glanced up. "Please, señorita, you said you were going to cooperate."

"Look at me, Cheena. I'm Amy Romano. I told you they arrested the wrong person."

"Are you saying you've never seen me before?"

"I've never seen you before."

"Never been to this office?"

"I've never been to this *puta* office."

She shook her head and went back to her Underwood, speaking as she typed. "Also known as Amelia Romano." She looked up again. "Matronymic?"

"I don't remember."

"You don't know your mother's last name?"

"I told you I don't remember."

She rolled her eyes. "What about occupation?"

"Gypsy *bruja*."

"You want me to write witch as your occupation?"

"No, that's too harsh. Let's go with … oh, Gypsy shaman, fortune teller, and spiritualist."

"You read fortunes?"

"More like precognition."

"What does that mean?"

"It means I know things before they happen. Do you play bolita?"

"Everyone in Tampa plays bolita. It's like a religion."

"If I were you, I'd put five dollars on number 83 at the Lincoln Club."

"I can't afford that kind of bet."

"Use my money. We'll split the earnings."

"I can't do that, señorita."

"You'll be sorry when they announce number 83 as the winner."

She wasn't sure how to spell spiritualist in English, and I didn't correct her when she wrote *espiritualist*. The questions went on—date of birth, address, next of kin, birthmarks, health issues. I told her the same thing I'd told Soledad and the doctor, that I'd been in an accident, lost my memory, and didn't know the answers.

"Let me see if I have this straight," she said, her fingers still on the keys. "You were in an accident, hit your head, and now can't remember crucial details about yourself. Right?"

"Right?"

"Then isn't it possible you're Carmen and don't remember?"

"No, Cheena, I'm a hundred percent certain I'm not Carmen."

"How can you be so certain?"

"Because I know. What's your next question?"

She typed "unknown" in the spaces and looked up. "Do you dance flamenco?"

"I'm pretty sure I do."

"I need a yes or no."

"All I can say is maybe."

She made a notation and looked up. "What languages do you speak?"

"Spanish."

"I already put Spanish. What about Gypsy?"

"Gypsy's not a language. We call it Romani, but in Andalusia it's called Caló."

"So you speak Caló? Right?"

"I can manage."

She typed in my answer and looked up again. "This is just too weird. Carmen sat in the same chair where you're sitting. She spoke Caló. You speak Caló. Carmen danced flamenco. You dance flamenco. You have the same bona fides … and you look just like her."

"Listen, Cheena, I am not Carmen. *Punto final.*"

She took the forms out of the typewriter. "They won't like your answers."

"That's their problem." I held up my cuffed hands. "Can you take these off?"

"They'll take them off in the interrogation room."

"Interrogation?"

"They'll want your entire life history. Did you say number 83?"

"At the Lincoln Club. Tonight. It's a sure bet."

She jotted down the number and then leaned back in her chair and began humming the tune, "I don't know why" as if all were well in the world.

"Do you like that song?" I asked.

"I love music, period. Can't live without it. That song's my favorite." She pointed across the room. "Oh, look, he's back." She stood and led me past more desks with clattering typewriters, around the three G-men who'd arrested me, and to a table in the corner. Behind it sat a mustachioed little man in a dark suit who looked like Groucho Marx.

"What's this about?" I asked him.

"*Huellas dactilares*," he answered. "For the files."

"Why do I need to be fingerprinted?"

"Please, señorita, I'm just doing my job."

He stood, took off his jacket, loosened his tie, rolled up his sleeves as if this was serious business, and arranged the ink and plates. But when he reached for my hands, I said, "No way, José. I just had my nails done. I'm not putting that nasty stuff on my fingers."

I waggled my fingers and said it again, louder. I thought the G-men would come rushing over. They didn't. They wouldn't even look at me. Nobody would look at me. *Nadia.* Cheena made it worse by singing her favorite song.

I don't know why I love you like I do.

I don't know why, I just do...

Damn them. They should give me the attention a criminal of my stature deserved.

"I'll be careful with your nails," Groucho said. "I love that shade of red."

I could have screamed. It was as if everyone had suddenly become Stepford wives.

The passion to wreck the place had gone out of me anyway, so I held out my hands for the fingerprinting. He chattered about the Lindbergh baby the whole time—Lindbergh himself arranged the kidnapping. The baby had a deformity. The wife and babysitter were also in on it.

"Wasn't Lindbergh," I said. "It was some German creep. Did it for the ransom."

"How do you know?"

"Because I'm a spiritualist. I see the future."

He and Cheena exchanged looks. Cheena shrugged and went back to her song. When Groucho finished, he cleaned my fingers with a smelly substance, shook my hand, thanked me for being cooperative and said, "You're teasing about who killed the Lindbergh baby, right?"

"Just keep reading the papers. A Kraut did it."

He burst out laughing. "A Kraut? You had me there for a second."

The mug shot was next. Again, I cooperated and was blinking away the blinding flash when Groucho came up beside me. "A Kraut," he said again and cracked up.

He was still laughing when five or six local cops showed up in their flared riding pants, this time waving what appeared to be a judge's order.

Everyone gathered around. I was so focused on what they had to say I didn't notice Natalia until she stepped out from behind them. Crazy Natalia in her Gypsy get-up, all scarves, ankle skirt, headband and jangling jewelry, looking like an escapee from a caravan.

"Not to worry," she said to me in Caló. "We're going to spring you."

CHAPTER 39

I knew that wasn't going to happen and would have stayed out of it if Gerhardt, who stood behind me with other agents, had kept his mouth shut.

"Damn greasers," he muttered. "Probably pissed because they paid for a night with her."

"I'd pay for a night with her," said the driver. "Look at that ass."

My face grew hot. I swiveled around and glared at them. They avoided my eyes. I wasn't about to let them off, so I turned to Cheena. "They're talking about me."

"Ignore them. They're the asses."

By then, the sergeant in charge, a heavyset man with a thin mustache, was making a speech about jurisdiction in Spanish. "*No hay derecho,*" he said at least three times, standing next to a photo of agents busting whiskey barrels with axes. "You don't have the right."

I liked his courage and struck off toward him, holding up my cuffed hands. Cheena followed like a little sidekick. No one stopped us. There was silence, all eyes on me as if waiting for snakes to drop from the ceiling.

"Let's go," I said to the sergeant. "They don't have the right. Get me out of here."

He looked as stunned as I was that no one had stopped me.

"Well, come on," I said and headed for the exit.

"Stop them!" yelled the older man with thinning hair. He grabbed my arm and spun me back in the direction I didn't want to go.

Natalia jumped in front and gave him a verbal blistering in Spanish, poking her finger in his chest. Other agents found their backbones and hurried to his side.

The sergeant and his men also got into the fray, pushing and shoving. "*No hay derecho!*"

A hat rack crashed to the floor. So did a water jug and a framed photograph of Machine Gun Kelly. Someone shoved a local cop. He fell against me and we both went down.

I screamed. I uttered every dirty word I knew in Spanish and Caló and probably would have thrown in a few English vulgarisms if the driver hadn't pulled me to my feet.

He sat me in a chair and clamped a hand over my mouth.

The shouting continued, Spanish on one side and English on the other, bringing people out of side offices, even postal workers in uniform. The man in thinning hair banged a heavy ashtray on a table and kept banging until things quieted down.

He identified himself as Chief Agent Rothman and explained in both English and Spanish that this was a federal case, a capital crime, whatever that was, but in the unlikely event I beat the murder rap the locals could have me.

"She wrecked a streetcar," said the sergeant. "Who is going to pay for the damage?"

"I'll pay for it," I said, trying to stir the pot.

Rothman and the sergeant got in one another's face and began arguing. While this was going on, Natalia came over and knelt beside me, bringing with her the smell of roses.

"Are you hurt?" she asked in Caló.

"I'm okay, just a little shaken. Why are you dressed like a Gypsy?"

"So they won't recognize me from this morning. Are they giving you a bad time?"

"That one is." I pointed at Gerhardt. "I put a curse on him."

She laughed. The agent behind me turned to the fingerprint guy. "The hell they saying?"

"It's Gypsy talk. Who knows what they're saying?"

The agent clamped his hand over my mouth again.

Natalia glared at him as if she were about to strike him dead. Instead, she stepped over to Rothman and the sergeant. They stopped their argument. Then, with everyone in the place gathered around, Natalia mounted a chair and raised her arms like a high priestess at a ritual.

"Everyone listen to me. Listen. Please."

She said these words in Spanish, and even before Cheena translated, the room fell silent. Natalia leveled an arm at me, bracelets jangling. "Don't you people know who that woman is?"

No, I wanted to shout. *Please don't say I'm Carmen.*

"Her name is Carmen Amaya, the most famous flamenco dancer in Spain. Someone kidnapped her … tried to kill her. She escaped. She was seriously injured. Her head is messed up. But beware how you treat her. Bewareeee. She has the power of the curse."

It became so quiet you could hear the swish of ceiling fans.

The sergeant broke the silence. "She should be in the hospital, not in your *puta* post office."

He motioned for his men to leave, and they marched out together, still grumbling. Natalia blew me a kiss, said "Abyssinia," and followed them out, scarves flowing.

Well, thank you for screwing me! I felt like yelling.

As soon as the door closed behind them, Rothman rolled his eyes and smacked his hands together as if he had dust on them. "Everybody back to work. Go, Go!"

He marched over to me and buttoned his jacket. His face was crimson. "Are you hurt?" he asked in Spanish.

"I want to file a complaint against your agents."

"For God's sake, woman, you're the one creating the fuss."

"I'll calm down when you tell me why you're arresting me."

"Do I have to tell you?"

"No, I just want to hear you make up some bullshit reason."

"We don't have to make up anything. You hijacked a streetcar. You endangered the lives of passengers and people on the street. There's also the matter of a murdered agent."

"You arrested the wrong person. I'm not Carmen."

"Oh, please. Even that Gypsy knows you're Carmen."

"Can I speak with you in private?"

"We don't do private."

He gestured to the agents who'd been standing behind me. They pulled me out of the chair and led me into a shadowy back room that contained a small table, a lamp, a few chairs and a photo on the wall of J. Edgar Hoover.

CHAPTER 40

I half expected them to slap me around, yell at me, beat me senseless. Instead, they sat me in a wooden chair at the table and left. No words. No threats. They didn't even look at me.

I looked around for chains and a dunking sink. But there was only a newspaper on the table, a high window with bars, and that damn photo of Hoover. Even as a young man he looked like a pit bull. I checked the door.

Locked.

Damn it. All I'd accomplished was to wreck a streetcar, alienate half the population of Ybor, and still end up in a dimly lit room with a throbbing headache. I was also hungry and thirsty, my time in the beauty parlor wasted, and my blood pressure was probably off the chart. Stupid, stupid, stupid. Why hadn't I just surrendered at the doctor's house?

Or gone home with Lafitte?

I sat back down and glanced at the headlines in the *Tampa Tribune*. Six dead in the shootout at El Dorado. Violence at the 40,000 man veterans' march on Washington, DC. Herbert Hoover re-nominated at the Republican Convention. More bank failures. A plunge in the Dow Jones averages to 44. Lindbergh's housemaid committed suicide.

And I thought I had problems.

God, I was tired. I cradled my head in my arms on the table and closed my eyes. Maybe I'd wake up in my bed in 2019 and discover it had all been a dream.

Darkness closed around me. From somewhere came the clack of

castanets. A guitar strummed. It became the "Habanera" from Bizet's *Carmen*.

"Amy."

I jumped up and there she stood in her tattered gown, her hair tangled and matted. Beyond her in the darkness, where before had been a cinder block wall, there now appeared a dark lagoon surrounded by trees, and beyond that, Lafitte's yellow biplane.

The girl motioned with her hand. I followed as if drawn to the hole, to Lafitte, but had taken no more than a few steps when the door swung open.

Lights flooded the room. The image vanished. So did the girl, and in marched the Untouchables in their hats and suits, bringing with them a cloud of smoke from their cigarettes.

It took a moment for me to realize I was still in the chair at the table, still cuffed.

Chief Agent Rothman, holding a thick folder, removed his fedora and was about to sit down when he noticed the newspaper. He picked it up and shook it. "Who left this in here?"

No one confessed. Gerhardt, along with the other agents who'd arrested me, sheepishly took up positions against the wall, avoiding my eyes. Cheena was there too, dressed in a power jacket. Behind her came another woman who could have been a weight lifter with her strong face, cropped hair, and heavy-set build. She plopped her black briefcase on a side table.

Here it comes, I thought, the whips and chains.

She unsnapped the briefcase and took out a notebook and pencils.

Cheena gave me a friendly nod, which further reduced the tension. Then Rothman put his folder and cigarette case on the table and took the cuffs off me. Another good sign, but as I sat there, rubbing soreness out of my wrists, trying to shake off the memory of the dream, he took a seat across from me and switched on the lamp, letting it shine in my face.

"Is that necessary?" I said, shading my eyes.

"It depends on how cooperative you are."

"Do I look like a threat? There are six of you."

"It's not numbers that matter. It's your attitude."

He turned the lamp sideways and began removing documents and photographs, placing them face down like a card dealer. With his balding head and thick glasses, he looked like a stone-faced judge about to sentence me to the gallows. He took out a cigarette, tamped it on the table, lit up, and introduced the other three agents by name. When Gerhardt's name was called—his last name was Hessler—he came to attention and snapped his heels together like a Nazi.

"For the record," Rothman said, speaking in halting Spanish, "my questions and your answers will be in Spanish. Cheena will translate. The lady over there is our, *como se dice,* stenographer."

Cheena translated his words into English. The stenographer scribbled on her pad.

Rothman leaned forward. "Please state your full name, occupation, and address."

"You already have that information."

"Please, señorita, this is for the record."

"Look, I'm willing to answer your questions. I'll even swear on the Bible, but there are a couple of things I want in return."

"This isn't a labor union negotiation."

"You could at least hear me out."

He sighed like a father in the presence of an unreasonable child. "What?"

"I'm starving. I haven't had anything to eat since breakfast."

He turned to Cheena. "Get her a ham sandwich."

"Not a sandwich. I want Caldo Gallego from Columbia. A big bowl."

Rothman let out a sharp breath and slapped his palm on the table. Before he could reply, I said, "Some home-made bread too. Warm."

I would have settled for the sandwich, but he gave the order. Cheena left the room and returned with a pitcher of lemonade. I took a few swallows. "There's one more thing," I said.

"Don't push it, señorita."

I pointed at Gerhardt, who by then was sitting in a chair against the wall, puffing on a cigarette and still wearing his hat. "I want that man out of my sight."

"Why?"

Gerhardt lowered his head. I explained what happened. Cheena translated with the energy of a woman who'd also been his victim.

"She's lying," Gerhardt said, his face turning red. "I never touched her. She's the one who molested me … put one of them spells on me, threatened me with—"

"Enough," said Rothman. "We'll discuss this later." He gestured with his thumb like a baseball ump. "Wait outside. I'll call if I need you." Cheena shot me a satisfied glance. Gerhardt trudged out. "You two as well," Rothman said, speaking to the other agents.

As soon as the door closed, Rothman opened his cigarette case and offered me one.

"I don't smoke."

"Since when?"

"I've never smoked."

He picked up a document—probably Carmen's bio-sketch—and consulted it. Carmen was a smoker. He knew it and I knew it, so he probably thought I was faking. He said nothing, but I could see uncertainty in his face. Finally, he put the document down and looked at his watch. "It'll take another half hour for your food to arrive, so let's get started."

CHAPTER 41

From outside the room came the clatter of a teletype machine. Cheena and the stenographer sat there waiting. And finally, Rothman said, "For the record, please state your full name, occupation, and address."

"My name is Luz Amelia Romano, but I can't remember—"

He held up a hand. "Stop right there. Is Carmen your stage name?"

"I'm not Carmen. I keep telling you that."

"If you're not Carmen, why were you running?"

"Because I was scared, that's why. I thought your agents would gun me down on the street."

"No one was going to shoot you, Señorita Romero. All we—"

"It's Romano, not Romero."

He glanced at the form. "As I was saying, we weren't going to shoot you. We wanted to question you in connection with the murder of Agent Pruitt."

"I don't know this Agent Pruitt. Never met him."

"Where do you live, Señorita Romano? Where are you from?"

"I was in an accident and can't remember."

"Tell me about your accident."

"All I remember is I was in a car and—"

"What kind of car?"

"I don't remember."

"Night or day?"

"Night … I think."

"Were you alone?"

"Only thing I remember is this, this … woman. She appeared out of nowhere. Middle of the road. I swerved, maybe hit a tree. Everything went black. When I awoke, I was alone. No road, no car, no corpse. I wandered around, bleeding. I must have found a road because someone picked me up. Next thing I know I'm at the doctor's house."

The questions went on. Who picked you up? Don't know. What kind of car? Don't know. Describe him. Can't. Who are your closest relatives? Don't know that either.

Sometimes he paced the room with his cigarette, or sat on the corner of the table, or leaned forward to stab out his cigarette in the ashtray. Sometimes I fanned away the smoke or pushed away the ashtray, and he asked me again, "When did you stop smoking?"

"I've never smoked."

"How do you know if you can't remember?"

"I just know. And you shouldn't smoke either. It causes cancer. Stains your teeth. Turns your fingers yellow. Makes you smell like nicotine."

He looked at the cigarette in his hand. "Are you a medical doctor, señorita?"

"I can't remember."

"A dentist?"

I shrugged.

"Let's see your teeth. Smile for me."

I gave him a fake smile. "See how white they are; no cigarette stains."

Cheena put a hand to her mouth, probably thinking it was time for a checkup. Rothman picked up an enlarged photo of Carmen in her flamenco dress and held it up. "This you?"

"That's not me."

"How could it not be you?"

"Not me."

He held up another photo, his eyes burning into mine. "Do you know this man?"

I almost choked at the sight of Clarence.

"Now we're getting somewhere," Rothman said. "Is he the man who tried to kill you?"

"All I can say is that photo scares me."

The photos kept coming—a woman who looked like a brothel madam, a well-dressed young man who was probably Pruitt, another gangster looking character, and then, Lafitte, the pilot.

"Is this the man who took you to the doctor's house?"

"I was barely conscious."

"Please answer yes or no."

"It might have been him or it might have been you. I don't remember."

He shook his head and put away the photos. "You told Cheena you're a soothsayer with pre-cognitive powers, and you can move objects with the mind. Is that right?"

"I had to say something."

"You even scared the dickens out of my people by claiming the power of witchcraft."

"I didn't call it witchcraft."

"Okay, let's call it the power of curses. Isn't that witchcraft?"

"Whatever."

He stood, walked around the room and sat back down. "Listen, Señorita Amada—"

"It's Romano. I'm not Carmen. How many times do I have to tell you?"

"Fine, but let's separate fact from fiction. First, you've been injured. It may have been a car wreck or it may have been an unnamed assailant. Which was it?"

"Car wreck."

"Are you certain it wasn't an assailant?"

"Didn't I just say car wreck?"

Cheena looked up as if she expected Rothman to start yelling. Instead, he took a deep breath. "Please, señorita, it would help if you'd be more cooperative."

"I'd be a lot more cooperative if you'd do something about Gerhardt."

"It's Agent Hessler, and this interrogation is about you, not him."

"So you're just going to ignore what he did to me?"

"I'll deal with it in time. But if you don't start answering my questions, I'll call off the interrogation until tomorrow or maybe next week."

"Does that mean I can leave?"

"No, señorita, you'll be our guest until you change your attitude."

"Fine. What's your next question?"

"The question is why were you running? Wasn't it because you're a wanted fugitive?"

"Carmen was the wanted fugitive, not me."

"Indulge me for a minute, señorita, please. Let's suppose you are in fact, Carmen Amaya, the flamenco dancer. You knew you were wanted in connection with the murder of Agent Pruitt, so you used your injury to feign amnesia. Further suppose you used your time at the doctor's house to invent this fictitious Amy Romano character."

"I'm Amy Romano and I'm not fictitious."

"Then how do you explain the dress?"

"What dress?"

He motioned to Cheena. She handed him the same tote bag that contained my wallet and hat. Rothman reached inside and pulled out my flamenco dress.

"Isn't this the dress you're wearing in the photo?" He waved it around like a prosecutor in a courtroom. "It came from the doctor's house. So let's be realistic here."

It grew quiet. I was defeated. I had only two cards left—that I spoke English, which Carmen didn't, and I didn't have a tattoo, which Carmen did.

"Can I speak to you in private?" I said.

"We've already had that conversation, Señorita Amaya."

I had my mouth open to protest when the door opened and in stepped Groucho, the fingerprint guy without his jacket, still with loose tie and his sleeves rolled up. He glanced at me over his spectacles and then whispered in Rothman's ear.

Rothman's eyes widened. "Are you sure?"

"Positive," Groucho said. "They don't match."

Rothman stood. "Sonofabitch," he mumbled and flung his folder against the wall. Then he stormed out with the fingerprint guy.

Cheena picked up the mess and was putting it back into the folder when another clerk popped into the room. "Who ordered Caldo Gallego?"

CHAPTER 42

The bread was still warm. Caldo Gallego had never smelled so good or tasted so delicious, and those famous lines from the "Habanera" played in my head like a victory march.

The bird you thought you'd caught
Flapped its wings and flew away.

How sweet to see the feds eat crow. I didn't even have to hike up my dress to show the tattoo I didn't have. With any luck at all, I'd be at the doctor's house in time for my date with Lafitte.

Cheena, who was eating a ham and cheese sandwich, had the look of a player from the losing team. "What a disaster," she said. "How humiliating for Agent Rothman."

"Not humiliating for me."

"That's not the issue, señorita."

"You can call me Amy."

"Fine, Amy, but here's the issue. Pruitt was the first and only agent to be murdered. Washington wanted Carmen's head. Wanted to make an example of her, send her to the chair."

I sopped up the remaining liquid in the bowl with my bread.

"We thought we had her," Cheena said. "The news went out over the wires. All that clatter of typewriters. Press releases. They were celebrating in Washington. The director himself was coming to be photographed with Chief Agent Rothman. You don't embarrass Director Hoover. You'd don't make him look bad. Nobody, and I mean *nadia*, crosses him the wrong way."

"How much longer are they going to keep me here?"

She put down her sandwich. "Have you heard anything I said?"

"Every word, Cheena. I'm sorry J. Edgar is pissed, but how about me? I never committed a crime in my life … well, except for that streetcar thing. Then I get dragged in here and interrogated like a common thief. If it wasn't for the fingerprints, I might be going to the chair. So don't think I'm going to shed a tear over somebody's *embarrassment*."

She picked up my empty bowl and left the room.

I waited, thinking she'd come back and tell me I could leave. She didn't. Neither did anyone else, and the only indication I had of time was the barred window high above. It went from shadowy to dark. I heard crickets and the warble of night birds, and I thought of Lafitte. He'd be arriving about now at the doctor's house for our big date tonight—candlelight and wine in a quiet little restaurant on the bay. Would I get out of here in time to see him?

The door opened and Cheena came back in, looking more defeated than before.

"You're spending the night."

"But why? I'm not Carmen."

"Look, they're not going to let you walk just because fingerprints don't match. They still want to know who you are. If you've got nothing to hide, then drop that 'can't-remember' thing."

"Can I at least make a phone call?"

"Maybe tomorrow. Let's go."

She led me down a corridor and into a small room with a bunk, a toilet, and a washbasin. It also had a high barred window. "Bed's already made," she said. "There's towels on it. Also a gown and some toiletries. They'll wake you for breakfast at six."

"Cheena."

"What, Amy?"

"I wish you'd believe me when I say I had nothing to do with Pruitt's murder."

"It's not me you have to convince. It's Washington. It's Hoover.

Rothman's on the horn with him right now. You can hear yelling on the other end."

She walked to the door, stopped, and turned back. "There's something else."

"What?"

"I'm not supposed to tell you, but…"

"But what?"

"Gerhardt. The agent you put the curse on."

"What about him?"

"Well, when he left here, he took the Ford and…"

"And what?"

"They found it a couple of miles from here. On fire."

I couldn't have been more shocked if she'd slapped me in the face. I was sure she was going to say Gerhardt had been burned to a crisp and I'd be blamed for another murder and have something else to explain to St. Pete. Instead, she said, "He's missing. We're checking local hospitals. I imagine they'll be asking about the curse."

She looked at me the way a padre might look at a condemned prisoner, then shook her head and went out the door, humming.

CHAPTER 43

I slumped down on the cot. Gerhardt missing? His black Ford on fire? My words were meant to scare him. It had to be a coincidence. But what if it wasn't? What if I did have the power of curse in this crazy new world?

Somehow, I managed to change out of my dress and corset into a gown. I brushed my teeth, washed my face, and was trying to figure out how to turn out the lights when a sharp rap at the door caused me to jump. It opened, and there stood Cheena, looking as weary as ever.

"Sorry," she said, "but Agent Rothman wants to see you again."

"Did they find Gerhardt?"

"All I can say is if Rothman catches you in a lie you'll be here a long time."

I changed back into my dress, sans corset, ran a brush through my hair, and followed her back to the interrogation room with its cloud of cigarette smoke, dreading what I might hear about Gerhardt. Rothman stood when I came it. The stenographer was at her table, and the two agents who'd previously been dismissed were back in their chairs, arms crossed and avoiding my eyes.

"Take you hats off," Rothman said to them.

They removed their hats but still wouldn't look at me. Rothman stated the time—10:14 PM—named everyone present, lit another cigarette and fixed me in a glare that said he wasn't happy. "We need to ask you some more questions, Señorita Romano. It will not go well if you don't cooperate. Understand?"

"I understand."

"Did you or did you not put a so-called Gypsy curse on Agent Gerhardt Hessler?"

"It was a joke. Nothing more."

"What's a Level One curse?"

"No such thing. I made it up."

"Why?"

"To annoy him … to scare him for…"

"For what?"

"Feeling my breasts, running his hand up my legs to my … you know."

When this was translated, one of the other agents said, "She's lying. That never happened. I was there, saw the whole thing."

"He's the liar!" I shot back. "He knows exactly what happened."

"Enough," Rothman said. "The issue here is what happened to Agent Hessler."

"What happened to him?"

"We're the ones asking the questions. Tell me exactly what you said to him."

I repeated what I'd said for the record. Cheena corroborated my explanation, but one of the other agents said, "She left out a couple of cuss words."

Rothman looked at me. "What other words?"

"I might have also called him a *puta pendejo*. I was angry."

"What was his reaction?"

"He walked away and lit a cigarette."

"That's not all," said the other agent. "She made the lights go out. Scared the dookey out of Hessler. Said he felt a jolt like he'd been kicked in the stomach."

They all looked at each other. Rothman consulted his notes, cleared his throat, and looked up. "Did you make the lights go out?"

"Are you seriously asking me that question?"

"Just answer the question. Please."

I slapped my hand on the table. "I did not make the damn lights go out. *Punto final.*"

"Tell me about that Gypsy lady who came in with the local cops."

"What about her?"

"You spoke to her in your Gypsy language."

"It's called Caló, and it's more accurate to say she spoke to me."

"What did you discuss?"

"She wanted to know how I was being treated."

"Did you tell her about the curse on Agent Hessler?"

"I told her he'd treated me badly."

"That was not the question, señorita. Did you tell her about the curse?"

"I might have mentioned it."

"Did you ask for her help in making the curse come to fruition?"

"Of course not."

"You told Cheena you have the power of telekinesis. I looked it up." He pulled a page out of his folder. "Here's what it says—to use the mind to move or create objects, to levitate, to reanimate corpses, to make an object explode or catch on fire." He put away the page. "You say it was all a prank, and yet the lights went out, Agent Hessler said he felt like he'd been punched in the stomach, and his vehicle caught on fire. Do you have an explanation for any of that?"

"How can I explain what I don't know?"

"Do you now or have you ever had any association with the KKK?"

"Are you serious? What kind of question is that?"

"Just answer, please."

"I do not, nor have I ever associated with those bigots. They hate Gypsies. They hate us Spanish speakers, and they hate Jews and African Americans."

Everyone looked up as if I'd used the n-word, and I recalled my grandmother saying it was offensive back in the old days to refer to blacks as Africans.

"Colored folks," I said. "Negroes."

"Let's see if we can get to the bottom of this," said Rothman. "What we know is you leveled a curse on Agent Hessler. There are witnesses."

"It was a joke, nothing more."

"Joke or not, it frightened him. We also know he left this facility at five in the afternoon in a Bureau vehicle. What happened next is murky, but here is what we know from witnesses. A few minutes after leaving, he was hijacked by five men wearing sheets and hoods."

"KKK?"

"The markings on their outfits are consistent with a local chapter. They set the car ablaze. They left a small burning cross on the side of the road. They took Agent Hessler with them."

I wanted to cry. The KKK. A burning cross. My God, what had I done? I again tried to make the case that my words to Gerhardt had been a harmless prank, and yet I couldn't help but feel partially responsible. *Curses work only if you believe in them.*

After a while, Rothman leaned in close and lowered his voice. "Are you running from something, señorita? Maybe a husband or a boyfriend who's been threatening you?"

"Of course not."

"How can you be positive if you can't remember anything before the accident?"

"I just know."

"I think you know a great deal more than you're telling us."

He shuffled some papers, took off his glasses, rubbed his eyes, and put his glasses back on. "Let me lay out a plausible scenario. Let's suppose you are in fact who you say you are. And yet you could pass as Carmen Amaya. Right?"

"Maybe."

"And since you have this beautiful dress it's also plausible you dance flamenco. Right?"

"It's possible."

"Let's further assume it's possible that Agent Pruitt never had a relationship with the real Carmen Amaya … that, in fact, his relationship was with you."

"That's absurd."

"Is it? Your past is a big fat zero, Señorita Romano, an empty cigar box.

So until you get back your memory or until we establish your bona fides, we can put anything we want in that box."

"You're ignoring the fingerprints. They don't match."

He arched an eyebrow as if to say it made no difference. Then he gathered his papers and quit the room. The stenographer and the other two agents followed him out, leaving me alone with Cheena. "What now?" I asked her.

"It looks like you could be here a while."

CHAPTER 44

It stormed all night, with flashes of lightning and boom of thunder that in my dream became explosions from German artillery. The scarred landscape mushroomed up and fell back down. Lafitte's yellow biplane was hit. It spiraled downward, trailing smoke. Yet somehow he regained control and landed next to a trench. Then he cut his way through barbed wire, kicked in the door, shot Gerhardt and two other Germans with Clarence's Luger, and led me out of the place.

And we were flying away in his damaged plane, trailing smoke, when a loud knock brought me back to reality. The door opened, my dream faded, and in came a surly-looking woman with a breakfast tray of black coffee, boiled eggs and burnt toast.

She said, "Good morning," but it sounded like "*Guten morgen.*"

"Is this all I'm getting for breakfast?" I asked in Spanish. "How about a newspaper? How about some cream and marmalade?"

"I don't speak Gypsy," she said and slammed the door on her way out.

"Damn Nazi," I mumbled, and sank onto the bed to eat. Through the barred window came the toll of a Sunday church bell, and as I sat there listening, I heard a message in each toll, a reminder of things gone bad—Gerhardt, Lafitte, the KKK, a wrecked streetcar, and burnt toast for breakfast. Worse, I could be stuck in this room for a long time. Damn them! I shoved away the food, stood, and banged on the door, thinking to ask for a newspaper."

Cheena stuck in her head. "Fifteen minutes," she said. "Rothman wants to see you."

I fixed myself up as best as possible, and by eight, dressed in a shapeless blue detention dress and feeling like I'd swallowed a lump of coal, I found myself back in the interrogation room with Rothman, the two agents, the stenographer, and Cheena. All their faces were buried in the Sunday newspapers, and all looked like they'd just lost a wrestling match with J. Edgar Hoover.

Rothman, always the gentleman, stood and motioned me into my chair. He looked so beaten, with pale coloring, that I almost felt sympathy for him.

"Have you heard from Gerhardt?" I asked.

"It's Agent Hessler, and all we've heard is this." He held up a newspaper with a photo of a burning car. I tried to read the caption, but all I caught was *KKK* before he put the paper down.

"Can I see that?"

"Not now."

"You could have sent a copy to my room."

"This isn't the Ritz. We don't have room service."

"Oh, no? Then how about a lawyer? What about habeas corpus?"

"We know the law, señorita. We know what we're doing. And I find it interesting you know about habeas corpus with your faulty memory."

He turned to Cheena. "Get her."

Cheena stepped out and came back with a garishly dressed woman who could have been a brothel madam from the Gatsby days, all rouge, feathers and red colors, her cigarette in a long holder, her glossy purse clutched to her chest as if afraid they'd confiscate it.

She froze at the sight of me. "*Por Dios.* Carmen?"

She tried to approach me, but Rothman blocked her way.

"For the record," he said to her in Spanish, "Please state your name and occupation."

"Rosita Contreras, owner and manager of Granada after Midnight. I'm also the employer of that lady sitting there. She should be in the hospital, not stuck in—"

"What is her name?"

"Her name is Carmen Amaya. Why have you arrested her?"

"We're asking the questions, madam. What does Señorita Amaya do at your … um, lounge?"

"She dances flamenco. Everyone knows that. Why are you asking?"

"What else does she do for clients at your establishment?"

"She's a dancer, señor, *punto final*."

"Are you sure the lady you've identified as Carmen Amaya is, in fact, Carmen Amaya?"

"There is only one Carmen Amaya in this world and as the Virgin is my witness that's her sitting right there."

"Thank you, señora. You may go."

Cheena opened the door. Rosa didn't want to leave and tried to come closer. One of the agents grabbed her arm. She jerked loose and mumbled a few words in Caló. At the door, she said, "Don't you worry, *dulce*, we'll have you back on stage in no time."

As soon as the door closed, I asked, "What was that about?"

"Bona fides, señorita, nothing more."

"You already know I'm not Carmen, so why did you bring Rosa in here?"

"Rosa? You sound like the two of you are friends."

"I've never seen her before."

He pushed the newspapers out of his way and looked up with bloodshot eyes. "After you've slept on it, are you willing to tell us more about yourself?"

"I didn't exactly sleep. I had a miserable night. Those cold boiled eggs didn't help. Neither did the burnt toast. And there was no cream for the coffee."

"That wasn't the question. I asked if you have anything further to tell us."

"Only in private."

"I told you we're not allowed to be alone with suspects."

"In that case, I'm not answering your questions. I don't trust your other two agents—and please don't have Cheena translate."

"Why?"

"Because they lie. All I need is a couple of minutes."

He stood, paced around the room, looked at the ceiling, and finally said, "You've got two minutes, but you'd better have something worth saying."

CHAPTER 45

He told Cheena to wait outside and to open the door in exactly two minutes. She smiled as she left. None of the others made eye contact. As soon as the door closed, Rothman looked at his watch. "Your two minutes just started."

"First thing I have to say is Carmen had a Gypsy tattoo on her thigh."

"Everyone in Ybor knows about the tattoo."

"I don't have a tattoo."

"I'll take your word for it. What else?"

"Am I correct in saying Carmen does not or could not speak English?"

"That's my understanding, but you're not Carmen."

"No, I'm not. I'm Amy Romano. I don't have a tattoo, and English is my native language."

"What?"

"I said English is my native language."

In case he missed it, I repeated it in English.

His mouth fell open. "Look," I said, still speaking English, "I wanted to hear what your agents had to say about me, and I got an earful. You should teach them manners."

"Our agents don't go to finishing school. Is that all you wanted to tell me?"

"No, what I want to say is I may have left out a few details, but everything I've said is true. I was in a car wreck. Lost my memory. I don't know anything about my background. I don't even know why people say

Abyssinia instead of adios or goodbye."

"What are the details you left out?"

"One of the pictures you showed me. I recognized him."

He pulled out a photo of Lafitte. "This man?"

"Not him."

"But you know him, don't you?"

I didn't answer. He shuffled through his photos and held up a picture of Clarence.

"Yes, him. After the accident, I was wandering around in the woods, lost and bleeding. He found me. He thought I was Carmen … tried to finish me off. Said he was working for some guy named Sal. I hit him with a tomato stake and got away. After that—"

"Wait, wait. You hit him with a tomato stake?"

"Knocked him to the ground, then I ran for my life, ended up at the doctor's house. But everyone still thinks I'm Carmen. It's bad enough that some mobster named Sal is after me. Then I learned the feds are also after me. Is it any wonder I was running? It's been a nightmare."

The door opened and Cheena stuck in her head. Rothman said, "Thank you, Cheena, we're okay." He waited for the door to shut and turned back to me. "Where is this wooded area you mentioned?"

"All I remember is someone saying we were near Tarpon Springs."

"North, south? How far from Tarpon?"

"I have no idea."

He sat there for the longest, saying nothing until Cheena opened and closed the door again. Then he gathered up his papers. "I'm going to open the door, but before I do, I think you should know obstruction in a federal investigation is a serious matter."

"What obstruction? What are you talking about?"

"Withholding information about your native language. And since you were misleading us, how can we be certain you're telling the truth now?"

"That's the most twisted logic I've ever heard. I was misleading because I was scared."

"Every criminal in the world is scared, so they run and they lie."

"I was running because I'm innocent."

"Look, let me remind you again." He shook a hairy finger at me. "You've been saying you have amnesia, that you don't remember anything. If that's true, then it's conceivable you could have been involved in Agent Pruitt's death. You just don't remember."

"That's absurd. I had nothing to do with—"

"Hold on, let me finish. The only thing certain is English is your native tongue, you don't have a Gypsy tattoo, and you are not Carmen Amaya. So here's the bottom line. Until we unravel this case—and believe me, we will unravel it—I'm giving you a choice."

"What choice?"

"First, what you just told me is going to remain our secret. When I open that door, people will hear us speaking Spanish. *Español, señorita*. You do not let on to anyone that you speak English, not to Cheena, not to the other agents. Understand?"

"Why?"

"Would you please listen and stop asking questions? The second thing I want you to do is water down your protests that you are not Carmen."

"You want me to pretend I'm Carmen?"

"That's exactly what I'm saying. It will work to your advantage."

"How can it work to my advantage? Carmen is a wanted fugitive."

"Let me ask you something, Miss Romano. Would you prefer to walk out of here as Carmen Amaya or spend the rest of your life in the Big House?"

He let that thought hang in the air like a dark cloud, then said "Abyssinia" and left the room.

Cheena bounced back in, grinning as if she had a new boyfriend.

"You were right," she said. "I should have listened."

"What are you talking about?"

"Bolita. I put a dollar on number 83. Won a hundred dollars."

She kept yapping, pulling me out of my Carmen thoughts, and was asking if I had more numbers when the door opened a crack.

"Cheena?" called a woman's voice.

Cheena excused herself and stepped to the door. She spoke quietly to whoever was there and then rushed back into the room, her eyes big as saucers.

"What?" I said. "What's going on?"

The door swung open and in marched J. Edgar Hoover.

CHAPTER 46

I didn't realize I was standing until Agent Rothman, who followed him in, motioned me into my chair. Cheena scooted away and shut the door behind her. Rothman also looked like he wanted to bolt. He mouthed the word "English" to me. Hoover said nothing, didn't smile or grunt or even acknowledge my presence. Instead, he sank into the chair where Rothman had previously sat, opened a folder, took out a few sheets of paper, and began reading.

He took his time, which gave me a moment for my heart to stop racing and to notice he was dressed in a dark suit with a white shirt and vest. He was also well proportioned and taller than I thought, with a full head of dark hair, but his face seemed permanently fixed in a scowl.

At last, he put the papers back into the folder and glanced up.

"Do you speak English?"

"Yes, sir."

"It says here you speak only Spanish and Gypsy Romani."

Rothman answered for me. "It's part of her undercover, sir. We thought it best for Miss Amaya to keep it secret. That way she could learn more."

"You should make that notation in her record."

"Yes, sir."

Hoover turned back to me. "Where's the frock?"

"The what?"

"The flamenco frock."

He opened his folder and showed me a photo of Carmen in her flamenco dress.

180

"I'll get it," Rothman said. He raced out of the room and came back with the dress.

Hoover unfolded it and examined it the way a woman might do in a clothing store, rubbing his hand over the fabric and along the lace, turning it this way and that. He even smelled it. "Nice stitching. Where did you have it made?"

"I … uh … locally, I think."

"A frock like this is expensive. How would you not know?"

"She was in a bad accident," Rothman said. "A head injury." He touched his head for emphasis. If there was ever a good-cop, bad-cop, moment, this was it.

Hoover folded the dress and put it on the table. "Do you know who I am?"

"Yes, sir. Everyone knows who you are."

"What is my name?"

"You're Mr. Hoover, head of the FBI."

Rothman said, "Director Hoover, and it's BI, Bureau of Investigation, not FBI."

Hoover shot him a shut-up look and turned back to me. "What's the F for?"

"Uh … feds, federal. Everyone calls you the government men, so I naturally thought it was the Federal Bureau of Investigation."

"Federal?"

"Yes, sir. Bureau by itself sounds tepid. But if you add Federal, it'll give it more of that, um … *je ne sais quoi*. You know. Strong, authoritative. Like the Marines."

Rothman rolled his eyes. Hoover picked up an ink pen and jotted the word "Federal" on the folder. Then he fixed me in a withering gaze. "Let me see if I have this straight. You injured your head. A concussion, and now don't know if you're Amy something-or-other or Carmen, the flamenco dancer. Is that right?"

"Yes, sir."

"Are you still having doubts?"

I glanced at Rothman. He gave me an almost imperceptible nod.

"You can call me Carmen," I said.

Rothman looked relieved. Hoover leaned back in his chair and crossed his arms. "Let me describe a hard reality, Miss Carmen Amaya. Are you listening?"

"Yes, sir." I sat straight in my chair.

"Someone murdered one of my agents with a shotgun. You might have been involved."

"But—"

"Someone else kidnapped one of my agents. You might have been involved in that one as well. So let's get this straight. You don't kill one of *my* men. You don't kidnap *my* men. Someone is going to pay dearly." His face went from pasty white to crimson, his voice got louder, and even the cords on his neck stood out. "Are we clear on that?"

"Yes, sir, but I didn't have anything to do with—"

"Just shut up and listen. In the Bureau, guilt or innocence doesn't matter. What's important are results. Innocent people have gone to the chair."

"That's not right," I said.

He slammed a fist on the table. "Are you calling me a liar?"

"No, sir, I'm saying it's not right to execute innocent people."

I thought he'd come over the table. Instead, he asked, "Are you a priest, Miss Amaya?"

"No, sir."

"The Dalai Lama?"

"No, sir."

"Then don't lecture me on right and wrong. Understand?"

"Yes, sir."

He drew a sharp breath and picked up my flamenco dress. "I'm told that you, the flamenco dancer, are helping us crack an illegal operation in the Tampa area. Is that right?"

I glanced at Rothman. He nodded. I answered, "Yes, sir."

"It was a purely local matter … until my agent got murdered. Now my office is involved. Do you understand what I'm telling you?"

"Yes, sir."

"There was also that second matter, which was even more important to the Bureau."

"What second matter?"

He turned to Rothman. "You haven't told her?"

"No, sir. I was waiting for—"

"Have you questioned her about it?"

"No, sir, that was next on my list."

Hoover slapped his open palm on the table. Rothman looked like he wanted the earth to swallow him. Hoover turned back at me. "So here's the deal, Miss Amaya. You can continue your denials, your obfuscations, your obstruction, and get indicted on the evidence we have, or you can continue helping us. Which is it going to be?"

"May I ask you a question, sir?"

"Make it brief. I've got a plane to catch."

"Don't you know who shot Agent Pruitt?"

"We have a pretty good idea."

"Why don't you just haul him in? Sir."

He turned to Rothman. "Didn't you explain he's already been brought in?"

"Not yet, sir. She's only been here for—"

"That there were no other witnesses and that she's the only one?"

"There wasn't time, sir."

"And that his lawyers got him off."

"We were going to explain that today, sir."

Hoover's face turned so red I thought he'd catch fire. He closed his eyes as if trying to contain his anger, and finally looked back at me. "Does that answer your question?"

"Yes, sir."

"Good, and please don't say we should gun him down on the street. That's what the Soviets do. This is America." He slapped a hand on the table for emphasis. "We want the evidence." Another slap. "We want a trial." Slap. "We want the world to know we're coming after you if you mess with our agents." Slap. "Then we're going to send that sonofabitch to the chair. And anyone else who had anything to do with his killing."

He leaned so far across the table I smelled coffee on his breath. "Do you understand what I'm telling you, Miss Carmen Amaya?"

"Yes, sir."

"So are you going to help us or not?"

By then I'd have jumped on the table if he'd asked me. "Yes, sir."

"Good. I don't want to have this conversation again. Are we clear on that?"

"Yes, sir."

Hoover rubbed his hand over the fabric on the flamenco dress again, then picked up his folder and stood. Rothman jumped to his feet. I also stood, but if I'd expected a handshake or a thank-you-for-agreeing-to-endanger-your-life-in-the-service-of-our-country, it didn't come. Instead, Hoover marched to the door like a commanding general and shut it behind him, leaving me alone in the room with Rothman.

I fell back in my chair and breathed again. Rothman, who looked like he'd just been spared exile to Siberia, also sat. He bowed his head as if to thank the gods and finally lit one of his Lucky Strikes, which he hadn't dared smoke in Hoover's presence.

"Thank you for cooperating," he said. "Are you okay?"

"I will be when my heart stops pounding. What's this second matter he was talking about?"

"Give me a minute."

He closed his eyes, leaned back, and took several cancerous drags on his cigarette, fouling the room with his smoke. The door opened and Cheena came back in. Rothman waved her away. "Not now. Give us five minutes."

As soon as the door closed, he stabbed out his cigarette in the ashtray. "What I'm about to tell you is strictly between us. If it leaves this room, you'll be in greater danger than you already are. Understand?"

"No, I don't understand. Please tell me."

"You're not going to like it."

CHAPTER 47

He stood and paced around the room, rubbing his chin, driving me crazy. *Get on with it!* I wanted to scream. Finally, he looked at the chair where Hoover had sat, pushed it away like it was toxic and pulled over the chair where he'd been sitting.

"The director's obsessed with his priority," he said, "so we have to deal with it."

"What priority?"

"It's a delicate matter."

"Just tell me, please."

"Well, you know how serious the crime problem is in Ybor. We've got Salvatore Provenzano, Charlie Wall, Santo Trafficante, Ignacio Antinori, Tito Rubio. The Klan too. But the director thinks they're just common bootleggers, criminals, smugglers and bigots."

He lit another cigarette. By then I was ready to strangle him.

He took a long puff. "Here's the bottom line. We—meaning this office—we're up to our necks with these criminals. But Director Hoover's more concerned about protesters on the street. They're the real threat, at least according to him."

"How are they a threat?"

"Because they're spreading like cancer. They've even got war veterans marching on Washington, demanding money for their sacrifices. Director Hoover thinks Moscow is financing the turmoil, pushing for a revolution like they had in Russia."

By that time I felt like I also needed a cigarette. "So what does that have to do with me?"

"It means the director expects you to do the same thing Carmen was doing."

"You already told me that."

"I'm not talking about the mob; I'm talking about the other thing she was doing."

"What other thing?"

"You don't know?"

"I'm not Carmen, for God's sake. How would I know?"

"Well, Carmen either was, or pretended to be, in sympathy with the workers. She went to factories. Talked to workers. Danced for them. Made friends with labor leaders, newspaper editors, and anyone else who backed labor. They loved her. That's the information the director wants. Names. He keeps a list. He calls it his … well … it's not a nice name."

If I'd been standing, I'd have had to sit. My great-grandmother Carmen a snitch, a mole, a Benedict Arnold? Helping the feds create an enemies' list? Good God, I'd always imagined her on the street with the protesters, hurling bricks and smashing windows, waving placards.

"It's a dangerous job," Rothman said. "Some of those labor men are as violent as the mob. If you were discovered, you could end up—"

"In the swamp?"

"It's possible that's what got Carmen killed."

"So what happens to people on the director's list?"

"Let's just say I wouldn't want to be on his list."

He picked up the dress Hoover had left on the table and headed for the door.

"Wait. Are you releasing me or not?"

"Up to you, *Carmen*. You can tell Cheena if you'll do it or not."

"And if I say no?"

"Do you want me to convey that message to Director Hoover?"

I felt like throwing a chair at him. Bastards. They were sending me on a suicide mission. J. Edgar frigging Hoover and his electric chair on side, and the labor thugs, the mob and the bootleggers on the other. Well, to hell with that. I had other plans. I was going to hit the bolita clubs, make as much money as possible and get out of Dodge, go to New Orleans or Spain or some other place, possibly with Lafitte.

Cheena came back in and led me to her desk, humming the whole time. Only five or six other workers were in the place, all with loose ties and rolled up sleeves, banging away on their typewriters. Cheena pulled out a bunch of forms, placed carbon paper between them, and adjusted the forms in her Underwood.

"Well," she said, "is it a yes or no?"

"Yes or no what?"

"Oh, please, señorita, it's Sunday. I don't want to be here either. Just tell me yes or no."

"Doesn't look like I have a choice. Does it?"

"I need a simple yes or no."

"Affirmative."

She punched a single key, turned the roller, made a couple of adjustments, and began typing, speaking as she typed. "The below-named informant, Señorita Carmen Amaya, has stated in my presence that—"

"Wait, you're putting on paper that I'm an informant?"

"Either that or suspect. Which would you prefer?"

"How about individual?"

"Individual is not an option. I have to choose suspect or informant."

"Fine, call me an informant."

She went back to her Underwood, clickety-clack, still mouthing the words: "Said informant has both read and understands the conditions in this document … and is willing and able to perform the duties laid out to her by Agent Rothman … and is fully aware of the hazards associated in the performance of the tasks and the consequences of failing to comply…"

This went on for several minutes, right down to Carmen's identifying tattoo and her Andalusian accent. She then pulled out the document and handed it to me.

"Read and sign, please."

"It says here you're paying me eighteen dollars a week."

"That's more than the *tabaquera* girls earn. Here, use this pen."

"And that I have to report to my contact once a week."

"That would be me. I'll want a written report at each meeting."

"Also that I have a Gypsy tattoo on my thigh."

"A minor detail. Have you read everything?"

"Enough," I said and signed it, knowing full well I wasn't going to snitch on the workers.

Cheena excused herself and left the room, and while I waited, wondering if I'd get out in time to see Lafitte, one of the agents who arrested me came in—the loud-mouthed, lying driver.

CHAPTER 48

He saw me and hurried away as if I had leprosy. Bastard! He'd driven the car. He'd participated in the nasty comments about me. And he'd lied to Rothman to protect Gerhardt.

"What are you scared of?" I called out loud enough to get everyone's attention. "Afraid I'll hex you for lying to Rothman?"

He didn't look at me, probably because he didn't understand Spanish. No one else would look at me either, *nadia*, like I didn't exist. I toyed with the thought of pulling Ma Barker off the wall or chanting in Romani. Maybe they'd all run out of the room.

Or maybe they'd shoot me.

At last, Cheena returned with an envelope containing my first snitch payment of $18, which required another signature. She also returned my tote bag, wallet and flamenco dress.

"Just a few more things to do," she said.

"Like what?"

She lowered her voice. "That curse you put on Gerhardt. Was it real?"

"It was a coincidence."

"Are you sure?"

"No, Cheena, I'm not sure. Maybe it was God. Maybe it was the devil. Can we move on? Can I change out of this stupid blue frock and get out of here. I'm starving."

"Fine, okay. But we're not finished yet."

"What else do we have to do?"

"That winning bolita number you gave me. How did you do that?"

"Didn't I tell you I have the power of precognition?"

"You also shared a number with friends at El Dorado."

"How do you know what I did at El Dorado?"

"Shhh, not so loud. You're not the only informant in this city."

"Are you saying you had spies at El Dorado?"

"We have more eyes in Ybor than Carter has little liver pills."

Oh, great, I thought, Amy Romano, Agent 007. But before I could reply, she said, "We were talking about winning numbers. Can you tell me another one?"

"I might for a price."

"If it's illegal, you can forget it."

"Isn't bolita illegal?"

"Bolita is like jaywalking. No one enforces it. What's your price for another number?"

"Simple. You place the bet and we split the winnings."

A grin as big as Cuba crossed her face, and when she stood and thrust out a hand, I knew I had her. "Before you get too excited," I said, "there are a couple of other conditions."

Her smile vanished. "What conditions?"

"Secrecy. You never breathe a word to anyone. You never share the numbers."

"I'm not crazy. What else?"

"You bet only the amount I tell you. Small bets. These places are run by gangsters. If they think for a minute you have inside information, they'll come after you."

"You're not telling me anything I don't know. Anything else?"

"Only this. You have spies. Gypsies have spies. You'd be surprised if I told you the names of people in this city with the blood. We share things. We meet secretly. There are rituals."

"Why are you telling me this?"

"Point is you may be watching me, Cheena. But guess what? I'll be watching you."

"Stop it," she said, waving a hand. "I don't want to end up like Gerhardt."

"So we agree?"

"A thousand percent."

We sealed our ungodly pact with a handshake, and then I asked if I could use her phone.

"Not yet. We're not finished."

"What else do we have to do?"

"Wait here." She stepped to the exit door, opened it, glanced into the hallway, and came back. "They just got here," she said.

"Who?"

"Paco and his assistant. They say he's the best."

"The best what?"

The door swung open and in marched a little pig-tailed man with a black carrying case. He had earrings in both ears and tattoos on his face and arms. His female assistant also looked as if she'd escaped from a tattoo circus, right down to her mulberry colored hair, dangling earrings, and body piercings. Typewriters stopped clattering. Everyone in the place stared. Cheena escorted them to the room where I'd spent the night and came back.

"It'll take them a couple of minutes to set up," she said.

By then I was ready to dash for the exit. "Wait, Cheena, what is this about?"

"Didn't Rothman tell you?"

"Rothman didn't tell me anything. What's going on?"

"Carmen had a tattoo on her thigh, a Gypsy spoke wheel."

"I'm not Carmen—and I'm not going to get a tattoo."

She motioned me into the interrogation room and closed the door. "Let's get something straight, señorita. Didn't you just sign a bunch of federal forms to the effect that you're Carmen Amaya? In front of a Bureau of Investigation witness?"

"Yes, but…"

"But nothing." She waved her copy of the form in my face. "It says here … and I quote, 'Identification markings: Spoke wheel tattoo on right inside upper thigh.'"

"I don't care what it says. I'm not getting a tattoo."

"Is that your final word?"

"Final word. Tell J. Edgar to kiss my Spanish Gypsy rear."

She took a deep breath and sank into the chair where Rothman had sat. "You're making a big mistake, Amy. The only thing between you and freedom is a little tattoo. Do you want me to go out there and call Rothman?"

I paced around the room. I cursed. I slapped the wall. I knocked over a chair. Finally, I sat back down in front of Cheena.

"Is it going to hurt?"

CHAPTER 49

If anyone tells you it doesn't hurt to get a tattoo, they're lying. The needles, the endless little punctures, the dye, Paco bending over me with a cigarette dangling from his lips, the high-pitched whining of his tattooed assistant, holding up a sketch of a Gypsy wagon wheel.

No, Paco, the spokes are green.

No, Paco, it's this needle, not that one.

It didn't help that Cheena serenaded us the whole time, or that Paco had bad teeth, bad breath, and smelled like an ashtray, or that his assistant had a nasty smokers' cough. It hurt even more because it was the tender flesh in my inner thigh, a place that only my ex-husband and Ramón had touched. Lafitte too, but it was only a touch. Gerhardt didn't count.

At last, they swabbed on a disinfectant, covered it with a bandage, gave me instructions on care, and left me on the cot with a towel between my legs like an assault victim. Cheena brought me a big glass of lemonade and the clothes I'd been wearing when I was first arrested.

"Don't you have something stronger than lemonade?" I asked.

"We've got coffee."

"No, Cheena, I don't want coffee. Can I make that phone call now?"

"Not to the doctor."

"Why not?"

"Later. Right now you need to get out of that smock."

She waited outside while I changed, and when she came back in, she had on a shoulder holster with a pistol. "What's the gun for?" I asked.

"Protection. Sal's got a big mouth. He talks with his buddies in clubs and restaurants. He's terrified to know you're alive. Says he has to finish the job. Is it okay if I call you Carmen?"

"If I'm going to be Carmen, I might as well answer to the name."

"You should never have gone to El Dorado the other night. People saw you."

"Tell me something I don't know. Can I call the doctor now?"

"No, Carmen. Sal knows you were staying at the doctor's house. You wouldn't be safe going back. Neither would the doctor."

"So where am I supposed to go?"

"A friend's house."

"What friend?"

"Your sister, Natalia. She's outside now, waiting."

If there was ever a wanting-to-scream moment, that was it, sitting painfully on the cot in that little holding room. They were going to stick me with crazy walking-disaster Natalia. Better to beg Cheena to board me in the post office until we worked out another solution.

"Why?" I asked, trying to keep my emotions in check.

"Because she lives in a safe house near the Columbia Restaurant."

"Is she also one of your snoops?"

"The less you know the better."

I sighed in defeat. Cheena said, "Here's the plan. The driver … he's out there now … he'll drive the three of us to Centro Español. It's on Setima, close to Natalia's house."

"What's at Centro Español?"

She pulled on a jacket to hide her pistol. "Let's go."

I grabbed my tote bag with the flamenco dress and other belongings, and followed her down the hall to a side door, wincing from the burning in my thigh. Cheena glanced outside as if checking for lurking enemies, then led me to one of their black Fords.

CHAPTER 50

The motor was running, its exhaust stinking up the place. I climbed into the back with Cheena and we sped away. The driver avoided my eyes. Natalia, who has sitting in the front, didn't look that happy either, and we were soon rumbling along the backstreets of Ybor, running stop signs and blowing the horn at pedestrians and animals, everyone glancing behind and all around as if expecting men in white sheets to come after us in a tobacco truck.

"With any luck at all," Cheena said, "they'll try to kidnap or kill us."

"Who will try to kidnap or kill us?"

Natalia twisted around. "Don't you get it, Carmen? Didn't you hear what happened to that agent you hexed? And that's only part of the problem."

"What's the other part?"

"For God's sake, girl, where's your brain? Sal knows you've been locked up. His thugs are on the lookout. You're poison. You could get us all killed."

I tried to settle back. Was this going to be my life from now on—hiding, glancing into shadows? Maybe Natalia had the right idea—kill the bastard before he killed me.

"The house where we're taking you is safe," said Cheena, sitting next to me, "but we'll make a few rounds during the night anyway." She handed me a card. "Here's my horn number."

"Why aren't you staying with us?"

"Because that's not what we do."

"Not to worry," said Natalia. "We've got a twelve-gauge shotgun—double-barrel, double-aught buckshot. It'll stop a horse."

"Will it stop men with Tommy guns?"

She didn't answer. The driver took us past the Columbia where I'd wrecked the streetcar. I expected to see a mess, but the only sign of the accident was a scorched sidewalk in front of Paco's Tattoo Parlor. Everything else looked normal—cables in the overhead, lamp posts upright, a family of homeless sitting on a blanket. It was as if the accident never happened.

"Cigarette smoke is burning my eyes," I said. "Can I roll the window down?"

"No," Natalia answered. "Sal could toss a stick of dynamite into the car."

"Just toss it back," Cheena said and rolled down the window.

We drove on and were almost at the Centro Español when a noisy group of women protesters marched out of a side street, waving placards and beating drums.

"Shit!" said the driver, and stopped the car.

A huge ribbon identified them as the Ladies Sobriety Society of Ybor City. One of their placards read: LIPS THAT TOUCH ALCOHOL SHALL NEVER TOUCH MINE!

"Stupid women," said the driver. "Like anybody would want to touch *their* lips."

Natalia, who didn't understand English, turned around to Cheena. "What did he say?"

"Said if he had a bottle he'd guzzle it in front of them."

"I thought G-men were teetotalers."

"Ha, you should see the bottles they confiscate. The only ones they destroy are for the cameras. They also throw wild parties with *putas*. Get roaring drunk."

The procession passed; the noise faded. Then we pulled into the parking lot of the Centro Español, an imposing building with red bricks, wrought-iron balconies, and a decorative Moorish entrance. "Why are we stopping here?" I asked Cheena.

She still didn't answer. The driver looked around and motioned us out. "All clear," he said.

The three of us hurried into the front door. We passed muster with the door guard and then followed a long corridor toward the rear. From somewhere came piano music, the buzz of conversation and mouth-watering smells of food. Yet even in this magnificent building with its mosaic tiles and Moorish arches, I glanced into shadows and doorways like a fugitive.

"Can we slow down?" I asked Cheena.

"What's wrong? That tattoo hurting?"

"It's killing me."

"Oh, don't be such a sissy," Natalia said.

We passed a room in which sat a large gathering of Ybor citizens at their tables, all dressed in their Sunday finest, the women in their ridiculous hats and white heels.

"Wonderful organization," Natalia said as if I cared at that moment. "They've got the largest mutual aid society in Tampa. Also a hospital and cemetery."

"Here," Cheena said and stopped at a door marked with the number 12. "This is where we're meeting tomorrow, 0900 sharp."

"You brought me here just to show me where to meet?"

"No, I brought you for something else."

She opened the door and motioned me in. And there, at a table with bowls of food, fruits and drinks, and a large flower arrangement in the center, sat Soledad and the doctor, dressed as if they'd just come from Sunday Mass.

CHAPTER 51

W̲e kissed and hugged. Soledad was pretty as ever in a red outfit that contrasted nicely with her dark Cuban features, but Dr. Antonio's left eye was purple and swollen.

"G-men did that to him," Soledad said. "Punched him in the face."

Gerhardt, I thought and would have complained to Cheena except the door was closed and neither she nor Natalia had followed me in.

"Eat," said the doctor. "You must be starving."

I wasn't hungry, not after the torture I'd endured or the prospect of living with Natalia, but I eased into a chair anyway and filled my plate.

"Does Lafitte know what happened?" I asked the doctor.

"Not everything. He came last night, waited around until midnight. We were worried sick. Then this morning Natalia told us you'd been arrested for hijacking a streetcar. A streetcar, Amy? What were you thinking?"

"It's a long story."

"I'm sure it is." He reached into his breast pocket and took out an envelope. "Here, this is from Lafitte. He left it for you."

I opened it and took out the eight hundred dollars I'd won at the Dorado. There was also a poem in the envelope titled FLAMENCO ABYSSINIA, written inside a heart symbol.

Run away with me and be my bride,
And we will into the heavens fly.
Tell Ybor City and the bad men in it,
Adios, au revoir, and goodbye.

The glow that had been building inside me from the moment I saw him burned right down from my heart to my entire body. Oh, those kisses that night in the car, the passion, the yearning. I clutched the note to my breast and read it again and again, imagining I could hear his voice, his accent, and feel his breath on my neck.

"I think he's in love," said Soledad, grinning, and handed me another envelope.

"What's this?"

"Five hundred dollars from your other bolita winnings."

In all the excitement, I'd forgotten about asking her to place a bet, and tried to give the money back as payment for all they'd done. She refused. So did the doctor. "Besides," Soledad said, "I placed a bet and won a hundred dollars. How did you do that?"

"A dream. Didn't I tell you?"

The doctor shook his head as if he knew better. Soledad had no problem with my explanation, so I enlisted her as another bolita partner, and while we ate, I told them about all my adventures, leaving out only the tattoo and the unholy deal I'd struck with the feds for my freedom.

"Wait," said the doctor. "You hijacked a streetcar. They think you're Carmen. And yet they're letting you go? I don't understand."

The door opened and in stepped Cheena. "Sorry to break this up."

"What's wrong?" I asked her.

She pulled me into the corridor and lowered her voice. "Gerhardt," she said with a look of disgust. "He's with the hobos down on the docks, babbling to himself. He's also drunk, all messed up. We've got to get him."

Justice, I thought, and I could almost picture him wrapped in trash bags, sleeping on a sewer grate, and down to his last pint of moonshine. But at least he was alive.

"I probably shouldn't tell you this," she said, "but…"

"But what?"

"Well, he's ranting about a Gypsy that put a curse on him, saying he's not going to rest until he puts a bullet in you or you get burned at the stake, or words to that effect."

CHAPTER 52

I had so many enemies that a pathetic loser like Gerhardt didn't concern me. Besides, I had more immediate problems, like how to get along with Natalia in a house protected with a double-barrel shotgun. So I grabbed my tote bag, said adios to Soledad and the doctor, and followed Natalia to a back door.

It opened onto a narrow alley with overhanging foliage and underbrush so thick we could have been back in Brooker Creek. "You live in a forest?" I said.

"Oh, just shut up and follow."

She set a fast pace, looking around as if there were monsters in the shadows.

"Would you slow down?" I said. "I'm hurting."

"Christ, Amy. Don't be such a baby. We need to get out of sight."

A car entered the alley behind us. I hurried to the side, ready to plunge into the bushes, but the car turned out to be Cheena and the driver in their black Ford. They passed us slowly, tires crunching on the shells, leaving behind the smells of cigarettes and exhaust fumes.

"Why couldn't they drive us?" I said.

"Why should they? The house is right here."

She guided me into a narrow side path through the foliage, telling me to watch out for poison ivy. We pushed away vines and spider webs until we reached a dilapidated gate covered with creepers. Beyond it, surrounded by overgrown shrubbery and live oaks with bromeliads and draping

Spanish moss, stood an unpainted clapboard house.

"This is the back," said Natalia. "It fronts a busy street."

She pushed through the gate. I lingered a moment. Was this Abuelita's house? Yes, smokehouse and all. Same green shutters. Same back porch with four columns and a swing. I'd spent the happiest days of my childhood here, in the swing, climbing trees, playing with friends.

"Is this your house?" I asked Natalia.

"My mom's, but she had to move out. Bastards at the bank. They're foreclosing in a couple of weeks. Carmen's stuff is still here."

"But you live here?"

"Depends."

"Depends on what?"

"For God's sake, Amy, would you stop interrogating me? And if it makes you feel better, Vito doesn't live here either. He has his own place. It's a lot more luxurious than this shack."

I followed her around the clothesline and a vegetable garden gone to weeds, up the rotting back steps with its green mold, across a sagging wooden deck, through a screened door that screeched, and into a breezeway that led to the living room with high ceilings.

It had the same pungent fireplace smells I remembered from 2019, and I could almost picture my grandmother Sonja in her rocker, endlessly relating the story of her famous mom, Carmen, whose picture hung over the fireplace.

What happened to her, Abuelita?

Who knows, mija? They say the mob got her.

"It's you," Natalia said, nodding at the picture of Carmen. "The dress, your face, posture and all. You see why people get confused."

I didn't want to get into a discussion about Carmen or the dress, so I ignored her and picked up a framed photo of a grinning little girl with white hair tied back with a ribbon. "Who's this?"

"That's Sonja. Carmen's little girl. Just turned two."

Sonja? My abuelita? I'd never seen the picture. "Where is she?"

"In a boarding home with my mom. If it wasn't for me, they'd starve."

"What about Sonja's father? Why isn't he helping?"

"Ha, good luck with that. Carmen wasn't exactly the Virgin Mary."

"You don't know who the father is?"

"Probably that writer."

"What writer?"

She stepped over to the bookcase and took out the Spanish language version of Hemingway's *The Sun Also Rises*. "This writer. Isn't he your friend?"

I sat down, my head spinning. Hemingway my great-grandfather? I had a sudden urge to mix myself a stiff drink and go deep-sea fishing.

"Don't look so shocked," Natalia said. "Carmen was shameless." She switched on an electric fan and moved it so that its airflow rippled the curtains, then she hitched up her dress and took out a small pistol that had been concealed in her stocking.

"Stocking gun," she said. "A two-shot Derringer. You should get one for yourself." She laid the Derringer on the mantel and was heading toward the bathroom when the phone rang—two short rings and one long. Natalia ignored it.

"Aren't you going to answer?"

"Not our ring."

"What do you mean, not our ring?"

"It's a party line."

"What's a party line?"

"For Christ's sake, Amy, don't you understand anything? A party line means six or eight houses on the same line. We each have a special ring. Ours is a long ring. Oh, but I forget. You had an accident. Head fucked up. Don't remember a thing. Right?"

"Did anyone ever tell you what a bitch you are?"

"Don't get sassy with me, girl. I'm just trying to help."

"Maybe I don't need your help."

"Fine. Go ahead and hijack another streetcar." She dismissed me with a wave, but then said, "Carmen's bedroom is over there. It's your room now. Got everything you need. Clothing, shoes, even wigs. There's also a suitcase packed with your things. Soledad brought it."

"Soledad knows about this place?"

"How else would she bring it?"

"I thought this was a safe house. How many people know about it?"

"Oh, stop whining and check the damn suitcase."

CHAPTER 53

The furniture in Carmen's bedroom was the same as in 2019—same brass bed, same armoire, same dresser. The only difference was the stark wooden walls and a poster of flamenco dancers. Soledad's red suitcase lay on the bed. I opened it and found my toothbrush and toothpaste, nightgown, underwear, slippers, the forty pages I'd typed in English, and the dress I'd worn two nights ago at the Dorado.

My cell phone was there too, inside its blue leather case.

Had Natalia seen it? Did it still have power? I didn't dare open it with her in the house, so I stuffed it back into the suitcase and was about to close it when I noticed a small book—Pablo Neruda's *Twenty Love Poems and a Song of Despair* in Spanish. Had Soledad put it there?

I opened the book and began reading:

I can write the saddest poem of all tonight.

To think I don't have her. To feel that I've lost her.

What does it matter that my love couldn't keep her?

The night is starry and she is not with me.

I sighed and thought of Lafitte. Would he come? Would I ever see him again?

"Amy?"

"I'm back here, still in the bedroom."

"What's taking so long? We need to get started on your lesson."

I closed the book and went back into the living room where Natalia was brushing her hair. "What lesson?" I asked. "What are you talking about?"

"I'm talking about your accent, for God's sake. That god-awful, flat-toned way you speak Spanish. There's no music, no poetry. It's worse than Cuban talk. Worse than Mexican with all their *chingas*, and sure as God created blue skies above Spain, it's not the beautiful Castilian we speak in Andalusia. If you're going to pretend to be Carmen, you've got to speak like her. Act like her. Otherwise, you could end up like her. Do you understand what I'm saying?"

"I may speak with an accent, Natalia, but I don't hear with one."

"Didn't I tell you to not get sassy with me?"

"You treat me with respect and I'll do the same for you."

She put down her hairbrush and paced around as if trying to work off her hostility. If I had to stay with her much longer, only one of us would come out of this house alive.

At last, she said. "Fine, we're stuck together. Might as well get along."

The phone rang again, three short rings. I waited for it to stop ringing and said, "Before we work on my accent, I want to ask you something."

"I may not answer."

"Are you working for the G-men?"

"If I was, I wouldn't tell you."

"Why was Carmen working for them?"

"Because she didn't have a choice, that's why. Neither do you. So get used to it." She pointed at the bookcase. "Which one do you want? We've got books by lots of famous Spanish writers—Machado, Martinez Ruiz, even Cervantes."

"What are you asking?"

"For God's sake, girl, don't you get it?"

"No, Natalia, I told you I don't read minds. Tell me what we're doing."

She closed her eyes and took a couple of deep breaths as if trying to contain her temper, and when she spoke, her voice was softer, like a frustrated mother trying to explain a simple task to a child. "Listen, Amy, you choose a book, any book. You open to any page. You read aloud. I'll help with your pronunciation. Let's do that a while. *De acuerdo?*"

"Okay, fine by me."

She slapped her head. "No, no, no. Stop saying 'okay.' It's an *Americanismo*. The Spanish word is *vale*, or *bien*, or *de acuerdo*. You never say 'okay' in Spanish. It's as bad as those damn frogs like Lafitte saying *non*. 'I make you coffee, *non*. I kiss you down there, *non*.'"

I beat back a strong desire to hit her with a book, but just to annoy her, I stepped over to the bookcase and pulled out Unamuno's *Tragic Sense of Life*. "Look, here's a book by your favorite socialist. Let's do this one."

"*Por favor*, Amy, I'm not into egalitarianism."

"You said to pick any book."

"Not that one."

I put it away and pulled out Hemingway's book.

"Good choice," she said, sighing. "Love affairs, a promiscuous woman, bullfighting. Oh, to be back in Spain in the Twenties."

Her reminiscences went on and on—sangrias and sunshine, fiery flamencos, the wines of Málaga and Alicante, and love atop wine casks in the backrooms of little bodegas—as if she'd been Hemingway's inspiration for Lady Brett, getting it on with a hot matador.

I stopped her with a wave of the book. "Do you want me to read or not?"

"Go ahead. I'm listening."

I opened the book and began reading in Spanish. Natalia paced the floor and listened, sometime jumping into the dialogue as if she were one of the characters, correcting my pronunciation in every other sentence.

Give the R's an extra trill, for God's sake. Rrrrrrr. Roll it.

Put a lisp into your Z's and S's like you have a speech impediment.

Put cadence into your voice, rhythm, up and down inflections.

How long this torture lasted I don't know. Surely Eliza Doolittle didn't suffer as much in *Pygmalion*, and I was ready to ask for a break when the phone mercifully interrupted us with a long single ring. "That's us," she said and scurried away to answer.

She spoke to someone in a low voice and came back. "I've got to go."

"Go where?" I asked, alarmed at the thought of being alone.

"What difference does it make? You're a big girl. You know where the kitchen is. There's food in the pantry. Frigidaire has milk, butter, cheese. You've got books. A Victrola. A Marconi. There are also matches on the kitchen counter and extra candles. Oil lamps in all the rooms."

"Oil lamps for what?"

"Good God, girl, where have you been? Power goes out. Power comes back on. Goes out again. Lights go out. Lights come on. Just like in Spain."

She stepped closer and looked into my face. "Oh, Amy, please. Don't tell me you're scared of the dark. There's nothing to worry about. The G-boys will make their rounds."

"Does Sal know about this house?"

"No, Amy, Sal doesn't know, but if it makes you feel better you can sleep with the shotgun."

"Are you serious? I don't know how to shoot a shotgun."

She left the room and came back with it anyway—a double-barrel shotgun and a box of shells. "Here, already loaded. See these two hammers. Just pull them back until they click. You aim, you pull the trigger. Boom. Nothing to it."

"That's it … just pull back the hammers and shoot."

"Didn't I just say that? This thing will stop an elephant." She showed me how to reload, and asked if I'd given any thought to her suggestion about getting rid of Sal. Yes, I told her, I'd been reconsidering. She said, "*Bien*, we'll talk about killing the sonofabitch tomorrow." Then she took her purse and headed for the door. "If anyone knocks, don't answer. It'll probably be someone selling bolita tickets."

"Are you coming back tonight?"

"No, Amy, so it's okay to lock the door."

"What if the phone rings?"

"Don't answer. Don't make any calls either. It's a party line. Nosy neighbors listen. Oh, and one more thing. Under no circumstances are you to leave the house."

"What if it's on fire?"

She rolled her eyes, opened the door, said "Abyssinia" and left, leaving me on the sofa with a double-barrel shotgun cradled over my lap.

CHAPTER 54

The doors were the same as in 2019, wooden and flimsy, easy to kick down. Even I could have busted into the place. The screened windows were no better. They were old and rotting and partially open for air circulation.

And they called this a safe house?

I closed and locked all the windows anyway and barricaded the doors with furniture. Not that furniture would stop an intruder, but there'd be noise if anyone tried to break in.

The phone rang—one long ring. Our ring.

Natalia had said not to answer, but suppose it was Cheena? I eased down the hall with my shotgun and stared at the phone. A piece of art, in brass, a ringer on the box, no dials, the receiver hanging from a hook on the wall.

It kept ringing, long, shrill rings, like a fire alarm. I reached for the receiver and stopped. Suppose it was Sal, checking to see if I was home?

The ringing stopped. Did phones in the Thirties have voice mail? There were no flashing lights, nothing. I picked up the receiver and pressed it to my ear.

"*Numero, por favor?*"

Good lord. Was that the way to make calls? Speak to an operator?

"Someone was trying to call me," I said. "Can you tell me who?"

"Sorry, señorita, we don't have that information."

I thanked her, hung up, and headed for the bathroom. The last time I'd had a bath was before my date with Lafitte. Since then I'd been almost crushed in a shootout, stumbled through a smelly tunnel, walked a couple of miles in a nurse's outfit, crashed a streetcar, been molested by Gerhardt, yelled at by J. Edgar Hoover and spent a night on a smelly cot in the Ybor Post Office. What I needed was a good scrubbing.

But Paco said to keep the tattoo dry, so I cleaned myself with a washcloth. I also shampooed, dried my hair with a towel, combed out the tangles, and sat in front of a small table fan in the kitchen, holding the shotgun over my lap.

Shadows crept across the room. Thunder rumbled. I lit a couple of lamps in case of a power failure, changed into one of Carmen's frilly nightgowns and came out of the bedroom in time to hear the phone ringing again. One long ring.

Damn it. Again I stepped down the hall with my shotgun. The ringing stopped and started again—shrill, grating. I clenched my teeth, picked up the receiver as carefully as if it were a bottle of nitroglycerin, and pressed it to my ear, my hand over the mouthpiece.

No one spoke, but there were sounds in the background. And men talking.

In Italian.

I slammed down the receiver, panic rising in my chest. The caller would have heard me pick up. Stupid me. In my imagination, I could see Sal and his buddies piling into their gangster Packard, all Tommy guns and dark hats.

What happened to her, Abuelita?

Who knows, mija? They say the mob got her.

I shoved another piece of furniture against the doors, turned off all the lights, and stared out the windows into the darkness, into occasional flashes of lightning.

A car passed. But no one came.

Nothing.

I fixed a cheese sandwich I couldn't eat. I picked up a book I couldn't read. I read Lafitte's poem again. I cursed Ramón for getting me into this fix, and Natalia for leaving me alone in the house, and Sal and Clarence for wanting to kill me.

And when I ran out of people to blame, I turned on the radio.

Unlike the doctor's radio, which was a Marconi, this was a beautiful floor-model Blaupunkt, all dials and little lights, switches, pushbuttons, and the names of international cities like Amsterdam, Zurich, Berlin, Paris, London, and Rome.

Like you could actually tune to those places.

It came on with a hum and the pop of static. I waited for it to warm and turned the dial until I heard the beep-beep of a telegraph and a man with a nasal New York accent.

Germany had granted citizenship to an Austrian thug named Adolf Hitler.

The US should never let a German boxer like Max Schmeling fight in America.

More banks were failing.

Hooverville hobo villages were spreading.

Mexican *Federales* were shooting priests again.

It began to rain, drumming on the roof and blowing against the windows. Something hit the side of the house—debris, I hoped—and the voice on the radio identified himself as Walter Winchell. He railed against General MacArthur for setting fire to the shanties of bonus marchers in Washington DC and driving them away with bayonets and gunfire, and he kept at it until I imagined I could smell the tear gas and see soldiers with gas masks on horseback and MacArthur in his boots and riding britches.

He was describing the blazes over Washington as so bright they lit the night sky when a sharp crack of thunder caused me to jump out of my chair.

The power went out. So did the whiny voice of Walter Winchell.

Wind howled. Windows rattled. Flashes of lightning lit every corner of the room. This was like one of those teenager horror movies—a woman alone in the house, a raging storm, a stalking killer. A stupid woman who goes outside looking for the fuse box.

A slow panic eased in. I backed into a corner and hugged the shotgun a little tighter.

In time, the storm abated, leaving behind the smell of fresh damp air.

Too scared to go to bed, I crept into the bedroom with a lamp, fumbled around in the suitcase, and took out my cell. Shit, only 56 percent battery power and no way to recharge.

I opened the archived newspaper pages I'd downloaded in 2019 and began jotting down bolita numbers. There were more than three hundred bolita establishments in Ybor, but the *Tribune* published only the ten largest. I finished with Monday's results and made quick work of Tuesday and Wednesday, and was working on Thursday when a car drove into the driveway, its headlamps lighting the room.

My heart almost stopped. Without thinking, I blew out the lamp and grabbed the shotgun.

A door slammed. A man's voice. Footsteps on the front porch. Then a rap at the door. Loud. Like Sal was outside with his mob and ready to kick in the door.

What happened to her, Abuelita?

CHAPTER 55

I crept out of the bedroom like a combat veteran, feeling my way to the living room in the darkness, and knelt behind the sofa with the shotgun, ready to pull back the hammers.

The knock again, this time louder.

"Amy, are you in there? It's me, Soledad."

Good Lord, I'd been on the verge of shooting a nurse, an angel. "Hold on, I'm coming!"

I re-lit a lamp and noisily shoved away furniture I'd so carefully placed as a barricade—an easy chair, a side table, a coffee table, and three heavy dining room chairs.

"Amy, what are you doing?"

"Almost finished. Hold on."

I unlocked the door and discovered that it opened outward.

Outward, mind you. What good was an interior barricade? How embarrassing.

Soledad stepped out of the darkness and came inside, bringing with her the freshness of outside air. "Is someone moving?" she asked, looking around.

I was so flustered I didn't notice Lafitte until he stepped into the light, his leather jacket wet from the rain, looking like the prince of every woman's dream. Donnie Sue was there too, she of the Brooker Creek swamp, now dressed in a yellow and green outfit that gave her a respectable appearance. Which made me painfully aware that I was in a nightgown.

"Bet you didn't 'spect to see me," she said with a grin. "I got a story to tell."

There were hugs and kisses. Lafitte said he'd have come alone but didn't know the way, and was dying to see me and learn the details of my adventures with the streetcar and the feds.

"Are you okay?" he whispered. "I missed you."

My heartbeat picked up. The glow came back, but before I could answer, Soledad said, "We tried to phone you. No one answered. Didn't you hear it?"

"I answered, but all I heard was someone speaking Italian."

"That's because we were at Luigi's. It's a bistro near the house."

I rolled my eyes. Stupid me. Soledad lit more lamps, drawing moths to the light and filling the room with the smells of scented lamp oil. I raced into the bedroom to pull on a robe and check myself in the mirror. Lafitte rearranged the furniture, and we were soon seated in the shadowy light in the living room, Lafitte next to me on the sofa, and Donnie Sue telling us in her tortured country accent why she ran away from Clarence.

He'd turned meaner.

Slapped her around like a dog.

"I prayed to Jesus for protection. He musta heard me 'cause he saved me. Too bad he didn't save them other girls."

"What other girls?"

"Ones he dumped in the gator hole. Made me wanna puke. Purty little thangs. Clarence says Sal plays games with the girls … you know, when they doing it. Ties 'em up. Puts a red strap around their necks … sometimes it gits rough. Always claims it was a accident."

My hand went instinctively to my throat. Lafitte looked like he was ready to throw up, and Soledad seemed to be struggling to understand Donnie Sue's English.

"How many girls has Sal done this to?"

"You was the third. Well, maybe not you, but the one they thought was you."

She kept talking about the "gator hole," telling Lafitte and Soledad the same thing she'd told me back at the shack—that the hole was haunted, that you could see lights at night and hear the screams of the girls. "The coloreds won't go near it. I can't take it no more. Clarence threatened to do the same to my skinny neck if I tattled, but Jesus came to me in a dream. Said to git away 'fore Clarence fed me to the gators. That's why I run to Frenchie."

"Frenchie?"

"Lafitte. Clarence calls him Frenchie. Anyhow, I snuck off with Frenchie while Clarence was sleeping off a drunk. Now I'm here. You told me you might git me a job at Rosa's."

All of us looked at each other. Was she aware the only jobs for girls like her at Rosa's were in the upstairs bordello?

"You promised," she said with pleading eyes. "I'll do anything to git away from Clarence."

"What about going home to your family?"

"Ain't no way."

"Why not?"

"My daddy. I ain't gonna tell what he done to me. Said I was white trash. Gonna burn in hell for tempting him and he was gonna light the fire."

Her story of poverty and childhood abuse went on until I was almost in tears. When I translated for Soledad, she asked Donnie Sue what happened to the dad.

"They say I blasted him with a double-barrel. My pitcher's in ever post office in Jones County. They'll fry me certain if they catch me."

Lamps burned. Moths flitted around the light. Thunder rumbled. After the shock wore off, Soledad told Donnie Sue she could help around the doctor's house. I wanted to do something for her too. Then it struck me. Bolita. I could use another partner.

Not just Donnie Sue, but also Lafitte and Soledad.

"I've got an idea," I said.

I explained the same way I'd laid it out for Cheena—a fifty-fifty split, the need for caution. Donnie Sue said to count her in "…long as I ain't gotta kill nobody," so I took a lamp, went back to the bedroom, tore out three sheets of paper, and began transferring the Monday numbers to the paper, two numbers for each of them at two different establishments.

Lafitte knocked on the door. "Amy, *c'est moi.*"

I stuffed the pad under a pillow and was about to open the door when I noticed the cell I'd so hastily dropped on the bed. It was still on, battery power at 43 percent. Damn it, what was wrong with me? First the botched door barricade and now this.

I powered it off, threw it under a pillow, and opened the door.

"Can we talk?" he said, concern in his face.

I pulled him inside and shut the door. "What?"

"Is dangerous what you do with bolita. Look what happen to Carmen."

"I didn't get the numbers from gangsters. Okay?"

"Then where?"

"Look, I'll tell you everything. I promise. But not now. Please trust me. Please."

We looked into each other's eyes and came closer. The temperature in the room rose. He pulled me into his arms and we kissed and fondled the way we'd done in his flathead V-8. His lips found their way to my breasts. The warmth inside me turned to fire, and if I hadn't pushed him away, he'd have had me undressed on the bed while thunder rattled the windows and moths with death wishes flung themselves against the lamp globe.

We straightened up and went out, trying to act as if nothing had happened, though I could see the hint of a smile in Soledad's eyes. I handed each of them the paper on which I'd jotted the numbers, but my plan to go into detail had dissipated in those moments with Lafitte. We said our goodbyes and promised to meet again on Tuesday to settle up.

Lafitte also hugged me. "Twenty minutes I come back," he whispered.

I nodded but didn't answer, and when they went out the door and drove away I plunked down on the sofa and asked myself if this was the right thing to do. I'd gone to bed with only two other men in my life, Ramón and my ex-husband, and in both cases I'd jumped too soon. Now I was doing it again. Was it love? Lust? Or was I just too damned scared to spend the night alone?

All the above, I figured, and headed to the bathroom to freshen up.

CHAPTER 56

The bed that would someday be my grandmother's creaked like it was falling apart. Lightning flashed. The wind howled. The nightstand rattled, though it may have been caused by thunder. I heard my cries and the rhythmic slap of flesh against flesh.

Lafitte asked if I liked it. I said yes. I was Carmen, I was slut, so needy and wanting his love that I wouldn't have stopped him even if the tempest blew the roof off the house.

In time our passion gave way to tenderness and an occasional spasm, and I began to notice things I hadn't noticed before—like the flickering candles, the dying storm.

Clarence's Luger on the nightstand.

"Where did that come from?" I asked, sitting up and pulling a sheet about me.

"Soledad. She say is yours … not to shoot yourself. Her English not so good."

He propped himself up on an elbow and faced me, his body pale in the candlelight. "You know how to shoot Luger?"

"Who is Luger?"

"The pistol, Amy … nine millimeter. I show you how use, but now I have other plans."

We did it a second time, and a third, in ways that were probably illegal in much of the world, right there in the bed where I'd slept as a child. He said he couldn't get enough of me, that he'd fallen for me the second he saw me in that alligator-infested swamp, and he couldn't get me out of his mind and had tortured himself wondering if I felt the same about him.

"Do you?" he asked.

"Not really. I just wanted to see what it's like to sleep with a Cajun."

It grew so quiet I could hear the drip of rainwater from the roof. "Oh, come on," I said and jabbed him in the ribs. "I was only teasing. Why else would I be in bed with you?"

He took a deep breath. "Why you steal streetcar?"

I told him about the streetcar hijacking, and the curse I'd laid on Gerhardt, and my unholy pact with the feds. And he told me something I didn't know—that Carmen's reports to the feds about labor unrest were either bogus or doctored because her sympathies were with the workers.

"How do you know that?" I asked.

"Natalia tell me. Drive her crazy. She hated it."

"Tell me about you and Natalia."

"Ancient history. Nothing to tell."

"How long were the two of you like—?"

"Amy, please."

"Okay, you don't want to talk about Natalia. Tell me about Clarence."

He didn't want to talk about Clarence either, except to say they'd met during the war, and that his airplane, which he called a Spad, had been shot down, and Clarence and other American soldiers saved him from the Germans. "After the war, Clarence, he go home to Mississippi, close to New Orleans, make living by moonshine in the swamp. We write letters. We—"

"Wait. What happened during the war with Clarence?"

"Long story."

"We have all night."

"Amy, please."

I sighed and gave in, and then we were talking moonshine again, Lafitte telling me in his broken English all the problems Clarence had in trucking his whiskey to New Orleans—bad roads, break-downs, hijackings by other moonshiners, payoffs to the highway patrol.

"So Clarence, he ask me meet him in New Orleans. Make new plan."

"Bootleg by airplane?"

"But I have no airplane, no money. So Clarence, he introduce buyers in New Orleans. Tell them I famous war pilot, shoot down a hundred Germans, when truth is I shoot down only six and get shoot down myself. Anyhow, they loan money. I promise to pay back in six months. Everybody happy—Clarence, me, the men in New Orleans. We make lots of money. But after two months Clarence, he get in big trouble. Has to run. Goodbye, moonshine."

"What kind of trouble?"

"Donnie Sue trouble."

"For killing her dad?"

"Husband too."

"What?" I sat up in bed.

"Man named Dillard. See, Clarence, he want Donnie Sue. And Donnie Sue, she want Clarence. Big fight. Bang, bang. Dillard dead. They run away together. Disappear. Now I have expensive airplane but no moonshine, no money, and bad men in New Orleans who want payment."

"Why couldn't you just give them the airplane?"

"Ha, I try. They laugh. Say give back money or me too bang, bang, dead. Then Clarence, he write me from Florida, place called Tarpon Springs. So I run, fly away and change name to Lafitte. From here I send money to gangsters in New Orleans—six hundred dollars. Not enough, they say. They want fifteen hundred."

"Or what?"

"What you think? Now I wanted by gangsters and by G-men."

"Same as me. We're like Bonnie and Clyde."

"Amy and Lafitte. We look good together on wanted poster. *Non?*"

We made love again, Amy and Lafitte, and again when the power came on and lit the room, and again when I heard the jingle of the neighborhood watchman's bells. We opened the window to let in fresh air and the sounds of outside, and that was when he opened up about his wartime experiences with Clarence—running and hiding from the Germans and getting help from French civilians. There were girls and stolen kisses and hunger and tender moments of love in a barn. Which might explain why I wanted him again when we were awakened by crowing roosters.

We lay in one another's arms until the first rays of light wrapped around the window drapes, and he reminded me that Monday was a workday, he had deliveries to make, and it was a long drive over a bad road to his airplane near Tarpon Springs.

Not that we could have slept any longer. I had a nine o'clock meeting with Cheena and there was a terrible racket coming from the street—the bolita vendors and fresh bread hawkers, and someone offering to sharpen knives. There were also shrill sounds of whistles like a referee in a ball game, and an ungodly clanging that might have been pots and pans.

"Are you coming back tonight?" I asked.

"Not sure. I let you know."

That wasn't the answer I wanted. Was he tired of me already?

He kissed me on the cheek, climbed out of bed, and pulled on his clothes. I got up, straightened myself in the bathroom, and followed him out the door like a woman sending her man off to war. Here the vendor racket was even louder, held in by low-lying fog. Lafitte gave me a hug, another kiss, said to keep the door locked, then climbed into his car, went through the motions of starting it, said "Abyssinia," and drove into the morning mist, leaving the smell of exhaust behind. No words of love. No promises. No talk of a future.

Damn him. Was I just another conquest? A hopeless romantic? No wonder women had cats and dogs to keep them company.

The phone was ringing when I went back inside—one long ring followed by another. It stopped, then started again. I picked it up without saying hello, and heard Cheena on the other end. "Amy, are you okay? Otis called to say a car just left."

"Who is Otis?"

"The driver. He called from the club. He's waiting for me to call back."

"Call him back and tell him I'm fine."

"We need to meet earlier … soon as you can. I'm leaving now."

"What the rush?"

"I can't tell you over the phone. Just get out of there. *Apúrate!* Go through the back. Otis will pick you up in the alley. And bring the Luger."

"How do you know about the Luger?"

"Just bring it, please, and stop asking questions. Lock the door and give Otis the key."

CHAPTER 57

For at least the third time, I pulled myself together in a hurry, put on one of Carmen's wigs and dark glasses, stuffed the Luger into my tote bag, and was about to leave when I noticed the towels on the floor. Good Lord. What if Otis came into the house? I tossed the sheets and towels into a hamper, drew in a deep breath, and hurried out the back door.

Otis was waiting in the alley, leaning against the black Ford in his dark suit, smoking a cigarette, his hat pushed back on his head. "Nice getup," he said.

I shrugged and handed him the house key.

"Change door locks," he said in a loud voice as if that would help a non-English speaker like Carmen understand. "Check the windows. Better for you. Understand?"

I gave him another don't-understand shrug, hoped he wouldn't check the clothes hamper, and a couple of minutes later I was back in Room 12 of the Centro Español.

Cheena was already at the table, her face buried in a copy of the *Tampa Tribune*. "That damn MacArthur," she said. "He's as bad as what his father did in the Philippines." She pushed away the paper and motioned me into a chair. "Well?"

"Well, what?"

"Your Cajun friend. You're playing with fire, Amy. It's only a matter of time before we find his operation, and when we do, that expensive airplane will be ours and he'll be in jail."

"He doesn't make moonshine; he hauls it."

"Would you listen to yourself, girl? Transporting is the same as producing. Do you know about him and Natalia?"

"What about them?"

"Do I have to draw you a picture?"

"He says they're ancient history."

"Ha, that's what they all say. Did you bring the Luger?"

I felt like shooting her with it, but took it out of my bag and put it on the table. She photographed the pistol from different angles, wrote down the serial number, said something about Lugers being a collectors' item, and handed it back.

"How's your tattoo this morning?"

"It smarts."

"I'm sure it does after last night."

"What's that supposed to mean?"

"Oh, please, Amy. I wasn't born yesterday."

The door opened, and in came servants with trays of breakfast—rice and beans, fried bananas, boiled eggs, fresh bread, fruits, juices, and other delicacies, as well as coffee and warm milk in silver pitchers. They spread napkins on our laps like we were honored patrons, and as soon as they left, I said to Cheena, "I thought this place didn't allow Cubans or Asians."

"That's why I asked you to bring the Luger. We might have to shoot our way out."

When I stopped laughing, she said, "It's for Spaniards only. No Cubans and no brown skins—people like me—but do you think for a minute they're going to argue with J. Edgar Hoover?"

She talked as we ate, yammering about the need for discretion and not to breathe a word about our investigation into labor unrest, saying I could end up like Carmen. I tried to listen, but thoughts of Lafitte and Natalia kept intruding. Had they made love in the same bed? Was I just another conquest?"

"Amy?"

"What?"

"Are you listening?"

"What was your last question?"

"I asked about Don Ignacio, the man you met the other night at El Dorado."

An image of a balding little man with a potbelly and heavy jowls popped into my head. "How do you know about my meeting with him?"

"Oh, please, Amy, didn't I tell you we have eyes everywhere? You're scheduled to perform at his factory this coming Saturday … a flamenco performance."

"That was Carmen's job, not mine. I'm not about to go there and—"

She cut me off with a wave of her hand. "Let's get something straight. You're Carmen now. It's your job. As soon as we finish here, you'll go to Rosa's and work out the details."

"But—"

"Just shut up and listen. You heard about those two missing workers, didn't you?"

"What about them?"

"Labor agitators. They used to work for Don Ignacio. But guess what?"

"What, Cheena?"

"The man that got shot inside the Dorado. He was one of the agitators."

By then I'd lost my appetite for breakfast. "What does that have to do with me?"

"Everything. Don Ignacio was sweet on Carmen."

"How sweet?"

"Carmen wasn't exactly a virgin."

She took a manila folder out of her bag and slapped it on the table. "This is Carmen's report. It says Don Ignacio complained to her about agitators at his factory … said he and his friends would take care of them and to not be surprised if their bodies turned up with bullets in their heads. We'd like you to follow up."

"You can't be serious."

"It's part of the agreement you signed."

"I hope you don't think I'm going to get cozy with Don Ignacio."

"Up to you, Amy." She shoved the folder across the table. "Here, read it."

I began reading but saw nothing in it Cheena hadn't told me already. When I finished and handed it back, she said, "Just one more thing."

"What?"

"Don Ignacio locks the door when Carmen is in his office. Likes for her to sit in his lap. Don't be surprised if he asks to see the tattoo."

She let that unsavory thought hang for a minute and said, "Let's talk about Sal."

"What about him?"

"Today is Monday, right? On Mondays he has lunch at the Columbia. You and I are going to lunch there as well. It's time to confront him."

CHAPTER 58

I almost choked on my coffee. "Wait. First, you hit me with Don Ignacio. Now we're having lunch with Sal. I might as well shoot myself with the Luger."

"No, Amy, you don't have to shoot yourself. Did you bring the numbers?"

"What numbers?"

"Bolita, the winning numbers."

"Wait, you just dumped Sal on me. Suppose there's a shootout?"

"We'll come back to Sal in a minute. Do you have the numbers?"

I reached into the purse that had been Carmen's and took out the numbers I'd prepared for her. "Five dollars on each," I said. "Not a penny more."

She looked over the numbers and location and shook her head. "I still don't get it. You say these numbers come to you in dreams. Or a crystal bowl. Really?"

"What difference does it make?"

"None." She stuffed the numbers into her purse. "Let's eat."

She slathered strawberry jam on a slice of bread, ate it, and tapped her fingers on the table. "There's something else you should know."

"What, Cheena?"

"It's about Gerhardt. He knows where you live. He's on the loose and he's dangerous."

"What? Yesterday you said you were going to pick him up."

"Couldn't find him. That's why we're changing locks on your doors and windows. Also why I'm going to show you how to use the Luger."

By then I could have run out of the place pulling at my hair. It was bad enough that I had Sal, Clarence, and J. Edgar frigging Hoover after me. Now I had Don Ignacio and crazy Gerhardt.

There were also the doubts she placed in my head about Lafitte.

I shoved away my plate and tried to pay attention to her Luger instructions—slap in the magazine, pull back the lever, aim, fire.

"Got it," I said.

"No, señorita, you don't have it. Never chamber a round unless you're going to shoot, and never leave a cartridge in the chamber. Take out the clip, pull back the lever, eject. Otherwise, you could shoot yourself … or shoot an innocent bystander. Got it?"

"Got it."

We practiced until I told her to stop, then we came back to Gerhardt. "Strangest case I've ever seen," Cheena said, pausing to bite into a slice of pineapple. "He was *perfectamente normal* until you put that curse on him."

"Is it perfectly normal for an agent to run his hand up my leg and feel inside my panties?"

"Rothman would fire him if we could get corroboration, but that's not the issue."

"What's the issue?"

"The curse, Amy. Where did you get the power? You caused the lights to go out. You turned Gerhardt into a blathering idiot."

"I didn't make the damn lights go out. As for Gerhardt, maybe the Klan drugged him."

"No, dear, there are too many weird things about you. No background. No history. Winning bolita numbers. Power of the curse. Telekinesis." She leaned forward and fixed me in her gaze. "And you're a dead ringer for Carmen. What is it you're not telling me, Amy? Who are you?"

"You need to stop calling me Amy if I'm to be Carmen."

"You're right, Carmen. So who are you?"

"Are you going to interrogate me or tell me how we're going to confront Sal?"

She sighed, shook her head, and said, "Fine. Let's talk about Sal."

She started with a long discourse about his background—born in Italy, served in the US Army, worked his way up from street thug to big-time mobster—and this went on for so long I had to hold up a hand to stop her. "Look, Cheena, all I care about is the here and now. What's to stop him from pulling out a gun and shooting me?"

"No, Amy … Carmen. Gerhardt might do that. He's out of his mind. But Sal's too crafty. He's not going to shoot you in front of witnesses … at a restaurant."

She explained what she had in mind—how to dress, how to approach him, what to say—but no matter how much she tried to assure me the plan would work, I couldn't get that restaurant scene in the *Godfather* movie out of my head.

"Are you okay?" she asked. "You're shivering."

"I'm shivering with happy excitement."

She managed a smile and took out the note on which I'd jotted the winning bolita numbers. "Here's something to think about. Once we get Sal off your back, maybe we can keep this bolita thing going a few days. Right?"

"Right."

"Make as much money as we can, then both of us can go to Spain. Right?"

"You'd quit your job with the Bureau? Aren't you an agent?"

"I'm a girl, Carmen. The Bureau doesn't take girls. Don't take brown-skinned Asian-Cubans either. I'm just a flunky, the coffee girl, the translator."

"I thought you were Rothman's assistant?"

"If it was up to him, I'd be a full-fledged agent. But tell that to Hoover. As far as the Bureau is concerned, I'm a nobody, a *nadia*, another *guajira* from the Cuban cane patches."

Her face turned even darker, and she began pouring out her grievances like a drunk in a bar. How could the Bureau be so stupid as not see the value in her? She was as smart as they were. Street savvy too. She could out-shoot any agent, drive a car better, and speak three languages.

"But no, I'm just a girl. That's why I'd walk out if I had the resources."

I raised my glass of orange juice. "Fuck the Bureau."

Her scowl turned to a bubbly smile. We clinked our glasses together. Both of us said, "Fuck the Bureau!" and downed our Florida orange juice.

CHAPTER 59

Rosa's flamenco lounge was only a short hike away, in a two-story building with all the trappings of a small Moorish palace. It had arched colonnades, ornate tiles along the lower walls, and Arabic script above the arched portal. The only hint of a business establishment was a modest sign set into stucco near the entry—GRANADA AFTER MIDNIGHT.

I didn't want to come here, didn't want to do anything except go home and think about my meeting with Sal. But Otis was at home, changing the locks, so I rang the doorbell and hid from pedestrians behind a column, feeling uncomfortable in spite of my dark glasses and wig. Across the street, a young boy in knickers was hawking the morning *Tribune*.

"Extra, extra, MacArthur attacks bonus marchers with bayonets!"

I pushed the ringer again and was about to give up when the door opened and there she stood: the madam herself in a red nightgown, rubbing her eyes and looking at me as if to say, "Who the hell are you?"

I took off my glasses. "It's me, Rosa."

"Oh, my God," she said, and threw her beefy arms around me, bringing with her the smells of tobacco and perfume. "We were worried sick about you."

She led me into a reception room that was as ornate as the exterior, with cushions, lounge chairs, colorful accent tiles, and murals of dancing girls that looked like scenes out of a caliph's harem. An enormous black cat lay on a cushion, and all around were floor pots with blooming flowers.

"Thank goodness you're back," she said. "We need to set up that performance for Don Ignacio. He was here this morning, asking about you. I let him break in one of our new girls."

"Why was he asking about me?"

"You don't know?"

"I was in a serious accident, Rosa. Head injury. Can barely remember my name."

"It'll come back. Not to worry. Now come on back and say hello to the girls."

She lit a cigar, and I followed her through an arched door with dangling beads into a room with dark wood floors, wines casks around the walls, rough wood tables, and posters of bullfighters and flamenco dancers. The sweetness of perfume hung in the air like a fine mist, blending with the ever-present tobacco smells, and I could only imagine how it would look at night, smoke-filled and packed with noisy guests for the girls and the performance.

"*Muchachas!*" Rosa called out. "Get down here. It's Carmen. She's back."

Down the stairs they came, one at a time in brightly colored nightgowns and fluffy robes. Rosa introduced each by a fake Moorish name—Jasmine, Jade and Amber, and Fatima, Alisha and Zafron. There were hugs and kisses and happy smiles as if they genuinely cared for Carmen. I mentioned the car wreck and my faulty memory, and they were all gathered around saying how glad they were to see me again when Rosa looked up the stairs. "Where is Nura?"

"Cleaning up after Don Ignacio."

"Nura's our new girl," Rosa said. "American. Can't speak a word of Spanish. Not very bright either, but she's blonde, blue-eyed and cute. That's what our Spanish customers like."

"There she comes," said one of the girls.

Donnie Sue came bounding down the stairs like she'd never been happier.

I could have thrown up. Donnie Sue in a Bordello? Servicing a disgusting little creature like Don Ignacio? Enjoying it? As if that wasn't bad enough, she knew I spoke English and that I wasn't Carmen.

"Come on," Rosa said, motioning with her hand. "Get over here and meet Carmen."

I nodded at Donnie Sue, praying she wouldn't recognize me in my wig.

"Amy," she said, grinning. "I know'd it was you the minute I seen you."

Rosa turned to me. "What did she say?"

"I think it's English. Do you mind if I talk with her … in private?"

"You speak English?"

"I've been studying it. Maybe I can get some information for you."

Rosa took a puff on her cigar and said to go ahead, so I took Donnie Sue's arm and led her to a side room. "What the hell are you doing here?"

"Making money, that's what. Had my first customer this morning. They say he's a big shot."

The knot in my stomach twisted tighter. "Do you realize what kind of disease you could get from a mobster like that? Haven't you heard about Al Capone?"

"That was Al Capone?"

"No, Donnie Sue. That was Don Ignacio. What I'm saying is he's as bad as Al Capone, and Capone has syphilitic dementia."

"What's that?"

"A deadly sexual disease. Is that what you want?"

"Can't be no worse than Clarence. I prayed to Jesus he'd stop his whoring and drinking, but I don't know if he rightly heard me 'cause he just gits worse."

I rolled my eyes. "Listen to me, Donnie Sue, and listen good. Are you listening?"

"Yes, ma'am."

"I want you out of here and back at the doctor's place tonight. Understand?"

"Why?"

"Did you enter the bolita numbers I gave you?"

"I was fixing to do it this morning."

"Those two numbers will win you a thousand dollars, half for you and the other half for me. Tomorrow I'll give you two more numbers. And maybe two more the next day. That's a lot of money. But here's the rub. If you don't leave this place and leave today, you can forget about it. No more numbers, no more money except what you get for whoring."

"All I know is I ain't going back to Clarence."

"You don't have to, child. How old are you?"

"Almost nineteen."

"You follow my instructions, do what I tell you and you'll have enough money to do what you want. A lot more than you can make here. Understand?"

"I reckon so."

"What does reckon mean?"

"It means, yes, ma'am."

"Good, and one more thing. You keep your mouth shut about me. Don't give me away. I'm supposed to be Carmen. Carmen doesn't speak English. I could be in big danger if they learn I'm not Carmen. Then we'll both be fucked. Understand?"

"Yes, ma'am."

"Good, now go out there and pretend we couldn't understand one another. Then you get dressed and leave. I'm calling the doctor's house tonight. You better be there."

"Yes, ma'am."

I walked out and found Rosa holding the cat in her arms. "You were right," I said. "That girl is dumber than a light post. I couldn't understand a word."

"No problem as long as she brings in customers." She led me into her office, motioned me into a chair, and said, "We need to talk about your performance at Don Ignacio's. I'd prefer *La Malagueña*. It's about a penniless *campesino* telling a woman from Malaga he wants to be with her but understands her rejection because he's poor."

"I can do that one, but—"

"No, Jezebel, stop it!"

"What?"

"It's Jezebel. She's licking herself again. She gets fur balls and throws up on the rug. What were you saying?"

"I said I can do *La Malagueña*."

"Don Ignacio wants the other number. Stop it, Jezebel!"

"What other number?"

"Oh, Carmen, *pobrecita*, what did they do to your head? It's the one you choreographed."

"What did I choreograph?"

"The 'Habanera' from Bizet's *Carmen*. Don't you remember anything?"

CHAPTER 60

Cheena was waiting for me at the house, watching Otis install locks on the windows. She had changed into a dark suit jacket for our meeting with Sal and looked more like an attractive office executive than a tough wannabe agent with the Bureau. Otis avoided my eyes, but I got the creepy feeling he was watching me.

Cheena handed me a new door key. "We need to hurry," she said. "It's almost noon."

"Why can't I just threaten Sal on the phone?"

"No, Carmen, not with your voice. He needs to see you … in a public place."

"Whose idea was this, yours or Rothman's?"

She glanced at her watch. "Are we going to do this or not?"

I plunked down on Carmen's dresser stool to catch my breath. My heart felt like it was in my throat. "Hurry up," Cheena said. "We need to get moving."

I dabbed on a touch of what Cheena said was Carmen's favorite perfume—Shalimar—then went through Carmen's jewelry box and picked out hoop earrings, jangling bracelets, and a large sapphire finger ring. Cheena helped me choose an ankle-length skirt with enough vibrant colors to make a Gypsy proud. Also a white blouse with ruffles, a waist-length jacket of the style Spanish ladies wore at bullfights, and a jazzy little French beret that looked like what Garbo or Dietrich would wear.

"You're Carmen," Cheena said, standing back for a look. "No doubt about it. Sal will have a heart attack when he sees you."

"Why would he have a heart attack?"

"Because he's telling people it's impossible you're still alive, that he finished the job himself. Strangled you to death with a belt. Dumped you in the swamp."

"How many women has he done this to?"

"We don't know. Women disappear all the time. All we know is he's a sick bastard."

She squeezed something out of a tube that smelled of cinnamon and chocolate. "Your bruise," she said and used the cream to make a barely perceptible streak on the left side of my neck.

"Isn't there some other way to do this?"

"Well, you could shoot him with the Luger, but you'd never make it out the door." She let that thought hang for a minute, then pulled out her pistol, ejected the clip, and popped it back in. "Colt forty-five," she said. "Not as accurate as your Luger, but it'll drop a horse."

"Why are you showing me this? Is there going to be gunfire?"

"It's a just-in-case." She glanced at her watch. "We better get going."

I thought Otis would drive us, but Cheena had brought her car, a 1928 Model-A coupe.

"Yours?" I asked.

"My husband's."

"You're married?"

"Not anymore."

"What happened to him?"

"Don't ask."

She settled into the driver's seat and began clicking and pulling things, muttering about fuel switches and spark levers. She set the throttle, choked it, and stepped on the clutch with one foot and the floor starter with the other. The engine whined and whirred and finally sputtered to life, not with the throaty vroom of Lafitte's V-8, but with a wimpy clattering pulse.

"Relax," she said, "it'll be fine. Did you bring your Gypsy scarves?"

"Got them."

"Heater?"

"What?"

"Your Luger."

"It's in my tote bag."

"Loaded?"

"Would you stop scaring me? Yes, it's loaded."

"Cigarettes?"

"I don't smoke."

"You do now." She handed me a pack of Gitanes. "Carmen's favorite. Light one for me."

"I didn't know you smoked."

"Only when I'm tense."

"Wait. You've been telling me to relax; now you're saying you're nervous."

"Just light the damn cigarette." She handed me a box of matches.

The drive took us through the business part of Ybor, past the usual trolley stops and protesters and Seminoles and the homeless sitting on blankets or leaning against buildings. The news out of Washington had fired up the protesters, and they were shouting and waving placards in both English and Spanish at every intersection and trolley stop.

SUPPORT THE VETERANS!

WE WANT WORK. MUST WE STARVE?

I tried to relax, taking deep breaths with the windows open, but Cheena's cigarette and her obsession with pistols was getting to me. My panic grew worse when the Columbia loomed up before us, right there on the corner of East 7th Avenue and 22nd Street, looking like a Sultan's palace with its colonnades, arched portals, and Spanish tiles. Even there, a little boy in rags was holding up a sign. WHY CAN'T YOU GIVE MY DAD A JOB?

"*Mierda!*" Cheena said and slammed her palm on the steering wheel. "It's Big Tony."

"Who the hell is Big Tony?"

"Tony Palermo." She nodded toward a thick-necked man leaning against the wall. "Sal's driver. It means Sal's already inside."

"Is that a problem?"

"Tony's bad news. He's the one who…"

"Who what?"

"Cleans up after Sal." She took a right on 22nd, drove a half block and parked in the rear of the Columbia, in a dirt lot that didn't exist in 2019. "We'll have to use the service entrance."

"Wait, what do you mean about Big Tony cleaning up after Sal?"

"Do I have to explain? He's the one who took the body to the swamp."

"Whose body?"

"Your body. He's going to faint when he sees you."

By then I was ready to jump out and run. Again Cheena assured me it would go well, but I could see from her jerky movements and wide eyes, and the way she kept glancing around, that she was just as jittery as I was. As if that wasn't scary enough, she took out her pistol again, racked the lever to chamber a round, and stuffed it back into her shoulder holster.

"Why did you do that?" I asked.

"Just in case." She flicked her cigarette out the window and opened the door. "When we go in, they'll be seated to your left. Keep your head turned away. Don't let them see you until you go to their table. Got it?"

"Is it too late to back out?"

"Would you just stop it? An hour from now we'll be laughing."

CHAPTER 61

T he service entrance was locked, which didn't help my anxiety. Neither did the midday heat of the parking lot or the sight of a homeless woman digging in the garbage.

Cheena pounded on the service door. A young man wearing a floppy chef hat and white apron opened it, letting out the pleasant smells of roasting onions and peppers.

"I'm Cheena," she said. "Don Fernando is expecting us."

The name seemed to carry magic, and a moment or two later a slim man in a tuxedo appeared. "They're here already," he said, thumbing over his shoulder. "Charlie's with them. So is Santo."

Alarm bells went off in my head. "Santo who?" I asked.

"Santo Trafficante. He's with Charlie Wall. Looks like a conference."

Again I felt an urge to run. Cheena had assured me it was it going to be only low-life Sal and a couple of his gutter thugs. But now … now we were going to disturb a pow-wow of mob bosses.

"I'm holding you to our agreement," Don Fernando said to Cheena. "No fights and no shooting. This is a respectable restaurant."

"All we're going to do is talk."

Don Fernando didn't look convinced, but he led us through the kitchen and into the dining area anyway. Even in my panic, I noticed it was just as majestic as in 2019, with ornate chandeliers, potted palms, and a railed balcony. Off to our left, against a tiled wall on which hung a large painting of flamenco dancers, sat six or seven men in dark suits beneath a cloud of cigar and cigarette smoke. "Is that them?" I asked Cheena.

"Shut up and keep walking."

They glanced up. Someone must have made a crude comment because they laughed. I turned away, and a moment or two later, Don Fernando had us seated at a corner table. A server brought menus and water, and even he looked like he was ready to bolt. Only a few other tables were occupied, which I'd heard was typical of the depression years.

Cheena put on her glasses and stared at Sal's table over her menu. I shifted my chair for a better view. "Looks like a Corleone mob meeting," I mumbled.

"What?"

"I said which one is Sal?"

"Short one at the head. The others are Charlie Wall, Ignacio Antinori, Tito Rubio, Jimmy Lumia, Joey Vaglichio, and Santo Trafficante. Also bodyguards against the wall. Too bad we don't have a bomb. One big explosion and we could clean up the city."

The words were scarcely out of her mouth when a ghostly figure in white strode through the front door and seemed to float across the room, right past their table. None of them looked up. Cheena didn't notice either, which made me wonder if panic was creating an image that didn't exist. I fumbled for my distance glasses, and by the time I realized I no longer had them, the figure was gone.

"Are you okay?" Cheena asked. "You're shaking."

"How could I be okay? That bastard over there wants to kill me."

"Look, just calm down." She picked up a folder I hadn't noticed before, took out a single sheet of paper, and handed me a pen. "Here, sign it as Carmen. It's already notarized."

"What is it?"

"An affidavit. It came with our menus. All you have to do is sign it."

The affidavit stated that I—Carmen—had written a full account of the attempted murder of myself and the actual murder of Agent Pruitt, and that I'd placed the account in sealed folders in different law firms in the Tampa area, and in the event of my untimely death or disappearance, the folders were to be provided to the Bureau of Investigation.

"Are you saying this will get him off my back?"

"Absolutely. Just hand him the folder and walk away. No words necessary."

"Wouldn't it be better if I called him a murdering son of a bitch?"

"Don't push it in front of his friends. He has a temper."

I was signing the affidavit when she said, "*Mierda!*"

"What?"

"Big Tony. He's coming this way."

I buried my face in a menu. Behind me, I could hear him shuffling around like a restless dog, his footfalls blending with the clatter of dishes and the buzz of conversation.

"He's checking the customers," Cheena said. "Don't look."

He came so close I smelled his aftershave. Cheena glanced up and lifted an eyebrow. "Lose something, big boy?"

He grunted, and then his footfalls faded away. "*Huevón,*" Cheena hissed.

I breathed again. Cheena said, "Don't look now, but there's a waiter up there on the balcony. Except he's not a waiter. He has a camera. Also a heater. Are you listening?"

"I'm listening."

"Table off to your left. Three men having lunch, dressed like cigar factory workers. They're Bureau. One of them is Rothman. They're backup, just in case. Feel better?"

"Not really."

She shook her head in frustration. "You're not going to faint on me, are you?"

"No, Cheena. Let's do it."

"Good. Put on the headscarf."

I took off the beret and wrapped the red scarf over my head like a Gypsy fortune teller.

"Waist scarf."

I wrapped the green scarf around my waist.

"Now I want you to slide your chair behind the column so they can't see."

I had no idea what she was up to but did as she said. She reached in her makeup kit and took out a powder puff and white powder. "You're dead, remember? A walking corpse."

"Are you crazy? Why didn't we discuss—"

"Just shut up and cooperate." She began applying white powder to my face, and while this was going on I closed my eyes and begged God, Jesus, the Virgin, and all the saints to get me through this. When she finished, and my face was as pallid as a corpse, she took out the same tube of coloring paste she'd used to make the faux bruise on my neck. "Your eyes," she said. "Dead people have dark circles underneath."

"God, give me courage."

"Perfect," Cheena said, leaning back to inspect me. "You look like you just climbed out of a casket. Sal is going to shit in his pants when he sees you."

"Can we just get this finished?"

"One more thing." She reached back into her tote bag and took out an envelope that was sealed with tape. "You're not going to like this."

"What, for God's sake?"

"First, I want you to light a cigarette."

"I don't smoke."

"Damn it, Carmen, would you please just cooperate?"

I took out a cigarette and lit up, using the candle on the table.

"Perfect," Cheena said. "A dead woman that smokes. Now I'm going to open the envelope."

Even before she tore it open, I got a whiff of death, like a dead rat. "Snake Lily," she said. "From my oriental garden. Flies love it. Stick this in your pocket. It's to enhance the effect."

"You can't be serious."

"Rothman's idea. Not mine. Here, take it."

I wasn't going to touch the envelope. For all I knew it really was a dead rat. Cheena leaned over and stuffed it into my side pocket. "One more thing."

"You keep saying one more thing."

"Yes, but this is the best. You're a zombie. Right? Zombies don't walk like normal people. They stumble, they shuffle. They drag their feet, they mumble to themselves."

"Since when do zombies smoke cigarettes?"

"Carmen was a smoker."

"You people are bat-shit crazy."

"This is going to be good," Cheena said. She handed me the folder that contained the affidavit, then twisted around and looked at Rothman.

Rothman nodded his head.

Cheena placed her Colt .45 under her menu and squeezed my hand. "Go," she said.

CHAPTER 62

I stood. People around me looked up from their tables. I feigned a stumble and made a little jerky motion with my arms, thinking how ridiculous I looked. The stench of Snake Lily followed me. So did every eye in the restaurant. A server stepped aside as if I'd escaped from the cast of the *Walking Dead*. I tried to drag my feet, but my legs already felt like jelly. Yet, somehow I crossed the room without falling, with only the clack of my heels disturbing the silence.

The bodyguards didn't intercept me. Sal didn't whip out his pistol and shoot me. He didn't even move until I leaned over him and stabbed out the cigarette in his ashtray, lingering long enough for him to catch a whiff of Snake Lily.

By then, the restaurant had grown as quiet as a funeral home at midnight.

"Hello, you little prick," I said, surprised at my audacity. "Remember me?"

He sprang out of his chair and backed away, his mouth open.

I waved the folder in his face, and when I spoke, I tried to feign the voice of a woman with a vocal cord injury. "When you get back your *cojones*, read this."

I slapped the folder on the table.

Big Tony, who I'd ignored, came plodding over to protect his boss but stopped short when he recognized me. From his expression, I thought he'd faint. I shook a finger at him, my bracelet jangling. "Touch me again, you *hijo de puta*, and you're dead."

I should have retreated at that moment, should have left them with the smell of Snake Lily in their nostrils. But their expressions emboldened me. My face grew hot with rage, the same as when I'd throttled Clarence with a tomato stake. Damn them for what they'd done to Carmen and those other girls. And damn them for the scare they'd put into me.

I turned to the other men and pointed to the faux bruise on my neck. "This is what that little shit did to me. Strangled me to death with a belt. Then he sent Big Tony to dump my body in a swamp. But guess what? I'm back from the dead. And now they're going to pay."

I dragged out that last word—*paaaaay*.

No one moved. There was nothing but wide-eyed stares. I swiveled back to Sal and Big Tony and raised my arm. "You're cursed. Both of you are good as dead." *Deaaaaad.*

I snapped my arm straight as if hurling a lightning bolt.

The lights in the restaurant flickered, went out, and came back on. A bulb popped. The large painting of the flamenco dancers fell off the wall.

Everyone at the table jumped to their feet, pistols drawn, glancing this way and that as if the feds had burst into the place.

"What the hell?" someone said, and then Big Tony clutched his chest and sagged to the floor.

The lights dimmed and came back on. There were gasps and mumbling and someone yelling, "Call a doctor!" Big Tony began foaming at the mouth. Another bulb popped as if announcing the arrival of the Grim Reaper. His body stiffened. He tried to speak, maybe ask God's forgiveness for the pain he'd inflicted on others, but the words spilled out in a torrent of foam. He jerked a few times and lay still, and if I live to be a hundred I'll never forget that parting glimpse into the face of evil—Big Tony's bulging eyes, his mouth open in a silent scream.

Diners hurried for the exits. Others gathered around for a look—cooks, servers, guests, mobsters, and even Rothman—glancing from the body to me. Had I caused all that havoc? Did I scare Big Tony to death? And what about the girl of the swamp? Had I really seen her?

Cheena took my arm. "Come on, girl, *vamos*. I've got your tote bag."

We hurried through the kitchen, out the back door, and into the Model-A that had grown hot in the noonday sun. I tossed the envelope with the Snake Lily out the window. Cheena started the engine, and we were soon speeding down Setima like a race car, away from the Columbia, past the protesters with their placards and the homeless in rags, scattering chickens, Cheena laughing and slapping her hands on the steering wheel like a lunatic.

"We did it!" she said, cackling. "Light me a cigarette."

I lit two cigarettes, one for her, another for me, then I mopped the makeup off my face.

"You're smoking," Cheena said. "Are you all right?"

"No, I'm not all right. I've never killed anyone."

"You didn't kill Tony. He had a heart attack. Adios and goodbye. Too bad it wasn't Sal. She slowed for a traffic light, looked both ways and ran it.

"How did you do it?" she asked.

"Do what?"

"The lights, the popping bulbs, the painting that fell off the wall. How'd you do that?"

"I thought you guys did it."

"Hell, no, we didn't do anything. Who are you, Amy?"

CHAPTER 63

I wanted to go to the house and jump into the shower, scrub away the smell of Snake Lily and the memory of Big Tony. But Cheena said she was hungry and drove us to Gino's Bistro on 8th Avenue, a little hole in the wall place not far from El Dorado. I used the bathroom to get myself together, and when I came out, she'd already ordered tea and the special of the day.

"Gino makes the best gnocchi in Ybor," she said as if we'd just come from the movies. "You'll love it." She reached over and wrapped her hand around my wrist.

"What are you doing?"

"Just making sure you're real."

I yanked away. "For God's sake, Cheena, I'm not a ghost."

"Then how do you explain all those happenings?"

"How do I know? This tea doesn't have ice."

"You need ice to help you explain?"

"I need ice for my tea."

"They charge extra. They have to chip it. Are you going to answer my question or not?"

"What question?"

"The lights. The popping bulbs. The picture that fell off the wall."

"How do I know? Maybe it was the girl of the swamp."

She looked around as if she expected to see Carmen's ghost in the shadows.

"Let's put it to the test," she said.

"Put what to the test?"

She pointed to a painting on the wall. "That's *Il Duce*—Mussolini. Look at him. Got on his military uniform with eagle's wings, soaring over the city of Rome. Smirking like he's God. Italians love him. Everyone else thinks he's a fascist menace. Go ahead and do it."

"Do what?"

"Put a curse on the bastard. Make him fall off the wall."

"That's ridiculous."

"No, it's not. Prove it."

"Curses work only if you believe in them."

"I'm half Cuban and half Philippine. I believe in curses. Humor me."

"Fine, if it'll shut you up."

I pointed at the painting, lifted my right arm, and snapped it straight, just as I'd done to Gerhardt and Big Tony. "You're cursed, you fascist pig."

Nothing happened. Cheena twirled her finger. "Come on, Carmen, concentrate."

"No, Cheena, this is silly."

"One more time, please."

I rolled my eyes and tried to think of something sinister to say. All that came to mind was Humpty Dumpty falling off a wall. But that was before the candles on the table flickered and died. And then … then, the words came into my head as if Carmen herself had whispered them in my ear, in English. Again I lifted my arms toward the painting.

In Ybor City, does Mussolini, in a framed picture smirk.

Spell from hell, tear him down, put him in the dirt.

Cheena burst into laughter.

"What's so funny?" I asked.

"Gino. He thinks you're saluting Mussolini, the way you snap your arm straight." She waved him over and pointed to my tea. "My friend wants ice in her tea. Also a slice of lemon."

"No problem, señorita. You like Il Duce?"

"Ice and lemon, please."

As soon as he left, Cheena asked, "Since when do you speak English?"

"Only when I get worked up."

"Do it again."

"Do what?"

"The chant, Amy. English, Spanish. Whatever. Just make the painting fall."

"If that damn painting hasn't fallen yet, it never will."

"Oh, come on. I'll chant with you." She waited for Gino to return with the ice and leave. Then the two of us chanted like witches at a Sabbath:

In Ybor City, does Mussolini, in a framed picture smirk.

Spell from hell, tear him down, put him in the dirt.

We did it a couple more times, with arm snaps that probably looked to Gino like a salute, but Mussolini remained on the wall, still smirking.

"Maybe you're not trying hard enough," Cheena said.

"Would you let it go?" I picked up an ashtray on the table. "I could throw this."

"Fine," she said and shrugged in resignation. She still stared at the painting and didn't turn away until Gino, who had changed into a clean white apron, returned with our gnocchi.

"My wife is artist," he said in his Italian accent. "She sell painting for three dollars. You need more ice or lemon for your tea?"

"No, I'm okay."

"For you I give special price. Only two dollars. What you think?"

"For iced tea?"

"No, señorita, for painting of Il Duce."

I didn't want to hurt his feelings—he seemed like a nice little man—so I told him with a straight face that I loved the colors and the symbolism of the duce soaring over Rome.

"One dollar, fifty cents."

"Very kind of you, Gino, but not today."

He trudged away as if the world was coming to an end. Cheena muttered, "He should pay us to haul away that piece of shit." She spooned a dollop of gnocchi into her mouth and smacked her lips. "Told you he makes the best gnocchi in Ybor."

I wasn't that hungry, not after what had happened back at the Columbia, and tried to push the image out of my head. It didn't help that I caught a whiff of Snake Lily. Or that Cheena, who never knew when to shut up, kept up the chatter as we ate, reliving every moment of our adventure, saying she felt confident Sal would leave me alone.

"My curse didn't stop Gerhardt," I said. "Why should it stop Sal?"

She didn't have an answer, and what was worse, I knew from my research that Carmen had disappeared a second time, not long after she'd been seen with Hemingway. What happened to her—or to me in this case? Did the gangsters get me, or did I leave Ybor for good?

What happened to her, Abuelita?

Who knows, mija? Maybe the mob got her.

"Amy?"

"What?"

"Are you listening?"

"I'm thinking about Big Tony."

"Oh, to hell with Big Tony. If he was here he'd be saluting Mussolini. You want dessert?"

"I'm full. Can we go now?"

We finished our gnocchi and conversation, paid the bill, and were standing to leave when the lights flickered and Mussolini fell off the wall.

CHAPTER 64

Cheena's reaction when we got back into the Model-A was an endless string of who-are-you and how-did-you-do-that and what-is-going-on, and didn't end until I told her to just shut up and that I needed to go home and shower off the smell of Snake Lily.

"Otis is still there."

"Okay, then take me to Rosa's."

"Are you serious? Rosa's is open for business. Go there now and you could get propositioned and fucked. Then you'd really have something to tell your boyfriend."

She parked in the shade of a tree, lit another cigarette, and turned to face me. "Besides, we need to talk about an escape plan. It won't be long before the mob figures out what we're doing."

"What do you suggest?"

"Change our bolita money into gold. Get on a ship and leave the country."

"And go where?"

"Spain. But first, we need to change our dollars into gold."

"Where do you get gold?"

"Oh, Amy, poor Amy. Any Gypsy can tell you take your paper to a bank and trade it for gold. Says so right on the bills. You can also buy rare coins—Spanish escudos, Mexican pesos. French francs. You pay a premium, but you can also sell them in Spain for a premium."

We schemed for another hour or so, and she dropped me off at Rosa's.

"Use a rubber," she said, laughing, and drove away.

A beefy guard at the door stopped me. "Where you going, *dulce*?"

"An appointment with Doña Rosa. She's expecting me."

"Name?"

"Mata Hari. I'm in a hurry."

He seemed to like what he saw—a woman in a wig, sunglasses, and beret—and motioned me into a world I'd never entered: an open brothel in Ybor that also featured flamenco.

A haze of cigar and cigarette smoke hung in the air, stirred by ceiling fans. Men and working girls in their little feathery outfits stood around with drinks or sat on cushioned sofas, and somewhere in the back, a female vocalist was belting out a soul-wrenching *cante jondo* in a mixture of Spanish and Gypsy Caló.

Listen to me, and I'll sing you a song

Of love turned to heartbreak

And things gone wrong…

Story of my life, I thought and looked around for Donnie Sue. She wasn't there—unless she was upstairs servicing a customer—but Rosa was easy to spot in her flowing red outfit with the feathers and scarves. She motioned me over, and I was heading her way when a balding older man with a cigar in his hand grabbed my arm. He had stained teeth and dandruff like almost every other man I'd seen in 1932, but his smile seemed genuine.

"Hola, señorita. How about the two of us go upstairs?"

"And do what?" I asked as if I didn't know.

"Well, for starters, we'd remove your sunglasses. Then we'd unbutton your blouse. Then…" He leaned closer and must have caught a whiff of Snake Lily because he straightened up and blinked his eyes. "Excuse me," he said and drifted away.

By then, Rosa was at my side. "Thank goodness you're back," she said and stabbed out a cigar in the ashtray. "We need to get you back to work. We need you, Carmen."

She told an assistant to keep an eye on the place and led me through dangling archway beads into her office. It reeked with the smells of unemptied ashtrays. Her cat on the armchair glanced up, sniffed the air, and scooted away. Rosa hugged me but then stepped back.

"Oh, my God, what is that?"

"My skirt. I spilled water on it from an old vase of flowers."

"You need to change it, girl. You're scaring Jezebel. Can I get you a drink?"

"I've only got a minute. How's your new girl working out?"

"That ingrate little slut. She took her money and left. You can't trust people nowadays. All these gangsters and bootleggers. Crooked politicians. If we were living in biblical times, God would rain fire and brimstone on this city."

"Maybe He'd destroy this place as well."

"God wouldn't touch it. We provide an honest service for our customers."

She complained a while longer and said we needed to rehearse Bizet's *Carmen* for my performance at the cigar factory.

"I'd rather do *Malagueña*," I said. "It won't require much practice."

"No, no, no. Don Ignacio asked specifically for *Carmen.*" She clapped her hands. "Jezebel, get over here!" She picked up her cat. "It's all right, *dulce*. Carmen's not going to bite you."

I rolled my eyes. "I don't want to do *Carmen.*"

She put down the cat. "Look, it's not a matter of what you want. I have to keep Don Ignacio happy. If it wasn't for him and Santo, I couldn't keep this place open. They protect me. They protect the girls from predators like Sal." Her eyes watered and she put on the piteous expression of a beggar. "Please, Carmen. Do this for me."

I stood, walked around the room, and thought about it. With any luck at all, I'd get out of Ybor before the Saturday performance.

"Fine," I said and headed for the door.

"Wait. Where are you going?"

"A bank."

"Since when do you trust a bank? Didn't you lose a fortune when Citizens went under?"

"All I want is exchange paper for gold."

"How much are you talking about, *dulce*?"

"A thousand now, maybe more tomorrow."

She cocked an eyebrow, lit another cigar, and gave me a fellow-conspirator kind of nod. "First National down the street. Used to be Bank of Ybor. Went under in '29. Ask for Don Rafael. Tell him Rosa sent you. He's used to large transactions. Keeps his mouth shut. No questions. And for God's sake, get out of that stinky skirt."

CHAPTER 65

There wasn't time to change, so I trailed the scent of Snake Lily into the bank and kept my distance from other customers. Don Rafael handled my request with hardly a word, and by six, I was back at Carmen's house, lugging three pounds of $20 gold coins in my tote bag.

Natalia met me at the door, dressed in flared riding britches. "What the hell is that stench?" she asked. "You smell like you climbed out a grave."

"Snake Lily. Didn't you hear about Big Tony?"

"I heard. The whole world heard. You need to take a bath."

"Who told you about Big Tony?"

"Everybody. Why didn't you shoot Sal when you had a chance?"

"Are you crazy? There were seven of them. Bodyguards too."

"So what? You had the Untouchables on your side. Could have wiped out the whole mob."

"For God's sake, Natalia. I could have been killed."

"You could still be killed. Big Tony was like a brother to Sal. Don't think for a minute that your little affidavit hoax will work. That's Katzenjammer Kids' stuff." She nodded at the bulge in my tote bag. "What's that?"

"Luger and extra ammo. I might have to go down shooting."

"A Luger is too big. You need something small … like my Derringer."

I thought she'd want to hear my version of what happened. She didn't. So I hurried into the bedroom, closed the door, and was about to strip off my rancid clothes when she called out, "I'm leaving. Don't forget to lock the door behind me. It's got new locks."

"Where are you going?"

"Don't ask."

"Are you coming back tonight?"

"And mess up your night with the Cajun? No, *dulce*, but if I were you, I'd open some windows and take a long shower."

I locked the door and was glad she'd left, but had second thoughts when the house became so quiet I could hear the sounds of traffic over on Setima. Back in 2019, I wasn't that superstitious, but after a sinkhole, the girl of the swamp, Gerhardt, and things falling off the wall, it wouldn't surprise me at all if Big Tony's ghost dropped by for a chat.

I took out my loaded Luger and glanced up at the wall poster that faced the bed, an eye-catching image of flamenco dancers.

Could I make it fall off the wall?

Don't even think about it, I told myself. I didn't have the power. It had to be Carmen. She was following me around like a guardian angel and could be here now, standing beside me.

The thought raised goosebumps on my arms.

Suppose she suddenly materialized?

Good Lord, it was bad enough to worry about Sal and Clarence without having to be terrified of ghosts. If Lafitte didn't come tonight, I'd never be able to sleep.

I dumped my gold coins onto the bed. Now what? There were fifty coins, a mixture of Liberty and St. Gaudens, secured in paper-wrapped stacks of ten each. Fifty gold coins weighed more than three pounds. If I kept winning at bolita, I'd have ten or fifteen times as much by Saturday, enough to fill a pirate's chest.

But where to hide them? Under the mattress? In the attic?

Maybe gold wasn't such a good idea.

I stuffed the coins into a shoebox, stripped off my clothes, picked up both the Luger and shotgun and padded into the bathroom. It had a flimsy hook latch, so I shoved a chair against the door. No way was I going to be caught naked behind a shower curtain like Janet Leigh in *Psycho*. I had guns, loaded guns. And they were damn well going to go off if someone tried to break in. With that thought in mind, I ran water in the tub, climbed in, and tried to scrub away the smell and foul experience.

Afterward, I changed into one of Carmen's frilly house robes, sank onto the living room sofa with Pearl Buck's *The Good Earth*, and waited for Lafitte.

Eight o'clock rolled around. The phone rang several times, but not our ring. It grew dark, and darker still when thunder rattled the windows. I lit candles and lamps just in case.

At nine, when I heard the first jingle of the night watchman making his rounds, I put away the book and conjured up excuses for Lafitte. He'd had a flat tire. He'd crashed his plane into the swamp. He was stuck in a traffic jam—as if such things existed in 1932—but the excuses dissolved in the swish-swish of the fan blades.

Another crack of thunder, and out went the lights.

Damn it. Where was Lafitte?

The loneliness came back, the self-doubts, the insecurities. To him, I was just another easy conquest. He was probably sitting in a smoky tavern in Tarpon Springs this very moment with a little Greek beauty, drinking Ouzo and eating moussaka.

Or maybe they were getting it on at his place on Spring Bayou.

Bastard. I should have known better.

A sound on the front porch startled me.

Lafitte? I froze and listened, waiting for a knock.

Nothing.

The doorknob rattled and turned.

Shit!

I blew out the lamp, grabbed the double barrel and Luger, and ducked behind the sofa.

The room seemed to turn icy cold. From somewhere came an earthy odor, like damp soil and decay. Then a shadow brushed by as if a spirit had entered the house. A chill ran up my arms and down my back. I swung this way and that with the shotgun, my senses on full alert.

Nothing. No one. But someone or something was in the house.

Big Tony?

Carmen?

My heart pounded so furiously I felt it in my head. The doorknob rattled again. I heard a man's voice. Loud. Like he was reading from the Scriptures.

"Let no one be found among you who practices sorcery. Or casts spells. Anyone who does these things is DETESTABLE TO THE LORD!"

CHAPTER 66

I aimed the shotgun but didn't dare fire while he was outside. Even in my panic I knew it wasn't a good idea to shoot one of J. Edgar's agents except in self-defense.

The lock on the door clicked. Did he have a key?

"Spawn of Satan! Whore of Babylon!"

The door swung open and there stood Gerhardt, silhouetted against flashes of lightning.

"Witch, I know you're in here. Time to settle with the Lord."

A light appeared to my right.

There was shriek, like a terror-stricken woman being attacked by vampires.

Gerhardt fired.

My shotgun went off—both barrels—creating a blinding flash and ear-shattering noise. The barrel slammed into my face, knocking me senseless. I thought I'd been shot, that it was over, that I'd never see Lafitte again or dance flamenco or go to Spain, but when my senses returned, I realized I was still behind the sofa, my ears ringing.

Had I hit him? I'd been so intent on shooting the crazy bastard that I had my finger on the triggers while I was thumbing back the hammers.

Where was he?

And what was that shriek?

No footfalls. No mumbled curses either. Only the lingering flash deep in my brain.

Fire the Luger? No, that would show him where I was hiding.

In the movies, a character in a bad situation would throw an ashtray or some other object, hoping to get the bad guy to show himself. I didn't have an ashtray and wasn't about to crawl around looking for one, so I flung the empty shotgun.

It clattered on the hardwood floor.

No response. No movement.

Was he dead?

I peered through the space beneath the sofa. It was an antique Duncan Phyfe, high enough off the floor that I could see a portion of the living room during flashes of lightning. The front door was open to the outside, letting in a breeze, and I could see tree limbs and Spanish moss dancing in the wind. But no humans. No one on the floor either.

Was he gone?

Or hiding in the bedroom?

Damn it, what to do? I'd have to expose myself to get to the wall phone. Did it even work during a power outage? Maybe I should dash out the door and run.

But what if he was on the porch?

How long I waited behind that sofa, cowering in the darkness, I don't know, but it was long enough for my heart to stop pounding. Long enough for my labored breathing to return to normal. Long enough for the ringing in my ears to stop.

The wind whistled. Lightning flashed. I heard the jingle of the night watchman's bells and was wondering if I should scream for him when a car pulled in the driveway, its headlights momentarily lighting the room.

Lafitte?

A door slammed, but the car drove away.

What was that about? Had someone come for Gerhardt?

There were footfalls on the porch. The crunch of broken glass.

I aimed the Luger.

The silhouette of a man appeared in the open doorway.

"Amy! Are you here? It's me."

Lafitte, standing there like a rock, holding my universe together.

I flew into his arms and told him what happened. He took out his pistol and together we crouched in the darkness, listening for sounds.

"You not call police?" he asked.

"Couldn't. I was hiding behind the sofa."

"He still in house?"

"I don't know."

"Wait here. I check."

"No. Lafitte. He's got a gun."

He checked anyway, going room to room like a cop on a drug bust. I followed him with my Luger and flashlight, and together we looked in closets, under the beds, inside cabinets, and any other place an intruder could hide.

"Not here," Lafitte said. "Gone."

No blood either, but there were plenty of signs he'd been there—like the transom I'd blown out with the shotgun, and the hole in the living room wall from the bullet he'd fired.

We traced the trajectory and saw that it came out inside Carmen's bedroom closet, blowing a hole in the wood big enough for me to insert my fist. The bullet had also passed through Carmen's clothing and lodged in the wall.

"Caliber 45," Lafitte said. "Best you call your friend at the Bureau."

"Are you sure? Aren't you on their wanted list?"

"Is worse you not call."

He was right, so we lit lamps and checked the phone. It worked, and a few seconds later I had Cheena on the other end.

"That idiot," she said. "Don't touch a thing. I'll be right over."

"I have company."

"Look, I don't care who you're sleeping with. I'm on my way. Don't shoot me when I drive up ... and don't try to hide your Cajun friend either."

CHAPTER 67

We waited in the dim light, Lafitte telling me it was such a long drive from Tarpon he'd flown his airplane and left it in the field near the doctor's house. Soledad had driven him over.

"We need to get you out of Ybor," he said. "Is dangerous for you here."

"Can we leave by Saturday?"

"Why Saturday?"

"Don Ignacio. He's expecting me on Saturday. He's a disgusting little character. They say he and Carmen might have been lovers."

He made a gagging gesture. I told him I felt that way too. He said, "Okay, here's what we do. You pack bags. Have everything ready by Friday. I make arrangements."

We were still hatching our plan when Cheena drove up in her Model-A and trotted into the house, pistol in one hand and flashlight in the other. She was dressed in slacks and a light jacket over a low cut white blouse that blended nicely with her dark complexion.

"Are you okay?" she asked. "Did Gerhardt hurt you?"

"I'm fine. Just scared."

She walked around with her flashlight, shining it on the broken glass. "No blood. How could you miss with a shotgun?"

"It fired before I was ready. Somebody should have warned me about recoil."

She shined the light on my face and studied it, coming so close I caught a whiff of perfume. "There," she said and touched a spot over my right eye. "It's a little red."

She turned to Lafitte. "Do you understand Spanish?"

"*Un poco.*"

"Were you here when it happened?"

"I come later."

"I don't see a car."

"A friend drove me."

"Do you have a gun?"

He took the pistol from his jacket and handed it to her.

"Colt 45," she said, "1911 semi-automatic. War issue. They used these on my people in the Philippines." She sniffed the pistol and handed it back. "You need to get out of here."

"Why?"

"Otis. He's on the way with other agents. They'll say the shooter was you."

I felt like kicking something. Otis and Gerhardt were friends. Otis had lied for him. He'd shared biblical quotes with him, and for all I knew he'd given the door key to Gerhardt.

"Was it necessary to tell Otis?" I asked Cheena.

"Would you listen to yourself, Amy? One of our agents broke into your house. Tried to kill you. We have to investigate. It's a big deal."

She told Lafitte to go to the Buen Gusto coffee house on 7th Avenue, just a couple of blocks away. "Wait there. I'll let you know when we're finished."

Lafitte grabbed his bag, zipped up his aviator jacket, and trotted into the rain. Cheena watched him go. "*Guapo*," she said. "I'd fall for him too, even if he is a bootlegger."

I didn't know how to answer that and didn't have to because Otis pulled into the driveway with two other agents. They jumped out and began looking under the house, in the trees, in the bushes and even on the roof, yelling to one another in the dizzying arcs of their flashlights.

"All clear here."

"Here, too. Maybe he's in the house."

Otis charged inside as if assaulting the place, barking orders like a

Marine sergeant, water dripping from this oilskin jacket and black hat. They swept the house with drawn pistols. They checked my shotgun and Luger. They discovered the lodged bullet in the wall and got so excited you'd think they had found the Hope Diamond. Then they closed all the drapes, lit more lamps and candles, and began bickering with each other.

"She had a twelve gauge. How could she miss?"

"Maybe 'cause she ain't stupid," said an agent in a deep Southern drawl. "Hell, Hoover'd drag her off in chains, throw her in a damn dungeon."

"It's Director Hoover," Otis shot back. "Show some respect. And we don't know for sure it was Gerhardt. Could have been Sal."

"Not Sal. She hexed the little bastard. Scared the dookey outa him."

"Hex didn't stop Gerhardt, did it?"

Cheena passed around towels. Otis, his hair messed up from the toweling, took off his jacket, loosened his tie, and opened a notebook. He glanced into the shadows as if looking for ghosts and finally said to Cheena, "Tell her we need to ask a few questions."

"She knows that. What's your question?"

"I want her to tell us exactly what happened."

Cheena motioned me onto the sofa and translated. Otis leaned forward in his chair. A crucifix dangled from his neck on a silver chain.

"Are you Catholic?" I asked in Spanish, pointing at the cross. *Catolica*?"

"What'd she say?" Otis asked.

"She asked about your cross … if you're Catholic?"

He pushed it back into his shirt. "It's from my wife. Says it'll keep me safe."

"Really?" I said when Cheena translated. "Did she also give him a wooden stake and mallet?"

"Please, Amy. They're trying to be civil. They're scared of you."

I sighed and shut up. Otis repeated his question. Cheena again translated. I answered and was reliving the horror of Gerhardt opening the door when something slammed against the house.

All of us shot out of our chairs, the agents yanking out their pistols.

Cheena pulled me down behind the sofa.

There was a scratching sound at the window, and as if that wasn't terrifying enough, something or someone screeched on the back porch.

The same screech I'd heard before.

CHAPTER 68

We doused lamps and candles and crouched in the darkness, watching the doors. The storm picked up. Rain beat against the windows, and it wouldn't have surprised me at all if the door burst open and the girl of the swamp floated into the room.

After a while, the agent they called Alabama spoke from the darkness. "So we just gonna sit here all night in the dark?"

"No," Otis answered. "We're going outside to investigate."

"It's storming out there."

"You're an agent, hayseed. Since when are you scared of rain?"

"It ain't rain I'm scared of. He could ambush us."

"You knew this was dangerous work when you signed up."

"I signed up to bust bootleggers, not fight one of our own."

"We don't know it was Gerhardt. It could be Sal."

Otis gave instructions, and off they went with their pistols, two agents out the front and Otis out the back. I expected to hear gunfire or the rat-a-tat of Tommy guns, but all I heard was wind blowing through the open doors, bringing with it droplets of mist and damp earthy smells. "Why didn't they close the doors?" I asked Cheena.

"Men. They don't put down the toilet seat either."

I tried to remain calm, sitting there with my back against the sofa, telling myself it would be okay. But nothing had been okay for the last three days. Suppose they didn't come back? Suppose someone or something nabbed them? Like the Klan. Or Carmen's ghost.

Cheena, as if reading my thoughts, snuggled closer. "What was that screech?"

"Might have been a cat."

"Did Carmen have a cat?"

"Haven't seen one."

"God, I hate this job."

"Why do you do it?"

"Because I have to make a living. Do you know anything about Philippine history?"

"Not a lot?"

"Well, Manila is also overrun with gangsters. I was forced to marry one of them when I was only fourteen. He dragged me off to Cuba. I escaped. That's why I'm here now."

"What happened to your husband?"

"Same thing that happens to all gangsters."

She stopped talking. The grandfather clock struck ten, and not long afterward I heard movement on the back porch. "That better be them," Cheena said and aimed her pistol.

There were footsteps. "It's us!" Otis hollered. "We're coming in. Don't shoot."

They tromped in with their flashlights, their faces wet, brushing water and debris off their jackets. "Broken palm frond," Otis said. "Wind blew it against the house."

"What took so long?"

"Checking the back alley."

"What about the screech?"

"Cat. We saw it on the porch."

"Black as Satan," said Alabama. "Don't witches have cats?"

"What's that supposed to mean?" Cheena asked.

He nodded at me. "Maybe she caused that screech. Maybe she caused that limb to break. Maybe she wants to scare us out of here."

"Better shut up. She might turn you into a frog."

The chatter went on until candles and lamps were lit, the doors locked, everyone with a towel, and we were seated around the sofa. The flickering lamps lit up only part of the room, yet even in the poor light not one of them would make eye contact with me.

Otis took out a notebook again. "Rothman said to take notes."

"Be careful what you ask her," Cheena said. "You don't want to antagonize her."

The three agents exchanged glances. Otis said to Cheena, "Tell her we're just doing our job."

Cheena translated, and then the questions began.

What makes you so sure it was Gerhardt?

Did you get a good look at his face?

How was he dressed?

They did not dispute me or make disparaging comments, not even when I told them I didn't see his face, didn't see how he was dressed, and the only way I knew it was Gerhardt was by the sound of his voice and the words he'd spoken.

Otis jotted down my answers and asked a few more questions, most of which I couldn't answer, then they began discussing the matter among themselves in hushed tones.

"You think she's telling the truth?"

"Why would she lie?"

"Maybe she wants round-the-clock protection from Sal."

"You gonna accuse her of that?"

"I ain't accusing her of nothing. You saw what she did to Big Tony."

They were still debating, talking about me as if I wasn't there, when the grandfather clock began its chimes for eleven. Each stroke reminded me of Lafitte waiting at the coffee house.

Lafitte in his wet clothes.

Looking at his watch.

Wondering what was taking so long.

When the strokes ended, I spoke to Cheena in Spanish. "Can't we get them out of here?"

"Well, you could make books start flying off the shelves."

"I can't do that, but I can do something else."

I took the shawl from my shoulders and wrapped it around my head like a fortuneteller.

"What are you doing?" Cheena asked.

"Just watch. Play along with me. Act scared."

"I'm already scared. Please don't put a curse on Otis."

"What's she saying?" Otis asked, his face crisscrossed with worry.

"Says she's hearing voices. Scary stuff."

"Like what?"

"Maybe you don't want to know."

It grew so quiet, I could have said, "Boo," and scared them away, but by then the Gypsy in me had broken free. I pointed at the fireplace and began chanting, in Caló.

God is good, but the devil will have his due.

God is good, but the devil will have his due.

The outside wind picked up. There was another bloodcurdling screech from the back porch. The candle on the coffee table flickered and died. Then Cheena, who must have been an actress in a former life, made the Sign of the Cross. "Shit," she said. "We better go."

"What's happening?" Otis asked, the whites in his eyes showing. "What's she saying?"

"Gypsy talk, same thing she was doing at the Columbia, just before Big Tony dropped dead."

Otis was the first out of his chair, grabbing his hat and jacket. He told Cheena to leave the mess for them to fix tomorrow, then he and the other agents retreated out the door, across the broken glass, and into the rain.

CHAPTER 69

After Lafitte kissed me goodbye the next morning, I disguised myself in a red wig and slipped out the back door for the short trek to the Centro Español for my meeting with Cheena.

She wasn't there. The server said she'd be late. He poured coffee, laid out breakfast, and handed me copies of *La Gaceta* and the *Tampa Tribune*. There was no mention in the papers of Big Tony, but Lou Gehrig had hit four home runs in one game, Amelia Earhart was being honored in a ticker-tape parade, John D. Rockefeller had turned against prohibition, and Hemingway's *Farewell to Arms* would soon be a movie starring Gary Cooper and Helen Hayes.

The door opened and in walked Cheena with Chief Agent Rothman.

They were bleary-eyed and rumpled as if they'd been partying all night. Rothman, who smelled of cigarettes, poured himself a mug of coffee, stirred in sugar and cream, and sat down facing me. From his expression, I knew he hadn't come for coffee and conversation.

"There's good news and bad," he said.

I cringed and waited.

"Good news is we found Gerhardt. He was stumbling around on 7th Avenue in his drenched clothing, babbling about witches. He's in the hospital."

"And?"

"Well, you were right about it being him. He admits it."

"I hope you're going to charge him with attempted murder."

"His story is a bit different from yours."

"In what way?"

"Well, that's the bad news." He took a long sip of coffee, lit one of his Lucky Strikes, and turned to Cheena. "You tell her. Your Spanish is better than mine."

Cheena drew in a deep breath and squirmed as if she didn't want to deliver the bad news either. "You're not going to like it," she said.

"Just tell me, for God's sake."

"Well, here's what he told us. The Klan got him—men in hoods and white sheets. Says it was your fault because of the hex. They took him to a barn, told him they were going to burn him on the cross for destroying the livelihoods of hardworking Christians. Forced him to drink a potion. Last thing he remembers is the taste, like sassafras root and castor oil. Everything went black. Can't remember a thing after that."

She yawned, shook her head, and continued. "Now he's got a bad memory, same as you. Except the memory loss in your case wasn't caused by the Klan."

Rothman rolled his eyes. "Excuse me, Cheena, but we're talking about Gerhardt."

"Sorry, I had a long night. Anyhow, like I was saying, the potion knocked him out. When he got his senses back, he found himself in front of your house … well, Carmen's house. Had no idea how he got there. Says he was scared. Believes God sent him to make amends."

"Make amends how—shoot the witch?"

"No Amy … I mean, Carmen. He said he wanted to apologize for being rough. Wanted to ask your forgiveness. Beg you to lift the spell. So he knocked on your door—"

"He didn't knock. He just opened the door and came in, cursing, calling me the whore of Babylon. That door had a new lock. Somebody must have given him a key."

Rothman held up a hand. "He's a Bureau agent, Carmen. He knows how to open locked doors." He turned to Cheena. "Go ahead."

"Like I told you," she said, "he knocked on the door. You opened it …

at least that's his story. Says you took one look and dashed into the darkness. Then you appeared again off to his left, wild-eyed, screeching like a demon, all lit up with a shotgun."

"Lit up?"

"Like somebody shined a light on you. Like a ghost. His exact words. You aimed the gun. He fired, point-blank. You should be dead. But you shot back. He panicked, thinking you were the devil. Or maybe that swamp apparition. Ran so fast he lost his pistol."

They both stared as if to ask, "Who the hell are you?"

"Now he's back to babbling *tonterías*," Cheena said, "ranting you ought to be burned at the stake … like they burned witches in the old days. You messed up his head."

I turned Rothman, sitting there with his coffee in one hand and a cigarette in the other. "So who are you going to believe—me or bat-shit crazy Gerhardt?"

He pushed back in his chair, stood, and downed his coffee, "Stenographer will be here soon to take your statement. We'll have to report to Director Hoover. All I can say is it's a good thing you didn't shoot an agent with that shotgun."

He yawned and left the room.

Cheena flung her table linen at the closing door. "Can you believe that shit? Gerhardt's a blathering idiot, but he's one of J. Edgar's idiots. They'll take his word any day over yours.

You're screwed as soon as that report gets to Hoover."

"How long will it take?"

"They'll wire it when they get your statement."

She pulled up a chair and sat beside me. "I've got an idea."

"Your last idea killed Big Tony."

"Who gives a shit about Big Tony? Here's what we're going to do. When Peggy comes in—Peggy's the stenographer—you say exactly what happened. I'll mistranslate. Make deliberate mistakes. Peggy will take it to the office to type. You get to read it before you sign it tomorrow, Tuesday. No, no, today's Tuesday. What am I thinking? Tomorrow's Wednesday."

"Then what?"

"Then you throw a fit. Refuse to sign, saying it's mistranslated. They'll have to retype it. That means it won't reach Hoover until Thursday. It'll take him a day to respond, so we're good at least until Friday. By then we'll be ready to head to Spain with our bolita winnings."

"But what if Rothman reports it by phone?"

"He won't. He's terrified of Hoover."

"But what if he does?"

"Trust me, Amy. I know everything that goes on in that office. And I mean *everything*. If an order comes down to bring you in, I'll let you know."

We were still scheming when Peggy showed up, looking as wild-haired and beaten as Cheena, complaining it wasn't fair she'd been up all night taking Gerhardt's statement and now had to take mine. "No rest at all," she said. "They must think I'm a robot."

"She's right," I said to Cheena. "It's not fair. She could make mistakes. Why don't you tell her to get some rest and let's do this later?"

Cheena slapped her forehead with her palm. "Why didn't I think of that?" She turned back to Peggy and told her to go home, saying she'd take the heat from Rothman. Peggy thanked her, gulped down a glass of orange juice, grabbed a banana, and took off with her briefcase.

"Now we have until Saturday," Cheena said. "Let's eat and go collect our bolita money."

CHAPTER 70

I'd grown so accustomed to looming disaster I could hardly believe I made it to Wednesday and on to Thursday without anyone shooting at me. I even went back to writing about my adventures, thanks to a new Remington portable typewriter I bought for only $17.60.

Otis repaired the transom, cleaned the mess, and patched the damage in the living room wall from Gerhardt's bullet, but he overlooked the exit hole in Carmen's bedroom closet. Could I hide my gold coins there, inside the wall? Yes, perfect. I was earning between five and seven thousand a day from bolita, almost all of which I converted into antique Spanish escudos. I secured them in stockings, dropped them into the hole and plugged it with a wood fragment that had been blown off by Gerhardt's bullet.

But I felt so guilty about accumulating a small fortune while living in a soon-to-be-foreclosed house that belonged to my great-great-grandmother that I went to First National and settled her mortgage for five thousand in cash.

Cheena went to a dentist and had the stains removed from her teeth.

I paid another visit to Lola Milagro's and was welcomed like a returning war hero.

Yes, I told them, I wanted the pan shave.

No one at the Bureau questioned my complaints about the mistranslation of my statement, and it wasn't until Thursday that I signed it. Cheena said Hoover was so burdened with paperwork he wouldn't read my statement until Saturday or Sunday. So I was in high spirits when I walked into Rosa's to rehearse *Carmen* for a Saturday event I wasn't going to attend.

She ground out her smelly cigar and led me into her office through the archway with its dangling beads. No smile. No hug. No hello.

Even her cat looked hostile.

She plopped into her chair and scooped up her cat. "What's this I hear about Big Tony?" she asked. "You being dead, looking like you were dressed for Halloween, scaring the hell out of Sal? I never featured a dead performer yet."

"It was a prank. I never thought it would turn out that way."

"Maybe it was a prank, but now I've got to answer to Charlie and Santo and Don Ignacio. And that's not the worst part."

"What's the worst part?"

"Sal. The little bastard went missing. Just like that G-man you spooked."

"No one's heard from him?"

"Not a word. They checked his place. He's gone. So is his Packard. They're saying you put a hex on him. Made the lights go out. Is that true?"

"All I did was scare him."

She narrowed her eyes a moment. "There's more bad news," she said. "Don Ignacio wants us to perform at his factory tomorrow—Friday— instead of Saturday."

"Tomorrow? But we—"

"Tomorrow, Carmen. The big boys are going to be there—Charlie and Santo. They want to see you in the flesh. Know you're alive. Want to see that tattoo. We have to be there by one."

She stood and paced around the room with her cat, her face turning red. "It's an outrage. A sacrilege. They don't give a goat's turd about *our* schedule, *our* need for rehearsal. They don't care about tradition. Hell no. All they think about is *their* convenience. Bastards!" She kissed her cat. "Right, Dulcinea? You agree, don't you?"

I sat back and tried to absorb what she'd told me. "Why can't we just refuse?"

"You don't say no to Don Ignacio. Not to Charlie or Santo either."

She plopped back down and began fanning herself. "It's a nightmare, Carmen. We've got to do it. They want us there by one p.m. Please say you'll help me."

I didn't know how to answer. Lafitte and I had planned to leave early Saturday morning, *before* the performance. But now … now, I'd have to face the mobsters again.

"Well?" said Rosa. "Promise me."

The beads at the door separated. A beefy door guard stuck in his head. "Somebody asking for you, he said, nodding toward the door. "Says it's urgent."

"Who?"

"Chink girl."

I hurried out and found Cheena, looking up and down the street like a fugitive.

"What?" I asked, feeling panic in my chest.

"It's Gerhardt. Little bastard disappeared."

"Again? How'd he get away?"

"Who knows? But I'll bet my bolita earnings Otis had something to do with it."

By then I was ready to scream. Gerhardt on the run again, wanting to kill me. Sal also missing, probably wanting to drive a stake into my heart. A Friday performance for the most notorious mobsters in Tampa. What else could go wrong?

"Something else I have to tell you," she said.

"What?"

"Just don't panic on me. Okay?"

"What, Cheena? Tell me."

"Well, it's Hoover … J. Edgar. He read your statement and called Rothman."

"And?"

"He wants you brought in for more questions."

"Now?"

"Not yet. We're busy today with a moonshine bust."

"So when are they taking me in?"

"Tomorrow afternoon. Four p.m. I can't promise the outcome, but if I were you, I'd…"

"You'd what?"

She laid a hand on my shoulder and looked me in the eyes. "Disappear."

I paced around, trying to think. "Maybe I should head to the Greyhound station now."

"Don't even think about it. Hoover ordered Rothman to keep a watch on train and bus stations. They catch you running, it'll be a sure sign of guilt."

"So what am I supposed to do?"

"The performance, Amy. Tomorrow. Do it. I'll drive you there and back, but instead of driving you to the 4 o'clock meeting, I'll drive you to the airstrip."

"Who told you they switched from Saturday to Friday? I just learned myself."

"Natalia told me. She knows everything."

"Is she also a snitch for the Bureau?"

"Look, all I'm going to say is she and Rothman are like, you know…"

"Like an item? Like lovers? Is that how she gets her information?"

"I'm not saying another word. What you have to do is go home, get ready, work it out with your boyfriend, and meet me first thing in the morning. We'll iron out the details."

CHAPTER 71

By the time I kissed Lafitte goodbye on Friday morning and watched him fade into the mist, we had a plan. But what if Hoover decided to bring me in earlier? What if Sal showed up at the performance and wanted revenge for Big Tony? What if, what if…?

Cheena met me for breakfast at the Centro Español and seemed as jittery as I was. No, she told me, Hoover had not called and, no, they'd heard nothing more about Gerhardt or Sal. But, yes, she liked the plan and thought it would work.

"So why are you nervous?" I asked.

"I'm not nervous. Just want to be sure we've thought of everything."

"Have we?"

"This is Ybor, Amy. Things happen."

That wasn't what I wanted to hear, so we talked a while longer and then made our usual rounds—collecting bolita earnings, placing more bets, exchanging our money for gold coins, and trying to act normal. The only thing I did out of the ordinary was give Donnie Sue, Soledad, and Cheena an extra winning number for the Friday bet.

I also gave Cheena my Friday night tickets.

Afterward, she drove me home and used our telephone to call her office.

"No problems," she said. "No word from Hoover."

"What about Gerhardt?"

"Nothing. Maybe he went back to Ohio."

She helped me into my flamenco dress with its crimson ruffles, and at exactly 1 p.m., we drove into the parking lot of Don Ignacio's cigar factory and parked next to a mule and wagon.

The sharp smells of horse manure and tobacco didn't put me at ease. Neither did the trucks, wagons, mules, and people in the parking lot. The factory itself was just another red-brick, box-shaped structure that occupied the better part of a city block. But for me, it loomed up like Dracula's castle. The only thing pretty about it was a large sign over the entrance that showed a young señorita in a worker's hat smoking a cigar and pointing to lettering that read, HAV-A-HAVANA: THE BEST OF CUBAN CIGARS.

Cheena whipped out her pistol, ejected the clip, looked at it, and slapped the clip back in.

"Why did you do that?" I asked.

"There," she said. "On the landing."

I followed her gaze to a cluster of men in dark suits in front of large double doors—the mob bosses of Ybor—the same men I'd confronted in the Columbia Restaurant.

"It's my just-in-case," Cheena said and shoved the pistol back into her shoulder holster.

"Just in case of what?"

She opened her door. "Oh, stop worrying. Couple more hours and you'll be flying away from this damn place with Lafitte. Just wish there was space for me on that airplane."

When Cheena said not to worry, I knew we were in trouble. "I hope you don't expect me to walk like a zombie," I said.

"No, Amy, but it's okay to put a curse on the bastards. Now come on, smile. But watch out for horse shit. You don't won't to ruin your pretty shoes."

"God give me strength," I said and stepped out with my tote bag.

It seemed as if everyone in the parking lot stopped what they were doing—the workers in their white straw hats, the protesters with their placards, a man in a chef's hat selling deviled-crab croquettes, a family of Seminoles, the mobsters at the doorway.

Even the mules stared.

I nodded and smiled and tried to stay calm. *Please dear God. Get me through this.* And I was almost at the landing when Natalia rushed down the steps. Bitchy Natalia, all gypsied up in scarves, headband, jangling bracelets, enormous hoop earrings, and a long flowing skirt in colors ranging from red to purple.

"What took you so long?" she wanted to know. "Rosa was getting worried."

"She said to be here by 1 p.m."

"No, Carmen, we were supposed to *start* at 1 p.m. You don't keep the mob waiting. Rosa's in a tizzy. That's Charlie Wall up there and Santo Trafficante."

"Is Sal here?"

"No one's seen him, but there comes Don Ignacio. He's not happy you're late." She switched from Spanish into Gypsy Caló. "Don't let him take you back to his office, not unless you brought a bottle of mouthwash."

"What does that mean?"

"Do I have to draw you a picture? Now shut up and smile."

I'd only seen Don Ignacio once and remembered him as a portly little man with a balding head. Now, in the daylight, he looked like Alfred Hitchcock with a cigar. He waddled over and planted sloppy kisses on both my cheeks, bringing with him the smells of cigars and aftershave. He ignored Natalia and pointed to Cheena. "Who's she?"

"My bodyguard."

"Tell her to get lost. You're perfectly safe."

"She's also my makeup artist, and she's coming with me."

"*Bien*, Carmen. Whatever you say." He studied my face as if to convince himself I wasn't a ghost, and even ran his sweaty palm over my cheek. "Beautiful. We have so many things to talk about … in my office after the performance. Hmmm?"

If a mule had been near me I'd have mounted up and galloped away.

He took my arm like we were lovers, led me up the steps of the landing, beneath the Hav-a-Havana sign, past the staring mobsters, through the double doors, and into the factory.

CHAPTER 72

Back in my other life, cigar factory culture had been so romanticized you'd think it was the inspiration for the opening scenes of Bizet's *Carmen*. There were plays and academic lectures, and tours of old factories and mobster hangouts. I'd seen pictures in *La Gaceta* and the *Tampa Bay Times*, and colorful artistic depictions by Ferdie Pacheco.

I'd even gone to a wedding inside a converted factory. But nothing prepared me for the vastness of the building, the humidity, the smells, the eye-burning fog of cigar smoke, the bustle, the turning ceiling fans, the workers at their tables, and a lector on an elevated platform, reading loudly from Cervantes, almost shouting in a deep voice: "DO YOU SEE OVER YONDER, FRIEND SANCHO, THIRTY OR FORTY HULKING GIANTS?"

Workers looked up from their tables. But instead of seeing forty hulking giants, they saw the mob bosses of Ybor in their black suits and fedoras, and Rosa in her red outfit and feathers with a cigar in her mouth, and the skinny guitarists in their Spanish hats and black tights, and Natalia in her Gypsy get-up, and me—Carmen—on the arm of a disgusting little man with dandruff on his shoulders and gray hairs hanging out of his ears and nose.

They also saw our vixen squad of faux Moorish girls from the bordello in their *puta* outfits—Jasmine, Jade and Amber, and Fatima, Alisha and Zafron.

Thunderous applause welcomed us, not by handclapping—their hands were too busy rolling cigars—but by foot-stomping. The building vibrated. There were whistles and cheers, and chants of "Tattoo!" and "Carmen!" and it didn't end until Don Ignacio held up both arms to stop them.

"*Ya, basta*," he said. "*No más.*" He clapped his hands for silence.

Back to work they went—men and women, young and old—rolling their cigars, the floor bosses going from table to table like slave-masters on a Roman galleon, the lector reading Don Quixote's adventures in La Mancha.

I hoped we'd get right to the performance and get it over with. Get out of this damn sweatshop, but Don Ignacio said he wanted to show us how cigars were made.

Natalia rolled her eyes. Some of the mobsters merely looked at each other and shrugged. I drew in a deep breath of resignation, and then we followed our waddling host down the center aisle like a bunch of Road Scholar tourists, stopping here and there to listen.

"This is Carlos, our fastest worker. Rolls at least three wheels of cigars a day, sometimes four. Each wheel contains fifty cigars. Watch how he does it."

Carlos smiled and nodded and demonstrated each step:

Cut the leaves into squares.

Wet the square with an aloe solution and roll into a cigar.

Clip the ends with a knife called *chaveta*.

Trim the rough edges and stack the cigars into molds.

He was showing us a mold when Don Miguel spoke again. "Each man keeps five cigars a day for his use. He can either smoke them or sell them."

"What about women?" I asked. "How many cigars do they get?"

"Women get nothing."

"Why not?"

"Because women don't smoke cigars."

Rosa ground out her cigar on the floor. I said, "That's not fair. Women have boyfriends and husbands. What's wrong with giving them five cigars a day?"

Don Ignacio looked like he was going to choke. From the way everyone stared, you'd think I'd dropped an F-bomb. Natalia stepped up beside me. "The women workers despise him," she whispered in Caló. "They'd cut off his dick if they had a chance."

Charlie Wall, who was pretty much the caudillo of Ybor, twirled his finger as if to say, "Get on with it," so we moved along the aisle until Don Ignacio stopped at a table that was occupied by women. None of them looked up. He reached down and rubbed the shoulder of a young girl who looked like she should be in high school.

"This is Imelda," he said, "our fastest female worker. But she's also … well, with child. She'll have to leave when the baby is due."

"Can she come back after the child is born?" I asked.

"Not unless she's got an old *abuela* to look after the kid."

Imelda bent her head a little lower. Natalia touched my arm. "Ask him who knocked her up."

"Why don't you ask him?"

"Because I know. Look how pretty she is. All the pretty girls get regular trips to his office."

Imelda must have felt my outrage because she glanced up and gave me a half-smile, sadness in her eyes. I touched her shoulder, nodded as if to say I understood her grief and would have hugged her if Don Ignacio hadn't pushed us along to the lector's platform.

"Our lector is José Luís. The strongest voice in Ybor. Yesterday he read *The Jungle Girl* by Edgar Rice Burroughs. Most lectors were fired in '29. But we still have ours."

"And do you know why?" Natalia hissed, still speaking Caló. "Because the poor bastard married the boss's ugly sister. In here you pay a price."

Don Ignacio shot us a murderous glance as if he understood Gypsy talk and then marched us past bales of tobacco and other supplies, stopping at a table to show us stack wheels, the cigar press, molds, the glue, and the knife for cutting.

He kept talking in his gravelly voice, telling us the duties of different workers—the women who selected the tobacco, the floor bosses, the assistants, the rollers—and I think if Charlie Wall hadn't twirled a finger, he'd have lectured us on tobacco cultivation.

"One more thing," he said and pointed to a door marked *Gerente*. "My office. It's where I order the supplies and pay the bills."

"And molest the young girls," Natalia hissed beside me.

Mercifully, he did not show us his office, but he squeezed my arm as if to say, "That's where the two of us will soon be, *dulce*. You on your knees."

I pulled loose and backed right into the mobsters. They scattered away like frightened deer. Don Ignacio then asked us if we were ready for the performance.

Everyone nodded, so he led the group back down the aisle.

I lingered just long enough to hand Imelda a twenty-dollar bill, pretending to shake her hand, and caught up with the group at the lector's platform where tables had been cleared.

Everyone moved to their assigned places—Cheena to a position beneath the lector's platform, the mobsters and Don Ignacio to chairs against the wall, Rosa and the vixen squad off to the side, and our two guitarists, Pablo and Diego, to chairs near the platform with their guitars.

"Let's do it," Rosa said. "Let's bring some excitement into this place."

Natalia stepped to the center of the floor and struck a dancer's pose. I was about to do the same until the lector clapped his hands for silence. "Señorita Carmen!" he called out from his perch on the platform. "May I have the honor of your company up here?"

"Do it," Rosa said. "Let them see you."

Up I went with my castanets, holding the railing, praying I wouldn't fall. I'd performed many times and in many places, but never on a lector's platform in a cigar factory and never before an audience of mobsters with guns. And they weren't the only ones. Crazy Natalia had a Derringer in her garter belt. Rosa packed a heater in her purse. Cheena had my Luger and her Colt .45. And for all I knew, the lector, the vixens, and all the workers had guns.

Just one shot, I thought, and … well, this was Florida.

CHAPTER 73

There were more cheers and foot-stomping. The platform vibrated. Fifteen minutes, I thought. Fifteen more minutes and I'd be heading for my rendezvous with Lafitte and his airplane.

"Ladies and gentlemen," said the lector in his deep voice. "Fellow workers, Don Ignacio and distinguished guests. Today I have the great honor, the pleasure, to present to you the most celebrated flamenco performers in America—the dancers, the *cantantes*, and the guitarists from Granada after Midnight. But most of all, I have the honor to present to you the Mata Hari of Ybor City, the one and only CARMENNNNN."

Bizet's *Carmen* came to life in rousing strums and rhythmic stomps. I pulled in a deep breath, muttered, "God give me strength," and sashayed down the steps with my castanets. Maybe this was my last dance in Ybor. Maybe my last dance ever.

Flamenco Abyssinia.

Natalia, who'd stood on the floor like a frozen statue, came to life, stamping her feet and clapping her hands, swaying seductively. Then, just like Selena in my other life, she belted out her opening lines in Caló, as cracked as if she were performing in a thieves' den in Andalusia.

Love, love, love, is a rebellious bird,
That nobody can tame.

She motioned me over—this bitchy woman who made my life miserable—and we did a little fandango around each other, our hands in the air, stamping our feet in a rhythmic dance with the guitars. The vixen squad clapped with us. So did the mobsters, sitting back in the shadows.

One of our guitarists, Pablo, dressed like a torero in his embroidered vest and tight black pants, his hair pulled back in a ponytail, moved onto the floor with us, strumming his guitar and pretending to show a romantic interest in me.

This brought out our vixen squad.

She's not worth your time.

She'll break your heart.

I danced around Pablo in teasing fashion. The protests grew louder, hand fans wagging, thigh flesh flashing. "Get lost," I said to Pablo and gave him a dismissive shove.

He retreated to his chair, looking downtrodden.

Natalia rubbed it in with yet another scorched line from the "Habanera."

The bird you thought you'd caught,

Flapped its wings and flew away.

There was no cape throw-down like the Brooker Creek performance, and no angry wife either, only the story of Carmen the cigar factory worker, the little Gypsy trollop turning up her nose at one suitor and going after another.

Which I did by striking a castanet against my knee and dancing to the other guitarist—Diego—in teasing fashion, clacking the castanets and waving the rose in his face.

Please, dear God, let this go well.

Diego put away his guitar and took the rose, just as we had rehearsed. Pablo kept up the beat with his guitar. Natalia clapped and stomped her feet. I did a roll of castanets in Diego's face.

He stood. Pablo's guitar strummed.

Diego lifted his arms and brought his hands together in rhythmic claps.

"No!" cried the vixens in unity, screwing up their faces in pretend anger.

She's not worth it.

She'll break your heart.

Ruin your life.

This was the moment I dreaded—the moment when Ramón's smoldering Gypsy wife had come after me with a stiletto. The moment my other world had fallen apart.

Please dear God, please.

God must have heard me because there were no angry shouts or curses. Only the clapping, the foot-stomping, Pablo's guitar, Natalia's voice, an occasional "*Olé!*" from the workers, and the swirling vixens, a dazzling display of red scarves, fluttering fans, lace, and ruffles.

How long the performance went on, I do not know, but it was long enough for me to shed my demons and enjoy myself, and long enough to wonder why I'd been so afraid.

It ended with thunderous applause and foot-stomping. There were whistles and cheers, and chants of "Tattoo! Tattoo!" Don Ignacio came waddling over with his arms out as if to hug me, but Rosa got there first. "You've got to do it," she said. "Don't disappoint them."

"Do what?"

"The tattoo. Show them a little flesh. Do it up there, on the lector's platform."

If I'd been closer to the door, I'd have bolted. Flamenco is a professional art-form based on folkloric traditions of southern Spain. It was never a dance to show flesh, and I wasn't going to corrupt it for the benefit of mobsters and cigar workers in 1932 Ybor City.

The cheers and chants grew louder. Rosa kept motioning for me to climb the platform. I bowed, I smiled, I waved, and I might have done a little twirl if it hadn't been for Cheena rushing over with concern all over her face.

"Horn!" she hollered above the racket. "It's urgent."

"A what?"

"Telephone call in the office."

My heart jumped. "For me?"

"For you, Amy. Why else would I be telling you? Don Ignacio's secretary is waiting."

"Did she say who is calling?"

"Only that it's urgent."

CHAPTER 74

Cheena and Don Ignacio's secretary led me down the aisle toward the rear. Little Imelda mouthed "Thank you" as I passed. The other workers stomped their feet and nodded and smiled. I forced myself to nod and smile back, but all I could think of was that phone call. What was so urgent? Was it Lafitte, telling me there'd been a change in plans?

Or was it a warning about Hoover?

"We need to hurry," said the secretary. "The operators cut the call if they don't hear anyone." She pushed open the office door and pointed to a dangling wall phone.

I grabbed the receiver and said, "Hello. This is Carmen."

"Amy, it's me, Dr. Antonio. Something terrible happened. You've got to help me."

He blurted it out: Three men had come to the house with guns … roughed him up … kidnapped Soledad and Donnie Sue and forced them into a big black Packard.

He told me this in a strained voice, pausing for breath.

Cheena, standing beside me, said, "Who is it?"

I shook my head at her and asked Dr. Antonio if he knew the men. He didn't but described them in a way that left no doubt—Sal, Clarence, and one other.

"Did you call the police?"

Cheena's eyes widened. Dr. Antonio said, "They threatened to kill

Soledad if I called the police. Feed her to the gators. That's why I need your help. You may know where they took them. They were talking about a place called Booger Creek."

Booger Creek. Brooker Creek. The place of my nightmares.

"They know about you and Lafitte," said the doctor. "They'll kill him."

I tried to remain calm. My world was collapsing again.

"What?" Cheena said again. "Are you going to tell me or not?"

"Can you find them?" the doctor asked. "You and your friends at the Bureau?"

"I might know where they're taking them. I'll—"

"This is the operator," said a snarky woman's voice on the phone. "Your time is up. It's been ten minutes. Other clients need this line."

The connection went dead. I said, "*Mierda! Mierda! Mierda!*" and was telling Cheena about the call when Don Ignacio stuck his head in the door.

"Come on, Carmen. They're waiting. We're going to take pictures."

By then I could have shot him with my Luger. How could this be happening? Why?

"Tell them I'll be there as soon as I change."

"No, Carmen. We need you in that beautiful dress. We have photographers."

I slammed the door in his face. "Can we go out the back?" I asked Cheena.

"Not a good idea. Otis is out there with other agents."

"Why can't we tell Otis what happened … ask him for the Bureau's help?"

"Are you crazy? Would you listen to yourself? They're not going to invade a swamp based on your word. They'll want maps, plans, reinforcements. It'll take two or three days."

There wasn't time to argue. No time to go back to the house and get my gold and manuscript either. Not even time to change, so I grabbed my bag and followed Cheena out the door.

The workers and everyone else turned to stare. Don Ignacio was waiting at the lector's platform with Rosa, pointing at his watch as if I were one of his workers. Natalia was also there with the guitarists, the vixens, and a photographer with a camera on a tripod. Only three or four mobsters remained, among them Charlie Wall and Santo Trafficante.

Rosa rushed to my side, her face red as her lipstick. "What took so damn long? You can't keep these people waiting. It's disrespectful. What's so important about a phone call?"

"It was Hemingway," I said loud enough for all to hear. "He wants me to audition for another movie. It's in Key West. I need to leave right away."

"You're not going anywhere until we take pictures."

"Fine, I'll give you two minutes."

Don Ignacio mumbled something I didn't get. The photographer positioned us in front of the lector's platform, shifting us here and there, asking us to smile when all I could think about was the tragedy unfolding in Brooker Creek. And he was behind his camera, flashing away when Gerhardt burst through the double doors.

Crazy Gerhardt, waving a pistol.

"Bitch! Fucking whore!"

He aimed his pistol and fired.

CHAPTER 75

A splinter of wood from the lector's platform stung my cheek. There were screams and curses, everyone diving for cover. Cheena whipped out her pistol. I crawled beneath the platform and fumbled around in my tote bag for the Luger, wishing I could burrow into the earth. Then, as if the door to hell had opened, the place turned into a free-fire zone—detonations all around and above me, like a shootout in an old cowboy movie.

Glass shattered. A ceiling fan dropped onto a table, its blade still turning. The photographer's tripod took a hit and went down. Smoke and acrid smells rose up around me.

Please, dear God. Please get me out of this.

How long the madness went on I do not know, but finally, the shooting slacked and turned into a single shot here and another there.

"*Ya basta!*" someone yelled. "Stop the shooting. He's dead."

It grew quiet. I lifted my head and peered through the haze. The mobsters were scrambling out the door in their black suits, ducking and weaving like soldiers in a war zone. Rosa and her crew of vixens and guitarists also dashed out. Other workers began crawling out from beneath tables, coughing, snorting, and brushing themselves off.

"Cheena!" I yelled.

No answer.

Where was she? I tossed the Luger into my bag, wiped a smear of blood from my cheek, and crawled out in time to see little Imelda standing over

Don Ignacio with a small pistol. He lay on the floor in a pool of blood.

So did Gerhardt.

Imelda caught my eye, pocketed the pistol, and hurried out the door.

"Cheena!" I called out again. "Where are you?"

Natalia appeared at my side, her hair disheveled. "She's over there."

Cheena was sitting on the floor, gasping for breath, her back against a table leg, her shirt stained with blood, her pistol on the floor, her hand tight against her chest.

"He got me," she managed to say, her voice weak. "But I got him."

I dropped down beside her and took her hand. "Let me look."

"No, Amy. It's too late. Go … go before Otis gets here."

She coughed and spit up blood. "Pocket," she stammered. "Keys … car keys. Take the keys. Go. Please. Don't let them get you. It'll be bad. Hoover will…"

Her words trailed off. I reached into her pocket and found the keys. She coughed again and spit up more blood. "Cigarette case too. Tickets inside … bolita. My numbers, yours."

She clasped my dress. The light in her eyes was growing dim. My best friend in Ybor was slipping away, maybe my best friend ever. I held her, the tears running down my cheek, and I didn't turn her loose until Natalia pulled me up.

"Come on girl. She's gone. You need to get out of here."

"But what about her?"

"The Bureau will take care of her."

With tears in my eyes, I made the Sign of the Cross and trudged out the door with my bag, my ears still ringing from gunfire. This was the second time I'd done Bizet's *Carmen* at a flamenco performance, and the second time disaster had struck. That performance was cursed.

I was cursed.

A crowd had gathered near the entrance. There were stares and animated conversation, and words like "bolita wars" and "gangsters" buzzing around like angry hornets.

We pushed through them. Sirens wailed in the distance. Dogs barked.

Every branch of a spreading live oak in front was filled with kids. People perched atop cars and wagons, and still more came trotting down the street to see what the fuss was about.

I offered the keys to Natalia. "Here. You drive."

"Are you crazy? I'm not going with you. Just go. Get away from here. The G-men will be here any second. You're burned toast if they catch you."

I hastened around a mule and wagon, hopped into the driver's seat of Cheena's Model-A, and stuck the key in the ignition.

The passenger door opened and Imelda jumped in beside me—little Imelda with her protruding belly and sad Cuban eyes with the pistol still in her hand.

"No," I said. "Get out."

"But they'll send me to the chair."

"For what, *mija?*"

"For killing Don Ignacio."

"No one will know. Get rid of the pistol. Throw it in the bay."

I yanked it from her and stuffed it into my bag.

"Where are we going?" she asked.

"You're going home. Keep your mouth shut. Anybody could have shot him."

She broke down in sobs. Worse, people were gathering around the car.

"Shit!" I said again and handed her the bolita tickets Cheena had given me. Tickets that would earn three thousand dollars at midnight.

"Here, *mija*, these are winning tickets for tonight. Cash them in tomorrow."

"How do you know they're winning tickets?"

"Because I know. Because I have inside information. Now go, get out and go home."

"I want to go with you."

"God-dammit, girl! Get out before I shoot you."

She hopped out and trotted away, crying. Sirens were getting louder.

I turned the key in the ignition and tried to remember how Cheena started it.

Open the fuel line. But where?

There, under the dash.

Now what?

There were three levers on the steering column.

I pushed them all down.

The choke. Where was the choke?

There, a knob on the dash. I opened it and closed it.

Starter? Where was the starter? Not on the dash. Maybe the floor.

Yes, that little pedal on the right side of the accelerator.

Please, dear God, let it start.

I stomped on it. The car lurched forward. People jumped out of the way.

The car didn't start.

Shit! I'd forgotten to depress the clutch.

Or put the gear in neutral.

I did both and hit the starter again. It whined. I choked it again. I jiggled the levers on the steering column. I smelled gas. The engine sputtered but still wouldn't start.

A carload of local cops barreled into the parking lot. The cops jumped out and rushed inside. Then a black Ford wheeled into the lot and stopped behind me.

I panicked. I pounded on the steering wheel. I cursed the car. I slammed my feet again and again on the starter. It still wouldn't start.

The door swung open and there stood Otis and other agents in their dark suits and fedoras. A crucifix hung from Otis's shirt.

"Get out of this car, woman. Get the hell out!"

CHAPTER 76

They dragged me out and cuffed me right there in front of a crowd of Carmen admirers.

"Well, take a gander at this," said Alabama. "Three pistols in her bag."

He sniffed one of the pistols. "Yep, been fired."

It took me a moment to realize there should be two pistols in my bag, my Luger and Imelda's Derringer. Not three. How did a third one get there?

Before I could protest, the crowd of onlookers surged forward, a sea of angry faces, cursing and protesting in Spanish.

"*Malditas agentes federales!*"

"*Sueltala!*" Turn her loose.

An old man in a straw hat and grizzled face pushed forward and spoke in tortured English. "She *inocente*. Not do nothing. Why you take her?"

"She killed two of our agents," Otis said.

"Three," Alabama said.

Otis took my arm and shoved me toward his black Ford, and was reaching for the door handle when Natalia rushed up in her Gypsy outfit, accompanied by a local cop. "What is going on?" she shouted in Otis's face. In Spanish. "I saw the whole thing. She didn't shoot anyone."

The cop translated.

"Doesn't matter," Otis answered. "Director Hoover said to bring her in."

Natalia argued with him, getting louder, her face red, and when it was obvious she was losing the battle, she jumped into the back seat of his Ford.

"God-damn Gypsy!" Otis said. "Get your ass out of my car."

"Watch your mouth," Alabama said. "Her and Rothman are like…"

Otis pleaded with her to get out. The local cop translated. She wouldn't budge, saying she was going with me to the Bureau to explain to Rothman.

The local cop got into a shouting match with Otis, claiming jurisdiction. There was pushing and shoving, and it didn't end until Otis agreed to let Natalia go with us. "In the front seat," he said. "Alabama needs to sit in back with your sister."

Natalia climbed over the seat into the front. Alabama pushed me into the place she'd been sitting and slid in beside me. Otis started the car and away we went, horn blaring, onlookers pounding the car with their hands, shouting "*No hay derecho!*"

"Fucking spics," Otis mumbled. "Can't even speak English."

"Bet your ancestors didn't speak English either," Alabama said.

"My ancestors are Swedish."

"They speak English in Sweden?"

"Just shut up and keep an eye on the Gypsy."

"I ain't looking at her. Hell, no! You saw what she did to Gerhardt and Big Tony."

Natalia, her face still contorted in rage, twisted around and spoke to me in Caló. "You're screwed if they take you in. Hoover already wants blood. It'll be a lot worse when he learns you were in the middle of another shooting."

"I didn't shoot anyone. You saw what happened. There were witnesses."

"Ha, listen to yourself, girl. You're Gypsy. They'll blame you no matter what. You better start conjuring up some witchcraft."

"Like what?"

"You know how to use a gun, don't you?"

"I don't have a gun."

"Look under your feet. I put my little stocking gun there."

I glanced down and felt it with my foot, beneath the floor mat.

"Better hurry," she said. "We're only five or six minutes away."

Otis slammed his hand on the dashboard. "God-dammit to hell, Alabama, I'm trying to drive! Can't you make'em shut up with that foreign shit?"

"No, Otis, I ain't about to antagonize them. Just step on it."

Otis sped up, passing trucks and wagons and blowing his horn. I needed to do something fast, so I spoke to Alabama—in English. "Would you please do me a favor?"

He sat straight up. "What the hell? You speak English?"

Natalia twisted around. Otis looked in his rearview mirror.

"I speak every language in the world," I said, trying to sound sinister. "Witches have that power." I kicked the back of Otis's seat. "How about that, Otis. Want to talk to me in Swedish?"

He didn't answer so I kept talking, saying I was from Romania. "Place called Transylvania. Maybe you've heard of it, Otis. It's where Count Dracula lives."

"What is going on?" Natalia asked. "Are you speaking English?"

"Just play along," I answered in Caló. "I'm trying to spook them."

I turned again to Alabama. "I asked you to do me a favor."

"Don't do nothing for her," Otis said. "She'll hex you."

I kicked his seat again. "Shut up, Otis, or you'll get the hex." I turned back to Alabama. "Are you going to answer me or do I have to do something drastic?"

"What do you want?"

"A cigarette."

He reached into his pocket.

"Not your cigarettes. I want mine. They're in my cigarette case."

"Where?"

"In my tote bag … next to that pistol you planted."

He dug around and took out my iPhone, still in its leather case.

"Notice how heavy it is?" I said. "Do you know why?"

"Why?"

"Look at me and I'll tell you."

"I ain't looking at you. Why is it so heavy?"

"Because it's magic. The whole world is inside that little case. Open it and I'll show you."

"How does it open?"

"That little button on the side? That one. Press it."

"Don't do it," said Otis. "It could blow up in your face."

I kicked his seat again. "This is the last time I'm warning you, Otis." I turned back to Alabama. "If I wanted to hurt you, you'd already be dead. Now press the button."

He pressed it. The Apple Icon appeared. He yelped and dropped it on the floor.

"It won't bite," I said and scooped it up with my cuffed hands.

"What's going on?" Otis asked from the front. "What's she doing?"

"Her cigarette case lit up."

"Not a cigarette case," I said. "It's my magic wand. Let me show you."

I entered my four-digit code. All the familiar icons appeared. In color. News, settings, email, stocks, weather, calendar. Alabama's eyes widened. I held it up and did a selfie with him beside me. Then I showed him. "Look, it's us."

"Holy mother of God! How did you do that?"

"Witchcraft and vampires. I can even make it talk. I can turn it into a snake or a gun. I can make it blow up this car. And that's what I'm going to do if Otis doesn't drive me to Miami."

It grew so quiet I could hear traffic on the street.

"What's it going to be, Otis? Miami or BOOM?"

"You're bluffing."

"Oh, yeah? You think so? Are you willing to take that chance? All I have to do is press this little button and turn all of you into ashes. Not me, though. I'm already dead." *Deaaad.*

"What is going on?" Natalia asked. "What are you saying?"

I told her I was going to scream and toss the cell into Alabama's lap, hoping he'd panic long enough for me to grab the Derringer, and was asking her to scream as well when Otis slammed on the brakes. "Shit!" he cried.

Ahead of us, directly in the middle of 7th Avenue, marched the Ladies Sobriety Society of Ybor City—drums beating, placards waving, the ladies chanting in unison.

"LIPS THAT TOUCH ALCOHOL WILL NEVER TOUCH MINE!"

"Go around them!" Alabama said, leaning forward. "Go! Get us to hell out of here."

And that was when I scooped up the Derringer.

I thumbed back the hammer. It clicked. I poked it in Alabama's face.

"Magic," I said. "My little toy just turned into a gun."

He flung up his hands. Otis didn't notice. He was too busy trying to maneuver through the demonstrators. Couldn't hear us either because of the drums and chants.

"Do you want to live?" I asked Alabama.

"Yes, ma'am."

"Then I want you to take out your pistol and put it on the floor. Slooowly."

He did as I said.

"Now, I want you to tell Otis to stop. Then you open the door, jump out and run away."

"You promise not to hex me?"

"I'll hex you if you don't tell Otis to stop this car this second."

"Stop!" he yelled at Otis.

"What?"

"Just stop the goddamn car! Now!"

Otis stopped. Alabama bounded out and took off running. Otis twisted around and stared into the barrel of Alabama's big black ugly Colt .45 semi-automatic.

"If you want to live," I told him, "you better turn this car around and head west."

CHAPTER 77

Otis made a U-turn and on we drove, heading west. Natalia asked what was going on and what I had told them in English and where we were going.

"I'll explain later," I answered in Caló. "Right now I want you to act like I'm also holding you hostage. Otherwise, they'll know you helped me."

I pointed the pistol in her face and switched into English.

"Listen, bitch, I know you work for these bastards."

"What?" she answered, her voice hysterical. "What are you doing?"

"Take out his gun and toss it into the back."

I said these words in both English and Caló.

Natalia took his pistol and threw it into the back seat. Otis kept both hands on the steering wheel. "Good," I said. "Now I want you to reach in his pockets for the cuff keys."

"I don't have the cuff keys," Otis said.

"Where are they?"

"Alabama has them. Check my pockets. You'll see."

I said, "Shit!" a few times, kicked the back of his seat, and asked Natalia if we were heading in the direction of Tarpon Springs.

"What's in Tarpon Springs?"

"Stop asking questions. Just make sure we're going the right way."

Otis drove on in silence. Commercial buildings and residential neighborhoods gave way to open fields, some with grazing cattle and horses, others planted with corn. Here and there we passed red Burma-

Shave signs with their jingles:

Several million/ modern men/ will never go back/ to the brush again/ Burma-Shave.

We crossed a bridge and came to a shantytown on the right—shelters of cloth, tin, and wood, as well as wagons and mules, battered jalopies and trucks, and kids and adults in tattered clothing. "Here," I said to Otis. "Stop right here."

"You can't be serious."

"I'm dead serious. Stop the damn car."

No sooner had we rolled to a stop than we were set upon by barking dogs and ragged kids. Others came out in the open—skinny women in granny bonnets, bearded men in bib overalls, some of them with shotguns.

"This is not a good idea," said Otis. "They'll think we're here to confiscate hooch."

"That's your problem." I shoved the pistol against the back of his head. "Here's what we're going to do. Are you listening, Otis?"

"Yes, ma'am."

"Strip off your jacket. Also your shoulder holster."

"Why?"

"Because if you don't, something ugly will happen."

He took off his jacket and holster.

"Now, I want you to leave the motor running and step outside. Do not try to take the keys or I'll blow a hole in your head. Understand?"

"Yes, ma'am."

"Now get out and walk away."

"What about your sister?" he asked.

"She's not my sister. She's a hostage."

"Can I have my pistol back?"

"Sorry, Otis, it's mine now."

"You're not going to hex me?"

"Not if you get out right now. Go, before I change my mind."

He stepped out into the midst of begging kids and trotted off toward the shanties.

Natalia slid into the driver's seat, and away we went.

CHAPTER 78

Natalia drove and talked, asking who I was, what the iPhone was, and if I really had supernatural powers. "Who the hell are you, Amy?"

"It doesn't matter. The important thing is for you to get back and tell Rothman what happened at the factory. Let him know I'm innocent."

"Innocent? You kidnapped two federal agents. You took their guns and stole their car."

"Desperation. I didn't have a choice."

"How am I supposed to get back to Ybor? We're going the wrong way."

"Just shut up and drive."

We turned right, passed more Burma Shave signs—*You'll love your wife/ you'll love her paw/ you'll even love your mother-in-law/ Burma-Shave*—and came to an open field that was probably Raymond James Stadium in 2019. There was no traffic, nothing but a windmill and a couple of oak trees under which cattle had gathered.

"Let's do it here," I said.

"Do what?"

"Take off these cuffs. They're hurting me."

She pulled onto the shoulder and stopped. "How?"

"Pistols. We've got six of them."

"You're going to shoot off the cuffs?"

"No, you are."

"Are you fucking crazy? I've never shot a pistol. Why don't you make that gadget do it?"

"That gadget is a cigarette case with a mirror. Nothing more. Now, come on."

I chose the Luger and led Natalia across an open ditch through knee-high weeds to a fencepost. Angry clouds rose in the distance. Thunder rumbled. Cows trotted over as if expecting us to feed them. I held out my cuffed hands to Natalia. "Look, I'll hold the links across the top of the fence post. All you have to do is shoot off the middle link."

"Are you sure?"

"Just don't shoot my hand. Don't shoot a cow either."

"What about me? I could get shot."

"No, Natalia, you won't get shot." I showed her how to use the pistol. Still, she whined and complained. I asked her to wrap one of her scarves around my head and eyes as protection from splintering wood. "Put another scarf around your ears," I said.

"What about my eyes?"

Back across the ditch I went, back to the black Ford and my tote bag in the rear seat. I found Carmen's sunglasses and trekked back to Natalia. By then, the entire herd of cattle had gathered around the fence post, chewing cud and infusing the air with unpleasant odors.

I waved my arms. "Get away from here! Go!"

They didn't budge.

We moved to another fence post. The cows followed.

"*Puta bovines,*" Natalia said. "Just shoot one of them."

"No, Natalia. We will not shoot a cow."

"They'll get shot anyway if we use that fence post."

She was right, so we trekked a short distance down the road to a Burma Shave sign. The cows followed. I dropped to my knees. Natalia began wrapping the scarf around my head.

"Wait," I said. "Don't forget to pull back that thing on the top."

"What thing?"

"This one. It positions a bullet. Otherwise, the pistol won't shoot."

"I don't like guns."

"Dammit, Natalia." I took the gun from her, pulled back the lever, and let it snap into place. "Don't touch the trigger until you're ready to shoot. Okay?"

"Would you stop saying okay? It's not Spanish."

"Just shut up and do what I tell you. Okay?"

"Fine, but I don't like it." She wrapped the scarf around my head. "Suppose I miss?"

By then I was ready to pound her to death with the pistol. "Damn it, Natalia, just do it!" I handed the Luger to her, put my hands across the top of the Burma Shave sign, and spread them as far apart as possible.

Natalia leaned over me. I held my breath and closed my eyes.

BANG!

Dirt, debris, and splinters flew up against the scarf.

"Missed," she said, and burst into laughter.

"What's so funny?"

"The cows. They're running."

"Fine, the cows are running. Let's try it again."

"Hold on. My glasses are messed up."

She cleaned her glasses. "Do I need to pull back that thingy at the top again?"

"No, Natalia. It's ready."

She leaned over me again, bracelets jangling, and fired a second shot. More splinters and debris flew up against the scarf, but this time it worked. I yanked off the scarf and waved my free arms over my head. "Thank God. Let's get going."

I stripped off my flamenco dress, right there on the side of a road, beneath a sky that was getting darker, and changed into my flared riding britches, walking shoes and a pullover, all of which I'd brought in my bag. For good measure, I strapped on Otis's shoulder holster and tried to stuff the Luger in it. It didn't exactly fit, but it was good enough. Then I examined the two Derringers. They were identical, both with double barrels.

"Does Rothman know you carry a Derringer?" I asked Natalia.

"Of course he knows. He gave it to me."

Without thinking, I handed her Imelda's empty Derringer—the one that had shot Don Ignacio—and kept the loaded one for myself.

"We need to go," I said and climbed into the driver's seat.

The motor was still running. I figured out the gears, popped the clutch, and sped away, trying to get the heavy feel of driving without power steering or power brakes. Rain began to fall, heavy here, light there.

"Why are we going to Tarpon Springs?" Natalia asked again.

"Not we. I told her about the phone call from Dr. Antonio.

"And you're going alone? Are you crazy? They'll kill you if they catch you."

"They're not going to catch me."

"So what are you going to do … zap them with that little gadget?"

"I'll figure it out when I get there. What I need you to do is get back to Ybor and tell Rothman to send out a team of agents." I explained the Brooker Creek location as best I could.

"How am I getting back to Ybor?"

"Just wait."

We crossed a wooden bridge over a misty little bayou, passed around a truck with wobbly wheels, drove past a couple of clapboard houses, and stopped at a run-down Standard Oil station at the intersection with Hillsborough. Billboards for Coca-Cola and Lucky Strike hung near the screen door, and a dirty pickup was parked on the side. An old man in greasy overalls and straw hat came ambling out. "Fill'er up?" he asked. "Sixteen cents a gallon."

"No gasoline. I'm looking for someone to drive my sister to Ybor."

By then Natalia was outside the car in her swirling skirt with scarves, bracelets, and big hoop earrings. The old man stared at her. "She Gypsy?"

I waved a five-dollar bill in his face. "Can you drive her or not?"

"I gotta fire up the truck," he said. "Do you need a Coke?"

"Two, and make it quick. We're in a hurry."

Until that day, I couldn't stand Natalia, but if it hadn't been for her I'd be in cuffs at that damn post office, waiting for Hoover and possibly a date with Old Sparky. I took out my notepad and jotted down four bolita numbers at four different houses. "Here," I said and handed her the paper with a twenty-dollar bill. "These are tonight's winning numbers. Guaranteed."

"How do you know they're winning numbers?"

"Inside information. Now go."

"Amy?" she said.

"What?"

"Get Sal. Put a bullet in the bastard's head. Do it for Carmen."

CHAPTER 79

A handmade sign on a gate read PRIVATE PROPERTY: NO TRESPASSING. Was this the Brooker Creek entrance? Just to be sure, I drove past and kept looking, but there were only dense woods and a dirt road so narrow that cars would have to pull over to let another one pass.

I turned around, went back, stopped at the gate, and stepped outside with my Luger.

A choir of Mockingbirds serenaded me from the trees. Crickets chirred and frogs croaked, but there were no humans, no traffic, and no lookouts, only a rutted trail beyond the fence.

Do it, I told myself. But how? James Bond would go barging in, get captured, escape, save Soledad and Donnie Sue, get laid, then blow the place to pieces with a secret weapon. I wasn't Bond, and I didn't have a secret weapon, but I had a Luger, a Derringer, and three Colt .45 semi-automatics. I lightened my tote bag, keeping only my flamenco dress, currency, the Luger with an extra clip, and a few gold coins. Then I stuffed the Derringer into my garter belt and climbed through the fence.

Now, just like the time I'd driven my Prius down this same creepy trail, there were hoots and screeches in the trees and an occasional flash of lightning.

I pushed on, looking this way and that for Lafitte's airstrip, stopping here and there to listen and to watch for snakes or other hidden dangers. Deerflies swarmed around me. Spider webs got in my face. Thunder rumbled, and every shadow loomed as an armed moonshiner.

Then I heard the crows.

The airstrip? I hurried around a bend and there it was—a long narrow clearing. Lafitte's airplane wasn't there. Neither was Virgil's wagon, only the windsock, the runway, the circling crows, and a tin-roof storage shed on which vultures roosted.

Was Popsicle there? Maybe I could I enlist his help.

But suppose Clarence and Sal were in the shed, waiting for Lafitte to land?

Or for me?

The clouds grew darker. The crows and vultures scattered. Then the first drops of rain began to fall. The clearing was only about fifty feet across, so I dashed along the foliage, trying to stay in the shadows, and reached the place I'd first met Lafitte. Here, in the bushes next to the trail beneath the trees. Lafitte in his boots and aviator jacket.

Run away with me and be my bride/ and we will into the heavens fly…

A crack of thunder told me it wasn't a good idea to remain in the open, not in Florida, so I followed the same path I'd taken with Lafitte to the back of the shed.

Rain drummed on the tin roof. I pressed against the shed, beneath the overhang to escape the rain, and peeped through the cracks, hoping to see Soledad and Donnie Sue.

No one. Only a greasy dirt floor, tools, buckets, barrels, and the smell of motor oil. The door was unlocked. I stepped inside, grabbed a blanket, and within seconds I was back on the trail.

Raindrops spattered around me. Enormous trees loomed up like monsters, covered in creepers and Spanish moss. Was this the place I'd almost killed Clarence—behind that tree?

Bastard! I should have driven the stake into his heart.

A twig snapped. Something moved in the brush … and then a hideous shriek seemed to shake the surrounding foliage, so loud the forest fell silent.

I turned this way and that with the Luger. Was it Clarence? Was it a beast? Or was it the girl of the swamp, warning me of hidden danger? The racket of the jungle came back, the chirrs and hoots and screeches, but around me there was only the trees, the falling rain, and a rutted trail.

On I went, one foot in front of the other, pistol in hand, my senses on full alert. The pungent sweetness of wood smoke wafted in the air. Yes, that had to be blaze at the moonshine still.

Or the fire under Pearl's wash pot.

A few more paces and there it was—clapboard siding and rusty tin roof, barely visible through foliage and rain that was dripping through the trees.

I pulled the blanket over my head for camouflage and crept through a tangle of palmettos and vines. Every struggle brought down torrents of water. Every vine became a python ready to drop on my head. But at last I was close enough to see Virgil's wagon and the smokehouse. I stepped closer, holding the Luger in front. Now I could see Pearl's wash pot and clothes line and the black workers at the whiskey still in their overalls, working in spite of the rain.

A car was there too. Sal's Packard, glistening with dampness and luxury. There had to be another road, I thought. No way a Packard could maneuver though the trail I'd taken.

The rain stopped the way it started, with a trickle. Frogs came to life. I eased closer to the shack, moving from tree to tree like a combat soldier— pistol in hand, my tote bag strapped around my neck, the blanket over my head.

Did it have a back window? Yes, and there were bushes against it.

Sweat trickled down my ribs. My heart beat faster. I didn't want to shoot anybody, but if someone was going to get shot, I wanted it to be Sal or Clarence.

At last, I reached the bushes next to the window. Easy, I told myself. Blend with the shrubbery. No sudden movements.

I took a deep breath and peeped in.

Donnie Sue and Soledad sat on the floor, their hands tied to the bed— Soledad with her ponytail and red ribbon, and Donnie Sue with her battered face.

The window was open an inch or two. Open it more, I told myself. Get their attention. Smuggle them out. Get them back to the Ford.

I transferred the Luger to my left hand, put my right beneath the window, and eased it up slowly. Soledad saw me first and elbowed Donnie Sue. I put a finger to my lips. Their faces lit up with hope. But was anyone with them? I couldn't tell from where I stood.

"Watch out for that snake!"

Where Virgil came from I don't know. But there he stood in his checkered red shirt and bib overalls, pointing to the ground with a silly grin on his face.

"Clarence!" he hollered. "She's here. Clarence!"

I bolted, but hadn't gone more than a few paces when men with guns stepped out in front of me: Clarence's black workers, all bearded and grubby and smelling of swamp and sweat.

Clarence was there too, in boots, hat, and flared riding pants, his right hand bandaged.

He yanked the Luger out of my hand.

"Well, I'll be damned!" he said. "Me and you got a little score to settle."

CHAPTER 80

I thought he'd pummel me with his fists. He didn't. I thought he'd frisk me and find my phone, gold coins, Luger clip, and Derringer. Didn't do that either. Instead, he turned to the man closest to him and shoved him in the chest.

"Stupid son-bitch! Ain't you the boss? Wadn't you on lookout?"

The man backed away, fear and hatred in his face. Clarence followed him into the group, pushing this one and that one, balling up his fists and calling them every foul name in the English language.

Just shoot him, I wanted to yell, and I'd have shot him myself if I could get to the Derringer beneath my britches. "Don't blame them," I said. "They saw the G-men."

He swung around. "What did you say?"

"The feds. You don't think I'm so stupid to come here alone, do you?"

He glanced into the woods. "I don't see nobody."

"Go see for yourself. They were chasing me." I held up my hands to show him the broken cuffs. "See. I stole their car and got away. They chased me here. I was you, I'd be running."

He yelled to his men to get into the woods and hold them off.

"I ain't shooting no G-man," said the worker he'd first poked in the chest.

"Me neither," said another. "We're colored. They'll hang the lot of us."

The others chimed in, nodding in agreement. Clarence lit into them again, his face red, reminding them they worked for him and they'd god-damn well better do what he god-damn ordered or he'd lynch their sorry black asses, and he was still assailing them with curses and n-words when they backed away and melded into the forest with their guns.

"You work for me!" he raged. "I better hear some shooting."

Whether they were obeying or running, I don't know. All I know is he shoved me around the cabin toward the front, cursing and yelling for someone named Benito. Chickens scattered. Workers at the still looked up. We passed around Virgil's wagon, ducked beneath sheets on the clothesline, and came to the screen door.

"Benito, get your big ass out here. Hurry! Bring the girls."

The screen door opened with a creak. Out came scrawny little Sal in a dark suit in spite of the heat and humidity. He took one look and backed away as if I had leprosy. Behind him came a heavy-set man who might have been Big Tony's brother.

"What's going on?" he asked in accented English.

"I said get the girls, god-dammit. G-men might be coming."

Benito disappeared into the shack. There was screaming and protesting, and I was vaguely aware of Pearl staring from the wash pot.

Benito shoved Soledad and Donnie Sue out the door, both of them crying, Donnie Sue with swollen eyes, Soledad with a ripped blouse. Pearl came trotting over with her stirring stick. "Don't you hurt them girls. They suffered enough."

Clarence pointed the Luger at her. "Get back to your god-damn wash pot."

"Where you taking us?" Donnie Sue demanded to know.

"Just get in the car."

"Not if you taking us to the gator hole."

"I said get in the god-damn car!" He aimed his pistol.

"I ain't going nowhere with you, Clarence. You gonna shoot me, shoot me right here in front of God and everybody. That'll bring them G-men running."

"She's right," I said. "You should go while you can."

Clarence glanced into the woods again. Sal also looked terrified, and I was hoping they might get in the car and drive away until Benito said to Clarence, "Don Salvatore not to want blood in his car. We do it at the hole, get rid of bodies."

Soledad didn't understand, but Donnie Sue did. She set up such a fuss that Clarence knocked her to the ground. Then he turned to Benito. "Get the car. Back it up here."

Benito took out his keys and struck off for the Packard, and he was at the door, opening it when a bloodcurdling screech pierced the air.

Everyone turned, and there stood the girl of the swamp.

CHAPTER 81

In the past, she always appeared and disappeared in seconds. This time she just stood there, almost luminescent against the darkness of the forest, her hair wet and scraggly, her shapeless nightgown hugging the ground, her face white as death.

She lifted an arm and pointed at Sal.

The workers scattered. Benito also disappeared. Sal backed away, whimpering like a frightened dog, looking from her to me as if wondering how there could be two of us.

She came toward us, walking as gingerly as the dancer she was, closer and still closer.

Sal backed away so fast he tripped over the wash pot. It overturned, splashing him with scalding water. He screamed and cursed. The girl kept coming. Sal regained his feet, but only to back into the sheets on the clothesline. Sheets flailed and flew every which way. Sal disentangled himself, whipped out his pistol and began shooting.

Clarence also fired at her, and that was when Pearl struck with her wash pole.

The first blow caught Clarence on his broken hand. He yelped. The pistol went flying. The second blow caught him on the head. He went down. Then Pearl was on him like a predator. Blows to the head and body, blow after blow, pounding him so hard that her red bandana fell off her head and blood splashed from Clarence's wounds.

I dashed for the Luger. Donnie Sue got there first, even with her hands tied in front. Clarence was probably already dead, but Donnie Sue fired into his body anyway and kept on firing and screaming until the Luger was empty.

Sal's pistol was also empty. He flung it at Carmen. The pistol went right through her and landed on the ground. Carmen turned to me as if to say, "He's yours now," and dissipated into the damp air and smoke.

By then I'd fished the Derringer out of my garter belt. "I'm over here," I said to Sal, trying to sound sinister. "See." I thumbed back the hammer on the Derringer and began walking toward him the way Carmen had done.

"No!" he cried, "Go away."

I thought he'd bolt. Instead, he picked up an ax and charged like an angry bull.

My first bullet caught him in the chest.

He stopped and looked as if he could hardly believe a ghost had shot him.

The second bullet struck him in the head, just above the eyes.

He collapsed next to Pearl's wash pot, jerked a few times, and lay still.

"May God forgive me," I said and sank to the ground.

CHAPTER 82

In time, the sounds of the outside world came back—the birds and crickets, the frogs. The whimpering and sobbing of Donnie Sue, Pearl, Soledad, and even Virgil. A gust of wind whipped the sheets on the wash-line, and then a little green and yellow canary alighted on a tree limb and chirped as if celebrating the demise of two bad men.

It was over. Or was it? I turned to Donnie Sue. "What happened to Benito?"

She shrugged. Virgil pointed toward the Packard. "Last I seen of him, he was over there, behind the car. He might still be there."

All of us stared at the Packard. Even the canary stared. Benito had left in such a hurry that he'd left the keys in the door.

I took the Luger from Donnie Sue, popped in the extra clip from my pocket, and was glancing all around when there was a movement back near the whiskey still.

"That might be him!" cried Donnie Sue. "Shoot him."

I aimed the pistol and was about to fire when Popsicle stepped into the open, looking like a scary Apache warrior with his Bowie knife, long greasy locks, and earrings. He wiped blood off the knife, pointed back toward the bushes, and made a throat-slashing gesture. Then he came over and said something I didn't understand.

Soledad, who until that moment had remained silent, spoke up. "He says if we're looking for a big man in a black suit, his body is back there."

Donnie Sue raised her arms to heaven like a holy roller, praising Jesus,

God, and the Holy Ghost. Soledad crossed herself and mumbled thanks to her Cuban gods. Popsicle cut the ropes off their wrists. And I just stood there a moment, all wet and filthy, still shaking, listening to that stupid canary sing. Now all I had to do was get to the airstrip and wait for Lafitte.

"Are the G-men really coming?" Donnie Sue asked. "Or was you just bluffing?"

"It wasn't a bluff. They could be here any minute."

"Shit, we better git rid of them bodies. Ain't gonna be purty if they find a bunch of coloreds with guns standing over corpses of white men."

She was right. Some of the workers had already drifted back, including the armed men Clarence had pushed around. One of them spit on his corpse. Another kicked him. Popsicle dragged Benito's body out of the bushes and laid it next to the other two.

"Let's haul'em to the gator hole," said Donnie Sue. "No bodies, no evidence."

"How far to the gator hole?" I asked.

"Five minutes at most. We can haul them in the Packard."

"Why can't Virgil haul them in the wagon?"

"It'll take Virgil a hour just to find the damn mule. He might even forget what's he's looking for." She tapped her head with a finger. "He ain't right in the head."

She walked over to the Packard and yanked open the door, letting out the smell of cigars. I thought she'd drive, but she turned to me. "Git in and crank it up, girl. Back it to them corpses."

"Why can't you drive it? I need to get to the airstrip."

"I don't know how to drive this damn monster."

I climbed in and sank into plush leather seats. Everything about it was luxury, the shiny knobs, the beautiful two-tone paneling, a hood that stretched out before me. I inserted the key, fiddled with the gears, pedals, switches, and levers and soon had it pulsing like a NASCAR engine.

Reverse? Where was it? Here. I backed it to the bodies.

Donnie Sue didn't want to stain her expensive new possession with blood, so she ran inside and came back with Clarence's Klan hood, sheets, and blankets.

Virgil, Popsicle, and Pearl loaded the bodies. Soledad said she was going to the airstrip with Popsicle. I gave her keys to Otis's car, and told her I'd be there as soon as we dumped the bodies. We hugged. I thanked her for all she and the doctor had done for me, and had tears in my eyes when I hopped back into the Packard with Donnie Sue, Virgil, and three dead men.

CHAPTER 83

The trail was more solid than the one I'd followed from the gate, but as we approached the hole, the woods grew dark and spooky, with massive trees, overhanging limbs draped in creepers, and swamp off to the side. The corpses were also reeking of foul things, even with the windows open, and I had this horrible feeling one of them would groan and come to life.

"Don't go too fast," said Donnie Sue. "The trail ends at the hole."

She related the horrors of the place—trees that sank into the hole, lights in the water, man-eating alligators, the screams of the victims. "Some people say you can see that girl of the swamp here, but I ain't never seen her."

"What do you mean, never seen her?"

"Never, not once."

"Not back there a little while ago … at the cabin?"

"What kind of question is that? Maybe Sal seen her, the way he was acting all crazy."

I asked Virgil if he'd seen her. He said he hadn't seen her either. And the more I thought about it, the more I recalled that no one had mentioned her, not Soledad when she was talking with Popsicle, and not Pearl. Was I the only one other than Sal and Clarence?

"What about the screech?" I asked.

"Screech owl. Woods are full of them. Scares the dookey outa you. That might be why Sal went crazy on us." She pointed ahead. "Look, there it is. Slow down."

I stopped and jumped out, not wanting to spend another second with three corpses. Was this the place that swallowed my Prius in 2019? The place I'd awakened in 1932? It looked the same—a dark lagoon lined with cypress trees and rank vegetation at water's edge. A low-lying mist hung. Things croaking and hooting as if warning me to stay away.

"Don't git too close," Donnie Sue said. "Damn gators come right outa the water."

"Look out for that snake!" Virgil said.

He bellowed with laughter. Donnie Sue got right in his face. "God-dammit, Virgil. That ain't funny. Now, come on. Let's dump them bodies."

"Wait," Virgil said, cuffing a hand over his ear. "I think I hear it."

"Hear what?"

"Listen."

The sound was barely perceptible, competing as it did with the jungle's hoots, chirrs, shrieks, and other racket. The sound grew louder. It became a roar. The surrounding foliage vibrated. Butterflies and egrets scattered. A dark shadow appeared through the treetops.

Then it was overhead—Lafitte in his biplane.

I waved. A blast of wind shook the trees … then it was gone.

"Let's finish this," I said and hurried toward the back of the Packard.

"No, no," said Donnie Sue, trotting to my front. "You gotta turn around and back up."

"Why can't you drag them from here?"

"Virgil's got a bad back. He ain't much count for heavy lifting."

"Why didn't you ask the workers to come?"

"Coloreds won't come near this place."

She staked out a spot near the water and said she'd motion me where to stop. I climbed back into the Packard, thinking the motor was still running.

It wasn't.

Shit! I didn't remember turning it off. I sat there a second, trying to remember how I'd started it. Then I went through the motions and hit the starter.

It whined and whirred. The engine sputtered but wouldn't start.

Damn it, I needed to get to the airstrip.

Donnie Sue trotted over and stuck her head in the window.

"Maybe you ought to choke it."

I found the choke, pulled it and pushed it back, and hit the starter again. The smell of gas filled the car. It still wouldn't start. Worse, the starter began to drag.

Donnie Sue reached inside and yanked down a lever. "Now, try it."

I hit the starter again.

The engine roared to life, all twelve cylinders at full throttle.

The Packard lurched forward as if I were in a drag race, tires whining, heading straight toward the water. And there she stood—the girl of the swamp.

I tried to turn the wheel.

It was locked.

I hit the brake—or maybe it was the accelerator.

I screamed. I tried to open the door to jump out. But it was too late. The Packard splashed into the water. My head hit the steering wheel. The world flashed white. A loud ring filled my head. Darkness closed around me, and I had the awful sensation that this was how it would end.

Goodbye, Lafitte. Abyssinia in another life.

CHAPTER 84

When my senses returned, water was pouring through the open window like a breached dam. Water up to my thighs. Up to my waist. To my chest. Cool water, deadly water.

Alligator water.

Open the door and get out, I told myself. Swim back to Donnie Sue and Virgil.

But the door wouldn't open. Worse, the impact and downward tilt had tumbled the bodies forward, and Sal was hanging over the passenger seat. Another body pressed against the seat behind me, his floppy arm over my shoulder, trapping me against the steering wheel.

The car went vertical.

Down we went, sinking like the *Titanic*, the gloom of depth closing around me.

Bodies floated away. The pressure behind me diminished. I sucked in the last of the trapped air and pushed/pulled myself through the open window.

The Packard with its three bodies continued its downward spiral.

Even then, free of the car, the suction dragged me down. So did the weight of pockets crammed with gold coins, pistols, Luger cartridges, and my cell phone.

I struggled. I prayed. I fought against panic. I tried to empty my pockets, not thinking about alligators or anything other than getting air into my lungs.

And that was when she appeared beside me—my great grand-mother Carmen, my guardian angel, motioning me upward.

She took my hand and up we went, lights flashing around us, up and still up.

I burst through the surface, gasping, thanking Carmen and the Virgin and all the Saints.

But Carmen, if she'd ever been there, had disappeared.

"Donnie Sue!" I cried. "Virgil! Over here!"

I swam for solid ground, frantic to escape the alligators, hoping the commotion had scared them away. Even in my panic, I thought of Lafitte waiting at the airstrip, looking at his watch, wondering what was keeping me. I'd have to run, get there before the G-men arrived.

And we'd fly away from this cursed place. Go to Louisiana or Spain.

Not until I touched land did I realize it was no longer daylight.

How could that be? The sun had been shining only moments before. Now there were stars in the sky. The air was also cold, not cold-cold, but Florida winter cold.

I struggled out of the water and trotted away, desperate to put that damn hole behind me, but had gone no more than a few paces when I collided with something.

Down I went, crying, cursing. What the hell just happened?

I rolled over and felt it—a barrel—the kind used for traffic barricades. The realization hit me like an avalanche. Lafitte would no longer be waiting for me at the airstrip.

We wouldn't be going to Spain either.

I cried until my stomach hurt and my head throbbed, right there on the open ground under a starry sky. The surrounding air turned colder. Nausea came over me. I began to shiver in my wet clothing, and when I saw the lights of a passing airplane, I took out my cell.

Please, dear God, let it work.

Yes, it lit up with only six percent battery charge. It even showed the time—2:42—and began dinging with downloading messages.

I pressed the telephone icon and punched 9-1-1.

CHAPTER 85

Her name was Georgette, and she told me in a Greek accent that I was in Florida Adventist Hospital in Tarpon Springs. They'd been worried about a concussion and didn't want to put me under, but I'd fallen asleep and been out fourteen hours.

"Do you know your name?" she asked.

I tried to sit up, but the tubes got in the way, words wouldn't come out, and the movement brought on a sharp pain. One more head injury, I thought, and I was going to end up like Muhammad Ali. "Where is my cell?" I managed to ask.

"Locked away. Do you need the bathroom?"

"Yes, but I might need help."

She unhooked me from the IV stand, which protested with a beep, then put on a neck harness, and held my arm until I was in the bathroom and the door closed.

"Take your time," she said. "I'll get the doctor."

If I'd had any doubts about being back in the present, they were dispelled by the sight of modern fixtures—a tiled shower and lavatory, a toilet without a pull chain or overhead tank—but the image I saw in the mirror was enough to frighten small children. The only positive was they'd removed the cuffs from my wrists. What on earth would Lafitte say?

But what if there'd never been a Lafitte or Natalia? What if I'd been hallucinating like Dorothy in *The Wizard of Oz*? I looked for cuff marks on my wrists, didn't see any, and I was about to check for the tattoo when

Georgette knocked on the door.

"The doctor's here."

I went out and found three other people with Georgette, a female doctor with a stethoscope, another woman with a clipboard, and an African American guy who could have been one of Rothman's G-men except for his race.

No, I told them, I didn't feel like answering questions.

They looked at each other, shook their heads, and watched Georgette settle me into bed and get me reattached. The doctor asked everyone except Georgette to give her a few minutes. They hesitated as if not wanting to leave her with an unknown, but finally stepped outside.

The doctor introduced herself with a half-smile—I didn't catch her name—and did the things doctors do with their stethoscopes. "Sounds good," she said. "All your other tests are also good … X-ray, bloodwork. Hemoglobin count was a bit off, maybe blood loss."

She bent over me and looked into my face. "Did your airbag inflate?"

"I thought so. Why?"

"What kind of car?"

"Prius. It was new."

"You told the ambulance crew it was a Packard Twelve. What's that?"

A stab of fear shot through me. Had I told them about the bodies? "It was a Prius," I said.

"Well, they better check the airbag when they get it out of the water."

She and nurse Georgette administered what she called a neuro exam— pupils, hand grasps, alertness, response to pain. They pronounced me okay and said they'd do a CT Scan on my head. "Let's test your memory," said the doctor. "Do you know your name?"

"Amy," I mumbled, my voice hoarse.

"You told the paramedics your name was Carmen."

"What else did I tell them?"

"Ask Terri. She's the woman with the clipboard. Do you remember what happened? You've got a big bump on your forehead."

"Can we do this later? I'm exhausted."

"Of course, Amy. The important thing is you're alive. A lot of people don't make it out of sinking cars. They're death traps."

She left the room. Nurse Georgette said she'd get me something for me to drink and followed her out. No sooner had the door closed than it opened again, and in marched the woman with the clipboard and the guy in the suit.

The woman introduced herself as Terri and said she was with hospital administration. "I'm sorry to trouble you," she said, "but it's important we get some basic information." She glanced at her clipboard. "Do you have insurance?"

"I don't have my card with me."

"Is your name Carmen Amaya?"

"No, it's Amy."

"Amy what?"

I didn't want to tell her anything, not until I learned what they knew. "Where is my cell?"

"All your belongings are safe. Right now we need to know who you are and what happened to you. It's for your safety as well as ours."

"What do you mean, your safety? Am I a threat?"

She and the man stepped away from the bed and had a whispered conversation, now and then glancing at me. It didn't look good. When she came back, she said, "It's important you answer our questions. Otherwise, we'll have to move you to a more secure facility."

A vision of Guantanamo popped into my head, with Marine guards, barbed wire, and vicious attack dogs. "What's your question?"

"First, we need your full name and date of birth."

I told her in my weak voice. She also wanted my address, social security number, and insurance provider. I told her that too. She jotted it down and then fixed me in a serious gaze. "Are you running from someone, Amy? Are you in danger?"

"No."

"Are you sure? Maybe kidnappers? We need to know."

"No one is after me."

"That's not what you told the paramedics."

"What did I tell them?"

"You said you'd been kidnapped. You said you'd shot your kidnappers and escaped with their guns. And when we found you, you had guns."

My headache grew worse. In my fevered mind, I was sure she'd say they'd discovered the bodies. "I didn't shoot anyone," I said.

She exchanged looks with the man. He stepped forward. "Listen, Amy, you also had shackles on your wrists. Your clothing was … well, not what people normally wear, and your pockets were crammed with bullets, gold coins, and a wad of old currency."

Georgette came in with hot tea. The man waited for her to leave. "We had to notify the Pinellas County sheriff's office," he said. "They'll be sending someone around."

"Can I have my cell phone?"

"It might take a while. They limit our staff for the holidays."

"Today is a holiday?"

"Christmas. Didn't you know?"

"Today is Christmas?"

"No, it's Christmas Eve. Santa comes tonight."

Christmas? *Noche Buena*? Good lord. What happened to November? It was Halloween when I'd left the present. "What year?" I asked.

"You don't know the year?"

"If I knew, I wouldn't have asked you."

"It's 2019, Amy. Are you alright?"

"No. I'm not alright. I'm confused."

"Is there anyone you want us to notify?"

"My grandmother in Ybor City. Also a friend, Selena."

I gave him the numbers. He promised to let them know, and they were going out the door when someone in a Santa hat came rolling in with a large tray of Christmas Eve dinner.

Down the hall, a group of carolers was singing "O, Holy Night."

CHAPTER 86

The hospital Santa stopped by on Christmas morning to wish me a ho-ho-ho Merry Christmas. Not that I had anything to be ho-ho-ho about. Cheena dead. Lafitte 87 years in the past. Why was I even in this life that Ramón had destroyed? Here I had no one except my old abuelita, but her mind was so gone she probably didn't know I had disappeared.

The detectives didn't show up on Christmas. Neither did Selena or Abuelita, and it wasn't until the next day, Thursday, that Terri came in again with her clipboard. I asked for my cell, and she told me—again—that it was locked away with my guns and they needed approval from so-and-so to retrieve it. Except so-and-so was gone for the holidays. The room phone didn't allow me to make outside calls either, though I suspected it was only my room, my phone.

Not that I blamed them. Florida had more than its share of lunatics, and for all they knew I was an escaped convict from the women's ward at Lowell Correctional Institution. Which might explain why the door sometimes opened and that security guy in a suit peeped in.

They'd even planted him at the nurses' station.

I tried to take my mind off Lafitte by reading newspapers and watching TV. Yet no matter how hard I tried, I was tortured by memories. Did he escape and fly home to Louisiana? And what did the newspapers write about the shootout at the Hav-a-Havana cigar factory?

If I'd had my cell, I might access some old newspapers.

But I didn't, so again I cried myself to sleep and found myself back at the sinkhole with Donnie Sue, Virgil, and the girl of the swamp. Rain was blowing sideways, drenching us. I wanted to ask her why she sent me back to 2019, but she seemed to read my thoughts.

"Your work is not finished," she whispered to me in Caló.

"What work?"

"A guitarist, Amy. A dancer, a Gypsy named Ramón."

Her words shocked me awake. The rainfall I'd heard in my dream was blowing against the window. What did she mean? Surely she didn't send me back to reunite with that bastard.

Or was it just a bad dream with no meaning?

Nurse Georgette said the rain was caused by La Niña. The doctor said it was El Niño. I ate breakfast and was trying to push the dream out of my head when Georgette popped in again. "You've got company," she said, frowning as if this was bad news.

"Who?"

"Detectives from the sheriff's office. Do you want to see them?"

An image of G-men in dark suits and fedoras came into my head. "Do I have a choice?"

"Not really."

I shoved away my tray, pulled on a hospital robe, and was wishing the room had a back door when they marched in—a man in jeans and jacket and an attractive Hispanic woman with raven hair. The man didn't look as hostile or formidable as the G-men, even with his unshaved face, but the woman's designer jeans, indigenous features, and red nails reminded me of Cheena.

The man showed me his badge and identified himself as Detective Nick Thorsos. The woman's name was Monica, and she spoke with a Mexican accent. I motioned them onto a little sofa against the window. After an exchange of small talk, Detective Nick took out a notepad and leaned forward. "Do you know why we're here, Amy?"

"The guns?"

"That's just one issue. You told the paramedics you killed someone."

"All I remember is my car hit the water. I bumped my head."

"What kind of car?"

"Prius."

"Not a Packard Twelve?"

"It was a Prius."

"Why did you tell the paramedics it was a Packard?"

"My memory's been fuzzy since the accident."

"Who was with you in the car?"

"I was alone."

He looked at his notepad. "Who are Donnie Sue and Virgil?"

"Where did you hear those names?"

"The paramedics. You said you were helping Donnie Sue and Virgil dispose of bodies. Is that what happened? Were the three of you dumping bodies in the sinkhole?"

"Didn't they search the hole?"

"They looked, but there was no sign of a car going into the hole. No bodies. No tire tracks. No disturbances. Nothing but the barrel you pushed over. You also had broken cuffs on your wrists. They were ancient, a brand made by Peerless back in the 1930s."

I shrugged, not knowing what to say.

"You had two pistols on you, Amy, a 1914 Parabellum Luger and a double-barrel Derringer, both recently fired. That's in addition to"—again he glanced at his notepad—"the cuffs, a wad of old currency, some antique gold coins, several nine-millimeter Luger cartridges, and your 1930s clothing." He looked up. "Is it any wonder we're curious?"

"Is any of that illegal?"

"Do you have a carry permit?"

"Do I need one?"

He exchanged looks with Monica. "Listen, Amy, we just want to know what happened. Can you help us out here?"

"I told you I'm having a hard time remembering."

He let out a sigh. "Did Ramón kidnap you?"

"How do you know about Ramón?"

"We're detectives, Amy. We speak to witnesses. We also know about you tearing away in your Prius and damaging another car. Then you went missing for two months."

I didn't know what to say. After a while, Monica said, "Listen, Amy, your Prius disappeared into a sinkhole, presumably with you inside. There were witnesses. That's big news. Huge. Now, two months later, you crawl out of the same hole, but dressed differently. That's even bigger news. We need to know what happened. Did you swim out of the car and go into hiding?"

"I don't remember."

She shook her head, pulled a red folder from her bag, and took out a few sheets of paper. "Report from the ER. You were in bad shape when they found you—injured and suffering from hypothermia. It's a life-threatening condition, but you kept talking. In Spanish, like you were having a bad dream. Carlos—he's a paramedic—recorded your words on his cell."

"What did I say?"

"It's garbled, but with lots of names—Otis, Gerhardt, Lafitte. But here's the crucial part. You seemed to be talking to someone named Rothman. Who is Rothman?"

I shrugged. She put on her glasses. "I'm going to read you a portion."

I closed my eyes and listened, dreading what I might hear.

"'Dammit, Rothman. It was Gerhardt shot her, not me.'"

Monica looked up. "Who got shot, Amy? Who is Gerhardt?"

"What else did I say?"

She again read: "He captured me, but Donnie Sue … she blasted Clarence. Bang, bang with the Luger … kept on shooting. I shot Sal with the Derringer.'"

By then I felt like jumping out the window. Again Monica looked up. "Is that why the Derringer was recently fired, Amy? Did you shoot someone named Sal?"

"I didn't shoot anyone. All those characters come from a novel I've been writing."

Monica lifted an eyebrow. Nick stood and walked around, rubbing his chin. "Do you have a copy of this … novel you can show us?"

"Most of it is in my head. I dream about it, talk about it in my sleep."

Nick sat back down. "Here's what I find interesting. You can't remember what happened after you went into the sinkhole, but you remember the novel."

"Is that a crime?"

"No, but if you can't remember what happened, then maybe you don't remember there could be some bad people out there, waiting for you. No one wants you to disappear again."

"I'm not going to disappear. No one is chasing me. Can I at least have my cell back? I need to call my abuelita. Let her know I'm okay."

Monica gave me a pained look. "They didn't tell you?"

"Tell me what?"

"About your abuelita."

"What about her?"

"Heart failure after you disappeared. Passed away before they could get her to the hospital."

CHAPTER 87

Nick and Monica didn't come the next day. Neither did anyone else, which was just as well because my eyes were red and swollen from crying. Georgette removed the head bandage, replaced it with a smaller one, and said the cut was healing well.

"When can I get my cell?" I asked. "It's been three days."

"Your cell is at the sheriff's office. Didn't they tell you?"

I almost panicked. The password was only four digits—the day and month of my birthday. Any idiot could figure it out. Had they powered it up and seen photos of the Packard?

God, I needed a friend, a shoulder to cry on. But not Georgette; she was probably spying for Nick and the sheriff's office.

On Saturday morning, after another restless night of crying, I was sipping coffee in my room and watching the news when Detective Nick showed up with a Stein Mart shopping bag. "Clothes from Monica," he said. "Ready to bust out?"

"Now?"

"Now, Amy. I can drive you home if you like."

He left the room, saying he'd get my things. Georgette removed the tubes and needles. I showered and changed into Monica's designer jeans and black leather jacket—she had good taste—and was signing the hospital paperwork when Nick returned with a box marked "Evidence Release." He and Georgette watched as I took my belongings out of the box—iPhone, coins, currency, riding britches.

Granny bloomers.

Good Lord, how could I explain that?

The coins and currency were inside a cigar box. "Those coins are valuable," Nick said. "Especially the Spanish escudos. They sell on eBay for thousands of dollars."

"You're not returning my guns?"

"We need to keep them a while longer … ballistics tests, background checks."

I signed the receipt form and looked at my cell. It was at a hundred percent power, probably because they'd been snooping. I was dying to open it, to see pictures of Lafitte, to read my messages, but I didn't dare with Nick in the room.

Nick left to get his car. Georgette wheeled me out the door toward the elevator, past the security guy at the desk. "Abyssinia," I said and waved goodbye.

On the elevator, Georgette asked me why I had said Abyssinia.

"It means goodbye," I said and sang the lyrics to her:

I'll be seeing you

in all the old familiar places…

Nick was waiting in a black Ford Raptor that looked like it was made for crashing through barbed-wire fences. He helped me strap into my seat and then touched a button to start the truck. Amazing, I thought, lots of space and no choke, no spark or throttle, no fuel line to open, and no starter on the floor. "Do you like Greek food?" he asked.

"If you're asking me to lunch, I'm starving."

CHAPTER 88

We went to the Tarpon Springs Sponge Docks, which was only a short drive from the hospital. Holiday lights hung over the streets, red, green and yellow. Tourists in shorts and ball caps crowded the sidewalks, going in and out of little shops and restaurants. What a difference from 1932 when men wore jackets and fedoras and women wore dresses, and no one was overweight.

"There," Nick said and pointed to a sign that read Dimitri's on the Water.

We parked behind Mykonos, but before we got out, Nick handed me sunglasses and a Tampa Bay Bucs cap. "Here, put this on."

"Why? Do you think the mob is waiting to nab me?"

"There's another reason."

"What reason?"

"I'll tell you in the restaurant."

He took a long look around and, not seeing any bad guys, reached into the back seat for a large shopping bag. "Don't ask," he said, and a few minutes later we were seated next to a riverboat that was taking tourists aboard. The smell of water-meets-land permeated the air. Seagulls circled and fluttered, creating an abrasive racket, sometimes plunging to the water.

"Are those birds always that noisy?" I asked.

"Just don't toss any food their way."

Nick ordered Pastitsio. I ordered a Greek Salad. No sooner had the server left than Nick leaned forward. Here it comes, I thought. More questions.

"Nice nails," he said, touching my hand. "It weakens my theory."

"What theory?"

"That you'd been kidnapped and held hostage. Kidnap victims wouldn't have such nice nails. Your hair's also been recently trimmed."

Good lord, I thought. Did he also know about the Gypsy tattoo and the pan shave?

The server returned with bread and olive oil. Nick waited for her to leave. "Do you mind if I ask you about your … well, boyfriend, Ramón?"

"He's not my boyfriend. I made a horrible mistake."

He nodded. "I can see that, but I had to ask. It's just he went missing after your Brooker Creek performance. Some of the witnesses said his wife laid a Gypsy curse on you."

An image of that horrible moment flashed through my mind. The screams, the knife, the humiliation. "Horrible," I said. "Embarrassing."

"It wasn't your fault. I thought you were magnificent."

"You were there?"

He grinned, reached for the shopping bag, and pulled out a Spanish torero hat and black cape. He put on the hat, then twirled the cape and gave me a come-on kind of look.

"Oh, my God. Was that you? The Greek dancer?"

"*Sí, señorita.*"

"You saved me from a stiletto."

He poked a finger through a hole in the cape. "The cape saved you, not me."

"Did they arrest her?"

"Disorderly conduct. She spent the night in jail."

"What about Ramón?"

"Nope. He grabbed his guitar and left. It was a … well, lively evening. I wish you'd tell me what happened."

I buttered a chunk of bread but didn't answer. He finally gave up and we made small talk until the food arrived. We ate. Nick kept glancing around as if concerned about assassins. The folks at the next table received a dish that flared. Everyone yelled "Opa!" After a while, Nick said, "Listen,

Amy, don't be surprised if you get mobbed when you get back to Ybor."

"Why?"

"You seriously don't know?"

"No one told me anything at the hospital."

"Oh, boy," he said and again looked over his shoulder. "Here's what happened. After you left the performance, you drove the wrong way on a one-way road. Then you blew past an old couple and ran them into a ditch. They saw you miss the turn and plow into the barrel barriers."

"They saw the car sink?"

"Others saw it too. They called 9-1-1. Before long the place was swarming with first responders—police, ambulances, divers, TV crews. I was there. Saw the busted barrels. Saw the tire tracks. We searched for two days and came up zip. No trace of you. Not the Prius either, only the evidence you'd gone into the water."

I sipped my tea and listened, not knowing what to say.

"Your face was in the papers and on TV for weeks. Speculation was wild. The hole swallowed you. You were faking your death. There was talk of Gypsy curses and UFOs, even stories about Mayans who threw virgins into sinkholes. And now you're back. So, yes, when word gets out, the news people will be swarming over you like those birds."

He took a chunk of bread from the basket, broke it into small pieces, and flung it over the water. The birds swooped, making their awful racket. Not one piece of bread reached the water.

By then I was breathless. "What do you suggest I do?"

"Well, you could always come clean and tell them what happened."

"No one would believe me."

"Maybe they would. Florida's a loony state."

"You saying I'm looney?"

"What I'm saying is your circumstances are beyond weird." He waved over the server and asked for the check, then turned back to me. "We'll be driving past Brooker Creek. I'm pretty sure the preserve is open. Would you like to see where the paramedics found you?"

CHAPTER 89

The gate was open. A large sign read BROOKER CREEK PRESERVE, at the same place I'd left Otis's black Ford and set off on foot. Back then there'd been forest all around, and the entrance had been dark and scary with a barbed-wire fence. Now there was sunlight, a cow pasture, and an inviting entrance. "You sure you want to go in?" Nick asked.

"I'm sure."

We took the same trail I'd driven in my Prius two months ago. The same trail I'd walked with my Luger 87 years ago, or last week, looking for the airstrip.

I looked now, wishing Lafitte would step out from the foliage and flag us down. Even now I could see his face and hear his voice, feel his arms around me. Lafitte in his aviator boots and a leather jacket. *Run away with me, and be my bride, and we will into the heavens fly....*

"Stop," I said to Nick.

He stopped the truck. I climbed out, almost certain this was the place I'd first met him, at the corner of the airstrip? There was no airstrip now. No tin shed either, but there were crows circling and cawing above me. "Amy?" Nick said.

"Just give me a minute."

I followed a little footpath off to the side. Water dripped from the foliage. A breeze whistled through the pines. The crows cawed.

"Lafitte," I cried out.

He did not answer.

Was he out here somewhere? Waiting for me?

Would I ever see him again? Or was he only a bittersweet memory?

"Lafitte," I called again, louder.

Nick appeared beside me and glanced into the surrounding trees and brush. "What's wrong?" he asked. "You're crying."

I couldn't answer. How do you explain the god-awful emptiness of losing a loved one or the kick-in-the-stomach pain of finding yourself at a place with memories or the sudden impulse to call their name and welling up with tears at the stark reality of loss?

You can't. You just can't. "I'll be okay," I said.

We drove on. There were forested wetlands and pine hammocks, and signs that directed hikers to nature trails, and here and there a speed bump, or water running across the road, but nothing that resembled an abandoned airstrip. No fork either. How could that be? On the night of my performance, a fork had led me straight to the sinkhole.

"Where's the sinkhole?" I asked Nick.

He pointed to the right. "Over there, but it's not part of the preserve."

He took a side road, and there it was. Forest on one side, swamp on the other, moss-draped cypress trees, and a black lagoon behind a chain-link fence.

Men and women milled around the site, all in worker helmets and orange vests. Cables trailed into the water. A monitor had been set up nearby. There were trucks and a couple of official-looking vans marked Florida Department of Environmental Protection.

"What are they doing?" I asked Nick.

"Let's ask."

We climbed out and passed through the open gate. "This is where they found you," he said. "The gate was closed. Locked too. No tire marks, no disturbance. Just you, hugging a barrel."

A man with a short gray beard and glasses hurried over. "Off-limits," he said, holding up his hand like a traffic cop. "No spectators."

Nick produced his badge and introduced me as his assistant. "We're investigating the case of the woman who drove into the sinkhole," he said. "What's going on here?"

We shook hands. The man said he was a hydrogeologist with the Florida DEP and began explaining as if we were also geologists, saying they were testing the water for instability, using terms like karst terrain and soluble carbonate rock. "Sinkholes can be dangerous," he said. "They've killed at least seven people in Florida alone. This place has a reputation."

"What kind of reputation?" Nick asked.

The man looked over his shoulder as if he didn't want his colleagues to hear. "All kind of stories—moonshine operation back in the Thirties, a dumping place for bodies, a gathering place for witches. Locals claim they've seen a ghostly woman in white. If that's not creepy enough, they say you can hear voices at night, even see lights in the water."

"Lights?" I asked.

"Illumination. There might be a scientific explanation. Also an explanation for that young woman you're investigating. Have you spoken to her? Asked her what happened?"

Nick looked at me as if I should explain. I felt like saying Stephen Hawking would be at a loss to explain, but instead I said, "She was pretty battered. Says she doesn't remember."

"None of it makes sense," the man said. "We're sure she drove a Prius into the water two months ago. Two months. There were witnesses. So why on earth would she show up now?"

I shrugged. Nick said, "There's all kind of wild rumors floating around. Captured by UFOs, sucked into another dimension. Do you have a theory?"

"Look, I'm a scientist. I look at facts. All I know is I'd love to talk with that girl. Ask her if others were in the car with her. I'm even hearing she killed some bad guys and stuffed them into an old Packard … drove it into the sinkhole. But what's really weird is…."

"What?" I asked.

"The way she was dressed—in 1930s clothes—and armed to the teeth."

I pushed the cap lower on my head. "If there's a car down there, why can't you find it?"

He took off his helmet and mopped his brow. "Here's what happens. First, you've got a deep hole. Then you've got the weight of the water. Then you've got limestone at the bottom and all around. Limestone dissolves. Cavities open. Water pours in. This creates a drop in surface level. Embankment collapses. And when it goes, it takes everything with it—soil, trees, alligators, people. If that little Prius is down there, or a Packard, it's buried under tons of debris."

His cell buzzed. "I better take this. If you're going to look around, watch out for poison ivy. Don't get near the water either. Alligators. We saw a whopper."

He sauntered away, cell to his ear. Nick asked if I wanted to leave.

"Not yet," I said, "I want to check out the other side."

CHAPTER 90

We followed a footpath to the left into the darkness of overhanging foliage and moss-covered trees. "Interesting what he said about a ghostly woman in white," Nick said, swatting at deerflies. "You mentioned a swamp girl to the paramedics."

"What did I say?"

"I'd have to look at the transcript, but you called her the girl of the swamp … said she saved you from bootleggers. You don't remember?"

"I was hallucinating."

"Is she a character in your book?"

"Can we talk about this later?"

We traipsed on, swamp on one side, sinkhole on the other, birds singing, water dripping, things moving in the overhead. Was this was the place I'd awakened in 1932, beneath the trees? A dark mood came over me. Foreboding, depressing. I'd found my love in this jungle and now I'd lost it. I needed to tell someone, needed to pour out my soul. But not to Nick. He seemed like a nice guy, but he was also a cop.

And those bodies might still bob to the surface.

When we reached the opposite side from the entrance, I found what I suspected was there—traces of an ancient road that ended at the sinkhole. I stared at the trees and palmettos that lined its banks. At the movement that might be an alligator. Yes, this was it, the place I'd gone into the sinkhole in the Packard, and now I was back, standing amid the ghosts that haunted my memory, imagining I could see Donnie Sue and Virgil in the shadows, their mouths open in horror, staring at the disturbed water, wondering if I'd come back up.

I stepped closer and gazed into the murkiness. Lafitte was down there somewhere … in his aviator boots and leather jacket. In another time. Lost in dimensions. Waiting for me.

Run away with me and be my bride, and we will into the heavens fly….

A sudden breeze whistled through the trees. The water rippled. From somewhere came the clack of castanets. A guitar strummed. It became the "Habanera," and there she stood in her tattered gown, her hair tangled and matted, dirt on her face.

She motioned with her hand and waded into the water, deeper and still deeper. She sank beneath the surface. The clack of castanets grew louder. A sensation I'd never experienced came over me, magnetic, hypnotic, pulling me toward the water.

I took another step, not caring about alligators or the danger of drowning, thinking only of Lafitte, waiting for me at the airstrip, waiting to take me away. He was down there, in the water.

"Amy! What the hell are you doing?"

Nick pulled me away, asking what was wrong.

I jerked loose, fell to my knees, and cried so hard my whole body shook.

CHAPTER 91

Mercifully, Nick did not interrogate me during the thirty-minute drive to Ybor, and instead tuned his radio to Pandora and the soothing music of Armik's Greatest Hits. It should have calmed me, but I kept wondering about the magic of the sinkhole. What would have happened if I'd plunged in? Would I have gone back to Lafitte? Or drowned and been eaten by alligators?

I took out my cell, powered it up and looked at my old texts. There were dozens, mainly junk, but also messages from Selena and Ramón asking where I was and if I was okay, and Ramón pleading his innocence and undying love.

"Anything interesting?" Nick asked.

I put away the phone and didn't answer, and neither of us spoke until we rolled to a stop at my condo on 5th Avenue. Nick took out his pistol and chambered a round, just like Cheena had done in another life. "Does Ramón know about this place?" he asked.

"What's the gun for? Is he that dangerous?"

"I'll explain inside."

We hopped out and hurried to the door. It opened to my code. Nick rushed inside with his pistol, and then we were standing in a room with stale air amid a pile of unopened mail. Everything else looked just as I'd left it, even dirty clothes in the hamper.

Nick turned on ceiling fans and adjusted the thermostat. I found a credit card and cash in my dresser, then grabbed suitcases in my bedroom and began filling them with clothing, laptop, hairdryer, makeup kit and other things, trying to avoid looking at the bed where Ramón and I had made love, now wishing I could pour gasoline on it and light it up.

Nick stuffed the mail in a garbage bag and hauled it to his truck. He also cleaned the refrigerator of old perishables and took them to the dumpster. When he finished, he motioned me onto the sofa. "Ready to hear about Ramón?"

I sat down and waited, dreading what I might hear.

"What do you know about his background in Spain?" he asked.

"Only what he told me—that he was divorced."

"So you had no idea he has a crime sheet a mile long—murder, robbery, extortion?" The list went on and on, one horror after another, and what was worse, he'd recently robbed a local convenience store and almost killed a female clerk.

"I suppose you haven't heard about Selena either," Nick said.

"Is she okay?"

"No, Amy, she's not. She disappeared the day after you went into the sinkhole. We found her car in a parking lot. Ramón's fingerprints were all over it."

Selena gone? Maybe murdered? And I'd been selfishly thinking of myself.

I took out my cell and punched in her number.

No answer.

"Don't," Nick said and touched my arm. "Her body was in the trunk."

The tears came again. I went to the bathroom and kicked over the trash can. That bastard! Why hadn't I checked his background? Why had I fallen under his spell? Gypsy magic? No, it was needy woman syndrome, stupid woman. And now Selena was gone.

I washed my face and went out to find Nick consulting his notepad.

"Are you okay?" he asked.

"No, I'm not okay. I wasn't expecting this. Why didn't you tell me when I was in the hospital? She was my best friend."

"We didn't know how to handle it. You were already in pain from the loss of your abuela." He glanced down at his notepad. "There's something else I have to ask you."

"It can't be any worse than what you just told me."

"It's about your Derringer."

I sat down. "What about it?"

"We checked the registration. Guess who owned it in the 1930s?"

"Just tell me, Nick."

"Federal agent named Rothman. He was head of the local Bureau of Investigation in the early Thirties, the people who busted moonshiners. You mentioned a man named Rothman. You have his Derringer. It was recently fired, so the question is obvious."

He sat there looking at me, waiting for an explanation. By then I was so flustered and hurting I didn't care anymore. "Rothman gave it to his mistress," I said. "I got it from her."

"Wait. Are you saying his mistress is still alive?"

I stood. "I'll explain later. Can we go now? I'd like to get to Abuelita's before dark."

We gathered our things, went out, and were at the truck when the condo manager came trotting over, a dumpy little blonde named Sherrie. "Oh, my God!" she said in her abrasive voice. "Is that you, Amy? We heard you were—"

More neighbors arrived, everyone staring as if I'd climbed out of a grave. Questions flew at me from all directions. Nick opened the passenger door of the truck and motioned me inside.

"Your rent's two month's overdue," Sherrie said. "When are you going to pay?"

"Not to worry. I'll take care of it."

I jumped into the truck and closed the door. Nick buckled in and away we went. Behind us, almost everyone had a cell to their ear.

"That went well," Nick said.

CHAPTER 92

We drove past the Columbia Restaurant with its memories of Big Tony, and I had another bad moment when we took a right near the Centro Español. Was Room 12 still there? I could almost see Cheena at the table with her Asian looks. Poor Cheena and now Selena. Both gone, and it was partially my fault, something else to explain to St. Pete.

"Here it is," Nick said, and pulled into the drive of my abuelita's house.

From the outside, it didn't look that different. Big front porch with four columns. Shrubbery all around. Oak trees with dangling Spanish moss. Had I really lived here with Natalia in 1932 and spent my nights with Lafitte? God, how I missed him.

"See anything out of the ordinary?" Nick asked.

"Nothing."

I climbed out with my cigar box of coins and old currency and found the key in a flowerpot. Nick took out his pistol and we eased into the house.

The smells and furniture were just as I remembered when Abuelita lived here—and not that different from 1932. But something wasn't right. No mail on the floor, the refrigerator empty, no clothing or anything else in the closets or drawers.

"Someone's been here," I said.

"Ramón?"

"Ramón's a slob. Couldn't have been him."

Nick gestured at the picture of Carmen over the mantel. "Is that you?"

"Great-grandmother Carmen. They called her the Mata Hari of Ybor."

"Isn't that the dress you wore at the performance?"

I didn't want to get into a discussion about the dress. It was in my tote bag in a Packard Twelve with three bodies at the bottom of a sinkhole. Didn't want to answer questions about Carmen either. What concerned me were the gold coins I'd hidden in the wall.

"Would you mind bringing in my things?" I asked Nick.

I waited for the door to close behind him and hurried into the bedroom. The sight of the brass bed—our bed—almost brought me to tears. The "Habanera" started in my head again.

"Just stop it," I said and went to the closet.

It was empty, nothing but wire hangers where my grandmother's clothing had hung. The pull string light was burned out, so I ran my hand over the wall, feeling for the spot that had been damaged by Gerhardt's bullet. Yes, a rough spot was there, covered with wallpaper. But were the coins in the wall? I'd have to rip off the siding to find out.

Nick knocked on the bedroom door. "You okay? I found tea in the kitchen."

"Great, brew us a cup. I'm going to check the attic."

I raced up the stairs. The attic looked the same, a clutter of boxes, old furniture, rolled carpets, and the Blaupunkt floor model radio. The cedar chest was there too, beneath a pile of blankets and quilts. I took a deep breath, opened it, breathed in the smell of mothballs, and yanked out books, ancient copies of *National Geographic*, and clothing until I found a folder at the bottom—my manuscript, a hundred thirty pages, yellowed by age.

Thank you, God. Now I had a record of my 1932 life. I could polish it, update it, maybe get it published as fiction.

"Are you okay?" Nick yelled up the stairs.

"Fine, be right down."

I took the manuscript downstairs and put it in the dresser drawer next to the cigar box that contained my coins. Nick was still in the kitchen, so I sat on the sofa and opened the iPhone to my photos from 1932. Donnie

Sue, the whiskey still, Cheena, the selfie with Alabama, the Packard. Lafitte next to his yellow biplane.

The castanets started in my head again, with foot-stomping and strum of guitars.

"Dammit, just stop it!"

Nick came into the room with a tray of tea. "Are you okay?"

I put away the cell. "Would you stop asking if I'm okay?"

He handed me a mug of hot tea and sat in the same chair where Otis had sat on the night of the interrogation. "We need to talk, Amy."

"I told you everything I remember."

"If you haven't committed a crime, there's no reason not to tell me."

"So if I don't tell you, you'll assume I committed a crime?"

"There could be other reasons."

"Like what?"

"Like Stockholm Syndrome. Sometimes victims are too embarrassed to say what happened. Or they fall in love with their captors. Is that what happened? Did someone hold you hostage?"

Yes, I wanted to say, I'd been a hostage, but it was hostage by time, not by a villain. And, yes, I'd fallen in love and wanted to stay in 1932—and I wanted to go back.

"Was it Ramón?" Nick asked. "Did he kidnap you?"

"For God's sake, it wasn't Ramón. I haven't seen him and never want to see him again."

"If it wasn't Ramón, then who?"

"If I told you what happened you wouldn't believe me."

"Try me."

"It'll take a while."

"I've got time. Why don't you tell me about that Derringer?"

I stood with my tea and walked around, wondering how much I should tell him. "Okay, suppose a woman like me, a flamenco dancer, drives her car into a sinkhole."

"And?"

"Well, suppose she survives but crawls out to find herself in 1932."

He stared at me.

"See, I told you no one would believe it."

"No, just hold on. I think it's pretty intriguing. It would explain your clothing."

"It's fiction, Nick. I'm talking about my book, not reality."

"Are you saying this whole thing was fabricated for a book?"

"Maybe."

"You almost drowned yourself for a book?"

"Do you want to hear the plot, or do you want to interrogate me?"

"Sorry. Go ahead. Your character is stuck in 1932. Then what?"

"Well, suppose she becomes a victim of mistaken identity. She's a dead-ringer for her great-grandmother, Carmen." I pointed to the photo over the fireplace. "Except Carmen is dead, murdered by the mob. The mob wants to finish the job. She's also wanted by the feds."

"Why would the feds want her?"

"Accomplice to the murder of a G-man. Hoover wants to fry her. So she spends the whole time running and hiding, trying to survive."

"How does she get back to the present?"

"The sinkhole."

"In a Packard?"

I didn't answer. He stood and walked around. "Is there a love interest?"

"Maybe."

"Does he fly an airplane?" He looked at the cell in my hand.

The knot in my stomach twisted tighter. "You've seen the photos, haven't you?"

He shrugged.

"Can you do that without a warrant?"

He reached into his shirt pocket and took out a folded sheet of paper. "Here's a copy. You were in a coma. We didn't know who you were, who beat you up, or even if you'd live. We got the warrant and sent your cell to Cyber Crimes. It's a—"

"Damn it, Nick, why didn't you tell me in the beginning?"

I picked up the tea tray, took it to the kitchen, and slammed it on the counter, scattering the cups. I had suspected as much but to hear him admit it set me on fire. He and probably the entire sheriff's office had read my messages and seen the airplane, seen the Packard, the whiskey still, the pictures of Donnie Sue, Lafitte, and others.

Nick came into the kitchen as if to apologize, but his cell phone dinged. He looked at it. "Christ, I've got to go." He said he'd check on me tomorrow, and to keep my doors locked and to call him if I heard from Ramón. "He's dangerous, Amy. Be careful."

CHAPTER 93

As soon as he left, I rushed into the bedroom and checked the wall again. Were my coins inside? Nick was right. Gold Spanish escudos were worth thousands, and I'd placed a hundred or more one-ounce coins in the wall, coins that in 1932 had cost only $30-40 each.

I pounded on the wall, hoping to hear a jingle. Nothing. No sound. Damn it, I needed something to bust a hole. But not tonight. It was too late, and I was too tired.

I plopped onto the sofa with my cell and began browsing the archives of old newspapers. The cigar factory shootout was dismissed as just another battle in the bolita wars. The main suspect was Carmen—meaning me—and I was on J. Edgar Hoover's most-wanted list for murder, hijacking a government vehicle, and taking hostages.

Great, I thought. Maybe I should make a copy of the poster and frame it on the wall.

I kept browsing but could find no mention of a raid on Brooker Creek and nothing about Lafitte. *Nada.* What had happened to him? Did he go home to Louisiana or did he link up with Natalia and go to Spain? The thought haunted me—Lafitte and Natalia in Spain. Damn them!

Sometime after 2 a.m., after I'd searched for hours, I fell asleep in the bed where Lafitte and I had made love a hundred times. Lafitte with his funny accent and garbled syntax. Lafitte kissing me all over. Lafitte reciting his poem.

Lafitte with Natalia in Spain.

"Amy."

I sat up and stared at Carmen. The music from the "Habanera" started again, softly, with castanets and foot stomps. She motioned with her hand.

"Your life is not here," she said in Andalusian Spanish.

"Then why did you bring me here? I wanted to stay in 1932."

"Come with me. Let's go back."

I followed her out the door in my nightgown, across the city of Tampa, down streets, highways, and trails, into the Brooker Creek Preserve, and past the barricade barrels.

"There," she said and pointed to the sinkhole. She took my hand. The warmth traveled up my arm and into my heart like a romantic drug. The lagoon pulled me as if it possessed a magnetic quality, as if Lafitte himself was pulling me. I didn't resist, did not want to resist.

She led me to the edge. "Now," she said, and we both plunged into the water.

And I woke up, still under the covers.

It was daylight, Sunday morning at 9:47, and what I had thought was the lingering beat of the "Habanera" was someone pounding on the front door.

I jumped up and glanced out the window. In the driveway sat a large U-Haul truck, all orange, white, and blue. A heavy-set man in shorts, tank top, and a Green Bay Packers ball cap was there too, along with a dog and a young boy. The pounding grew louder.

"Hold on!" I yelled, and tried to rub the dream out of my eyes. I pulled on a robe, ran a brush through my hair, then stumbled to the door and slid back the bolt that had been installed by Otis.

A woman with cropped blonde hair stood on the porch. "Why was this door bolted?" she demanded to know, holding up a key. "Who are you?"

"I'm the owner."

"What do mean, you're the owner? We just bought this house."

She tried to push her way in. I blocked her, even though she was larger. "I have no idea what you're talking about," I said. "This house is mine."

"How can it be yours if we just bought it?"

"Because it belonged to my grandmother. I'm her only heir."

"They said she didn't have any heirs, said they were all dead."

"Who told you that?"

"The realtor."

"Do I look dead to you?"

She yelled for her husband, a guy named Charlie. I tried to explain, but Charlie didn't care. He'd bought this god-damn house for $315,000 ten days ago, paid ten percent down, driven a U-Haul all the way from Wisconsin to escape the snow, and he'd be god-damned if he was going to get ripped off by me or some shady-ass realtor, and why the hell was I now living in *his* house.

He shook a finger in my face. "Either you get the hell out now, or I'm calling the cops."

His dog growled and bared its teeth. The woman took Charlie's arm and tried to pull him away. He jerked loose. The little kid began crying. The mom yelled at the kid and dragged him away. My headache came back. So did the "Habanera," and I began to feel as if my life was unraveling again, right there in the doorway.

I slammed the door and bolted it.

"We're calling the cops now!" the man yelled. "Get your god-damn things and get out of my house," and he was still assailing me with curses when I collapsed onto the sofa.

It took a long time for my head to stop pounding and the music and castanets and foot stomps to fade, and when it did, I called Nick.

"Are they still there?" he asked.

"They left in their car, but the U-Haul is still here."

"Well, I'm not a lawyer, but I'm pretty sure if you've got a copy of the will, and the will was never changed, you've got a legitimate claim to the property. However…"

"However what?"

"Is it possible your grandmother changed the will after she thought you were dead? It happens. I didn't mention this, but I talked to her a few days after you went into the sinkhole. She wasn't well. Her mind was…"

"Was what, Nick?"

"Not functioning well. She said you'd joined the Peace Corps and was working with Gypsies in Romania. Then she said you were only eleven years old."

"Are you saying she might have changed the will without knowing what she was doing?"

"It's possible. Who's the executor?"

"I am."

"But you're dead … or were supposed to be. Is there a secondary?"

"Her lawyer."

"Call him, but don't leave your house. If they get inside, it'll be hard to eject them."

CHAPTER 94

I had a hundred things to do—like pay bills and file a claim with the insurance company for my Prius—but not now. Charlie and his wife might return with the cops and kick me out. I needed to bust open the wall and get my coins. But I needed tools, needed a crowbar and hammer, which I didn't have, and I didn't dare leave the house. Maybe I could find something here.

I glanced out the window again, and seeing nothing except Charlie's U-Haul, I changed into jeans and scooted out the back door to the smokehouse.

It was filled with old flower pots, empty Mason jars, a rusty barbecue pit, garden gloves and digging tools. I looked in boxes and opened drawers, and pulled things off the shelves, but the only thing that looked useful was a large screwdriver, rusted with age.

Not good enough. I needed a hammer, so again I went digging and turning things upside down. Would a brick do? I unearthed one in the garden bed. But it was only a half brick, red like all the other bricks in Ybor. It would have to do. I rinsed off the soil with a garden hose, put on gloves, and hurried back to the bedroom closet.

First I stripped off wallpaper that wasn't there in 1932. The wall beneath was wood—six-inch planks laid horizontal. What I needed was a power saw or a crowbar, or a man, but all I had was a rusty screwdriver and a heavy half brick. I sat on the floor and went to work.

The baseboard split and came loose in pieces, nails protruding like a medieval weapon. I shoved them away and started on the bottom board, driving the screwdriver between the joints, pounding and prizing until my hands hurt and my breath was coming in spurts.

The sound of a car took me back to the window. Not them, only a passing car.

Little by little the board surrendered in pieces, its nails protesting with screeches. I pulled it away and tossed it on the floor. Now there was a narrow dark space above the floor seal.

Coins did not spill out as I had hoped.

Please, dear God, let them be there.

It was too dark to see, so I inserted my fingers into the space.

Nothing, only emptiness. My heart beat faster. Was I looking in the right place, directly beneath the hole that Gerhardt's bullet had made?

Yes.

Maybe the coins were higher up. Maybe an obstruction had kept them from going to the bottom. I yanked off another board, and yet another.

Then I switched on my iPhone and peered into the space between the walls.

Nothing but open space.

Not a single coin.

Nada.

I shoved the boards away and beat back the tears. Now what was I going to do?

Natalia. It had to be that bitch. She'd found the coins and was living it up in Spain, maybe with Lafitte. Sangrias and sunshine, fiery flamencos, the wines of Málaga and Alicante, and love atop wine casks in the backrooms of little bodegas.

And me soon to become homeless.

A car drove in the driveway.

The pounding and shouts started again.

"Open this god-damned door or I'll kick it down!"

I drew in a deep breath and traipsed to the door.

Charlie and his moon-face wife were back, this time with a uniformed cop and a well-dressed lady in a red blazer. The woman identified herself as a realtor. The cop stared into my face.

"Do you own this house?"

"It belonged to my grandmother. I'm her only heir. She left the house to me."

"What is your name?"

"Amy Romano."

"Can you show me some identification?"

The realtor stepped forward. "Oh, my God, are you the sinkhole woman?"

I didn't know how to respond and didn't have to because Charlie shoved his way into the conversation. "Just tell her to get out of my god-damn house."

"We can't do that," said the cop. "Not without an eviction order."

Charlie exploded into curses and demands. The cop told him to step away and cool down. Charlie marched around the porch, cursing and mumbling, slamming his fist into his open palm. "Happy fucking new year," he said to no one in particular.

The realtor explained that Abuelita had changed her will for the benefit of a charitable organization. "They didn't want the property," she said, "so they listed it with me. You can save yourself and my client a lot of grief by vacating their property."

"It's not *their* property. This is my house. I paid for it and I'm keeping it."

"That's not what the register in the courthouse says."

"Would you please get off my front porch? I'm busy."

"Fine, you want to make this hard? We'll make it hard, but I'd advise you to get yourself a good lawyer. We'll be back with an eviction order."

She stalked away. I yelled after her to tell Charlie to get his U-Haul out of my drive.

CHAPTER 95

The first stories about me appeared in newspapers and television the next day, and by the weekend there were lengthy accounts of all the madness, everything from the humiliating flamenco performance at Brooker Creek to me climbing out of the sinkhole looking like Bonnie—as in Bonnie and Clyde—with my pistols and 1930s riding britches. They also showed pictures of a Prius, a Packard Twelve, a German Luger, a Derringer, the Brooker Creek Environmental Center, and me in my beautiful flamenco dress.

Reporters converged on the sinkhole and showed it in all its murky gloominess. They repeated the stories about flashing lights, ghost sightings, screams, and sudden water level drops, and even interviewed the DEP guy I'd met a few days before with Nick.

"Yep," he drawled on local TV, standing next to his truck in his orange vest and helmet, pointing to cables trailing into the water. "There could be a Packard down there with bodies in it, or maybe a Prius with bodies. We don't know yet, but we'll keep looking until the governor tells us to stop. He's taken a personal interest in this."

Gawkers stopped by the house to take pictures, and reporters showed up on my front porch. Since I wouldn't answer their questions, and neither would the hospital or sheriff's office, speculation began anew. I'd been kidnapped, held hostage, and was suffering from Stockholm syndrome. I was delusional, mentally ill, and needed treatment.

An anti-immigrant group in Clearwater called it a hoax I'd concocted with my "criminal boyfriend" Ramón to get a book contract. They posted pictures on their blog of the semi-nude paintings, and the two of us together, Ramón in his black outfit and me in my pretty flamenco dress, all smiles and happiness. And they claimed—without identifying sources—that I'd been schooled in the dark arts of deception, illusion, and criminal mysticism by a Gypsy mother from a cave in Granada and a Mexican illegal who worshipped pagan gods.

Never mind that I was born in Tampa many generations removed from the caves of Granada and my dad was a good Catholic who served in Vietnam as a US Marine and died from lung cancer when I was nine, and the only time I'd practiced the "dark arts" was in 1932 to save my butt from the bad guys.

A note appeared on my front door with an offer of money for nude photos. Another pervert left a voice message offering a hundred dollars for online sex. A woman who claimed to be the mother of the clerk Ramón had robbed and beaten left a message calling me a slut.

"Go back to Mexico," she railed. "We don't need your kind in America."

It hurt. It cut to the core of my being, but it also made me all the more determined to tell my story, so during one of those times when I sneaked out the back door to run errands—like buying groceries and getting a rental car—I went to Staples and had my manuscript converted to Word. I titled it *Flamenco in the Time of Moonshine and Mobsters* and added everything that had happened since my last day in 1932.

I paid my bills, but my bank balance dwindled. I had no income, and my assistantship at the university had been taken by another student. Worse, the eviction order came in the form of a registered letter that laid out the legitimacy of the house transaction, and I had a week to vacate. Charlie didn't come back to harass me, but his U-Haul did, and it was parked in a way that forced me to drive my rental car onto the grass.

My misery deepened. Why, I asked again and again, had I been brought back to the present when my sole desire was to remain with Lafitte in 1932? His poem, *Run away with me and be my bride*, became etched into my mind like a Biblical injunction. I tried to read poetry to ease my pain, but ended up reading the sadness in Pablo Neruda's love poems.

What does it matter that my love could not keep her?

The night is starry and she is not with me.

The music in my head became louder and more abrasive. I cried all the time. I could no longer write. I didn't care. As if that wasn't bad enough, the insurance company rejected the claim for my Prius. Not until they had validation that my car had in fact gone into the sinkhole.

And just when I thought it couldn't get worse, Nick called.

"Good news for your insurance claim," he said.

"What, Nick?"

"They found your car. Divers are in the water now, hooking it up. It'll take at least another hour. I'm here with Monica. Can you meet us at the sinkhole?"

"Why kind of car?" I asked.

There was silence. "Didn't you say it was a Prius?"

"Well, is it?"

"They didn't say."

I changed into jeans, grabbed a cap, rushed out the front door, and drove my little rental car as fast as I dared to Brooker Creek.

CHAPTER 96

The gate to the sinkhole was open. A light mist was falling, everything gray and gloomy, and even with the windows closed I caught the familiar smells of swamp, dampness, and decay.

Spectators stood around in groups with umbrellas and cellphones, watching the workers in their orange vests. There were also cars, vans, ambulances, SUVs and trucks. Some of the vehicles had TV logos on their sides. The ambulances were unmarked.

Nick and Monica trotted over as soon as they saw me. Monica handed me a poncho and pull-over cap. "Here, put this on. It's best they don't recognize you."

I looked around and saw my insurance agent, television anchors for local channels, uniformed cops, and ambulance crews in white. A crime scene tape barrier had been set up to keep them away from the action. "Crime scene?" I said to Nick. "What's that about?"

"Standard procedure."

"The ambulances too?"

He shrugged. "That's the sheriff over there—tall guy in uniform. They'll have to impound your car until everything's sorted out." He looked into my face as if taking in my gaunt appearance and the darkness under my eyes. "Are you okay?"

"No, Nick, I'm not okay. All these people are making me nervous."

"Don't blame them. You're big news."

Monica also had a troubled look on her face, as if she knew this wasn't going to turn out well. "What is it you're not telling me?" I asked her.

"I don't like all these people either. It's like a circus."

I pulled the cap lower on my head and followed them into the crowd. Cables trailed into the water from a boom that was attached to a large truck. Divers in black wetsuits stood nearby. After a while, the DEP guy strode into the open and asked everyone to move back. "For your own safety," he said. "We don't want you near those cables if they snap."

The cops herded us backward and adjusted the tape barrier. The DEP guy wished everyone a happy new year and gave a little press conference. He talked about Karst terrain, soluble limestone, and sudden water level drops, and said the sinkhole—which he called a pond—covered more than four acres of ground and had depths up to eighty feet, which was why it had taken so long to find my car.

A reporter asked, "What's your explanation for the woman who climbed out of the water?"

"I don't have an explanation, but I'd dearly love to hear her story."

A rumble of thunder interrupted him. He pointed toward the clouds that were getting darker. "We better do this before we get wet."

TV correspondents began speaking into microphones. The wench truck operators climbed into their cab and started the engine. The wench turned and whined. The cables pulled taut. The boom sank a few inches and shook as if struggling with a whale.

How long the cable pulled and whirred and prolonged my agony, I don't know. But it was long enough to for me to pray they were pulling up a Prius and not a Packard, long enough to deepen my suspicion that Nick and Monica knew more than they were telling me, and long enough for that damn music to start in my head again.

"Here it comes!" someone yelled.

An up-swell of bubbles disturbed the water. The rear bumper broke the surface. There were oohs and ahs and pointing fingers. Monica squeezed my arm. A shiver rolled over me, and out of the water came a drenched 1932 Packard Twelve looking just as shiny and new as the day I'd driven it into the sinkhole. With bodies piled against the windshield.

I wanted the earth to swallow me, wanted to evaporate, wanted to die. It was bad enough that I'd been sent back to the present, but why had that damn Packard followed me? It should be a rusted hulk by now. Clarence and Sal should be bones. But no, the bodies and the Packard were in better shape than I was.

The wind picked up, rippling the water and blowing debris over the area. Lightning flashed. Thunder shook the ground. The first drops of rain began to fall, and then we were all running to our cars.

Nick grabbed my arm. "Hold on. We need to talk."

"Damn it, Nick. You knew all along, didn't you?"

"No, Amy, we weren't sure until they pulled it up."

I thought he'd cuff me right there, read my Miranda Rights beneath an umbrella in a storm with rain blowing sideways. Instead, he yelled into my ear, "Get in the truck!"

I climbed into the back seat, dripping water. Rain drummed on the roof. Monica was in the passenger seat drying her face. Nick started the engine to get the heater going and blow away condensation, and for a moment I imagined myself behind bars in a concrete-walled room, just down the corridor from Old Sparky. No more Flamenco. No more Spain.

No more Lafitte.

Monica handed me a roll of paper towels. She looked as downtrodden as I felt. "Is there anything you want to tell us?" she asked.

"Am I under arrest?"

"You told the paramedics it was self-defense. Is that what happened?"

I didn't answer. Didn't know what to say.

Nick turned around to face me. "Look, Amy, right now we're just trying to figure out who owns that Packard, who was in it, how they died, and what your involvement was."

There was no way to deny it. They'd seen the pictures on my cell. They knew what I'd told the paramedics, and they'd soon find my tote bag, purse, and flamenco dress in the Packard. Monica spoke again. "You should tell us now, Amy, before they take the bodies for autopsies. If they find bullets, they'll go to forensics for testing, and if they match your guns…"

"I shot only one. He was coming at me with an ax."

Monica took out her notepad. "Who did you shoot, Amy?"

"I shot Sal—Salvatore Provenzano. He was a mobster."

"Was Ramón with you?"

"Ramón wasn't there."

"Where was this mobster from?"

"From Tampa … Ybor City. He murdered my great-grandmother, Carmen."

"Wait. Did you say great-grandmother?"

"Strangled her with a belt. Dumped her in that sinkhole."

"When was that?"

"A long time ago."

"What about the other two? Who are they?"

"I don't know the one with the slit throat, but the Anglo guy is Clarence Buckalew. Operated a moonshine still on Brooker Creek. He was in the Great War."

"Wait, wait," Monica said, looking up from her pad. "Did you say Great War?"

"First world war, a hundred years ago."

She looked at Nick. He shrugged as if to say, "See, I told you she was wacky." The music in my head started again, loud, abrasive, as if telling me to shut up, that I'd already said too much. "It's all in my manuscript," I said. "I'll email you a copy."

I hopped out and trotted over to my rental car.

I thought they'd try to stop me. They didn't. I thought they'd follow me. Didn't do that either, and if it hadn't been for all the vehicles and people, I'd have driven straight into the water. But I couldn't do that either, so I drove back to Ybor in the rain.

CHAPTER 97

A group of reporters stood in front of the house that was no longer mine, huddled beneath umbrellas like mourners at a funeral. They didn't see me and I couldn't face them. Didn't want to go inside and stare at the walls either, or wait to be arrested, so I kept driving around Ybor until a misty darkness fell over the city, looking for scenes of my 1932 life.

Rosa's Granada after Midnight had been converted to a restaurant and bar. I sat in my car for a minute in front, watching people going in and out despite the rain, and I thought of Rosa sitting in a chair with her cat, and the music and noise and smells and smoke, and the girls in their provocative dresses and cigarettes, and the men in their suits.

Gone now. All gone. None of them alive in 2019.

The El Dorado was also gone, replaced by a parking lot. No music or bawdiness or bolita. No Lafitte either. The cars in it looked as sad and lonely as I felt.

The house of Soledad and Dr. Antonio looked the same, and I cried at the sight of the giant oak under which Lafitte and I had sat in his flathead V-8, making out like teenagers.

The rain stopped and started again. I drove on, turned down a side street, and there it was, the Hav-a-Havana cigar factory, looming out of the darkness in the falling mist.

Images and smells marched through my memory like ghosts in a dream—Cheena and Natalia, the mobsters on the landing, little Imelda with the Derringer she'd used to shoot Don Ignacio, the workers in their straw hats, the horses and wagons and trucks, the chatter of Spanish, and the heavy smells of tobacco and horse droppings.

Now there were only broken windows and creepers, and an empty parking lot where weeds grew from cracks in the pavement and raindrops spattered the surface.

I stepped out into the rain at the same place where the G-men had dragged me from Cheena's Model-A. My body shook. Every outrage and indignity I'd ever suffered came out in belly-racking sobs. Damn the music in my head. Damn this world. Damn everybody in it who'd brought me to this point. My world, my life, my love was in 1932, and I wanted to go back. Wasn't that what the dreams and music were telling me to do?

My cell buzzed.

"Are you okay?" Nick asked.

"No, Nick, I'm not okay, and would you please stop asking?"

"Listen, Amy. We found a flamenco dress in the Packard. It looks like yours. You should come in now, voluntarily, and meet us at the sheriff's office."

"To be arrested?"

"To talk … for you to tell us what happened."

"Oh, please, Nick, you know as well as I do that no one is going to believe me."

A flash of lightning told me it wasn't a good idea to be outside in a storm in Tampa. I hurried back to the car, climbed in, and tried to dry my face and hands with tissues.

"Amy, are you still there?"

"I'm here, Nick. What's going to happen if I come in?"

"Questions, Amy, lots of questions. Don't wait until we put out an arrest warrant."

"So you're admitting I'll be arrested."

"Only if you don't come in. We need to get to the bottom of this."

"It's raining, Nick, pouring. I'm soaked. I can barely hear you. I'll call you later."

I clicked off. No way was I going to turn myself in. Hell, no! Some hot-shot prosecutor would create a story to fit the circumstances. Call it a modern-day hit job. There'd be an interrogation, maybe a trial, and the case would be presented by some cute little assistant D.A. in a power suit with blonde hair and a name like Heather or Brittany, and I'd end up in an orange jumpsuit mopping floors or making license plates with other wayward women. Even if they didn't convict me, I'd always be the humiliated flamenco dancer with a bizarre story that only conspiracy nuts and mystics would believe.

The only other option was to run—go to Spain or Mexico or some other flamenco-loving country and change my identity. But how could I do that without money? All I had were a few gold escudos that had survived the sinkhole. How much were they worth?

Maybe I should find out.

It was still drizzling when I drove into the driveway and maneuvered around Charlie's U-Haul, getting chilled in my wet clothes. The reporters were gone and everything was dark and spooky. I glanced around, cautious as ever, then jumped out and tracked water into the house.

The TV was on, tuned to a Spanish-speaking station.

Weird. I didn't remember turning the TV on, but I'd been in such turmoil that I didn't remember much of anything. I grabbed a towel and marched straight to the bedroom dresser.

The drawers were partially open.

Had I left it like that?

I yanked open the top drawer and pulled out the cigar box.

Empty. The damn box was empty. No antique gold coins or 1932 currency. No old engagement ring either. Not even my passport and credit cards. Nothing, nada, zilch.

"Why are you so wet?" asked a voice behind me.

CHAPTER 98

Ramón was usually a picky dresser who favored dark pants, form-fitting shirts, and elevated shoes. Now he was dressed like a beach tourist in baggy cargo shorts, flip-flops, a wrinkled black tee-shirt, and a Tampa Bay Rays cap turned backward on his head.

He hadn't shaved for a while either.

"Where the devil have you been?" he asked, speaking in a mixture of Spanish and Caló. "I tried to call you. So did Selena. I needed you. Needed your help."

I couldn't answer. Couldn't do anything except stand there with an empty cigar box in my hand and stare at the man who'd murdered Selena.

He kicked away a board that was still on the floor and got right in my face. "Answer me, woman. Where the hell were you? They're talking about you on TV."

I backed away and sat on the bed. "Why did you kill Selena?"

"I didn't do anything to Selena."

"You're lying, Ramón. Your fingerprints were all over her car. She'd been strangled."

"Who told you that? Have you been talking with the cops?"

He came toward me again, fire in his eyes. I held up the cigar box like a shield. He snatched it from me and tossed it away, then shoved me backward on the bed.

"Why do you give a shit about Selena? She was a fucking lesbian, a dyke. I asked her to help me, but no, she wanted to report me to the cops.

And you? Where were you when I needed you? They say you drove your car into the swamp but have been in hiding."

He drew back his fist.

"Stop it, Ramón. Give me a chance to explain."

He slammed his fist into the bed but still hovered over me, breathing hard, his breath smelling of cigarettes. "I'm waiting, Amy. What the hell happened? Where did you go?"

"Please, Ramón. Let me up and I'll explain."

He backed off. I stood and glanced around, wishing I had the Luger or a knife or even a tomato stake to drive into his evil heart, but all I had were my wits and the brick and screwdriver I'd used for ripping open the wall. Both were now atop the dresser.

"An accident," I said, trying to keep my voice calm. "Didn't you see it on TV?"

"What happened?"

"I was injured … stuck in the hospital. See this scar on my head?"

"Don't lie to me. You were with another man."

"No, Ramón. You're the only man in my life."

I put a hand on his shoulder, the way Natalia had done to comfort Vito on the day they'd shown up at the doctor's house. Ramón's expression softened.

"Why didn't you call me?" he asked. "Or answer my messages?"

"I couldn't, *amor*. I didn't even know my own name. All I remembered was what your wife said when she attacked me."

"That bitch is not my wife. I divorced her. I'm not even the daddy of her children. She's a *puta*. Sleeps with any man that wants her."

He went on and on proclaiming his innocence, getting louder and laying the blame for all his troubles on his ex-wife. I wasn't about to dispute him, not with his temper, but as he spoke, I eased along the bed, trying to get to the brick on the dresser.

He followed me, step for step, speaking in my face, sickening me with his lies and foul breath. "What's important is we're together now," he said. "Now we can run away."

"And go where?

"Mexico. They have flamenco. We can change our names and get a job."

He pulled me into his arms and put his mouth on mine, kissing me right there in the room where Lafitte had kissed me that first night.

"No!" I said and twisted away.

"Damn it, Amy, don't be like that." He wrapped his arms around me and backed me against the dresser. "I need you, *dulce*. Need you bad. You just don't know how I missed you."

"I missed you too," I said, and let him kiss me despite the hatred that raged in my heart. Let him run his hand inside my drenched pullover and fondle my breasts.

Let him bend over to pull down my jeans.

And that was when I whacked him with the brick.

It was a glancing blow, but he went down anyway. I tried to hit him again, but he grabbed my legs, lifted me up and slammed me against the wall. The brick went flying. The poster of flamenco dancers fell off the wall. Then we were rolling over the floor, screaming and cursing.

I kicked loose, rolled away, and reached for the brick.

He pounced atop me again. I bit him, scratched him, poked at his eyes, and tried to grab his *cojones*, but he was too strong, even after suffering a blow to his head, and before long he had me on my back with his hands around my throat.

His grip tightened. Blood dripped from his chin onto my face. I couldn't breathe. Still I squirmed and fought, and was trying to reach the brick when he slugged me with his fist. The fight went out of me, and as I lay there, trying to regain my senses, he straddled me.

"Bitch! Fucking *puta*!"

I thought he'd strangle me to death right there, next to the bed where Lafitte and I had loved and schemed. Do to me what he'd done to Selena. And what Sal had done to Carmen.

Instead, he unzipped my jeans and pulled them down to my ankles.

"One last time," he said and tugged at my panties. "Enjoy it."

371

The "Habanera" grew louder. Castanets clacked. Gypsies wailed. And even there, lying on the floor beneath Ramón, too weak to defend myself, a sense of injustice swept over me. Why? I wanted to scream. Why had Carmen brought me back to this nightmare? Why had she given me the love of Lafitte only to strip it away? Now I'd become another victim, another Selena.

I closed my eyes. Ramón's curses, so loud before, faded away. Warmth came over me. I heard the toll of a bell and even thought about Hemingway.

And then I saw her floating through the door in her tattered clothes.

"Amy," she said. "This is why I brought you back."

She may have been there, standing over us, or maybe not. She may have spoken, or maybe not. All I know is she—or something—communicated with me, not about dying, but about the board that lay on the floor beside me.

The busted one with protruding nails.

I reached over and clutched it in my right hand.

Ramón didn't try to stop me. He was too busy trying to rip off my panties.

With all my remaining strength, I slammed the board against the side of his head, nails first.

He sprang up. My vision returned in time to see him stumbling backward. He stepped on another nail and tumbled into the closet, atop the other boards.

I wasn't about to run like some frightened ninny in a movie. Hell, no! That sonofabitch ruined my life. He murdered Selena. And he'd kill me too.

I scooted over and grabbed the screwdriver atop the dresser, thinking to plunge it into his heart. But when I turned back, he wasn't moving.

Wasn't cursing either. The board was still plastered to the side of his head, blood oozing around it, and his mouth and eyes were open. I poked him with the screwdriver. No movement. I poked him again. "Bastard!" I screamed at him for what he'd done to Selena, and to me, and to others. "Bastard! Bastard! Bastard!"

Then I slumped against the side of the bed and broke into sobs.

CHAPTER 99

A crash of thunder brought me back to reality. There were flashes of lightning, the sound of rain blowing against the window, and the stench of blood and urine. The "Habanera" was also playing in my head as if saying to get out before Nick showed up at the door.

Up I struggled, holding the foot of the bed for support. My legs wobbled. My back ached and my hands shook, yet somehow I managed to pull myself together and get to the bathroom. The fight had left me with a busted lip, puffy left eye, and blood all over my face and pullover.

That bastard!

I ran water over my head, and then trekked back into the bedroom, naked from the waist down. I didn't want to touch him or smell him or get near him, but I needed the things he'd stolen, so I tossed a towel over his face and rummaged through the pockets of his cargo shorts.

Everything he'd taken was there—engagement ring, gold coins and 1932 currency.

He even had a cell phone and loaded pistol.

I threw the pistol into my purse.

What about his cell? No, leave it for Nick.

I hurried back to the bathroom, stripped off my pullover, and stepped into the shower.

When I came out, my cell was buzzing.

Nick. Damn him. He'd alert the local cops if I didn't answer.

I sent him a text—*Getting ready, Nick. Call U back in a few minutes.*

By then the "Habanera" was playing in my head like a fire alarm.

Hurry, I told myself. Get dressed. Get out.

The clothes I'd been wearing when I came out of the sinkhole were still in a box. The last time I'd put them on was on the side of the road in 1932, next to a Burma-Shave sign.

I put them on again—flared riding britches, white blouse with puffed shoulders, stub-toed shoes, socks, even the granny bloomers.

Then I made a quick mental inventory of things to take with me.

Swiss Army Knife. Check.

Cell fully charged and downloaded with 1932 gaming results. Check.

A cushion to soften the impact. Check.

Only one thing left to do. I powered on my laptop, keyed in a summary of the confrontation with Ramón, and emailed copies to Nick, Monica, and editors I knew at *La Gaceta* and the *Tampa Bay Times*.

My cell buzzed again.

"Are you okay?" Nick asked.

"No, damn it, I'm not okay. I just killed Ramón. His body is in the bedroom."

There was muffled silence. Then Monica came on the phone. "Are you injured?"

"I'm okay."

"Don't touch anything. We're almost there. One minute. Unlock the door."

One minute? Shit. What was I thinking?

I tossed everything I'd need into a tote bag and dashed outside to my rental car.

Sirens wailed in the distance. Rain was still pouring. I jumped into the car and was about to start it when Nick's SUV pulled into the drive behind me, stopping next to Charlie's U-Haul.

I lowered my head.

Nick and Monica jumped out, hurried around me without looking, bounded onto the porch, and went inside. As soon as the door closed behind them I started the engine.

The headlights came on. Shit!

Worse, that damn U-Haul and Nick's SUV were blocking the exit.

I drove onto the grass and barreled toward my neighbor's property—only to be stopped by a heavy line of shrubs. Damn it to hell! I spun around and headed toward my other neighbor's property. By then, Nick was out the door, Monica behind him. I floored the accelerator, bumped across the driveway, and flattened a little picket fence and a jungle of philodendron.

A moment or two later, I was back on 7th Avenue, heading west with plant debris hanging from the side mirrors, windshield wipers slapping.

A police car with flashing lights blew past me.

My cell buzzed again.

"Amy, what the hell are you doing?"

"It's in the manuscript, Nick. I sent you a copy."

"Don't do anything stupid. Just turn around and get back here."

"Sorry, Nick. I'm going to Spain. Don't try to stop me."

"That's crazy, Amy. They'll grab you at the airport."

"Abyssinia, Nick. Thanks for your help."

I clicked off and drove to Brooker Creek in the rain.

WHERE TRUTH MEETS FICTION

Flamenco in the Time of Moonshine and Mobsters was inspired in part by the adventures of my father, who operated three moonshine stills in the swamps of south Mississippi during prohibition and bootlegged by airplane to New Orleans. Some of the scenes are based on my mother's recollections of their run-ins with mobsters, G-men, and fellow travelers.

Clarence, Donnie Sue, Virgil, and Popsickle are also based on real people.

Brooker Creek Preserve is a beautiful 8700-acre, visitor-friendly, natural wilderness near Tarpon Springs, Florida. There are no sinkholes or mysterious lagoons on the property.

General Douglas MacArthur, who in 1932 was widely viewed as a villain for his part in putting down the Bonus Marchers, was promoted to a five-star General of the Army in World War II and awarded the Medal of Honor for his service in the Philippines campaign.

The Lindbergh baby kidnapping and murder in 1932 became the most publicized crime of the 20th century. Charles Lindbergh was then and remains a suspect, never mind that a German immigrant named Bruno Hauptmann was convicted and executed for the crime.

Ybor City in the early 20th century was populated by a dynamic community of immigrants from Spain, Cuba and Italy, most of whom were drawn by the booming cigar industry. They brought arts and entertainment, mutual aid societies, the Spanish language, and the culture of their countries, not the least of which were flamenco and bolita.

The Volstead Act of 1919, which established prohibition, created the opportunity for moonshiners and mobsters and, when coupled with the Great Depression, brought labor unrest, bloodshed, poverty, gangster competition for control of the city's vices, and an intensification of the existing hostility between the city's Cuban and Spanish immigrants.

In Spanish-speaking societies, a female with Asian looks is often called "China" (pronounced Cheena). Males are referred to as "Chino" (Cheeno). I used the phonetical spelling.

The correct pronunciation of Ybor is EE-bore.

The Hav-a-Havana Cigar Factory is fictitious in name only. More than 200 such factories existed in Tampa by the late 1920s and produced up to 600 million cigars a year. Many of the buildings—predominantly red brick—are still standing but have been converted to other uses.

Rosa's Granada after Midnight, although fictitious, is emblematic of many such establishments that thrived in Ybor City in the 1920s and 1930s.

Many of the mob bosses of Tampa did in fact hang out in the world famous Columbia Restaurant. It is still in operation and features flamenco entertainment.

The El Dorado was a high class brothel and casino in 1932, not the kind of place to take a nice girl. The location is now a parking lot for Hillsborough Community College.

Although the Volstead Act was repealed by the 21st Amendment to the Constitution in 1933, the mobsters remained. Sal, Big Tony, Vito, and Don Ignacio are fictitious characters. The other mob bosses mentioned in this work are not fictitious—and most came to a bad ending.

Charlie Wall, the undisputed master of Tampa's bolita empire, was a cold-blooded killer who eliminated his rivals and survived multiple assassination attempts. He was beaten to death with a baseball bat in 1955. His Spanish-speaking partner, Tito Rubio, was gunned down on the back porch of his Ybor City home in 1938.

Santo Trafficante controlled crime operations in Florida and Cuba until his death from stomach cancer in 1954. He was succeeded by his son,

Santo Trafficante, Jr., who died in 1987. Almost all the others—Jimmy Velasco, Ignacio Antinori, Jimmy Lumia, and Joey Vaglichio—were gunned down by unknown assailants.

La Gaceta, now a tri-lingual weekly newspaper (Spanish, English and Italian), was founded in 1922 by Don Victoriano Manteigo, a Cuban immigrant and former cigar factory lector. His grandson, Patrick Manteigo, is now owner and editor. The paper and its editors are strong advocates for Ybor City and the Hispanic community.

The Bureau of Investigation, headed by J. Edgar Hoover, was renamed the Federal Bureau of Investigation in 1935. In the early years, Director Hoover was more concerned with the threat of Communism and labor unrest than organized crime.

Ernest Hemingway may or may not have visited Ybor in 1932. His book, *For Whom the Bell Tolls*, about a young American in the Spanish Civil War, was published in 1940.

Ybor City is Tampa's only National Landmark Historic District. The mobsters, casinos, brothels, and moonshiners are gone, but the flavors of old Ybor remain in its vibrant night life, flamenco performances, Latin cuisine, the rich smells of Cuban coffee and cigars, and the availability of tours to mob hangouts, haunted places, and escape tunnels.

ACKNOWLEDGEMENTS

Flamenco in the Time of Moonshine and Mobsters would not have been possible without the support, encouragement, and critical eye of many friends, associates, fellow writers, editors, former students, residents of Ybor City, and family members.

In Cajun country, I am deeply indebted to my old friends in the Writers' Guild of Acadiana, as well as to Karen Ritter, Jessy Ferguson, Bea Angelle, Talis Jayme, and Cynthia Thomas.

Among my Peace Corps friends who listened, read my chapters, or otherwise shared their thoughts are George Pope and George Wildman.

A number of friends shared their thoughts and ideas on *Flamenco* or related personal adventures that found their way into the novel. Thank you, Dana Brown, Luzviminda Perón, Deborah Chong, and Lourdes Brindis.

In Florida, I am grateful to my friends in the Tarpon Springs Fiction Writers' Group for energetically critiquing *Flamenco* at our weekly meetings—Laurie Dalzell, Shannon O'Leary Beck, Micki Morency, Mark Turley, Laura Kennedy Bell, Liz Drayer, Beth Hovind, Frank Shima, Donna Lengel, Eleni Papanou, Dorté Zuckerman, Pamela Lopez, Laurie Cotrell, Debbie Brown, Bill Frederick, Tina Forcier, Louise Michalos, Linda Rodante, Raymond David, and Azra Alt. Also our deceased members: Roger Hoffine, Belva Green, and Bill Ciaccia.

My dear friends Gino Bardi and Elizabeth Indianos were always available for listening and lending a hand. Ditto for former homicide detective Ken Dye for his police expertise, and Bob Dockery for sharing his thoughts on the legal issues encountered by my characters.

Thanks also to Dr. Tom Carson of the Tarpon Springs Rotary Club for educating me on the protocol for unidentified patients admitted to a hospital. Joan Jennings and Joan Tobin, also of Rotary, read my manuscript and made many helpful suggestions. Among my other friends and associates at Rotary who commented on my books or offered encouragement are Ramona Pletcher, Ron and Patricia Haddad, Alleyne Newcomb, Sue Thomas, Sue Carson, Bill Grantham, the late Peggy Proestos, and my "Who dat" buddy, Dr. Alan Lane.

A BIG special thanks to Kit Duncan for finding and putting buckets of red ink on all the "opportunities for enhancement," big and small. Marina Brown, a talented dancer and author, taught me a thing or two about the art of flamenco. Pamela Tompkins provided source suggestions. Dr. Vilma Zalupski Fernandez (deceased) was kind enough to relate the experiences of her father, who worked at the Columbia Restaurant during the mob years.

A considerable portion of the background information on crime, moonshining, the cigar industry, and gambling in Ybor City during the Great Depression was derived from the internet. Additional background came from the many books on Ybor City (listed below) and period photographs and articles in *La Gaceta* and *The Tampa Bay Times*.

The love and encouragement of family always makes my job easier. Thank you, Chris, Julie, Alex, Davy, and Leza. Finally, my beautiful bride, Maria Nieves Edmonds, helped me develop the plot for *Flamenco* in the final months of her life. There are no words to describe my gratitude for her love, support and encouragement—or the sadness I feel at her loss.

FURTHER READING

Deitche, Scott. *Cigar City Mafia*

Deitche, Scott. *The Silent Don: The Criminal Underworld of Santo Trafficante, Jr.*

Frethem, Deborah. *Haunted Ybor City*

Gonzalez-Llandes. *Cigar City Stories: Tales of Old Ybor City*

Grismer, Karl. *Tampa, A History of the City of Tampa and the Tampa Bay Region*

Inglis. Tom. *The Guns of Tampa: Tampa's History of Notorious Underworld Slayings*

Kase, Ron. *A Time in Ybor City*

Lehane, Dennis. *Live by Night* (book and movie)

Mormino, Gary and Pozetta, George. *The Immigrant World of Ybor City*

Muniz, José Rivero. *The Ybor City Story, 1885-1954* (*Los Cubanos en Tampa*)

Pacheco, Ferdie. *Pacheco's Art of Ybor City*

Pacheco, Ferdie. *Ybor City Chronicles*

Reyes, Wallace. *Once Upon a Time in Tampa: Rise and Fall of the Cigar Industry*

Quesada, A.M. de. *Images of America: Ybor City*

Trebin Lastra, Frank. *Ybor City: The Making of a Landmark Town*

Wilborn, Paul. *Cigar City*

ABOUT THE AUTHOR

David C. Edmonds is the author of twelve books of fiction and non-fiction. He is a former Marine, Peace Corps Volunteer, academic dean, and Senior Fulbright Professor of Economics. He has spent considerable time in Europe and Latin America as a scholar and US Government official. His previous books have won more than a dozen prestigious literary awards. He currently lives in the Tampa Bay area of Florida.